Praise for Eagles and Dragons Publishing and author, Adam Alexander Haviaras...

Historic Novel Society:

"...Haviaras handles it all with smooth skill. The world of third-century Rome—both the city and its African outposts—is colorfully vivid here, and Haviaras manages to invest even his secondary and tertiary characters with believable, three-dimensional humanity."

Amazon Readers:

"Graphic, uncompromising and honest... A novel of heroic men and the truth of the uncompromising horror of close combat total war..."

"Raw and unswerving in war and peace... New author to me but ranks along side Ben Kane and Simon Scarrow. The attention to detail and all the gory details are inspiring and the author doesn't invite you into the book he drags you by the nasal hairs into the world of Roman life sweat, tears, blood, guts and sheer heroism. Well worth a night's reading because once started it's hard to put down."

"Historical fiction at its best! ... if you like your historical fiction to be an education as well as a fun read, this is the book for you!"

"Loved this book! I'm an avid fan of Ancient Rome and this story is, perhaps, one of the best I've ever read."

"An outstanding and compelling novel!"

"I would add this author to some of the great historical writers such as Conn Iggulden, Simon Scarrow and David Gemmell. The characters were described in such a way that it was easy to picture them as if they were real and have lived in the past, the book flowed with an ease that any reader, novice to advanced can enjoy and become fully immersed…"

"One in a series of tales which would rank them alongside Bernard Cornwell, Simon Scarrow, Robert Ludlum, James Boschert and others of their ilk. The story and character development and the pacing of the exciting military actions frankly are superb and edge of your seat! The historical environment and settings have been well researched to make the story lines so very believable!! I can hardly wait for what I hope will be many sequels! If you enjoy Roman historical fiction, you do not want to miss this series!"

Goodreads:

"… a very entertaining read; Haviaras has both a fluid writing style, and a good eye for historical detail, and explores in far more detail the faith of the average Roman than do most authors."

Sign-up for the Eagles and Dragons Publishing Newsletter and get a FREE BOOK today.

Subscribers get first access to new releases, special offers, and much more.

Go to:
www.eaglesanddragonspublishing.com

THE CARPATHIAN INTERLUDE

COMPLETE TRILOGY

ADAM ALEXANDER HAVIARAS

PART I

IMMORTUI

*For the Light in my life, without whom
I would truly be in the Dark.*

1

IMMORTUI

ctober - A.D. 8

"Hear us, great Father of Light! Receive our thanks for delivering us from the dark."

The words echoed off of the white-washed walls of the cave. All seventy men were silent upon their benches in that dark place, their heads bowed as they listened to the words. They had been eighty at one point but now ten walked in the light. Not bad, losing only ten.

Gaius Justus Vitalis spoke the words their Pater should have been speaking as their Saturn in the rites, but as he was away with the commander, it fell to the Heliodromus, the Sun Runner, to perform the ritual. The dark was lit only by two licks of flame behind him, on either side of the image of the tauroctony in which Mithras, Lord of Light, slew the great bull.

To the Heliodromus, the cave seemed smaller than usual, no doubt because of the size of the beast above him. He hoped the handlers had drugged it sufficiently. It was time.

"What time is it?" he called the question.

"It is the time of the season's death!" the men answered solemnly.

"Where are we going?"

"Into darkness!"

"What are you?"

"The Light! The Light! The Light!"

"And who are you?"

"Mithras! Mithras! Mithras!"

"Accept our offering…" he whispered as he thrust the gladius directly above his head into the soft flesh of the bull's belly. He sliced in four directions and the blood of the beast broke forth as water from a burst dam.

His arms held wide, eyes and mouth closed, Gaius Justus Vitalis, Optio of the third century of Legio V Macedonica, let the hot blood of the sacrifice wash over his entire person, staining his pure white robes crimson. He felt the power of his god in that sacrifice, as though he absorbed both light and blood in the ritual.

So this is what it feels like… he thought.

He then fought down the urge to vomit as the stink of the bull's punctured intestine spread. When the offal stopped falling, he stepped clear to accept a white towel from one of the Miles, his soldiers. The men began to file out of the cave, solemn, grateful to be alive as the sunlight that burned the fringes of some scattered clouds warmed their bodies.

"Vitellius," Gaius called to one of his men. "You and two others start cutting up the offering. Our century will dine on it tonight."

"Yes, Heliodromus," the man answered as they were still inside the sacred speleum, the cave.

"Be sure to wrap the thigh bones in the fat and offer them to Saturn."

"Yes, sir."

Gaius left the men to it and made his way out of the cave into the fresh October air. He closed his eyes when the sun touched his face. *One…two…three breaths…* When he opened his eyes he took in the expanse of the Danuvius and Porata rivers where the water fowl skirted their rippled surfaces in the morning breeze. The bald, grassy plains on either side of the rivers stretched on and on, greener now that the heat of summer had subsided. In the far northern distance, he observed the clouds where they clung to the Carpathian mountains, the slopes now awash with patches of green, gold and red.

"Better hurry, lads," he called into the cave. "The next century's going to be using the Mithraeum soon."

"Yes, sir," the three men answered in unison.

Gaius wrapped his gladius in the soiled towel and began making his way up the path to the legion's base, his bloody footprints fading as he got farther from the cave.

IT WAS THE THIRTY-FIFTH YEAR OF THE REIGN OF AUGUSTUS Caesar and the legions had been occupied the last couple of years in putting down a revolt in Pannonia and Dalmatia, from the Elbe to the Danuvius. King Maroboduus had finally been brought to heel with Tiberius leading the troops, ten legions in all, plus auxiliaries.

At the outset, when the fighting had proved grim and desperate, veteran and other legions had been called up, including the V Macedonica from the fortress at Troesmis in Moesia Inferior.

Gaius and his comrades had helped, it was said, to tip the scales in Rome's favour, and the men of the V Macedonica had returned to base honour-laden, if not exhausted, from a difficult campaign. There were many acts of heroism and decorations were to be given out at an assembly of the legion when everyone returned to base. Two cohorts had yet to return.

AN HOUR AFTER THE RITES IN THE MITHRAEUM, GAIUS EASED into the hot water of the caldarium to wash the rest of the blood from his hair, face and body, after having scraped most of it away with strigil and oil. In his small corner of misted mosaic and torchlight, the optio allowed his mind to drift away from the cold collection of timber and stone overlooking the Danuvius river, to his family in Rome. Fulvia, only two years his junior, would be approaching her thirty-third birthday which he would, of course, miss. He made a mental note to write and send her the Dacian bracelet he had acquired while on campaign. She always did love the exotic.

At six and seven years, he knew his wife would have her hands full with Faustina and Aemilia. He felt the loneliness then, as he thought of their childish laughter. Three years was far too long to have been away. He ran his hand over his close-cropped hair and splashed more water onto his face. He wondered how Fulvia would feel about the loss of his wild brown hair. She did love to run her hands through it. The outbreak of lice on campaign had spared no man, however, and the medicus had ordered all heads shaved. 'No use having men impaled by Germanic spears because they're too busy scratching at lice!' he had said. Gaius figured he had had a point as he wrote the order to shave his men on the wax tablet that hung from his cingulum.

"Thinking of home again, Gaius!" boomed a bloody great voice proceeded by a big splash. Gaius stood to attention as his centurion, Julius Lycus Vernus, rose like a titan out of the water.

"Sir! Yes, sir!" Gaius answered.

"Enough *sirs* for now, Gaius. We're off duty."

"Right. You startled me, is all."

"Ha. Nothing startles you." The centurion laughed and sat across from his optio.

Lycus was a monster of a man, scarred from many wars and tavern fights alike. He was brutal in battle and demanded the utmost of his men. As a career soldier, he was not one to accept mediocrity in his century and if he even caught a whiff of weakness, the crack of his vinerod would fix that. For a man as big and hard as a merchant ship, Gaius thought the bald head on Julius looked comic.

"Ahh!" The centurion rubbed his face and leaned back against the wall. "Good to be home!"

"Home…hmm."

"Oh stop that mumbling, Gaius. I know you miss your lovely wife and sprats. Believe me, I understand." Gaius doubted it since Julius always said that he would only marry after retiring and then, it would be to a girl forty years younger who would give him ten children. "But don't delude yourself. You're not going home soon. I wager there are more of those barbarian bastards deep in those woods, waiting to strike back. Mark me!"

"We whipped them pretty good though, sir."

"Aye, that we did. But you never know, do you? Besides,

I'm not ready to stop fighting. And I've got you to do all the grunt work. Ha!" He slammed a hammy fist into Gaius' oiled arm. The optio knew what was next: the compulsory encouragement talk.

"You know, Gaius, best thing I ever did was promote you to optio. I can trust you and you fight like a disciplined demon in the thick of it." At this point, Julius turned to the rest of the bathers. "Best fucking optio in the legions!" he bellowed, his parade ground voice echoing off the painted walls. "You'll see your family again. We'll be due a furlough at some point."

"The men could use it, to be sure. And me." Gaius never got his hopes up about that sort of thing. Too many cancelled furloughs over the years. They could both hear the wind howl beyond the high windows of the bath house. The centurion grew serious.

"How did the rites go?"

"Well," Gaius answered, the Sun Runner to the Pater.

"Do the men walk in the Light?"

"They walk in the Light."

"Good. I wished I could have joined you." He paused and looked curiously at Gaius, his voice low, honest. "Did you feel it? The power?"

"I did," Gaius bowed his head. "Mithras was with us."

"Amazing, isn't it?"

"Truly."

Without another word, Julius' naked bulk rushed from the hot water.

"We should join the lads back at barracks now, The feast'll be ready. You set them to it right away?"

"Yes. Vitellius was in charge."

"Good. Let's go."

Gaius followed his centurion to the apodyterium to gather

their things, foregoing the cold waters of the frigidarium in favour of meat and wine. His thoughts of home, of family, would have to wait. As they dressed into fresh tunics and bracae, Gaius asked about the meeting with the consular legate fresh from Achaea.

"It was good. He's a new chap, lips puckered up to Tiberius. Son of someone close to Augustus."

"Any orders?"

"Just to hold our end of the frontier and keep a watch over the other side of the river. Any sign of trouble and we're to stomp it out."

"What about decorations for the men?" Gaius knew the men needed the encouragement for the blood they'd lost.

"Oh well, that…" Julius smiled. "III Century will be the most decorated."

"Really?"

"Yes. And Gaius Justus Vitalis, you are receiving three honours. Second only to myself, of course. I'll be getting four."

Gaius could not help but smile. "When?"

"Tomorrow, I think. The last two cohorts were spotted not half a day's march from here."

As they stepped out into the brightly lit street of the base, Gaius whistled his favourite tune, the one he whistled to his wife when they had first met. It always seemed to cheer him.

IT WAS NEAR TO MIDNIGHT. GAIUS STOOD ON THE TOP OF ONE of the towers facing the river. Their century had been handed second watch and the men, however reluctantly, had put their armour back on after an evening of roasted meat and wine. It was bad luck, but they had no choice in the matter. Julius and

Gaius had managed to gather the men and march them up to the walls and main gates of the via Praetoria and via Decumana. Julius was now making the rounds, rousing any man who dared to doze, leaning on his scutum or pilum. Gaius swore he could hear the crack of the centurion's vinerod somewhere on the other side of the fortress.

He set his five-foot hastile against the battlements and leaned on the cold stone. His breath fogged in the air before him and he pulled his crimson cloak tighter about himself. Above, a few raked clouds drifted across the night sky. The moon was a full, silver disc, its light blanketing the green grass of the plain in grey. Beneath Selene's light, the Danuvius flowed like quicksilver, wide and deep and cold. Gaius missed the heat of home, the colour of oranges and bougainvillea, of olive groves, and gleaming white marble. Long ago days by the turquoise sea were a far cry from the deep, midnight blue of the Danuvius.

"Mithras…" he whispered, "…light our way in this dark place. Make us strong…me and my brothers…"

His prayers were broken by a distant rhythm that he recognized as the jingle of soldiers' kit and tramping hobnails. The ominous wail of a cornu sounded in the night. Across the river, a wolf howled long, slow and sad. Gaius did not know if it howled at the moon or in answer to the cornu's wail.

On the plain, the two returning cohorts came into view, their perimeter lit by torches carried by auxiliary cavalrymen. At the front, the two tribunes rode side by side before their men, the vexillaria swaying in the air above their heads. A long line of legionary red appeared as the jingle of their equipment became louder. Gaius watched a moment longer then turned, donning his crested helmet and grabbing his staff.

"Cohorts returning!" he called out as he descended the

steps. "Open the gates!" he ordered as several of his men came forward to raise the great oak beams that barred the iron-studded doors. Gaius stood in the road as the gates creaked open, the torches whipping as the wind penetrated. He strode forward, six men at his back. "Salve!" Gaius saluted the tribunes as they approached.

"Optio," the one acknowledged from his horse.

"Welcome home, sirs," Gaius said officially. "The commander asked that you both report to the Praetorium before retiring for the night."

"By Jupiter, we need to sleep," complained the other tribune.

"As the commander wishes," the first agreed. "Optio."

Gaius and his men moved aside to allow the tribunes and their men to flow into the base, quietly acknowledging friends and acquaintances as they passed. When all the troops had passed beneath the gate, Gaius walked out onto the moonlit cobbles of the road and paused. Something niggled at him. It felt more vulnerable outside the walls, not quite right. He wondered if it was the full moon, for he had been outside the walls for months on the Pannonian campaign. It was as if - *there!*

Gaius cocked his ear, tried to hear past the sound of the wind and the rush of the river far below. The six men behind him looked puzzled. Then he heard it again, a whimpering like… *a child*! He wondered if the father in him took over then because he immediately called back to his men.

"Torches! There's someone down there!" He strode forward and followed the noise until he arrived at the edge of the rocky slope where it fell away to the river.

"Sir! Here, sir." Vitellius handed him a torch and Gaius held it out trying to see.

"There's definitely someone down there. Do you hear it?" The men all leaned forward, then Gaius lobbed his torch to the left of the sound where it landed in a splash of sparks on the rocks at the water's edge. Not ten feet away from it, Gaius could make out the shape of a small body clinging to a log.

"What is it, sir?" one of the men asked.

"A child. We need to get down there now! Antonius," he turned to one of the men. "Go and get a long rope from the gatehouse. Tell them there is a child that needs rescuing down by the river. Tell them to close the gate until we return."

"Yes, Optio!" Antonius ran off and returned a couple minutes later with a long coil of rope. They heard the gates close shortly after. Gaius had already removed his cloak and helmet and laid his hastile on the ground.

"I'm going down," he declared, tying the rope about his waist, making sure his gladius was free. "You men hold the rope and let me down slowly. I don't want to break my leg in a crevice." With that, Gaius took one of the torches and slid over the edge of the rocks. All six men strained under his armoured weight but let him down slowly, allowing him to safely plant his feet. As he descended, the dark water louder in his ears, he strained to catch glimpses of the child. It looked to be a boy. He was soaked. Gaius assumed he must have crossed the river clutching the log that his little body was clinging to.

"Are you all right?" he called. "Boy!"

Only a slow whimper.

When Gaius came to the bottom, he wedged the torch into the rocks and moved slowly toward the child whose face was hidden by long, sodden, black hair. There appeared to be no blood. The Roman reached out a tentative hand and brushed aside the hair.

The boy screamed and in a moment was up, shrinking back among the rocks, eyes wild, body shivering uncontrollably. Gaius held his hands out, showing he meant no harm.

"It's all right. I won't hurt you." The eyes searched beyond Gaius, across the river to the dark beyond. "Whatever it is, boy, you're safe. Shh..shh..." he soothed, holding his hand out. The boy reached out and in the flickering light of the torch, Gaius could see where the fingers were torn and bloody, like he had been scratching at something, or clinging to the log. "Do you have a name?" he asked in Latin. Nothing. "Onoma sou?" again in the Thracian dialect of Greek. The eyes recognized something, but no answer issued forth.

"Was someone chasing you?" At this, the boy began to whimper again and then moved toward Gaius just before fainting. Gaius caught him and swept him up.

"Optio!" Vitellius called down.

"I've got him! Get ready to bring us up!"

Gaius walked back to the first torch, carrying the boy under one arm. With the other arm, he gave a tug and held on tight while the men brought them up slowly. When they finally reached the top, he could hear Julius' booming voice approaching.

"What in Hades is going on here?"

Gaius knelt down, his arm aching from holding on and indicated the boy.

"Found him at the bottom of the cliff, sir. Seems to have crossed the river. He was terrified before he fainted."

"Whatever he is, Optio, you should have waited for me. What if you'd gone into the river or broken your neck?"

"Yes, sir. Sorry, sir." Gaius looked back at Julius' angry expression beneath his centurion's horizontal crest.

"Well, let's get back inside the base. That's enough

mucking around. The boy's your responsibility now, Optio. Get him to the medicus and then release the men to barracks."

"Yes, sir!" Gaius saluted, picked up the boy and began marching back to the gate. Julius stared across the river a moment longer before turning and seeing the others all safely back behind the fortress walls. Though he did not say anything, his soldier's gut told him that the appearance of a terrified boy from the other side of the river did not bode well.

"Gods, I need a drink!" he muttered.

"MITHRAS, LORD OF LIGHT. WATCH OVER US ON THIS FAR away edge of the world. Let us not fall into darkness. Though only we men of war worship you, I ask that you shine your light on my family in Rome."

Gaius felt his prayers stunted as he lay on his bed in his quarters. Sleep did not bless him, unnerved as he was by the discovery of the boy. *So young...so little...* he thought. It made him long to hold his own children, ensure their safety. He lit a chunk of incense in the flame of the clay lamp and set it before the image of Mithras that occupied the central space of the table along one wall of his room. He wondered if Julius was stewing in anger in his quarters at the other end of the barracks block.

AT THE SIXTH HOUR OF DAYLIGHT, THE ENTIRE V Macedonica was gathered in a massive chequered formation on the grassy plain outside the walls of Troesmis. In the early autumn breeze that swept down in a rush of leaves from the distant mountains, the insignia and vexillaria of all six cohorts and auxiliary regiments jingled and swayed, a plethora of red, bronze, gold and copper. The entire legion had turned out for parade with red cloaks, polished helms, oiled straps and buckles, sharpened gladii and pila. All the men's eyes were on the dais that had been constructed of rough pine timbers for the occasion. Gaius could smell the dripping resin from where he stood. In the middle of the dais was the aquilifer, holding aloft the legion's sacred eagle, polished to blinding brilliance. Beside the aquilifer, the imaginifer held the image of Augustus, their Imperator.

Beneath these sacred images of Rome's power stood the legion's legate commander, Iulus Maximus Sabino, and, newly arrived from Athenae, the consular legate for Macedonia and Achaea, Corwen Constantio Arruns. The latter was flanked by two lictors carrying the fasces which indicated his ability to dispense justice and punishment. Both commanders wore impressive cuirasses of hardened black and brown bull's hide decorated with silver and gold with matching pteruges and ornamented greaves. The commander, wearing a thick red cloak of the legions, stepped forward to speak before the consular legate. Cornui from the edges of the dais rang out and the tribunes of the six cohorts, standing beside tables of decorations to be distributed, turned to salute their commander, their horsehair crests cutting the air with every movement. The men of the legion followed suite, hailing three times.

"Maximus! Maximus! Maximus!"

The commander saluted his men in return and made to speak.

"Men of Legio V Macedonica! We have had many hard months of campaigning in Germania with Tiberius." At the mention of Tiberius, another cheer went up. "The battle was hard going before we got there, but after that? Well...we showed those barbarian bastards a thing or two about Roman arms!"

The commander smiled as his men, his legion, whooped and hollered, pounded pila shafts on their scuta. Gaius could see the consular legate stifle a yawn. The man was obviously unused to the colder climes of the frontier compared to sultry Athenae. The broad purple stripe of a senator and patrician poked out, carefully visible from beneath the infrequently-used armour. The commander was about to speak again and Gaius silenced some of his men.

"I want you *all* to know that I am proud of you, men of V Macedonica. No leader could have asked for a better command. You are disciplined and skilled…and you can fight like the whoresons I know you are!"

Laughter and cheers erupted once more and the commander saluted his men before stepping back for the consular legate. The man held his cloak like the folds of a toga and when he stepped forward to address the legion it became apparent he was well-trained in oratory.

"Hear me, men of Legio V Macedonica!" Clearer than a cornu, his voice grabbed every man there and all voices fell away with the passing leaves. "I come to you by order of our most victorious Emperor, Augustus Caesar. He has commanded me to come to you with more rewards for courage than have been given to any one legion during this campaign.

More cheers. Constantio waited and then began again.

"In a moment, you shall receive your rewards from your tribunes. But first, I am also here to inform you that for your outstanding service to the Empire, you shall all receive a bonus of a full year's salary!"

At that, even Gaius and Julius let out a yell, especially

since they received at least twice the regular pay. Gaius thought of what he could do for his family with that money. Fulvia would be able to fix their domus the way she had always dreamed, perhaps a new lyre and clothes for the girls...

The cornu sounded again and before anyone knew it, the consular legate was leaving the dais with his lictors. The commander remained, ordered some of the men to carry the tables onto the dais so the tribunes could distribute the awards.

"First cohort!" the senatorial tribune called out. Gaius stood still and waited as the men of the double-strength cohort received their honours. After a time, he began to think of the boy. He had placed him in the care of the medicus, Stefanos. The boy had not woken but, at a glance from Stefanos, appeared to be free of major injuries. Gaius had stopped to see him before the gathering and told the medicus that the boy appeared to respond to Greek.

"I shall send word to you if he wakes, Optio. Go now and be honoured."

Gaius had gone, giving a nod to a statue of Aesclepios on his way out.

"Second cohort!" their tribune, Marcus Misenus Orban, bellowed from the dais. As the names of his comrades were called out, Gaius watched the sun burst out from behind a cloud, its light blinding, reflecting off the end of the bronze orb of his hastile.

"Third century!" Julius suddenly called, and then they were marching forward to the dais.

Gaius watched with Julius as many of their men, including Vitellius and Antonius, went up onto the dais to be decorated with various armillae and coronae. Gaius could remember the instances that merited the honours; a line being held despite enemy cavalry, the rescue of a fallen comrade etcetera, etcetera. So many deeds.

"Gaius Justus Vitalis!" their tribune called. Gaius mounted the steps to a roar from his men. "Optio," the tribune began. "I present you with this armilla and this torc as symbols of your courage in battle, your leadership and discipline." Gaius felt the weight of the ornaments about his neck and wrist. How they gleamed!

"And I, Optio," the commander began, "present you with this corona muralis for being the first to reach the top of the palisade in one of our major victories. Well done, Optio!"

"Thank you, Commander. Tribune." Gaius saluted them and turned to his century to see his men cheering and Julius grinning broadly like a proud father. Before leaving the dais, Gaius, on seeing the mass of a legion before him, wondered at the power given to a man who commanded so many skilled warriors. He felt, at that moment, that a legion could indeed conquer the world.

Back among his men, Gaius watched, also with pride, as Julius was awarded two armillae, and two coronae by the Commander, making him the most decorated centurion in the legion, more than the Primus Pilus of the first cohort. Julius beamed, a rare occurrence, and even smiled as he raised his vinerod to his men, and to the sun in the sky. He then pointed it at Gaius in loving salute and at that moment, the optio never felt more affection for his gruff mentor.

By the time Gaius, Julius and the rest of the century were making their way back to barracks, the men had been standing for hours, the price to pay for so decorated a legion. Now, all looked forward to a feast on extra rations of beef and pork, fresh bread, and amphorae of wine for each century.

The two friends were grateful that their century had not drawn the night watch this time.

"Now the lads can drink and dice until they pass out and not worry about it." Julius mused.

"That is until you crack their skulls at first light for drills."

"Aye. Of course. And they won't be easy drills either. Misenus said the commander ordered the drills to be tougher than ever now, so as to avoid the men getting fat and lazy on success. We'll have tough days ahead, Gaius."

"Tomorrow will be the worst of it."

"Sirs!" a voice came from behind them as they stepped onto the via Decumana.

"Medicus." Julius nodded to Stefanos as he approached, wiping bloody hands on his surgical apron.

"Centurion. Optio. I've come to tell you that the boy has awoken," he said, already walking away. "You'd better come!" he called back.

"Well?" Julius arched the bushy eyebrow that had a scar running through it.

"I'll go," Gaius said.

"I'll join you." Julius followed. "I want to see if this boy has anything useful to say."

The hospital was busy, full of medical staff tending to those troops who had returned from the front with varying degrees of injury and infection. Gaius looked away as they passed a door where one man was having a gangrenous leg amputated. It seemed as though it was taking six men to hold the trooper down. Gaius held his breath as the smell of the rotten limb clawed into the corridor. Stefanos finally stopped at the end of the corridor where he began to unbolt the wooden door.

"You locked him up?" Gaius asked, shocked. "Was that really necessary?"

The medicus rubbed his beard with a blood-stained hand. "He's had a terrible fright. I thought it prudent to prevent him from running away." He paused before opening. "Speak slowly, Optio. Go easy and give him time. He may speak, he may never. He just needs time, and to feel that he is safe."

When the door opened, the room was dark but for a little light through a square of glass at the top of the wall. Gaius and Julius removed their crested helms and stepped in. The boy was propped up against two pillows on the straw mattress of a bed set in the corner. A plate of bread and cheese lay untouched on the table beside him. Gaius took in the pale white skin accentuated by the black hair which had been combed back. But it was the eyes, fearful, darting this way and that, which poked Gaius with pity. He was thankful Julius hung back, unused as he was to children.

"Hi there, little one," Gaius began, kneeling down to eye level with the child. No response. He switched from Latin to Greek. "Hello. Do you remember me? I found you by the river." The eyes came to rest on Gaius, still. A slight nod. The boy began to shake and Gaius took a wool blanket from the foot of the bed and covered him with it slowly. "Do you have a name?"

"Ask him what happened," Julius said in a deep voice from behind.

"Not yet. He's unable to speak, I think."

"Ask anyway. We need to know." Gaius relented, knew an order when he heard one.

"What happened to you? Do you remember?" The boy

began to whimper and his eyes began roaming again as he clutched the blanket to himself, tried to sink farther into the corner. "I think we should leave for now, sir." Gaius turned to Julius.

"Yes. Let's. You can check on him later." Julius strode out into the corridor and Gaius turned back to the boy.

"Do not be afraid. You are safe here and I will come back later to check on you. All right?" Gaius left the room, the boy's eyes watching him all the while as he closed the door and slid the bolt home.

"I hope he speaks up soon," Julius said as they made their way to the barracks.

"Me too. Something's scared that poor boy to Hades."

That evening, while Julius feasted with the other centurions, tribunes and commanders in the Praetorium, Gaius joined the men of the century in their own raucous celebration. Wine flowed and platters of roasted meat, fresh bread, cheeses and olives hovered up and down the length of the barrack block. The hot food was good and rich, the wine better. Gaius had been sure to note on his wax tablet that each of his men had received their bonus after the required deposit in their legionary accounts. There was plenty left over after that, and so, following several helpings of food, the men settled down to the serious business of gambling with their new-found wealth. Many others opted to head outside the walls to the civilian vicus where the brothels were no doubt doing a booming business.

"How is the boy doing, sir?" Antonius asked Gaius as they passed a wine jug back and forth. The younger man was red in the face from too much food and drink, swayed where he sat.

Gaius laughed a little at his tenacity in trying to maintain a level of decorum despite being far gone.

"He won't speak yet, if he is even able. Medicus says it'll take some time." Gaius took a swig. "He's seen something awful though. I've never seen anyone look so afraid. Not even on the battlefield."

"He must have family or someone..." Antonius mused, even as he tipped backward into the wall.

"Must have..." Gaius answered absently. He slapped the unconscious man on the leg and rose shakily on his own feet. "Sleep well, Antonius." He turned to some of the others dicing nearby. "If he doesn't wake up, put him in his bunk, will you?"

"Yes, sir," the men mumbled.

Gaius grabbed a fresh jug and a last hunk of bread before stepping out into the street to go down the block to his room. As an optio, he was given his own room, unlike the troops who bunked eight to a room, or Julius who had his own suite of centurion's rooms.

He drank more as he dodged drunken men in the street, some singing bawdy songs, some gambling on the cobbles, some puking.

"Gonna be rough tomorrow, lads!" he said to no one in particular. "Go easy!" he laughed, knowing he would feel it too. When he arrived at his quarters, he stepped inside, lit the oil lamps a little clumsily, and bolted the wooden door. He removed his cingulum from about his waist and set it and the attached wax tablet on his desk. It slipped off the edge onto the floor but Gaius left it. His mood was melancholic. He reached for the small wood-painted portrait of Fulvia and his girls. On the wall opposite his bed, the image of Mithras slaying the bull wavered in the lamplight. He took a long draft of the wine and leaned back. His eyes travelled between the images of his god and his family.

"What are you doing just now..." he whispered to his wife, her eyes, her hair, her smile, "I miss you…"

HIS GLADIUS FELT AS IF IT WERE MADE OF STONE, FOR AS HE ran, Gaius strained with every fibre of his musculature to keep his pace. The grassy earth was uneven, pocked with rodent holes, and scattered moss-covered boulders. He tripped and fell into the face of a large rock. He gasped for breath, lungs burning with effort, his winded body aching with exhaustion. He looked back at the woods climbing up the mountains, toothy, jagged.

Sleep, just sleep... he thought and then the still air was rent by howls of pain, of rage, and he cried out, ripping himself from off the rock to run toward the distant sun. Behind him, the air grew darker, more roilsome, chaotic. Gaius looked down as the earth grew softer with his every step. From the mossy earth flowed blood from beneath grass, root and rock. His boots sank and he strained more and more with each stride.

Run to the Sun! he told himself. *Run to the Sun! Sun Runner!*

Hot breath came at him, raising hackles on his neck and seeing no way out, the Roman leaped atop a fallen log and turned, his sword raised as a wave of blood and bodies slammed into him, drowning out the sun, drowning him.

"OPTIO! OPTIO!"

It was not so much the voice of his men that woke him,

but rather the thud and flex of steel as his pugio embedded itself in the beams where he had unknowingly thrown it.

"Optio, sir!" came the voice again.

Gaius sat on the edge of the bed, cursed at the spilled wine jug where it had pooled on the floor. He stood and went to the door, retrieved his dagger and opened.

"Yes, yes. What is it?" he said, wondering if he had over-slept. "Don't tell me I'm late for drills." He knew Julius would have his hide for it.

"No, sir. We're just into the first hour of daylight."

"Good. So? Why do you wake me?" Gaius was not usually so curt with his men, but his head pounded and his tongue felt like he had cleaned the latrines with it.

"Sir. Another civilian from across the river, sir."

"Another?"

"In hysterics, sir. He had blood all over himself."

"So? Why wake me? Sixth cohort was on guard duty."

"I was told to come get you, sir, because the man we found recognized the boy you saved. Seems they may be from the same village."

"All right. I'm coming. Wait outside."

"Yes, sir."

Gaius turned into his room after closing the door. Feeling his stomach lurch, he moved to an empty basin and puked.

"You all right, sir?" the soldier asked.

"Good gods, man! Let me vomit in peace!" he barked back.

"Sorry, sir."

He shook his head after the final purge, hearing Fulvia's voice when she told him to go easy on the drink. *You can't match your men when it comes to drinking, my love. Stick to swords and spears. Mithras and Mars, dear. Not Bacchus.*

Gaius splashed cold water on his face and dressed in a clean tunic. He put on his cingulum and gladius and threw his crimson cloak about his shoulders. He had slept in his boots.

"Take me to the boy!" he said to the trooper when he stepped out. "I want to see him first."

When they arrived at the boy's room, the medicus was with him, calming him.

"What happened?" Gaius asked.

"Ah, Optio. Seems our young guest is acquainted with a man we've taken from the river. "Gaius looked at the boy, he had obviously been crying.

"Does the man say anything?"

"It's incoherent. He's insane, it seems. But, he did recognize the boy whom I was bringing back here after washing. The man ran toward us and made to grab the boy. The troopers accompanying him held him fast. The boy was afraid, but he did recognize the man. I don't know what he said, but the boy has been crying ever since."

"We'll talk to him…or try. First, notify the commander. He'll want to know. And send for Centurion Lycus also."

"Yes, Optio." Stefanos snapped his fingers and an orderly came running. He was gone a few moments later to the Praetorium. Gaius knelt down beside the boy's bed and held out his hand. The boy grabbed it and held tightly as he buried his face in a pillow and continued to cry.

TWO GUARDS STOOD WATCH OVER THE DOOR WHERE THE NEW arrival had been placed. The yelling was audible as Gaius approached, though he could not make it out. The boy stayed behind him with the medicus. Gaius nodded and one trooper opened the door.

"Wait!" Julius' voice boomed down the hall. "Hold, Optio." Gaius stopped short.

"Sir."

"You'll not go in alone. Who knows what madness is on him."

"After you, sir." Gaius stepped aside. It was not time for pleasantries. He could tell Julius was in a mood, most likely because all the men were hung over.

Inside the room, the first noticeable thing was the smell, of stale sweat and faeces, of fear. In a corner the man sat mumbling to himself, one inaudible word, over and over. His eyes took in the big centurion and the others, then lingered on the boy a moment longer. He closed his eyes and shook his head.

"Oi! You there!" Julius stepped up, his vinerod smacking into his hand. "Do you understand me? What happened to you?" Nothing. "By Mithras!" Julius cursed. "When will these Thracian bastards learn Latin?" He stepped back frustrated. "Optio, you try. You know some of the dialect."

"Yes, sir." Gaius stepped forward, his hand on the pommel of his gladius "Pios isse?"

Immediately the man's eyes fixed on Gaius, imploring, fearful. Then he pointed at the boy who clung to the medicus' hand.

"Ime o theeos tou. Ap to horio."

"He says he's uncle to the boy," Gaius translated for Julius. "That he is from the same village."

"Ask him what happened. I want to know what in Hades has these two cowering like beaten whores." Julius looked back at the boy and then to the man. "Go on, Optio. Ask him."

Gaius hoped the man would say something soon. Julius could be a kind old bear, but he could also lash a man to within an inch of his life to get the information he wanted. He turned back to the man.

"Pou ine to horio sas?" The man answered. Gaius translated. "He says his village is beyond the river, to the north and west, in the woods on the slope of the mountain."

"You came that far?" the medicus asked in Greek of both the boy and the man. They nodded, seemingly understanding his own educated dialect. Gaius looked into the man's frightened eyes.

"Ti synevi?" Gaius asked him what was wrong. He didn't know if it was the question or the memory of the answer that did it, but the man rose up on the bed and yelled at the boy.

"Oli necri! Oli necri!"

"He's saying they're all dead, sir."

"Who, Optio? Tell him to sit down or I'll have him beaten!" Behind Julius, Stefanos was comforting the boy who now bawled full-on.

"Stamata!" Gaius told him to stop. "Pios necri?" At this, the man fixed on the boy, tears burning his reddened face. "Who is dead?" Gaius repeated.

"Oikogenia mas!"

"He says their family is dead. Oli? All of them?"

"Oli." The man pursed his lips, hunched his body. "Oikogenia mas! Oli necri!" After this he launched himself at the door. "Athan-" but fell flat when Julius' vinerod caught him on the side of the head.

"That'll shut him up! Good gods! What a racket."

"Sir," Gaius interrupted. "The boy is distraught at news of his family. Perhaps we should let him rest?"

"I can give him a sleeping draught," Stefanos added, his hand on the boy's shoulders.

Just then there was a flurry of activity in the hall. Julius went out to see their tribune, Misenus, coming up.

"Lycus!"

"Yes, sir!" Julius answered, saluting.

"The commander wants you and Justus to report to the Praetorium immediately. You're to bring the boy and the man." He looked down at the limp form on the floor. "Wake him up."

"Yes, sir. We'll be there right away." The tribune stalked off, his red cloak billowing about him as he turned a corner. Julius looked down and beckoned the two guards. "Bring him along, you two. Let's not keep the commander waiting."

The two troopers hauled the prostrate man up by the arms and went after Julius. Gaius, Stefanos and the boy followed.

The Praetorium was bustling as usual, a steady flow of messengers going in and out of the tribunes' offices. The commander came out of his larger meeting space into the courtyard to see Julius, Gaius and their two stray Thracians.

"So, Lycus, what's this we have here? Who are they?"

"Two Thracian settlers from across the river, Commander. The boy was pulled out of the river two nights past by my optio, and this man was found swimming across today by sixth cohort. Optio Justus discovered from the man that he is the boy's uncle, that they are from the same village in the mountains, and that their entire family is dead."

"Dead?" The commander stepped forward. "All of them?"

"That's what he said, Commander."

"Did he say what happened?"

"No, sir. He made a run for the door before I clubbed him." The commander looked at the boy and at the man hanging between the two guards.

"Well, wake him and ask him now. We need more information." By now the other tribunes and several legionaries had come out to flank the commander.

"Optio." Julius nodded to Gaius who went over and spoke to the man. When he made no response, he slapped him.

"Ti synevi?" Gaius asked, indicating he should repeat for the commander. The man looked confused and startled for a moment at all the red cloaks about him. He strained lightly but the troopers held him. "Who killed your family?" Gaius asked.

The man fell to his knees, weeping.

"Athanatoi," he mumbled through his grief, his fear.

"Ti?" Gaius asked, straining to hear. "What?"

The man fixed wild eyes on him. "Athanatoi," he said clearly this time, pronouncing each syllable in frightening tones.

"What?" Gaius looked back at the boy. Stefanos shook his head, unbelieving.

"What did he say, Optio?" the commander asked.

"Commander, sir. I asked him who killed his family and he says…he says… *Immortui*."

Some of the men gathered gasped, others laughed. It was the laughter that set him off for, gazing about at the laughing Romans, the man grew angry. In a moment, he shot up from the ground, shoving his guards aside and charged for the commander's throat.

"Athanatoi!" he yelled.

It was his final word before the commander, in one swift, smooth motion, drew his gladius from his side to impale the maddened man on the end of it.

Gaius looked on in shocked horror at the transfixed body, the man's last word burning in his mind. *Athanatoi*. Undead… Immortui.

The Praetorium was in an uproar as men rushed to pull the body away, to bicker about what the man had said before attacking their commander.

"Enough!" the commander's voice seemed to crack the very walls of the courtyard. He handed his gladius to one of his staff to clean and stepped up to Julius. "Centurion."

"Yes, Commander."

"We've been charged by the Emperor to keep a close watch on the Danuvius frontier, to stomp out any resistance." He rubbed his chin, pacing the cobbles before his men. "I don't believe this rubbish of immortui. No end of superstition among the Thracians. If this poor boy's family has been massacred, whoever did it has got to pay. We're going to extend our Pax Romana across the river, and we can't have that threatened."

"Yes, Commander," Julius said. "My thought was that it is likely some renegade barbarians fresh from defeat at Rome's hands. They must have been moving east."

"We are of like mind, Centurion." The commander stopped pacing. "I want you, Centurion Lycus, to take half of III Century across the river tomorrow. I want you to find this village and root out these dregs. Put them to the sword or take them prisoner. Whatever is easiest. Just put a stop to this before they attack any other settlements.

"Yes, Commander!"

"Optio Justus can remain behind with the other half of your men." He looked at Gaius and then went into his offices followed by the tribunes.

After a few minutes, the only people left in the courtyard were Julius, Gaius, Stefanos the medicus, and the boy who stared at the small pool of blood on the cobbles where his uncle had died. Gaius put his hand on the boy's shoulder and led him back to the hospital.

"Gaius, you can't be serious! Immortui? Really? I thought you were an educated man," Julius chided him as he gathered his kit for the following day. After the men had been dismissed for the night, Gaius had gone to the centurion's quarters to talk.

"What if there's something to it, Julius?"

"The man was out of his mind, Gaius. Come now, the Undead? More like bastard Dacians, or something like that."

"The boy isn't mad. What about him?" Ever since his uncle said it, he's been saying the word too. *Athanatoi* is no small thing to these people."

"And I'm the new Croesus!" Julius mocked. "Listen, my friend." He put his beefy hands on Gaius' shoulders. "The boy's lost his whole family. He's the only survivor. Of course he's going to be lashed with grief. He's only a child!"

"Exactly!" Gaius agreed.

"That's why I'm going to march up to those mountains and make those baseborn bastard sons of devils wish they'd died in Pannonia." Julius slammed his gladius home in its scabbard. "Now, if you don't mind, Heliodromus, Saturn is setting out at first light and needs his sleep."

"Yes, Pater," Gaius answered, using the Mithraic title.

"And you have first watch of the day before drills."

"Great."

Julius led Gaius to the door. "Don't worry." He smiled. "I'm the most decorated bloody centurion in the legion!"

. . .

Dawn was close to stroking the sky with her rays when Gaius stepped out of his room in full uniform for the first watch of the day. Sleep had eluded him, his thoughts plagued by what had happened at the Praetorium. The dream he had had flashed through his mind continually. Most of all, he was rocked with pity for the boy. Gaius figured he must have known his family was dead but that perhaps the confirmation of this by this uncle had hit him hard. He had tried soothing him with vain words of comfort and vengeance the night before as Stefanos had mixed the sleeping draught. The boy cried still but in a more exhausted way.

"Pio ine to onoma sou?" Gaius had asked him his name. Whimpering, the boy had muttered "Daxos."

Gaius had been grateful for that much.

"Up, lads! First watch!" Gaius pounded the doors of those men who remained behind with his hastile. Julius had taken four contubernia, forty men, leaving Gaius to command thirty. Gaius knew Julius would already have his men mustered in the space before the gate, readying themselves to cross in groups on the barges. The bridge building had experienced delays since the legion had been called west. His men began to emerge from their quarters, lining up along the barracks' walls. Gaius walked along, inspecting belt buckles and scabbards, helms and pila in the early morning light.

"Right. Let's go! III Century to the watch!" he called down the line before leading them around the perimeter of the walls, leaving troops at regular intervals the whole way before climbing to the top of the gatehouse with Antonius to look out over the Danuvius.

The river fought the morning light with its dark depths as Gaius watched the first of the barges begin its crossing, the cloaks of the ten legionaries on board like splashes of crimson paint far below. In the distance north and northeast, the mountains raked upward to black, cloudy skies. It would take Julius and the men at least two days, maybe more, to reach the foothills.

When the final barge was ready to push off, Julius turned toward the gate house and saluted.

Gaius returned the salute, then watched as the men on the far bank raised the vexillum and began the long march. The increasing light of dawn glinted on their helms as forty beacons of light.

"Mithras go with you, brothers," Gaius said before making another round of the walls.

The remainder of the day was all routine for Gaius and the rest of the century. After the watch, he led the men in drills which included testudo formations, and a mock engagement with some men of the sixth cohort. Though outnumbered, Gaius' men's discipline won out against their opponents'. However, tempers ran high and soon Gaius and the other optio were pulling men apart. The other optio had cracked his man so hard across the back with his hastile that the buckles of his lorica snapped and he was taken to the infirmary. Gaius put his man on latrine duty though it was in fact the other century's fault that the brawl had started in the first place.

It was a relief to get to the baths afterward, to ease tensions, and let worries melt away. The men of the two centuries became friends once more while Gaius, the other optio, named Valens, and the centurion, Bosco, soaked in the caldarium.

"Sorry about that scuffle today, Justus," Valens said. "Our

men were sore losers, I guess. I thought it would make them feel good to beat some of old Lycus' men for a change."

Gaius laughed. "Did you now? Good thing we were under half-strength then."

"Pa!" Bosco spat. "I think we should rematch with your whole century once the rest are back. The men will try harder knowing all of you are there."

"They weren't trying?" Gaius asked, wary of making Bosco angry. The man was a brawler and things had only been stopped by Valens because Bosco had been called to the Praetorium.

"I didn't ask you, sir. What were the orders from the commander?"

"Ach! We've got to march over the Durostorum to pick up and accompany some magistrate and his family back here. Apparently they're making a tally of needs after the campaigns." Bosco stretched his arms up and back. "Just another shite escort job. Hopefully the wife will be something pretty for the men to look at. Not like Julius' plum job, eh? Search and destroys are always good for morale and better training than any drills. Lucky bastard."

Through half-closed lids, Gaius watched Bosco, wondered if he was right or simply mad, in love with blood.

"Lucky bastard…" Bosco repeated, the words splashing off the walls as he got out of the pool.

In Julius' absence, Gaius drilled the men doubly hard, so much so that they dropped at the end of each day, sore and unconscious, going to sleep like a babe to its mother. Gaius felt too that he'd never worked so hard in his life and put it down to his not wanting to disappoint Julius. The centurion was present, if not physically, then at least in his mind, barking orders in his usual, gruff manner. Gaius only found real peace when, at the end of each day, he led his men to the Mithraeum. As Sun Runner, he performed his duties to the god and to his men, and as optio, he ensured they were all ready for action. One day, after prayers, Gaius sat on a boulder outside the Mithraeum watching the westering sun blaze downward.

Mithras had not yet granted him an explanation of his bloody dream from before. Gaius wondered if Apollo would not have been a better judge as the God of Prophecy, but he quickly dismissed the thought. Mithras had always been the receiver of his prayers and offerings, the one who stood beside him in the heat of battle as he faced death. Yet thoughts of the dream harangued him, like Germanic wraiths on the march, ever present, ever mysterious, never letting one rest.

Julius and the men had been gone for over a week and still no word had arrived. Gaius wondered if the distance had been farther than expected or if Julius and his men were cornered, dug in with no way to get out.

As he sat on that boulder looking at the disappearing sun, the changing colour and light about him, he spotted Stefanos and the boy, Daxos, walking toward him. Then it hit him. *Perhaps the boy will know something useful?* Indeed, Gaius and the medicus had been so adamant about not disturbing Daxos with any more questions that they had failed to realize he may hold some important intelligence that could help them.

"Optio!" Stefanos waived as they approached. Daxos held his hand as they walked. Gaius noticed his eyes had stopped looking about with panic. Now they were dark and focussed, the well of tears for his family run dry. "Optio. Daxos says he wishes to speak with you."

Gaius looked back at the cave, wondered if his prayers for guidance had been answered, and motioned for both of them to sit with him on the ancient stone.

"Tell me."

Gaius noted something of the Thracian warrior had come into Daxos's demeanour; his head was higher, his little shoulders were back and his eyes looked directly from one man to the other. He wondered if Daxos had been thinking of the father he would never again see or hear praise from, if the boy had now decided he was the head of his clan, as the sole survivor. Daxos sat on the flat rock, the setting sun orange on his face.

"Immortui..." he began, trying the Latin word he had heard used.

"Athanatoi?" Stefanos echoed in Greek.

"Yes. They are."

"So, it's true?" Gaius asked, leaning forward. Daxos nodded, plucked up his courage.

"Yes. True. They...they kill my oikogenia...my family."

"Tell me what happened, Daxos. If you are able."

"My father and brothers were hunting, up the mountains, the Carpathians. They were gone many days and no word. Then, one night, we hear screaming from up the mountain. Louder than wolves or eagles. Coming toward our village.

"Our men, and my father, they come running, screaming from down the mountain. They have blood on their swords and themselves. The screaming followed them. 'Athanatoi!' my father yelled to the village. My mama, she ask father quickly what happened. I hear them. He said the Dacians have a sorcerer, a sorcerer who makes Athanatoi, makes alive the dead killed by Romans."

"But that's not possible, boy. The dead can't be raised. Then ine Athanatoi! They can't be. It's superstition to scare children."

"No, Medicus Stefanos!" Daxos looked angrily at the Greek doctor, then back to Gaius. "It was immortui. During the fighting," he continued, "more and more coming from the woods. Our men and women dying fighting, children crying. My father grabbed me running by. He was hurt, his sword broken. He told me 'Go to Romans! Go to get help!' Then, after saying this, his face changed, his eyes, his mouth. He, my father, he attacked me." Daxos wiped a tear that was not there with a shaking hand. "I climb high up a tree to be safe, but I see all. My father, he…he killed my mother, tear her to pieces."

Gaius listened in disbelief, terrified and enraged. He was sick as the boy gave voice to the horrors that he had witnessed.

"My uncle, you know, he came with the axe and killed my father who fell on top of my dead mother. Then, my uncle run."

"What did you do, Daxos? How did you get away?" Gaius sat beside him, looking sidelong at his face.

"I…I spend night in the tree. Watching, hearing my whole village killed. Immortui, some of them eat the dead, and… others that were dead, wake up. When the sun came next day, they were all gone. Only silence and torn bodies. My…my mama and father in pieces below my tree. I run…I run, Optio Gaius…I run here, to Rome for help."

The tears flowed once more, real and full of feeling outside of his previous shock, and Gaius looked down with pity where the boy's bracae were wet with the terror of his tale.

"I can't believe this," Stefanos repeated. "It is just not scientifically possible."

"What if it is, Stefanos? What possible reason could a boy have for making this up?" Gaius looked back at the cave. "Mithras watches over us in the Dark. He is the Light. The Dacians and other barbarian tribes…they suffered defeat, but what's to say they have accepted it?" Gaius shook his head, his thoughts racing, hid blood hammering. "And now, Julius is out there with forty men. What's happened to them now?"

Daxos looked up. "Centurion is already dead, Optio."

Gaius stared at the boy and then at Stefanos.

"I'll go to Tribune Misenus. We need to march. At first light." Then he turned to Daxos. "I am truly sorry about your family. You are very brave, and I know your father would have been proud." Gaius knelt down in front of him. "Know this. We will march and we will fight. And, immortui or not, we will avenge your parents' deaths."

"WHAT IS IT, OPTIO?" THE TRIBUNE SAID FROM THE courtyard of his quarters. Gaius stood out on the street where the doors to the six legionary tribunes' homes were. It was dark by then and the torchlight only aggravated the scowl on Misenus' face.

"Sir. I have some intelligence on the Thracian village. Centurion Lycus and the men may be in great danger.

Misenus, wrapped in a long blue cloak, came closer. "We can talk in my office. Follow me." Gaius followed him across the courtyard, his hobnails clacking with each step behind the tribune's leather-soled boots. "So, Optio? What intelligence do you have?"

Gaius sat on a stool Misenus motioned to and looked about the room. Antiques and family heirlooms hung on the walls where they were not covered by shelves of scrolls or maps. Gaius did not know Misenus very well, but from the look of things he was one to seek promotion, which meant he would do little to endanger that.

"Sir, it may be difficult to believe, but I think that the enemies Centurion Lycus went after are in fact… Immortui."

The tribune's hands went straight to his temples, as though massaging a long-standing headache.

"That's ridiculous, Optio."

"But the boy said that-"

"The boy? You mean to tell me that your so-called intelligence came from the boy who could barely speak? A Thracian settler?"

"He witnessed the whole thing, sir. The horrors that boy has been through!"

Gaius went on to tell Misenus everything Daxos had told him about the hunting party, the screams, the carnage, the dead rising, everything. When he finished, he looked at the tribune for some sign, for the order to march at first light.

"I like you, Justus. The commander likes you. I know Lycus loves you like a son. But I can't go to the commander with a story like this when all we have is the word of a distraught child and a dead mad man who tried to kill the commander."

"But, sir!"

"Let me finish, Optio." Misenus held up his hand. "Lycus and the men have only been gone a week. The distance is far and the terrain unknown. The imperial map makers and engineers have not covered the area as yet. If Centurion Lycus is not back in another week, then, and only then, will I allow you to take the remainder of the men and go looking for him. Is that understood, Optio?"

"Yes, sir!" Gaius stood and saluted, biting his tongue as he did so.

"Good." The tribune nodded. "Now, if you don't mind, I'd like to sleep. I'm supervising your drills first thing tomorrow. I want to see why the men are all so exhausted."

"See you then, sir!"

"Dismissed, Optio."

OVER THE NEXT COUPLE OF DAYS, TWO COHORTS WENT OFF ON furlough, a reward for their hard-won fighting in the months passed. Gaius was thankful that their own had been kept back; he had requested as much from Misenus in case Julius did not return. Misenus had agreed and told Gaius he hoped the men did not find out as it would make things difficult for his command.

The men, of course, grumbled as they watched others pass through the gates, laughing, jostling and singing their marching songs on their way to warmer climes in the south. A lot of enjoyment was to be had in a three week furlough.

For Gaius and his men however, days of drills, hard training and guard duty continued. The pain began to leach away from their bodies as they became accustomed to the new rigours Gaius devised. At times, Gaius wondered if some Mithraic fibre guided him in the new techniques of individual fighting that came to mind. After all, Rome's armies rarely broke formations, for therein lay their strength. After drills with pilum, gladius and scutum, testudo and cavalry-deflecting formations, they trained, unusually, as gladiators out for individual glory. The other optios scoffed, but when the commander showed up to watch, gave a nod of approval and went back to the Praetorium, the laughter ceased.

Another observer was Daxos. The young Thracian insisted on watching the drills every day and though he was young, Gaius put a wooden practice sword into his hand and set Antonius to teaching him some basics. Daxos took to it quickly, true to his people but, at times, needed to be told to rest. The intense emotion with which he swung his rudus showed the pain that yet lingered in his damaged mind and heart.

In his cubiculum, Gaius Justus Vitalis knelt before the image of Mithras, clutching the painted picture of his family. The lamp's flame flickered and cast deformed shadows across the small table. Gaius felt that a darkness, long awaited, long feared, was close at hand, ready to reveal itself. It was something that came as light as the flutter of a black butterfly's wings at the back of his consciousness. It had come and gone, and only when he was at peace, focussed in prayer, did he perceive it.

Then Daxos popped into his mind, a quick flash of screaming red. Gaius jumped up, grabbed his gladius and ran out the door.

It was past midnight, the moon at its zenith on a quiet night. The hospital was not far, and it took Gaius only moments to reach it. When he entered the corridor where the patient rooms were, he sliped on something wet. He looked down in the dim light to see muddy tracks leading down the hall. At the end of the hall, he heard the orderly's voice.

"Hold it there! Authorized personnel only. Get away from that door, you."

A second later the orderly was screaming as the person he had been speaking to rushed him and was now tearing at his face and throat. The screams turned to choked gurgling and Gaius' feet could not carry him quickly enough. The attacker looked at the rushing optio and darted for the room opposite. Daxos' room.

"Guards!" Gaius yelled as he reached the door and kicked it in. The door slammed into something. "Daxos!"

"Optio!" the boy cried. He cowered in the corner, terrified. "Look out!"

Before Gaius could turn, he felt something like claws grabbing at his boots. He tripped and spun to see a bloody face of rage bearing down on him, eyes shot and yellow with a mad jaundice.

Gaius kicked up into the creature and found his feet. "Daxos, into the hall! Get out!"

The boy lunged for the door and just as he did so the creature lunged for him, held fast for a moment by Gaius' gladius in his side. It but slowed him and he came at Gaius with a fast, hard, left-handed swing. As the claw bore down, Gaius' blade found the wrist and left a stump. He jumped back to catch a breath, but as he did so the attacker's right hand swung in and Gaius swiftly removed that hand and followed it up with a kick to the chest so that the creature crashed against the wall.

Immediately the creature came back, roaring with rage and only as Gaius spun his gladius in a deadly arc did the creature fall silent. The head thudded in a pool of blood and puss beside the spasming body.

Stefanos and a guard burst into the room. "Optio!"

"Stand back," Gaius ordered.

"What in Hades is it?" the guard asked.

"Immortui," Gaius gasped, air filling his lungs as the adrenaline ran away. "I think…Medicus…that you have your proof." With the tip of his sword, Gaius rolled the head over to reveal Daxos' uncle's distorted face.

"But…he was killed."

"Yes. He was."

"By the Gods." The soldier made a sign to avert evil.

"Go immediately, but quietly, and bring the commander and Tribune Misenus."

"Yes…yes, sir!" the guard said, backing out of the room in horror.

When he left, Daxos emerged in the doorway. He walked up, silent, and spat on his uncle's head.

"Come away from here, Daxos." Gaius led him into the hall to await the commander and tribune while Stefanos examined the body by the light of a lamp.

A few minutes later, the commander and tribune stood looking down at the bloody mass on the floor of Daxos' room.

"What in Hades could do such a thing?" the commander asked. "Never in all my years…" the thought died as he recognized the killing wound he himself had given the man that was. "I sank my blade through this man's very heart. How?"

"Immortui, Commander sir."

"Immortui? You're serious, Optio?" Then he looked at Misenus. "Tribune?"

"Sir. Optio Justus came to me a few days ago with the tale of what had happened to the boy's village. It sounded so outrageous I thought it best not to trouble you with it."

"Well, now I'm troubled even more, Tribune." He looked

down at the body again. "He didn't even stop when you took his hands off?" he asked Gaius.

"No, sir." Gaius shivered at the thought. "He didn't even flinch, just kept coming at me. Only after I took his head off…" Gaius stopped as Daxos peaked around the corner.

The commander pulled Gaius and Misenus close so that only they could hear what was said.

"I don't want word of this getting out. You hear me? It'll cause a superstitious panic that I don't need in my legion. We can't afford to send all our men out to take this on if we *want* to be discreet. A third of the legion is on furlough and we've been ordered to hold this frontier and fortress at all cost."

"What shall we do, Commander?" Misenus asked.

"Tribune, you shall do nothing. You have five more centuries to worry about. You'll remain here." He turned to Gaius. "Optio?"

"Yes, sir?"

"I want you and your men to go to this village and find Centurion Lycus and the others. Bring them out of there, and if possible destroy these immortui spawn. They cannot, at all cost, be allowed to spread. I don't know how it happened or what is responsible, but whatever it is, it is a threat to the Empire." He paused. "Are you up to this fight, Optio?" With thirty men are you confident you can discover what has happened?"

Gaius looked at the body on the floor, and in that moment fear seeped into his veins like fire. He fought to control it, the thoughts of what he stood to lose. This was no ordinary battle. This was that unknown darkness he had long dreaded. He turned to see Daxos in the door and his anger rose at what had been done to the boy, the ruin of his life that remained. He thought of Lycus, his friend, Saturn of their order.

"Centurion Lycus would do no less for me, sir. I'll prepare the men."

"Good. You'll leave under cover of darkness to aid discretion, early the day after tomorrow. Take whatever you need from the armoury and quartermaster and," he looked at Daxos, "take the boy and medicus with you."

"Sir?"

"You'll need a guide to get you there as quickly as possible if Lycus is to have a fighting chance, Gods willing."

"But, sir. The boy has suffered overmuch already. Can't he-"

"I'll go!" Daxos came into the room nodding. "I want vengeance, Optio. For my family, my mother and father. The commander is right. I can get you there faster-" he stopped, realizing he had burst in on their conversation. The commander looked down on Daxos from beneath furrowed brows.

"Good lad," he said, ruffling his hair. He turned to Gaius again. "Optio, if you run into more enemies than you can handle, if the frontier is threatened in anyway, or if you feel that…that all is lost, get word to me by any means you can so that we can be ready. Do you understand?"

"Yes, sir!"

"Good man. Now go and rest. You have a busy day of preparations tomorrow. Medicus?"

"Yes, Commander," Stefanos said as he entered.

"You heard my request?"

"Yes, sir."

"Are you willing to go?"

A pause and audible swallowing. "Yes, Commander."

"Good. Take the boy to another room for now. I'm doubling the guards. You," he spoke to the guard outside the door. "Get another you can trust and gather up this filth." He looked on the bloody corpse below. "Burn it outside the walls."

"Yes, sir!"

"Everyone dismissed." Commander Maximus stalked from the room with Misenus in tow, leaving Gaius, Stefanos and Daxos in grim silence.

"HEAR US, GREAT FATHER OF LIGHT! ACCEPT OUR PRAYERS, Mithras!"

"Mithras! Mithras! Mithras! The men repeated in the torchlit dark of the cave in answer to the Sun Runner's voice.

"We, your devout soldiers of light ask for your help and guidance as we march once more into darkness. Aid us in the rescue of our brothers and our Pater. Give us the strength to defeat the enemies of Rome."

"The Light shall overcome the Dark," the men chanted. "The Light shall prevail."

Gaius turned then to the altar where one of the Miles held a small ewe.

"Accept our offering Mithras, Lord of Light. Accept this blood." With a quick slice of the curved blade, warm blood poured over the altar to run in the stone-carved channels about the animal's shuddering body. All thirty-one of them in that cave were silent then, with their prayer. Gaius turned to speak again.

"Brothers," he began as he walked among them, his white robe stained with blood. "You have been preparing this entire day to set out. Your gladii and pila are sharp, your armour secure, your helms polished, and yet you do not know where we're headed. Though I guess you all suspect." Several heads nodded. "Commander Maximus asked for complete secrecy with regards to our mission, and I know you will be discreet yourselves. Tomorrow, before the sun rises on a new day, we will be marching for the mountains across the river to find Centurion Lycus and our brothers. There has been no word. But..." *How can I say it?* "...we now know that the stories of immortui are true. The man the commander killed emerged from the pit where he had been buried outside the walls." There were several gasps, but no scoffing this time. They believed him as they fought back the fear they were surely feeling. "The beast, for he was no longer like a man, came to attack young Daxos who has lost his family. Only after I had removed the thing's head did it stop coming at me."

Silence.

"Brothers. This enemy is strong, dangerous and speaks of powers we know not of. But! By Mithras, we will find them and we will make them pay for what they have become!" Several men roared at this, their courage up again with thoughts of their brothers' plight. "We will march against this darkness and come back into the light with the blood of our enemies upon our blades. Pluck up your courage, my brothers, for tomorrow we set out!"

Outside the Mithraeum, in the gathering mist of dusk where ravens whirled and cawed, the voices of the men within could be heard clearly. None knew what to expect and yet, not one of them made the request to remain behind.

WHILE THE STARS YET TWINKLED IN A COLD BLACK OCTOBER sky, Gaius and Tribune Misenus inspected the men by torch-light. They were fully equipped and armed for campaign. Each soldier carried his pick axe, shovel, pot, pan and food rations in addition to two stakes, pilum, scutum, gladius and pugio. Loricas had been tightly cinched and oiled, and each man wore his helmet, thick red cloak and wolf pelt arm bands to ward off the mountain cold. Those whom Gaius had identified as having mountaineering experience also carried long wreaths of hempen rope.

Gaius himself had affixed a new horsehair crest and feathers to his helmet and carried an extra two wax tablets for messages that might need to be run back to base. Even through his double-thick cloak, he could still feel the cold. Daxos followed him closely too, never leaving his side while Stefanos figured out the best way to hoist his medical gear. He felt clumsy with a gladius at his side rather than a scalpel.

Gaius finished looking over the last man and turned to Misenus.

"We're ready, Tribune."

Misenus nodded. "Good. Optio, I wanted to say that… well…I'm sorry I didn't believe you before."

"That's all right, sir. It was pretty unbelievable."

"True enough but…not all tribunes are arrogant bastards." Gaius smiled and nodded. "I'll keep a watch out at all times for you, Optio. If it comes to it, we'll be ready."

"Thank you, sir," Gaius answered, not a little shocked by the change in Misenus.

The tribune saluted Gaius and the men, and turned to the guards.

"Open the gates!" he called. The massive oak and iron doors creaked open and at Gaius' signal, all thirty-three of them marched out.

At the commander's order, it had been given out that the men of III Century, II Cohort, were setting out on a routine patrol, but as the gates closed again, the young tribune atop the wall wished fervently that that was not a lie. Misenus watched the dark as Gaius' men and their torches crossed the river and headed to the northwest, slowly and methodically, like wolves in the dark.

IT HAD BEEN A FRIGID START TO THE MARCH AND SO, WHEN the sun finally rose on that late October morning, the men were relieved to have its rays warming their backs. They all felt a certain amount of pride in the young boy. Daxos was keeping admirable pace. He wore woollen clothes that had been procured for him, as well as a thick cloak. Beneath was a black leather cingulum with a pugio that served for a sword. Few spoke as they marched, each man lost in the thoughts that flowed with the soft tramp of their hobnailed boots. A buzz of words did not really emerge until Gaius called a halt for the night on a patch of higher ground. They had made much better progress than he had expected. The mountains were much closer now, the dark gnarled forests of the slopes within view.

"Antonius!" Gaius called his trusted man.

"Yes, Optio?"

"I want everybody to work on a moat and stockade. I don't want any surprises during the night."

"Yes, Optio." Antonius saluted and set about giving the order. Gaius looked to the south-east for the base and found it out of sight. They had marched far and now they camped where Julius and the others had camped; the earth was pocked with the ghostly outlines of their fire pits.

Gaius removed his pack and lay down all his gear except for his gladius, pugio and shovel. With the latter, he jumped right in to help the men shift the earth to form a ditch and rampart. The going was easier than usual with the soil having been loosened by Julius and his men. When the earth was packed, every man's sharpened stakes were driven into the top of the rampart to form defences. Each of the three contuburnia raised their tents and lit their cooking fires. Gaius raised his own tent which he would share with Stefanos and Daxos who, all this while, stood staring at the dark slopes in the distance.

"Don't worry Daxos," Gaius said as he came up next to him. "We'll light torches and have a contuburnium on watch all through the night."

"I don't worry about tonight," the boy answered. "It is what we will find the night after next that scares me."

"We'll be there so soon? At your village?"

"Yes…yes…"

"I won't let anything happen to you, Daxos. Do you believe me?"

The boy did not answer. He simply reached for Gaius' hand. Gaius thought he looked so very small at that moment.

THAT FIRST NIGHT PASSED WITHOUT INCIDENT. AND THE NEXT. The men had become accustomed to their fear of what lay ahead, and even Stefanos joked about how they would someday have wonderful stories with which to scare their future children to bed, or, all the women they would be able to scare into their own beds.

On the afternoon of their third day on the march, they approached the edge of the forest - a world of deep green and teal, of shades of black walnut and forest fern. It was a world that light did not often penetrate. Daxos pointed to an over-grown cart path that wound up into the wood.

"How far is it to the village?" Gaius asked him.

"Half a day up the mountain. There is a flat part where the village is built. From there, another half day to the top of the first peak. Valley beyond, and then more mountains."

Gaius listened to the clipped description and knew they may not make it to the village before nightfall. And what if Julius and the men were not at the village? Gaius knew they could not return without some proof of what had happened.

"Make camp three hundred yards from the tree line," he ordered. "We'll set out for the village before sunrise."

That night, the moon hid itself behind thick veils of grey cloud so that all the men could see was the faint orange light outside their defences cast by the torches of the watch. The howling of wolves was much louder as they keened for Selene where she hid from their sight. Owls screeched around them, diving for mice and other rodents, and foxes barked here and there among the dark of the trees.

Gaius sat sharpening his gladius with a whetstone by a fire at the centre of camp. Antonius, Vitellius and Stefanos sat with him.

"Medicus?" Vitellius spoke suddenly.

"Yes?"

"We know these immortui are of a dark art, but...I mean...how did the boy's uncle come to change? Or his father?"

"Hmm. I have puzzled over this myself, Vitellius." They all turned to listen. "I inspected Daxos' uncle's body afterward, and from what I could see, apart from scrapes inflicted by tree, rock and thorn, there were three jagged, almost claw-like marks on the back of his calf muscle. It may be, and this is but a guess, that one of the immortui lunged for him as he ran and transferred the magic's poison that way."

Gaius looked up, his whetstone still. "You mean to tell me

we could catch this…this…I don't know what to call it. But we could end up like them? Immortui?"

"How else to explain it?" Stefanos threw up his hands, having obviously mulled it over and come to no better conclusion. "I believe it may be like to when a maddened dog bites a child or adult, and the subsequent fever that sets in. Some are killed, others go mad with rage and the burn of illness. We should tell the men to avoid close quarter combat at all costs. Especially avoid being bitten as, I suspect, it spreads more quickly that way than by a scratch."

Gaius slammed the point of his sword into the ground. "It won't be easy to avoid getting close, Stefanos. You saw that the only way I could stop that thing was to lob its bloody head off."

"I know. I told you, Optio." I was just guessing. I would suggest making the head your primary target."

"Mithras, help us," Antonius finally spoke, as another chorus of wolfsong broke out on the mountainside. It was a long sad note, as though they wept for something. Then it was silenced.

Before dawn, the camp was torn down and the men arrayed two abreast. Normally, Gaius would have had them tear down the ramparts and fill in the ditches, but he opted to break from procedure in case they needed to fall back on a strong position.

They began their slow progress into the forest then, each man listening to the pumping of his heart as he strained his ears in the silence. The cart path was little more than a narrow track that meandered up the slope, and each man took his turn stubbing a toe by tripping over an exposed stone or one of the thousands of red roots that veined the path.

"We should watch for bears, Optio."

"Bears?" Gaius looked up at Daxos where he stood on a large boulder by the side of the path. "Are there many bears in these parts?"

"Yes. Though my father said they leave us alone. Unless it is the mating time, or before hibernation. Then they are angry, especially the males."

Great, Gaius thought. *That's all we need.* He moved on and noticed the sun was directly above. "We're almost there, aren't we?"

"Yes," Daxos answered. "Just around the next turn." The boy jumped down to press on ahead, but Gaius stopped him.

"I'll go first. You go back to stay with the medicus." Gaius turned and whispered. "Antonius, Vitellius, on me in front. Everyone leave your stakes, pots, and satchels here. Gladii, pila and scuta at the ready."

Gaius nodded to Daxos and the others then started up, his hastile in his left hand, gladius in his right, the point sharpened to a deadly killing edge. Antonius and Vitellius flanked him while the rest came up behind, Daxos and Stefanos in the middle.

The first thing Gaius noticed was the faint smell of charring mingled with dead leaves and putrefaction. Not overwhelming but enough to perk up his warrior's senses. His cloak began to weigh on him and he felt sweat trickling down the ridge of his spine beneath his tunic and lorica. Then he noticed something and held up his hand to halt the men.

Absolute silence.

The forest held its breath as not a rabbit, fox, or bird moved about or called. All sound had been sucked out of the scene. Gaius stopped at the entrance to the village, marked by a ram's skull set upon a post, the empty sockets a grim warning. Gaius waited, listening as he scanned everything.

He counted twenty-odd stone dwellings with rough thatch and bramble roofs. They were all of varying sizes, scattered like a stray handful of pebbles about the large flat area of the plateau. Tall pines and beeches reached up above the rooftops. In the centre of the village was a well. All about, debris was scattered pell-mell, broken buckets or farming implements, axe handles, chairs, even part of a table. It looked like a group of Germans had indeed sacked the place, but then Gaius remembered the feral look in Daxos' uncle's eyes and knew it was no raiding party.

"Spread out!" he called back. "Keep an eye out for survivors, tracks, anything." The men fanned out in either direction, shields up to deflect a rushing attack, pila ready to launch.

"Not a soul about, sir," Antonius whispered.

Gaius held up a hand, wiped the sweat from his brow. Then he spotted something near the well and made his way there. Vitellius and Antonius watched his back as he examined it. With the point of his gladius he raised the item out of the mud and dead leaves.

"A legionary cloak," he whispered.

"One of ours?" Antonius glanced over his shoulder at the shredded material.

"Yes. They were here." Gaius slammed his hastile point down in the ground, its brass orb glinting in a bit of stray sunlight.

"Sir!" one of the men called from a nearby dwelling. "A helmet, sir." Gaius at once knew it to be another of their century.

"Optio!" came another voice, a trooper holding up a lorica breast plate that appeared to be torn in half. Then it seemed all at once, men began holding up pieces of their comrades' broken armour, weapons and gear.

"What in Hades happened here?" Gaius cursed as he looked at all the debris. Then his eyes fell on Stefanos and a trooper where they stood at the base of a tall pine. At their feet knelt Daxos, his weeping softened by the foliage and the hands muffling his face. Gaius strode over to him and found him keening over two skulls and a scattering of bones.

"His parents," Stefanos said as Gaius came up.

He knelt down and put his arm around the boy.

"There, there now. We will honour their bones if you wish. Do the Thracians still burn their dead?" Daxos nodded. "You two!" Gaius called two men over. "Gather some dry wood and make a pyre near the open area around the well."

"Yes, sir!" the men set to and Gaius turned to Antonius and Stefanos.

"Help Daxos carry his parents to the pyre."

"No!" Daxos stood up suddenly. "I do it myself."

"Very well," Gaius said. "If you need help, let me know."

"Optio, a word," Stefanos leaned in. "Not sure if you noticed but the bones have been picked clean."

"So? A fox, or crows perhaps?"

"Not so cleanly, I think, and decomposition would not happen so quickly. A fox would remove the bones to a lair. All the bones appear to be present here."

"You don't think that-"

"Optio! A bear!" two of the men shouted, shattering the deathly silence. Gaius, Antonius and Vitellius ran the to the other side of the village where some of the troops were moving in on a massive brown body on its side, in the last part of the village to be searched. One trooper threw his pilum into the bear's bulk with a thud and turned back to his companions.

"It's dead!"

He did not have time to see the red-yellow eyes rise, a face like a bloody moon on the other side of the carcass it had been quietly devouring.

The movement was so swift, the raging scream so chill that all the men froze momentarily as the creature sank its teeth into the trooper's neck in a spray of blood and pain. Antonius' pilum came whistling through the air to graze the creature, but it seemed only to enrage it.

"Take its head!" Gaius yelled as he ran. Two of the closer troopers moved in, cornering the creature but froze as they spotted the legionary tunic and bracae. Gaius reached them and before they could act, his gladius sliced through the neck, the head falling at their feet. "I ordered you to take the bloody head!" he yelled.

"But, sir. He's one of us!"

"Not anymore. He was immortui." Each man made a sign against evil as he stared at the corpse. "Don't hesitate! We do that and we're dead." Gaius looked down at the head and body, trying to see if he recognized the person it had been, but it was unrecognizable apart from the standard issue clothing. The skin was mottled, rotting, as if in the advanced stages of gangrene, and there were gashes in the flesh of the corpse. The latter were obviously no impediment to the creature, despite blood loss and the weakened state of body that such wounds would cause. It really was a walking corpse.

Stefanos was kneeling over the injured trooper, trying to stanch his bleeding when he was suddenly thrown back and the soldier's red-shot eyes turned on him, a sound of agony coming from his mouth as he writhed. Then, he was on his feet.

There was no hesitation this time and Vitellius' gladius swung fast into the neck of the man who minutes before had been one of them.

"By the gods," Gaius said under his breath, looking to Stefanos. "It took hold of him in minutes."

"Whatever happens," Stefanos called to the gathered men, "don't let them get close enough to bite or scratch you!"

"Nobody goes alone! Only groups of two or more! Now, finish searching the buildings. Cautiously! It's evident our men were here and that they were attacked by…immortui. But they may yet be out there alive. And if they are, by Mithras, it's our duty to find them. Get to it and keep looking for tracks."

The men set to and Gaius, having forgotten Daxos in the commotion, strode back to where he had left him. The boy stood by himself with the two troopers next to the pyre where he had laid the bones of his mother and father. Pity welled up in Gaius as he saw the boy standing, a white fist gripping the hilt of the pugio he wore. He stared at the bones of the people who had been his parents, the skulls he had lain in grisly affection, side by side.

Gaius stood beside Daxos and nodded to one of the troopers to strike a flint and light a firebrand.

"Are you ready, Daxos?" he asked.

"I…I am…yes."

The trooper handed Daxos the flaming branch and stepped aside as the son moved forward to burn his parents. "Mama… Baba…I pray to the gods that you are in Elysium now, as you always spoke of it. Don't worry about me." He glanced at Gaius. "I am safe."

As he shoved the stick into the base of the pyre, a thick smoke began to rise, and the flames took hold. Gaius then felt very protective of Daxos, and prayed to Mithras that he would not leave his own children so alone as the boy next to him. The flames became greedier, worked their way up through the branches until they licked at the bones. Though he struggled to do so, Daxos could not stem the tide of tears that streamed down his cheeks. But he did not whimper or cry out for fear of shaming the departed. Instead, his grip upon the pugio grew whiter and more intense, a channel for his young grief.

Gaius worried about the smoke's visibility, but knew they could not have left Daxos' parents lying there no more than carry the bones with them. Antonius came up to him.

"We've found some tracks, sir. Many leading up the mountain, on the trail and through the bush."

"Hobnails?"

"Yes, sir. Many of them."

"Have the men gather all their gear from where we left it. We've lingered too long and there are probably more immortui out there." Antonius set off to carry out the order and Gaius turned back to Daxos. "Are you ready?"

The boy wiped his face and nodded. Gaius pat him on the back. "Have your blade ready and stay close to the medicus. If things go wrong, run. Run as you did when you first came to us."

The houses had been searched and no more creatures had been found, only heaps of human bones picked clean in the darkness of the hovels. The bodies of the two dead Romans smouldered and stank on another pyre built by their comrades who would not leave without giving them to Mithras' light. Each soldier bade them farewell as he passed and started into the wood and up the mountain for a fight they all knew was coming.

It was dark again in the woods and progress was slow, cautious. Bits of Roman armour lay scattered as ghostly crumbs to a giant, their owners nowhere to be seen. Gaius had been keeping a tally of finds on his wax tablet, trying to determine how many men of Julius' forty had lost their arms, but he gave up on this after a while, for the remains were at times too broken or buried in leaves that he had no way of getting an accurate count.

Daxos had said the mountains were crawling with wolves, bears, lynx, and other predators, but of these there was no sign. It was as if nature herself had fled and all that was left were the trees, alpine sentinels that were toys for the cold winds from the North.

They should have returned to the base of the mountain, to the safety of the stockade for nightfall, but the remains of their friends that dotted the slopes drew them up and on until they reached the first peak. The trees broke into an open area where they rested, every other man set to a perimeter watch.

"The sun will set soon," Stefanos said as he and Gaius looked down into the thickly wooded valley on the other side.

"Yes. I'm afraid it won't be an easy night." Gaius turned to Daxos. "Have you ever been down into the valley?"

The boy looked out at the world and nodded. He said nothing at first. Indeed, all three were taking in the sight of the green and gold valley surrounded by jagged mountains which tore at the sky like titanic wolf's teeth. The ranges were long and jaw-like, and the reddening sun threatened to dip between two geologic canines.

"Yes, once I have been. With my father...long ago," Daxos finally answered.

"Do you remember what it looks like?"

"A little. I remember a village at the bottom, beside a stream. There are a couple fields and a small mill. But…"

"Yes? Listen, Daxos," Gaius knelt down. "I know you are scared, and so am I. But anything you can tell us will help so that we don't go in blind. If there is an open area, that is good. We can form up there. What were you going to say?"

"I remember after my father and I visited this valley, he said we would never return there."

"Why?"

"Because there was evil in the people. Because they had turned their backs on the gods, on Zeus, Apollo, on the sun."

Gaius stepped to the edge of the cliff overlooking the valley, his crimson cloak lashing him in a sudden gust of wind from below. He planted his hastile for balance. Then he thought he could hear chanting on the wind, mingled with a stench of rot so foul that bile rose from his guts.

Mithras, Lord of Light, he prayed inwardly. *Our men are down there, I know. But I know not what we will find. As the sun sets in the westering sky, do not desert us.*

"Form up!" he called out suddenly. We're going down into the valley." The men stood about, confused, fear etched on their battle-hardened features. Vitellius appeared beside Gaius.

"Optio, sir. Are you sure about this? What if we were to camp here for the night and go down in the morning with the light watching our backs?"

"The light does not penetrate that place nor anywhere beyond, Vitellius. Besides, if there are any of our men down there who are not immortui by now, they soon will be. They'll not last another night."

"Yes, sir."

"Gather the men to go down. I want those with mountaineering experience to lead the way." Vitellius went to do as ordered, and Gaius turned back to Stefanos and Daxos. "I want you both to remain here."

"What? But I-" Stefanos began to protest.

"No, Stefanos. No arguments. You know what we will face down there. I want you both up here in a tree for the night. If we are not back by mid-morning, you must go back to base without stopping."

"Impossible, Optio."

"No. Essential. Someone has to notify the commander and…" he turned to Daxos. "I want him safe. He is the last of his family." Suddenly, Daxos was clinging tightly to Gaius. "You will be my lookout. If anything happens up here, I want you to yell with all your might. Understand?"

"Yes, Optio. I hope your Mithras protects you."

Gaius nodded, looked at the boy one last time, and turned to two of his men.

"I want both of you to remain here with the medicus and Daxos. Keep a close watch." The men looked relieved. "Medicus will give you the rest of my orders. Mithras watch you, brothers."

"And you, Optio, sir," they answered.

"Let's go!" Gaius called as he joined the row of men pouring into the dark valley, their crimson cloaks like a trickle of blood swallowed by the jagged cliffs. Following the mountaineers down the safest path, Gaius turned to waive at Daxos before disappearing over the edge himself.

"This one will do," Stefanos said, standing at the base of a tall pine. "Up we go!"

. . .

THE MOUNTAINSIDE DOWN INTO THE VALLEY PROVED TO BE difficult terrain for Gaius and his men. Even the mountaineers lost footing at times in their search for a safe path. The ground, boulder-strewn and lichen-covered with trees sprouting at odd angles, was slick, made worse by the dying sun which barely penetrated the clouds that hovered above the valley.

They continued to find the odd bit of Roman armour or clothing, but no more bones, though the latter they could have missed. They were preoccupied with not plummeting down the mountainside to shatter their bodies on the rocks.

When they finally snaked their way onto the flat of the valley floor, the men needed some minutes to regain their balance, having fought back their vertigo for over an hour. Gaius motioned for them all to come closer and they encircled him, their Heliodromus.

"The flat area is about four hundred yards south west of where we are. We need to get there quietly and quickly. As soon as we are there I want a perimeter set up, stakes, no ditches." Several men had dropped their stakes on the descent and Gaius hoped that they had enough left. "We're going to establish that strong point and then, in smaller groups of five men, investigate the valley in sections." He looked up to where the moon hovered behind wisps of grey-black cloud. "If there is not enough moonlight, we'll light torches, though that may bring all Hades down on our heads."

Just then the lone, sighing howl of a wolf rang out from the jagged peaks overlooking the valley floor.

"You hear that, brothers? Rome's wolf is with us. And so is Mithras. Let's go and find our friends."

Gaius hoisted his pack and hastile, and set off, quiet and quick toward the flat fields of the valley. It was full dark now, unnaturally so. They stopped every so often to listen for immortui, but nothing reached their ears, not even the hoot of an owl or skitter of a mouse. They broke from the trees as the moon broke from the clouds and made for the centre of the field where they immediately set about driving the stakes into the ground at every pace. It was a small defence, but it would allow them a place at which to regroup and strike out from. Packs were piled in the middle of the circle. Each man chewed some rations, though with the foul stench seeping out of the very ground, it was hard for them to stomach anything.

"All right," Gaius began. "I need four volunteers to go with me for the first search." Four hands shot up and the men stepped forward. "Good. If anything happens we'll call out or make noise if we are able. Vitellius, you're in charge till I return.

"Yes, sir," Vitellius answered.

Gaius and the four men stepped out beyond the ring of sharpened stakes, faded into the darkness of the woods, and made directly for the village.

As Gaius and his men approached the village, the outlines of which were barely visible, the stench became unbearable, causing two of the men to retch. No fires burned anywhere. It was only foul, damp and dark. Sweat poured down Gaius' face and he dried his palms on his tunic so as to keep a firm grip on his gladius. The five of them went in the darkness, their shields up, pila prodding the air before them. Then it happened. One of the men tripped over something and landed against a tree. Something had been sleeping against the tree and in a moment, a blood-curdling roar ripped through the glade. The trooper cried out, fumbled for his gladius even as the creature drove its claws up into his belly to rip out a sheen of intestine.

The next man drove in and beheaded the creature, leaving only the savaged trooper wailing. At the same time, howls rent the air of the entire area. Gaius fought for control of his fear a moment, then strode to the fallen man who writhed in agony.

"Walk in the Light, brother," Gaius said to him before swinging his gladius through the man's neck. He turned back to the others. "Back to the stockade. Now!" he shouted as several quick shadows burst out of the bushes and a nearby dwelling. The immortui charged them, their aggressive amble animalistic, feral. One trooper held a creature at bay, impaled on his pilum while the next took the head and they retreated, shields and swords up. All around, the forest came to life. As Gaius and the men broke into the open space, torches flared around the stockade revealing the faces of their friends. Antonius was out with more men, waiting to go in.

"They're roused," Gaius told him, panting. "Otho is gone. He tripped into a sleeping one."

"Any survivors, sir?"

"Couldn't see… We but barely entered the village before they woke."

"I'll make another search," Antonius said. "We'll search the other side of the village."

"Don't stay long and watch the ground as you go," Gaius offered. They seem to sleep anywhere."

"I'll be waiting," Vitellius added, standing with his own four men. Antonius nodded and then set off at a run farther along the treeline before darting in toward the far end of the village.

Just then, Gaius thought he could hear laughter on the stale breeze, in the trees, and among the hills.

"Did you hear that?" he asked Vitellius.

"Hear what, sir?"

"Nothing. Let's get behind the stakes. Light torches!" he ordered. "We'll fight in the light!"

It seemed an eternity that Antonius was gone. The raucous noise receded into the distance and all was quiet for a time, but for the blood pumping in each man's ears. Gaius cursed, wished he had not needed to kill his man, but knew it was necessary else he became one of them. A chorus of roars pierced by screaming erupted from far away and Vitellius set off in that direction with his group.

The moon emerged then, where she had been hiding her face in cloud, and illuminated the flat of the fields. Immediately, Gaius spotted silhouettes on the flat, some with scuta and gladii, others bounding and clawing the air. Gaius knew they could not go on like this, going out and being massacred one by one. He turned to the others.

"There have to be some survivors! Let's call them! Call out to the III Century!" He yelled at the top of his voice. "Come to us, men of the III Century!"

All the men began calling, but began to despair until voices answered from the southern edge of the valley.

"Macedonica!" the voices yelled, getting nearer and nearer to the stockade. The fighting on the field subsided and Vitellius and Antonius returned with three men each.

"We can't fight them, sir!" Vitellius said, his voice desperate. "There are too many and they're coming on us."

"We can't even tell if they're Romans!" Antonius added, his chest heaving.

Out of the darkness at their backs came seven men, their eyes hollow and black, but when they came into the firelight, Gaius knew them to be survivors.

"Octavius?" Antonius called.

"Hail, Optio!" Octavius returned. "By Mithras, your arrival is blessed."

"Are there any more of you left?" Gaius pressed. The men came up and let their comrades see them in the light. "Well?"

"Don't know, sir. We've been up in the trees. It was…a right massacre, sir."

"What about Centurion Lycus?" Gaius prayed he was not dead.

"Don't know, sir. Centurion Lycus told us to hold up in the trees when he went with ten others to look for survivors." The man shook his head as if to wrench some malevolent vision from his head. "No one's come back, sir. No one at all. All we've done these past nights is listen to the immortui feeding and screeching." Octavius raised a shaking hand to his face.

Gaius' fears had come to fruition. Only seven survivors? Yet, he felt that Julius was out there and he could not leave without him. His mind raced, searched for a plan, a way to get his men out. But he needed to know if Julius was dead or worse.

One of the seven newcomers suddenly screamed and was thrown bodily ten feet away by the sudden impact of an immortui that now clawed at the trooper's throat which it ripped out and devoured just before a pilum arced out of the darkness to pin the creature to the ground. Suddenly they were coming from everywhere, out of the darkness like spawn of Hades, covered in earth and blood and oozing bruises and sores. Most, Gaius noticed, wore legionary tunics.

"Behind the stockade!" he yelled. "Attack!" Everyone squeezed between the stakes and hoisted scuta and pila to receive the immortui rush.

The faces were the worst, the dead, enraged faces of men the defenders had once known. They surrounded them in a wild mass, red-yellow eyes and rotting flesh all about the ring of fire and stakes. They kept coming despite stab wounds, hacked limbs and other injuries the Romans inflicted to hold them off. It was a scene of ultimate horror. For one brief moment, Gaius looked about, all senses except his vision deaf to what was happening. Even as he stabbed and cut, he felt he was in the eye of a blood-red storm. The men's faces and arms, his own, were awash with blood, their expressions contorted by agony and exertion.

"Look out, Optio!"

Gaius turned to see one of his men coming down on him from within the circle, his eyes aflame. Gaius brought up the ball of his hastile to hold the creature back and sliced through the neck leaving the head hanging by a string of tendons.

"Throw the body over the stockade!" Gaius yelled. Antonius and two others helped him. As soon as it landed, six immortui began devouring it, gorging themselves on blood and guts.

"We can't hold here, Optio!" Antonius gasped. "They're too many."

"I know, I know!" Gaius searched about. The stakes were giving and the men tiring. *Mithras, guide me*, he thought. More immortui were pouring from the forest now and, on the wind, that same laughter he had heard before. He turned, slicing at a mangled hand and bloody face covered in pustules and leaking sores. "We're moving out!" he notified the men. "On my count we'll make for the mountain path where we came down." The men nodded, scuta and gladii at the ready. All pila had been spent or broken.

"III Century! Form testudo!" Gaius and Antonius kicked out of the ring, their scuta up. Within moments, the Romans had formed a large rectangle of interlocking shields and were moving forward. Enraged bodies hurled themselves against the tortoise formation from every side and even from above, like waves from a violent sea slamming a breakwater.

The sound was deafening within and men hardened in years of battle shook like scared children as they chanced a cut or thrust between gaps to try and kill or lame any immortui that came near.

"Two hundred more yards, lads!" Gaius yelled. He hoped that when they reached the mountainside, the higher ground would give them an advantage if they had the strength left to climb. He turned to Antonius.

"I want you, when we reach the mountain, to go straight up to Stefanos and Daxos and tell them to wait in the tree until daylight. They're not to come down."

"What about you?" Antonius asked as his gladius shot out viper-quick into the face of a howling immortui.

"I'll be coming, after I make sure our men are all up."

The man next to Gaius fell screaming then, his ankle caught by one of the creatures. The gap was punctured immediately by other creatures and the testudo broke into chaos.

"We're almost there!" Gaius yelled. "Run! Run for the mountain!"

The Romans broke and ran, most tossing their scuta, too tired to carry them farther. Gaius spun, hacking and slashing, trying to see where his men were. A gift of moonlight pierced the clouds and he spotted them, the glint off of lorica and helm, the arc of their gladii. But he also saw them fall, one, then two, three and more bitten, torn or screaming as they were savaged alive.

"No!" Gaius ran in, Vitellius spotting him and going after.

"Optio, don't!" Such a rage had come upon Gaius that Vitellius thought him bitten, but his optio dove into the fray in a vain fit of vengeance. Heads fell, and legs and arms, but the immortui kept coming. Gaius felt one leap upon his back and there was a moment of panic that he was finished, but Vitellius arrived to grab hold of the creature.

"Ahh!" the trooper screamed as the beast sank its teeth into the side of his neck.

"Vitellius!" Gaius swung and met the red-eyes. "Walk in the Light, brother," he whispered, hoarse, before killing him.

Then Gaius ran, fiery eyes and death at his heels. The slope was in view, but the sounds of dying were all about, dizzying him with desperation and fear. Three more times he had to kill his own men who had moments before been infected with the evil that flooded the valley. He began to climb in the dark, uncaring of which way, as long as it was up and away from the nightmare below. The sounds of the dying and the clang of steel on stone echoed above and beside him.

"III Century!" he called out. This time, no one answered. They were broken and scattered. For a moment he thought he could hear a boy crying out in the dark and he stopped. "Daxos!"

He stopped on a flat rock some distance up the mountainside and listened. Sound blurred in his ears as did his vision. He was only leaning on the rock for a moment before something, an impact, racked his body with pain. Putrid breath filled his nostrils and as he swung his gladius out to kill the creature, Gaius lost his footing and stumbled into darkness, the moon above growing smaller and fainter with each crack of his body. All went black.

Light came, sometime much later. It pierced the crease of his eyelid, bright, almost white. Then rock came into view, clumps of moss, purple wild flowers and red leaves. Something flitted before his eyes, but Gaius Justus Vitalis did not dare move. There it was again, a tiny finch with shades of yellow and brown, perched on a twig before his face. The little head twisted and turned enquiringly, and chirruped once.

Then, laughter like clear water in a brook, playful, ever changing.

"I think he likes you, Heliodromus."

Am I dead? Gaius wondered. *Is this Elysium?*

"No. Not yet. You're not finished."

Gaius opened his eyes more now to see a man, golden-skinned and strong, in the prime of life. He wore white trousers, a white tunic, and brown leather boots. On his head was a soft Phrygian cap from under which sprouted auburn curls. A long golden-hilted dagger hung at his waist, but he made no move for it. In fact, he smiled readily at Gaius.

"Where am I?" Gaius asked. The man rose and knelt beside him. Gaius noticed a strong scent of cedar.

"You are on the mountainside." He looked up. "Quite a fall I should say."

"My men…my brothers…are they-"

The smile disappeared.

"Most of my Miles are gone or swallowed by the dark."

"All?"

"Most. Some have kept running, pursued by the black filth of the valley."

"I've failed," Gaius felt despair creeping in on him. "I… wait…did you say 'Your *Miles*'?"

The smile returned.

"Yes."

"Mithras," Gaius whispered. "By the Light. How can it be?"

"It is as it always shall be. You are never alone, Gaius Justus Vitalis, Sun Runner.

"Forgive me, Lord. I…I am broken."

The god stood up, looking down on his Heliodromus, and pitied him, a father's affection for a son who has fought hard but lost a battle.

"But the War is not over," Mithras spoke. "These mountains are dark…so dark…" For the first time the hand went to the golden dagger and the Tauroctony flashed in Gaius' mind. "As I said…" he tilted his head to listen to something on the wind. "…you are not yet finished. Listen, Sun Runner! You'll want to hear this!"

Gaius felt the god's hand on his chest a moment and then a flood of heat flowed into his body, his limbs, his mind. When he opened his eyes he was alone, his gladius leaning against the boulder next to him. He sat up with no trace of pain, mind clear, senses sharp.

Listen! his mind told him and then he heard them. Two voices. One harsh and guttural, the other soft and smooth and full of menace.

Gaius removed, ever so quietly, the smashed lorica and crushed helmet that had saved him, so that he now wore only his bracae, boots and belted, crimson tunic. Not much, but he realized that he did not then feel the slightest bit of cold. Gladius in hand, he followed a small path toward the sound of the voices, careful not to stumble upon rocks or to crack branches underfoot. The sun was behind clouds again, but there was plenty of light to see by.

He reached the edge of the path and crawled forward to peer over the edge into what appeared to be a small clearing just off the valley. He saw two men speaking in secret, with two guards nearby.

The first speaker, with the harsh voice, was as big as a bear and wore thick furs on his shoulders. His head carried a winged helmet and he wore a long-sword at his waist. The second speaker was tall and cloaked all in black, but from the way he stood and moved, his muscles were quick to action and full of strength. His face was concealed within the shadow of his hood.

"Tell me why you would help us," the first spoke. "And why we should seek help of the darkness." There was a pause and then an answer.

"Because, Arminius, Rome is the true poison in this world. It is spreading like a pestilence, and soon its power will be undefeatable. I cannot allow that to happen."

"Oh, you cannot!" the big man laughed, but in a second he was gasping, the other's hand around his throat, lifting him off the ground. One of the guards rushed forward to help his master, but the cloaked figure's free hand shot out to land a back-handed blow that snapped his neck instantly, sending the body spinning to the ground. He eyed the second guard who thought better of interceding. The cowled head turned toward the big man again.

"You and your people live only because I allow it. You would do well to remember that."

The big man rubbed his throat and stood face to face with the other.

"We do not want your immortui. Our gods will abandon us if we turn to your dark arts."

"There are no gods. There is only life and death, and I am master of both. Besides," he began to walk about casually, "the spell is cast and the immortui are sweeping the area. Last night was but a taste."

"The Romans didn't do that badly against your undead who, by the way, *can* be killed."

"Yes, they can be killed. But before they are killed, they will strike fear into the hearts of the Eagles. And fear, make no mistake Arminius, is the most powerful weapon. The immortui will haunt their thoughts, their dreams, everything. These mountains will be a barrier of fear to halt Rome's advance hereafter."

The big man turned, preparing to leave, and nodded to his remaining guard to get the spare horse.

"Very well. You distract the Romans, and soon my people and I will strike at them in the west. They'll never expect it so soon."

The black cloak laughed, and even in the recent warmth he had enjoyed Gaius felt fear slither up and down his spine. *That laugh...*

"You shall have, Arminius, more help than you expect when the time comes."

"What do you mean?"

"You shall see. Patience."

Arminius rode from the clearing with his man, leaving the other to laugh at his back. Gaius watched as the cloaked figure circled the clearing and then stopped. The cowl tilted up as if to smell the air, red and gold leaves falling to blanket the autumn ground. Black moths suddenly fluttered all about and as Gaius began to back away, the head turned and black eyes looked directly at him.

Gaius ran back along the path. *Not now!* Mithras's voice told him. He knew he had to return for Daxos and Stefanos, if they were still there, and make for Troesmis to warn the legions along the frontier.

First, he had to get out of the mountains.

. . .

THE CLIMBING WAS MUCH EASIER DURING THE DAY WITHOUT his kit and armour, but Gaius was not sure where he was, or how far from the others he had strayed the previous night. Occasionally, he came upon the disembowelled corpse of one of his men and twice he killed immortui who slept in pools of gore beside their kills. But he kept moving, pressed on without stopping except to get his bearings. He did not dare call out in case he roused the creatures, preferring to slay them unawares.

At last, along the ridge of the mountain, he spotted what looked like the tall tree near the path they had taken down the mountainside. He paused to catch his breath and chew some of the dried beef he had in the scrip at his waist. Birdsong reached his ears and he relaxed, breathed, and tried to remember Mithras' face. Gaius hoped the strength he had been given would hold out. As he pressed on along the ridge, the ground between boulders sounded hollow beneath his feet. He slowed as he approached the clear area about the tree and path, crouched in some bushes to listen.

Sunlight pierced a crack in the clouds, and rays angled their way down. He stepped forward, the point of his gladius prodding the air before him.

"Optio!" a voice called from above. "Over here!"

Gaius ran into the clearing and looked up the tall pine. He searched about for the two troopers he had left to guard Daxos and Stefanos, but there was no sign.

"Shh, boy." He heard Stefanos chide.

High up in the limbs of the pine, the two of them sat perched, white and shivering, for fear or cold Gaius could not tell.

"We're coming down!" Daxos began climbing.

"Wait!" Gaius yelled, but as soon as the boy landed, two

immortui, the troopers he had left with them, came out of the bushes. One darted for Daxos who hurriedly kept the tree between himself and the creature. The other made for Gaius. The men's faces were all holes and scratches, the arms covered with sores and bite marks.

Gaius stepped in quickly, stronger than the previous night, and made short work of the first, throwing the body aside.

"Optio, help!" Daxos cried out as he slipped on the dewy ground. The creature lunged and clawed at his leg and Daxos slashed at the hands with his pugio. Gaius landed on top of the creature, wrenched the head back just as it was about to bite, and sliced through the front of the neck until it stopped writhing. He let the body drop and knelt beside Daxos who threw his arms about him. The boy shook uncontrollably.

"I thought you were dead…I thought…hearing all the killing and screaming all night that…" he finished with sobs, his courage fairly spent.

"I'm well now, Daxos. But we need to press on. Can you do it?"

Daxos nodded, wiped his tears and sheathed his pugio. Stefanos landed beside them, having made his way down. Both smelled heavily of the pine resin that covered their arms, faces and hair. Gaius turned to him.

"We need to get back to base and warn them. There is an army of immortui in that valley. They decimated us. And there is a man…he…I overheard him and some German chieftain talking about attacks here and in the west."

"Let us go and use what daylight is left to us," Stefanos suggested.

"Did Antonius pass this way?"

"Yes. He told us to stay in the tree, but then ran off in the fighting. I don't know if he's alive."

For the first time, Gaius noticed the spread of blood all about the clearing, sweeping down the mountainside, plastering the trunks of trees.

"Come," Gaius wiped the blood off his blade. "We've got to go. If we get separated, you must both make for base, look for any patrols that might be out and warn them."

Down in the valley came a series of shrieks and roars as dark clouds settled over the world about them. Without another word, they set off down the mountain path toward Daxos' village.

THE THREE OF THEM MOVED THROUGH THE FOREST WITH great caution. It was unnaturally quiet and all trace of sunlight had been swallowed by waves of grey-black cloud.

We'll need a safe spot for the night," Stefanos whispered when they stopped for a moment. Gaius listened carefully, eyes closed and thought he could hear a rustle of leaves in several directions. Beast or immortui, they needed to get off the ground.

"Let's climb up there," he said, pointing to a gnarled oak which still retained some foliage for cover, and good wide limbs upon which they could rest. "Are you both able to climb?"

"Yes, Optio," Daxos answered, moving to the tree and accepting Gaius' closed hands to get up.

"How are your rations?" he turned to Stefanos.

"Two sticks of dried beef and a few apricots." He shook his head. "How are we going to make it back? The immortui are everywhere."

"We'll make it," Gaius stated, trying to sound confident. In truth, he felt he could on his own, but now he had two more to look after and he would not let a thing happen to Daxos. That he swore. "Let's get up before they start waking." The two men climbed up, struggling with the first high branch, and then each found a comfortable spot to rest his eyes.

Gaius looked to Daxos and smiled. The boy was already in a crook of the oak, sleep coming easily now that he felt more secure. Stefanos struggled for comfort and eventually succeeded, his breathing a bit loud and laboured from the exhaustion born of a night of terror. Gaius hoped the night would not hold as much horror as the previous one, but still kept his eyes on the path below. If anything approached, his sword was ready. He tried to think of light and Mithras' laughter, but another laughter intruded upon his thoughts, dark and foreboding, relentless.

As it turned out, the night was a restless one in which deep sleep proved impossible. Every sound made them all jump. That night however, it was not the sounds of desperate fighting, of the dead and dying, that rang in their ears like a horrifying chorus. It was the occasional rustle of leaves that startled them, the sound of ranging creatures sniffing at the air for their scent. The immortui were hunting them, hungry for blood. Gaius struggled to stave off the images of his men's guts being ripped out and devoured.

When dawn finally kissed the sky in the East, the forest lightened enough to allow them to scan the area. The surroundings seemed clear and Gaius looked up to Stefanos and Daxos.

"Let's get moving," he whispered. "We need to make the open plains before sundown." They nodded and he began to descend.

His heart stopped when he saw the red-yellow eyes glaring at him, the creature's mucus-ridden breathing making its body shudder. It waited as a shark with gaping jaws in a bloody sea battle. Then two more appeared from the bushes nearby.

"What do we do?" Stefanos said, his voice laced with panic.

Gaius looked down at the creatures he only knew for some of his men because of the torn crimson tunics they wore. Any other sign of the men he had lived and fought beside was long dead. Without a word, Gaius slashed at the eyes of the first as he dropped from the tree. The creature reeled only briefly, but long enough for Gaius to decapitate it and get out of the way of the other two who collided with each other screaming with rage to get at him. Gaius slashed out, cutting bits of rotten flesh from each and by the time he had cut the leg off one of them, Stefanos had severed the head of the third. The medicus then moved toward the one over which Gaius stood, but the optio spoke up.

"No. Leave him."

"Leave him? You can't be serious!"

"He can't follow us, and if others are coming they'll stop to feed on him."

Stefanos had no words as he turned and vomited.

"The village is not far now, Optio," Daxos stood at the base of the tree. "We should go." Just then, harsh cries crashed through the foliage.

"Let's go!" Gaius set off down the path to the village with Daxos and Stefanos behind. They barrelled down the path, dodging roots and boulders as they went. Gaius tried to listen for pursuit, but all he could hear was the racing of his own pulse. Then it reached him, a clear ring of metal on metal and cries in Latin. "They're in the village!" Gaius called back to Daxos and Stefanos, picking up the pace.

"Retreat!" a voice called from somewhere ahead before being cut off.

"III Century!" Gaius called as he burst from out of the wood into the village.

Immortui and Roman bodies lay scattered about the village in various stages of death or consumption. A loud gurgling sound reached Gaius on the other side of the village. He raced over, ahead of Daxos and Stefanos, to meet a welcome sight.

The tall, familiar, brawny, armoured figure and centurion's helmet stood in the midst of a pile of bodies. In his hands he held a writing body by the jaw and shoulder.

"Julius," Gaius whispered, too surprised to speak louder. "Thank Mithras."

Then there was a crack and sound of ripping as the figure tore the head from the body he held, bare handed, with the sword still hanging at his side. Gaius stopped ten feet away, looking with great relief upon the heaving, mailed shoulders covered with the phalerae his friend had been awarded. The centurion's horizontal crest hung slightly askew with the tilt of his head. He still wore his uniform, though it was crusted with blood, mud and offal.

Daxos and Stefanos caught up then and stood behind Gaius who stepped forward slowly, not wanting to startle his friend.

"Julius? By the gods, man. Are you all right? I never thought to see you again." Gaius moved closer, his left hand reaching out.

"Optio," Stefanos whispered, holding Daxos.

The massive shoulders turned with the helmet, like a bear looking over its shoulder. Gaius was so awash with emotion that he did not notice the raging, blood-shot and jaundiced eyes, or the powerful forearm that swung round like a catapult arm into his chest, heaving him off the ground.

Time slowed horribly as he tumbled through the air like a ragged doll to land against the well head at the centre of the village.

"Run!" Gaius called after Daxos and Stefanos as the massive creature bore down on him, its pocked face roaring. Gaius rolled out of the way just as a fist slammed into the stonework, an audible crack of bone renting the air.

"Julius!" Gaius called, getting to his feet. "Julius Lycus Avernus! It's me! Gaius!" More words were cut off as a large log came to crash into Gaius' shoulder sending him sprawling again. "Pater! By Mithras, stop this!" But the creature had no ears for it and bore down on Gaius, teeth bared to rend the flesh of his face. Gaius got his feet up to hold off the crushing body and when the teeth gnashed down, the eyes bulging with the approach of slaughter, Gaius held up the blade of his gladius. The teeth tore at the metal and Gaius kicked out as hard as he could, sawing with his blade.

"Stop this! Julius, it's Gaius! Your friend!"

Uncaring of the blood pouring from its mouth, the creature came again, faster, until it had Gaius by the fabric of his bloody tunic, running to slam the man against the wattle of one of the hovels. Gaius held his gladius at the creature's throat and pushed the forehead back with his other hand. The mammoth hands reached for his own throat and Gaius felt the pressure increase, his legs kicking out wildly but in vain.

"Julius…it's me…Gaius…"

Just as the world began to blur, Gaius felt the pressure slacken and his vision return, though he was still pinned to the wall. The creature shook its head as if harassed by wasps, shut the eyes tightly and screamed. When the eyes opened, they were Julius'.

"Kill me! Kill me, Gaius! Help!"

Gaius watched his friend fight, struggle to come through the darkness.

"Julius! You can fight it! By Mithras, you can beat it!"

The head shook again, wildly, the eyes as tight as a vice, but when they opened, the rage that poured forth was stronger than ever, full of anger, and hate, and bloodlust.

As the grip on his throat began to tighten again, Gaius cut deeply with all of his strength to saw through the neck of the man he had called friend. They fell in a heap, and Gaius rolled away, his vision blurred this time by tears of desperation. His chest heaved and he vomited, weeping.

He had not lain there long, but when the raucous cries of more immortui pierced the mountain woods about the village, Gaius jumped to his feet. He could hardly recognize the form before him now, the rotting corpse that he knew he would never see as a man again. Gaius leaned down and removed the badges of honour Julius had won, the armillae and the torc, and put them on the easier to run. Then, casting aside the sword he had used to kill his friend, he drew Julius' blade from the bloodied sheath. Despite years of use, the killing edge was still fine and deadly.

"Walk in the Light, Pater..." he whispered.

His running was not as a man's as he crashed down the mountain path, through brush and over boulders. His flight was instinctive and animal-like. The sky, the forest, seemed to become darker as he went. Now and then, that chill laughter nipped at his heels, followed by the rush of immortui on the dead leaves. Twice, one of them pounced from the covering ferns and twice his gladius licked out to finish them as he passed, something to slow others as they stopped to gorge themselves.

Before long, Gaius broke from the wood onto the open plain and slowed at the small rise where they had made camp previously. In the circle, two men struggled and screamed. As Gaius approached, he saw the immortui lashing out at Stefanos. Gaius slashed and the creature fell, black blood pouring from the severed neck.

"Stefanos? Are you injured? Where's Daxos?"

The medicus was on his hands and knees, gasping for breath, grunting from exertion for a few moments before he stopped and stood.

"No…" Gaius muttered, more angry than sad.

A second later that feral look appeared. Before it took a step toward Gaius, its hands were grabbing at the space where its head had been.

"Daxos!" Gaius yelled to the open plain. "Daxos! Keep running!"

A wave of immortui broke from the forest then. Gaius turned and began to run, toward the breaking clouds, away from the mountains and the dark laughter taunting him.

It was as a dream, his long run for life, his only thought being Daxos and warning the legion. Gaius Justus Vitalis did not know how long he had been running, only that he had to keep going, arms and legs pumping in unison, the blade of the gladius whistling as he drove himself across the windy plain.

As long as the sun holds out, he thought.

He chanced the occasional glance back over his shoulder

only to see the ranging black dots of the immortui hunting him, getting closer.

"May I run with you?" the man next to him said, no trace of breathlessness in his clear, youthful voice. Gaius looked to see that smile, enjoying the running, the auburn curls bouncing beneath the Phrygian cap. Mithras' muscular stride reinforced Gaius, and leant him strength. Together, the god and his Sun Runner raced over the grassy plain toward the light.

"Good! Good!" Mithras laughed joyfully. "Run with me, my Heliodromus! Run!"

Immortui closed in quickly, pushed on by the dark power lashing at their backs. When one drew even with Gaius, the god no longer there, Gaius slashed its leg and others slowed to feed before continuing. Mithras reappeared and ran again with Gaius who no longer felt pain in his mortal body, only heat and a will to run.

"You are nearly there now," Mithras said as the sun ran red in the west. "The charioteer is driving over the edge of the world, but you must go on. Keep running!" He smiled. "All will be well in the light."

And then, he was gone. Gaius despaired a moment, but kept his pace despite the howls of bloodlust at his back.

Shortly after, in the dying light of the sun, he saw distant shapes massing, and feared then that he had been surrounded. Part of him believed he could do no more, mortal doubt creeping in like a poison. He thought of the boy he had come to love like a son, of Daxos, and asked Mithras to watch over him.

Ahead, a single fallen tree trunk lay like a titan on its side, and Gaius made for it. He would not go easily. He would die with a bloody gladius in his hand and warm thoughts of his Fulvia and the girls in his heart. Several shadows closed on him then, five, six…seven immortui grunting and slavering like rabid dogs.

Gaius reached the fallen tree, leaped atop it and turned to face them. The sky was crimson and revealed wave upon wave of immortui in the distance. He steadied himself and slashed at the first and then second immortui as they reached his position. The other five pounced, and with what strength and speed the god had given him, Gaius slashed and cut and cried out before falling backward from the trunk. When he landed there was a sudden sucking in of air, and then the sky lit up with fire as of comets and shooting stars tilling the fields of the heavens until his vision went red and then the entire world disappeared into silence.

It was the sound of a bird, a single ray of bright sunlight through the small window, that woke him.

Elysium…was the thought. *The Light*… It was his home in Rome, the painted walls with visions of olive and acanthus. He heard voices, but could not make out the meaning of the words. He tried to speak. *Fulvia? Aemilia? Faustina?*

Then the walls of his home wavered as a fog, and turned to the white and red of his room, his cubiculum at Troesmis. He felt a small hand grasp his and chanced a turn of the head to see Daxos looking at him, his smiling face lit by the sun now filling the room. The boy's hair had been cut. He had been washed and dressed in a new brown tunic with matching bracae and a black cloak. Gaius smiled back. Then, a thought.

"Am I dead? Ime…necros?"

The boy shook his head. "Then ise necros. You…not dead." He squeezed the large scarred and callused hand. "You alive, Optio."

"What happened? How long have I been here?"

"You've been here for seven weeks."

"Antonius?" Gaius tried to sit, but fell back down.

"Optio." Antonius saluted and smiled.

"Was I sleeping for so long?"

"A fever. The medicus, Croesus, said he doubted you'd pull through, your heart was so weak, but Daxos here," he ruffled the boy's hair, "convinced the commander that you would pull through. And now you have."

Antonius sat down while Daxos went to pour water into a clay cup and handed it to Gaius. The soldier's head hung and though he was well enough, his hair had greyed. His eyes were two dark circles, a sign of sleepless nights.

"How many of the men returned?"

"Saving yourself, Daxos and I, ten."

"Ten only? Out of the seventy that remained?"

"Yes, sir."

"Tell me what happened, Antonius. How did you find me?"

"When we broke apart in the valley, I cut my way through to Daxos and the medicus. Then I ran. I hid up trees when the creatures ranged near, and killed several along the way. But they kept coming. Anyway, I somehow missed the village during the night, but ended up on the plain, about a mile from the path up the mountain. I ran, taking short breaks until I finally ran into one of the mounted patrols Tribune Misenus had sent out looking for us. I reported to the tribune what was coming, and he told the commander who mobilized the legion onto the plain to meet the immortui. The commander told the rest of the legion that German rebels were making an attack and that we needed to crush them."

"German rebels?" Gaius was shocked. "You mean the legion didn't know they were immortui until they fought?"

"They still don't know and the commander wants it to stay that way should fear run too deep in the ranks. I've been sworn to secrecy, as have the other ten survivors."

Gaius leaned back, shaking his head slowly, trying to remember. "Did you engage the enemy?"

"Yes, but not as you think. After I told the commander and Misenus how things had gone in the valley, they decided not to take chances. We brought all the artillery we had, including all the stores of naptha, and set the plain alight.

"Comets and stars..." Gaius remembered.

"What's that, sir?"

"The last thing I remember was a sky full of fire like comets and shooting stars."

"Well, we certainly lit up the place. And all the immortui as well. They ran around, mad and flaming until they burned away or were smashed by boulder and bolt. The only immortui bodies that were not fired were the seven you had killed, whose bodies lay all about you. Luckily, the commander, who was out front with Misenus, was the first to find you. He had me fire the bodies before anyone else looked too closely..."

Antonius' face darkened and Gaius spied the fear in him, the bitter mixture of remorse and guilt at living when so many had died, many having been killed by himself.

"What is it, Antonius?"

"It's the eyes, sir. I can't...I just see those bloody eyes wherever I look."

"I know, my friend." Gaius held out his hand and grasped

Antonius' forearm. "But thank Mithras for bringing us to the Light once again. He watched over us."

"*Someone* watched over you, by the Gods!" Into the room burst Commander Maximus. Antonius sprang to his feet and saluted and Gaius attempted a weak bow. "At ease, men," the commander said as Misenus entered the room behind and closed the door. "Thank Jupiter that you're awake, Optio. So long asleep I thought I'd soon have to notify your wife. Oh, don't worry. No letters have been sent." The commander sat on the edge of the bed and glanced at Daxos. "Daxos reached us as we were marching out to find you. Brave lad." The commander stopped, his hands working each other. "You saw Centurion Lycus?" He glanced at the polished sword by the bed, the armillae and torc that had been laid on the bedside table. Gaius nodded.

"I tried to bring him back, Commander. But…the darkness had taken too great a hold of him." The memory of Julius' last desperate words rushed back upon Gaius then and his body shuddered. How could he explain it all? "Centurion Lycus fought as he always did, with courage and force, right to the very end. But I couldn't save him."

The men were silent then as the sunlight filtering in enveloped the decorations that Julius had worn, and the blade he had wielded.

"He walks in the Light, now," the commander muttered, the men repeating the words. "When you are well enough, Optio, come to me and tell me all that you remember."

"I will, sir. But to be honest, I don't recall much at all."

"Never mind now. Rest. Build up your strength." The commander rose, and Antonius and Misenus stood to attention. At the doors, he stopped. "Antonius has told you of the need for absolute secrecy, Optio?"

"Yes, sir. He has."

"Good…good," his voice faded away.

"Tribune!" Gaius called after Misenus.

"Yes, Optio."

"Thanks for keeping an eye out for us, sir."

Misenus smiled, nodded. "I'm only sorry I doubted you, Optio. It won't happen again."

When Antonius had left, Gaius motioned for Daxos. The boy came slowly and sat on the stool next to the bed. Gaius held out his arm and Daxos laid his head on it, his eyes closed.

"Thank you for standing by me, Daxos," Gaius said, tears burning his eyes.

It was another two weeks before Gaius had enough strength to walk about. He had been in bed for so long that his limbs had come dangerously close to atrophy. It was, he believed, only some reserve of Mithras' strength that had ensured his health. It would take time, he knew, to regain his former state of physical fitness, and so he looked forward to getting back to the gymnasium and drill hall.

There were only twelve left alive from III Century and each man among them was dealing with his personal demons of that night in the valley. Gaius had made it a point to have each man brought to him so that he could speak alone with them. All experienced nightmares, all lived now with a greater sense of paranoia, guilt and an anger that drove them near mad for vengeance. But against whom? The immortui were all dead, and the scouting parties into the forest and up the mountains had found nothing except wolves, bears and the bones of the slain.

Then a memory rushed upon Gaius' mind like that final, red tidal wave of undead creatures. Laughter, dark and terrible, from a black cowl. Gaius started in his bed, nearly knocking over his oil lamp.

"Daxos!" he called, and the boy came running from his cubiculum.

"Yes, Optio?"

"Go and get Antonius, quickly. I must speak with the commander." Daxos put on his cloak and ran to get the trooper.

"What is it, Optio?" the commander asked, sitting behind his desk in the Praetorium. Antonius and Tribune Misenus stood to either side of Gaius with Daxos lingering near the door.

"I've remembered something vital from the valley. I can't believe it didn't come to me sooner, Commander, but it was as though something was intentionally hiding the memory of it from me."

"Well? What?"

"Arminius."

"Who?" the commander asked.

"He's chieftain of the Cherusci, is he not?" Misenus asked. "I think I've heard the name. He's one of Quinctilius Varus' trusted men."

"I don't know what tribe, sir, but when I was alone in the mountains, I got separated from everyone in the night and fell during some fighting." Gaius accepted a cup of wine from Misenus and drank, unaware of the whiteness of his complexion. "I had heard voices. One was Germanic, without a doubt...the other... I don't know. It was a voice to chill the hardest of men. They were speaking of a rebellion, an attack the likes of which Rome had not seen. The German was Arminius and the other, robed and hooded in black, said he was the one allowing the German tribes to live in the mountains. He told Arminius that he would give the Germans the help they needed to stop Rome once and for all." They were all silent but for the flickering of the lamp flames as the commander stood, his fists on the map-strewn table.

"My gods, Optio. Who was this other person with this Arminius?"

"I don't know, Commander. All I do know is that he is the one who created the immortui." The laughter rang in Gaius' head and he closed his eyes to shut it out. "And if he can do that, then Rome will face an enemy unlike any other since Romulus and Remus first took up arms."

"Did you overhear when this attack would come?" the commander asked, standing straight now, his mind searching for a way to send warning without causing panic.

"No, sir."

"We need to send word to the western legions of Arminius' plans."

"Shall we signal them, sir?" Misenus asked.

"No. Signals could be read by the enemy. I'll send my best riders."

"Will you tell the generals of this other enemy, Commander?" Gaius asked, keenly aware of the lateness of his remembrance of this information.

"No. Only that there is word of a renewed rebellion under this Arminius of the Cherusci. We've taken care of the immortui here so there is no need for superstitious panic. I just hope we're not too late."

Misenus and Antonius nodded their agreement, but Gaius

hung his head, suddenly weary, full of uncertainty at the commander's words. He said nothing.

"Optio?" Gaius raised his head.

"Yes, sir!"

"I'm promoting you to the rank of centurion."

"Sir? Shock registered on Gaius face. "I…I can't. Centurion Lycus-"

"Is dead, Optio. He walks in the light now. And we need good men in the centurionate."

"I don't know what to say, sir."

The commander came around the table to stand before Gaius and placed his hands upon his shoulders.

"You can say 'yes'. And 'Thank you, sir.' Besides, Justus, as an Optio Centuriae, you were in line for the promotion.

The commander looked at Misenus and then back at Gaius. "It was Centurion Lycus' last request, should he not return, that you be promoted and that you inherit his wealth and property as he was without issue."

"Yes, sir." Gaius said, standing tall. "Thank you, sir! I won't let you down."

"I know that, Centurion." The commander held out a scroll to Gaius. Your papers. He paused. There is one more thing."

"Sir?"

"I'm sending you home on furlough."

"Home? To Rome, sir? But what about the Germans? I must be in the fight, sir."

"You are in no condition to fight, Centurion. What you need is to heal and build your strength again. There is no better place for that than with your family in Rome. You'll have four months.

Gaius nodded, inwardly happy to see his wife and children, but outwardly downcast.

"Centurion. We need time to replace all of your men. So many dead…you twelve survivors will return to duty, never fear. I would not be willing to lose such men as you. But by Mithras, you need time."

"Yes, Commander. I understand."

"Good. Misenus will make arrangements for your to return to Rome.

"Sir…" Gaius started, uncertain. "May I ask that Daxos accompany me if he is willing?" He has been of much help to me."

The commander looked at the boy at the back of the room, smiling and nodding eagerly.

"Yes, Centurion. By all means. Now, I should get those riders out. Misenus, stay here. Centurion Justus, Legionary Antonius, dismissed."

The men saluted and, followed by Daxos, went out into the moonlit night and back to the barracks.

"What are your plans for the centurion and his men, sir?" Do you think they'll be able to serve?" Misenus asked when they were gone.

"Oh yes, Tribune. They'll be able to serve. In what capacity I do not yet know. What I do know is that their experience and resilience has made them a unique group."

"Unique enough to fight this mysterious enemy, sir?"

"Perhaps, Tribune. Perhaps."

BACK IN HIS QUARTERS, WITH DAXOS SLEEPING SOUNDLY ON his little cot, Gaius sat down by the light of a lamp. His mind raced as he went over the turn of events. He could almost feel

Julius in the room, ghostly congratulations on his lips. But it was of little comfort.

So many dead…so many.

Gaius unrolled a papyrus scroll, dipped his stylus into the ink pot, and set to writing.

MY DEAREST FULVIA,
I am coming home…

PART II

LYKOI

To the Shades of the Fallen,
Those who have fought for Good
in the dark corners of the world.

2

LYKOI

October - A.D. 9

THE RAIN FELL HARD UPON PUBLIUS QUINCTILIUS VARUS AND his remaining men. They were exhausted and hungry, but they had to keep moving at any cost. They had to reach an open space where they could dig in and fight.

With the rain and the onset of night, the Romans could no longer see their pursuers. But they could hear them. Oh, yes. They could hear them. A sound to chill the Gods themselves.

"Use the last of the pitch to light torches, Tribune," Varus commanded. The man obeyed without a word and within minutes, a ring of fire encircled the shield wall that protected the legate, his few remaining officers, and three broken centuries.

How is it possible? Varus wondered. *Three centuries left of my three legions...*

Varus removed his helmet with the broken crest and looked up at the three golden aquilae of his savaged legions. Firelight played on the golden breasts of those symbols of Rome's might. The commander thought they still looked proud, strong.

His men were anything but.

For three days they had been harried through the Teutoburg forest, that Germanic Hades. The legions had been ambushed over and over and over…from all sides, at all hours. For days, all Varus had heard were the cries of his men in the black, gnarled woods.

The nights were the worst.

That sound… an incessant howling that tore into one's person as efficiently as any gladius. Varus closed his eyes in the face of the sputtering rain-slapped torches and tried to imagine his villa at Baiae, the scent of jasmine, the heat of the sun.

But all he felt was the cold, and the wet. All he heard was the terrifying sound of ripping flesh, and the harsh breaking of bones like dried twigs.

"Commander!" The tribune came up beside Varus. "They're forming up for a charge, sir!"

"So they are, Tribune." Varus opened his eyes and looked at the surrounding tree lines where black shapes cursed in ugly guttural intonations, spears, scythes, and clubs waving madly at the Romans.

"What shall we do, Commander?" the tribune pressed.

"We shall die, Tribune. Like all the rest."

The tribune shook his head in frustration and moved past Varus. "Form up! Prepare to receive attack!" he ordered as he placed his helmet on his head and hefted a pilum.

Varus hears the insubordination in the tribune's voice but

thinks only of the eagles and the rain upon his face. He no longer thinks of Arminius and how the man had betrayed him, and Rome. He cares little for the civilians he had abandoned to the Germans once the attacks had begun.

When the pained, tormented, and raging howls of the enemy begin anew, Quinctilius Varus thinks only of the ancestral gladius at his side. When the barbarians' visages begin to transform, when the teeth begin to gnash and rip through Roman shields, armour, and bone, then does Varus draw his sword and plant the handle in the deep mud.

As the beasts rush in, huge and dark and matted with gore, Varus watches his men crumple on all sides. The body of Varus' last tribune flies over his head as he drops on his old knees and places the tip of his blade beneath the rim of his ornate cuirass.

Varus falls on his sword, even as Arminius struts up to him and hacks the head from his body without hesitation.

The hunt comes to a violent end as the moon cuts through the clouds and shines upon the field.

It is full, and bright, and all at once, several thousand of the enemy begin to bay at its light.

THICK MIST SHROUDED THE EARLY MORNING FIELDS THAT surrounded the city of Rome. Peasants and slaves were making their way to the places of their assigned tasks - tilling fields, moving animals from one pasture to another, fixing a water wheel, or loading a wagon. They all moved around in ignorance of the world beyond their everyday.

Gaius Justus Vitalis ran past them every day since he had returned to Rome. But he ignored the labouring drones by the wayside.

He only ran, was driven to do so.

Every morning, Gaius plunged into the pre-dawn darkness to run out of the city along the Via Appia almost all the way to Tarracina, to the south. There, he would drink water, and then return to Rome.

His legs drove on, relentless. His arms pumped hard, timed with his breath.

The peasants and slaves beside the road stared at the shirtless soldier who raced past them every morning as though the Furies were at his heels. He never stopped. His eyes were always forward, his mind elsewhere. They made the sign against evil as he passed, though they knew not why. They did not know of Mithras, or of immortui, nor that the Heliodromus who sped by them had run with a god out of the very depths of Hades.

When he came to the white tomb of Caecilia Metella, Gaius Justus Vitalis, centurion in the legions of Emperor Augustus, lashed himself to a speed unattainable by most men.

Run with me, Sun Runner, the voice in his mind said, urging him on faster and faster until he was at the city gates.

The soldiers had come to know the running centurion well and waved him through at a jog.

Gaius poured sweat as he passed the cliff of the Palatine Hill where the emperor was building his sprawling palace complex. He pressed on up the Caelian Hill to the home that had been in his family for generations, and where his wife and daughters now waited for him to break their fast together.

He rapped on the door and immediately Ludo, the door slave, opened. Gaius entered, touching the image of Mithras on the wall as he passed into the small atrium.

"Did you have a good run, Master?" Ludo asked, running a hand over his closely shaved head.

"Yes, Ludo. I did." Gaius accepted a towel and dried his face, chest and arms.

"I do wish you would take Pugio with you, Master. There are bandits on the Via Appia."

Gaius smiled at the old slave who had been his father's.

"Worry not, Ludo. There are no bandits that would bother me. Besides, Pugio cannot keep up with me. Gladiators are not meant for long distance running.

"Nor are dearly-missed husbands who leave their wives' beds in the small hours."

Gaius turned, smiling for the first time that day, to see Fulvia coming toward him. She wore a silver and blue stola, and her hair fell loosely about her shoulders.

She was the most beautiful woman Gaius had ever seen, and though he had been home over two months on his furlough, he felt each sight of her as sharply as the first time, when he had finally come home to her arms.

Ludo slipped away, beckoning to Nisica, Fulvia's body slave, to follow him.

Gaius took his wife into his arms and kissed her. She did not shrink from his sweating body.

"Good morning, my love," he said.

"Good morning to you. It would be even better if you stayed abed, you know." She smiled and ran a finger between the muscles of his chest. "I've had too many lonely mornings these past years."

Gaius gazed at the floor a moment and then stood back a half step.

"I had a particularly brutal dream, and needed to run it out."

"Another?" Fulvia stepped closer to him. "Why do the Gods torment you with these dreams every night?"

"I don't think it's the Gods, my love."

"Who then? What?" She looked at her husband and remembered him momentarily as he had been - dark and curly of hair, strong, muscular, and calm. Now, Gaius' hair had gone more to grey and was short. His body was still beautiful and well-muscled, but scarred, angular, tight, and quick as a wild beast's.

"I don't know," he lied. The laughter of those mountains where his men had been slaughtered, where he had killed his friend, Julius, still echoed in his mind. And with the laughter, dreams of blood, of death and dying, and crimson waves thrashing him.

"Gaius?" Fulvia's hand was on his cheek and he realized he had been away for a moment.

"It's nothing." He forced a smile. "Go rouse the girls and I'll bathe quickly."

She smiled a little pitifully, turned, and went to their daughters' cubiculum.

"Master?" Pugio's great bulk appeared down the corridor. "You bathe now?"

"Yes," Gaius answered.

Pugio handed him a fresh towel and strigil, and followed Gaius down the hall.

A short time later, Gaius and Fulvia were seated in the triclinium with the table laid out with fresh bread, cheese, boiled millet, figs, and honey. They enjoyed the rare moment of peace together on the couch.

Soon, in came Aemilia and Faustina wearing pink and

yellow tunics. They walked arm in arm in mock regality, their heads high, and proud, and topped by delicate olive crowns with braided ribbons which Nisica had fashioned for them.

"Good morning, ladies," Gaius stood, his hands on his hips.

The two little heads turned to him slowly as if they had only just noticed him.

"And who is this before us, sister?" asked Aemilia.

"I do not know, sister," replied Faustina. "But he seems to have eaten most of our cheese."

Fulvia stifled a laugh behind her husband who furrowed his brow in anger. When the girls' act wavered, Gaius burst out in laughter and lunged for them, scooping them up and tickling them.

Their laughter rang through the domus and washed over Gaius like a healing rain, helping him to forget his blood-soaked nightmares for a time.

"You'll wake the whole Caelian!" Fulvia chided, however much it did warm her heart to see Gaius and the girls laugh together. Their home had been too quiet in his absence.

"Let the lazy folk wake!" Gaius roared with Aemilia slung over his shoulder.

"Oh, they shall," Fulvia gazed out to the garden where the builders' materials lay scattered about. "They already turn their noses at our run-down home."

Gaius stopped laughing. He knew Fulvia could handle any of their snobby neighbours, but their criticisms of their family home set his teeth on edge.

"Well, soon they'll have no reason to do so, our prickly neighbours."

"No," Fulvia smiled as Gaius and the girls settled themselves down to eat. "Calista!" Fulvia called their kitchen slave who came running.

"Yes, Mistress?"

"More cheese for the girls."

The slave nodded and went back to the kitchen.

"Are you happy with the architect's plans?" Gaius asked his wife. The bonuses and increased centurion's pay had made it possible for Fulvia and Gaius to retile the roof, redesign the perystylium and atrium, and to expand the triclinium. Fresh paint and frescoes were being added throughout the house as well as mosaics. The cost was great but now, it seemed, they could afford it.

"I'm happy to be able to brighten up our home, but nothing does so more than having you here."

"It will not last, I'm afraid."

"Then let's enjoy the time we have, Gaius. All of us."

He nodded, knew she was right. What good was the present joy if he only spent his time worrying over the morrow?

A shadow passed swiftly in front of the doorway.

Gaius jumped up, but calmed himself immediately. He was always edgy now. There was only one person missing from the gathering.

"I'll go." Gaius went out of the triclinium and into the sunlit garden to see the boy sitting against a column among the buckets and plaster trowels. "Daxos?"

The young Thracian sat there trembling, his eyes hidden by his long black hair.

"Why don't you come and eat, Daxos?"

"I not want to disturb you family, Centurion."

"Come now. You're our guest here."

"I had the dreams again. Of immortui eating. Of my parents."

Gaius breathed deeply, full of pity for the boy. He had thought bringing him to Rome and showing him the wider world would help him to forget.

He had been wrong. Daxos' nightmares had followed him, the horror more persistent than ever. It was something that they shared.

Gaius sat down beside Daxos, and stared at the same dusty plaster bucket.

"I have the dreams too. Every night."

Daxos looked up for the first time. "You?"

"Yes. Me. All twelve of us who survived will remember and have dreams." Gaius paused a moment as he thought of something. "You've not told your dreams to Aemilia or Faustina, have you?"

Daxos shook his head. "Your girls, they laugh at me."

"What?"

"I not belong here, in Rome."

"Why do they laugh?"

Daxos shrugged.

"Promise me something, Daxos."

"Yes?"

"That you will not say anything about immortui to the girls or my wife. Understand? It is too scary for women."

Daxos nodded. "I promise."

"Thank you. And I will speak with the girls about their laughing. All right?"

The boy nodded again and went back to his cubiculum before Gaius could ask him to join them for breakfast.

Gaius stood still for a moment in the shambles of a garden and felt the sunlight upon his face.

Mithras. Lord. Help me through this darkness, he thought.

"WHERE IS DAXOS?" FULVIA ASKED WHEN GAIUS RETURNED.

"He had bad dreams and went back to his room."

"Is he ill?" she asked.

"No. Just misses his parents terribly. Seeing us reminds him of what he has lost." Gaius turned to Aemilia and Faustina. "By the way, girls, have you been laughing at Daxos?"

"He speaks so strangely, father. He gobbles all of his words," said the younger Faustina.

"Why did you have to bring him home, father?" asked Aemilia. "He scares me the way he stares at things and cries all night."

"Girls…" Fulvia began but Gaius waved her down.

"My loves, you are kind girls, and I know you will understand that I brought Daxos here out of kindness. He has lost his family, his entire people. And without his help, I would not be sitting here with you now, or ever again. Do you understand?"

Aemilia nodded, but Faustina still needed plain words.

"You mean you would be dead if Daxos had not helped you?"

"Yes. That is what I'm saying, my girl."

"We will treat him better, Papa," Aemilia said, Faustina nodding with little tears on the edge of her lids.

"I know you will, girls. I know," Gaius soothed as he squeezed his wife's hand without thinking.

The girls finished eating in silence. The sobering thought of their father's near death had sapped the silliness from them.

Aemilia whispered something to Faustina and the two looked at their parents.

"May we be excused, Papa?" asked Aemilia.

"Yes, of course."

"Remember, girls. We're going to the Forum later," Fulvia added.

"Yes, Mama," they said as they left the triclinium.

"You and Daxos should come too, Gaius."

"To the Forum?"

"Anywhere. He's a lonely boy. We can't leave him locked away in this house with his memories. He needs distraction."

Gaius smiled at his wife. At first she had been upset he had brought the boy home with him, that they had to share Gaius' time with an outsider. But now, as ever, Fulvia was the kinder, wiser one among them. She too had imagined if the letter she had received from Troesmis had been a notice of Gaius' death rather than a letter saying he was bringing a guest.

The thought of the former was unbearable. It had seemed to her then, after that sobering thought, that helping the boy was the Gods' will. She knew Juno, Vesta, and Diana would smile on them.

As Gaius finished eating, she leaned closer to him. He had that vacant, faraway look creeping in upon him again.

"Have you decided to tell me what exactly happened to you in those mountains, my love?" She felt his muscles tighten and release.

"No, Fulvia. I can't."

"We always tell each other everything. At least we always did."

Gaius breathed deeply. He could not blame her. He knew

the changes in himself must be worrisome. He knew his strong woman wanted to help.

"I know. And I do tell you everything. You will always know my heart."

"Good," she smiled.

"But you cannot know these things. You should not."

"But why?"

"Just know that Mithras is with me. He protects me."

"How can I take comfort from a god no woman worships?"

"You have to trust me, Fulvia. Please."

She pulled away slightly, shaking her head, struggling with the anger that was rising in her breast.

"When I was fighting for my life in those mountains, it was not only Daxos who saved me by running ahead to find the army, or sitting by my bedside." Gaius took her lithe hand and kissed it. "Mithras was with me as I ran and fought, but what gave me a will to go on, to fight when my limbs were as lead, were thoughts of you and of our girls. If you trust in anything or anyone, trust in Venus and the deep love I have for you, the love she kindled in my soul the very moment we met. Can you trust in that at least?"

Fulvia stood and looked down at her husband. She smoothed the fabric of her stola and held out her hands to him. He took them and stood.

"Of course I trust in that. With all the power within me. I always will."

Gaius kissed her then, and for those moments, the dark laughter at the back of his mind was completely strangled, giving him some peace.

When they came out of the triclinium, the sound of laughter echoed off of the walls, loud and joyous.

"What's all this?" Gaius demanded.

"We're playing!" Faustina giggled as a ball bounced past her and off the wall.

Then Aemilia and Daxos came running around the corner, both smiling and laughing, cheeks flushed from the game. They stopped when they saw Gaius, but his smile put them at ease.

He caught the ball and threw it past them so that Daxos and Faustina charged after it.

Aemilia was about to run, but Gaius mouthed a 'Thank you' to her. She smiled back and went to rejoin the game.

"We should trust in our daughters too," Fulvia said as they went to get ready for their outing.

"They're full of surprises." Gaius laughed, looking back over his shoulder as they went up the steps to their cubiculum.

THE FORUM ROMANUM WAS BRIGHT AND BUSY THAT afternoon as Gaius, Fulvia, the girls, and Daxos walked about gazing at the vendors' stalls, greeting acquaintances, and admiring the slew of new buildings and improvement projects commissioned by Augustus and the Senate.

Rome had changed much in the few years Gaius had been away. Everywhere he looked, it seemed wood and stone had turned to marble. Statues stood sentry everywhere you looked. From atop the Palatine Hill, the sounds of workmen and their hammering spilled into the Forum.

"Why are they building so much?" Daxos asked Aemilia. He had been to the Forum another day, but this time he took things in.

"The Emperor wishes to make Rome pretty for the people, "Aemilia answered.

"And to reflect Rome's greatness," Gaius added behind them where he walked beside Fulvia. He wanted to hold her hand as they went, not ever let go of her, but he knew that was frowned upon. *If everyone had been through what I've been through, they wouldn't be so damned stuffy!* he thought.

So, instead of holding his wife's hand, Gaius, accustomed to a lorica and pteruges, spent his time trying not to let the folds of his plain toga fall apart.

They came to a stop in front of the Rostra where the girls began to explain to Daxos that the prows of the ships that protruded from the platform were from captured enemy ships.

Daxos gazed about awestruck by the sights, the smells, the history. Then his eyes came to rest on something in the crowd.

He bolted.

"Daxos!" Gaius called and went after the boy, cutting a swathe through the startled crowd.

"Where did he go, Mama?" Faustina asked,

"I don't know, dear. Let's wait here for your father to come back." Fulvia put her hands on the girls' shoulders and searched the mass of heads for a sign of Gaius.

GAIUS FOUND DAXOS CLINGING TO A MAN AT THE BOTTOM OF the steps of the Temple of Castor and Pollux.

"Antonius?" Gaius said as he arrived.

"Gaius! Erm… I mean, Centurion."

"Pah! We're civilians for now." Gaius spread his arms to show his toga. "Gaius is fine."

The two men clasped forearms in greeting and Antonius ruffled Daxos' hair.

"I was just coming out of the temple when this one came running up to me." Antonius smiled. "Scared me to death."

"Me too." Gaius gave Daxos a disapproving look. "Don't run off like that again. All right?"

The boy nodded and they began to walk back toward Fulvia and the girls.

"How come I haven't seen you in Rome these last months?" Gaius asked.

"I went south to see our family lands, make the rounds. You know, make sure the relatives know I'm not dead."

"Got it!" Gaius laughed.

"I also got married!"

"What? Well, congratulations, my friend. Who is she?"

"Her name's Vera. I met her through my cousin, Quintus. She's a butcher's daughter, and as pretty as Venus herself."

"Well, I'm happy for you. Speaking of Venus…" Gaius sped up to reach Fulvia whose worried look dissolved when she saw him coming. "My love, this is my optio, Antonius."

"I'm happy to meet you, Optio. I've heard all about you."

"Likewise, Lady Justa. And these young ladies must be Aemilia and Faustina. Correct?" Antonius knelt down smiling. Gaius noticed the shake of his hands before he steadied them on his knees.

"Optio," the girls greeted in unison.

"So, any news, Antonius?" Gaius asked. "How've you been?"

Antonius' eyes darted momentarily before answering. "Well enough. With a new wife to keep me busy, tired mostly."

"Erm." Fulvia looked at Antonius and then to the girls and Daxos.

He froze. "Apologies. Barracks life and all."

"Yes, well…" Gaius laughed. "How about you come to our home the night after next for a meal so we can catch up?"

"Sounds good," Antonius answered.

"And bring your wife, Optio," Fulvia added.

"I will, lady. Thank you."

With that, Antonius set off for his home on the Aventine, and Gaius and the family continued to stroll about the Forum.

Daxos remained close to Gaius at all times after that.

THE FOLLOWING DAY, GAIUS TOOK HIMSELF TO THE BATHS FOR a wash and some proper exercise with other off-duty legionaries.

When the centurion stepped onto the palaestra, several of the competitors took in his sharp, muscled physique and the array of scars criss-crossing his arms and chest. It was not long before a couple of younger, unseasoned lads asked if he would box or wrestle with them.

Gaius was not unused to younger men wanting to test themselves against him, but in Rome, many young citizens thought it entertaining to try and humiliate off-duty soldiers.

The tension and memory of dark laughter had set Gaius on edge that morning. He was feeling particularly punchy, so he accepted the challenge.

"Actually, boys," he said as he put his towel down, wearing only his loincloth. "I'm eager to get in the water, so I'll just take you both on at the same time."

It was not long before a crowd had gathered to watch, and the bets were being laid.

The two young men flexed and circled like game cocks while Gaius stood calm, watching each of them.

The youths were lean and fast, but it did not take Gaius long to see that they were not used to team fighting. They wanted individual glory.

Definitely not men of the Legions.

They charged him fast at the same time from either side.

When Gaius leapt out of the way at the last second, the first youth's nose exploded where his own friend had landed his punch. The stricken one screamed and Gaius shoved him out of the way while he squared up to the other.

A feint, and a combination of three blows left the second grabbing his head while it rang.

"Come now, boys!" Gaius teased. "I need some exercise!"

"Ahh!" the one with the pulped nose ran and punched Gaius clumsily on the shoulder. Gaius dodged the follow-up and sent him spinning to the ground.

"Your turn, old man!" the other spat. He was angry, rabid for all his humiliation. Gaius waved him on.

Old man?

When he came at Gaius, it was with a pankrationist's stance and attack to the leg.

The kick caught Gaius hard on the thigh, but he managed to duck beneath the closed-fisted swing to his ear, and then get behind the youth to wrap his arm like a vice about his neck.

"Yeah!" cheered some of the veterans from the sideline.

Gaius squeezed and spoke to the lad. "You're too angry. Not enough focus for fighting. Street brawls are sloppy."

The young man tried to swing at Gaius' head, but the angle was not right. When his body began to go limp, Gaius let him fall. He did not see the blade that was coming from behind in the hand of the nosey one.

"Centurion!" a voice called out, preceding a grunt, and then a distinct crack of bone.

"Ahh! Ahh!" the other youth fell to his knees clutching his broken wrist beside the enormous Gaul who had stopped him.

Gaius turned quickly, furious. But his smile returned when the Gaul bellowed with laughter.

"Vitorix!" Gaius recognized him. "Well-timed, as ever!"

"You didn't really need my help, Centurion. Just didn't think the little cock was playing fairly, is all."

"No, he wasn't," Gaius eyed the two bloody youths darkly. "I suggest you two stick to tavern brawls instead of real fighting."

As the two crawled to each other, guards came over to take them away. No weapons were permitted on the palaestra floor.

"Maybe next time I'll break a sweat," Gaius joked.

"Ha!" Vitorix laughed.

As one of the survivors of their journey into the Carpathians, Gaius thought it amazing to see his jollity intact. He too laughed, slapped the big Gaul on the back, and they went to continue their exercises.

After training with weights and going through the warm, hot, and cold plunges, Gaius and Vitorix submitted to the massage slaves' ministrations, grunting as the knots were hammered out of their muscles.

"So how have you been, Vitorix?" Gaius asked through closed lids.

"Hmm. Fine. Bored, I guess. I'd rather be fighting Germans."

"Same old Vitorix. You'll get your chance."

"Truth is, sir, I can't sleep. Not at all since…well…you know."

Gaius opened his eyes. "Not at all?"

"Nope. Not a wink until I'm so drunk I'm forced to fall over wherever I am. I'm drinking too much. Been mugged twice cause I'd fallen in the fucking Subura."

"What? Mithras, man. No sleep other than that?"

The Gaul looked embarrassed, so Gaius changed the subject.

"Seen any of the other men since our furlough began?"

"Hmm, Yes. Barna's here. He cries in his sleep. Like a bloody baby. Sabinus is in Rome too. But he's just always sharpening his gladius or pugio in some corner. Says he wants to keep'em sharp in case."

"In case of what?"

"Why, in case of immortui, sir." Vitorix whispered. The slave stopped suddenly but continued when Vitorix barked at him. "Saguntus, the Iberian, is also in Rome."

"Does he have any…problems?" Gaius asked.

"Always whispering prayers to Mithras. Never stops really, unless you speak directly at him."

Gaius felt for his men. He had known they were all affected by that ill-fated mission but had secretly hoped a few months of leisure would make it all go away.

It would seem not.

When Gaius and Vitorix parted ways after changing in the apodyterium, the Gaul went directly to his favourite tavern, having told Gaius he would get the others together and meet at the baths another day.

Gaius wished his trooper well and returned home, his heart heavy with the news of his men.

The Via Sacra was suffused with a pink light that reminded Gaius of youthful days of contemplation in the Forum. Times after lessons when he would sit and ponder the world about him, the people passing by. Philosophy had always had a melancholic effect on him.

He stopped at the fountain where he had been sitting when he had first seen Fulvia. The memory warmed him.

It was as though it was yesterday, his green days as an army recruit. So much had happened since; marriage, children, the deaths of parents, and war. A world of contrast, the beautiful and terrible, like oil and water in his mind. He had handled it all well and with pride, for years.

Until...immortui.

The experience had changed him, shaken his world. Gaius closed his eyes and leaned over the fountain to cup some water and splash it on his face. He imagined Fulvia and the girls as they laughed together. That made him smile, unaware of the increasing activity down the road.

He looked up and was about to thank Mithras for all his blessings when a single, dark blade of cloud cut across the sun's face.

"Look!" someone gasped behind him.

Gaius watched as an eagle that had been soaring high above the city began to plummet screeching to earth somewhere near the Capitoline Hill.

"An evil omen!" the person beside Gaius began to babble and covered his head with a fold of his toga.

The noise in the Forum turned to a series of wails and screams. People who had been milling about the Rostra for news began to run in every direction.

Gaius began walking toward the commotion, a sense of dread germinating in the pit of his stomach. He reached out and grabbed a trooper of the vigiles who was running by.

"What's going on?" Gaius demanded. "What's happened?" He shook the man.

"News...from Germania. "The man's eyes were wild and

he stared at the black cloud that hovered over the city, turning the pink light to a sickly grey.

"What news?" Gaius demanded, using his parade ground voice.

The man's eyes fixed on Gaius, wide and terrified.

"Three entire legions and all auxiliary cohorts under Quinctilius Varus have been massacred."

"What?" Gaius let go and the trooper ran off. *Mithras, help us... This has to be a mistake...*

But the omen and the panicked people shouted otherwise.

Gaius began to run like all the others. He had to get home to make sure Fulvia and the girls were safe. When Rome was in a panic, horrible things could happen.

When Gaius burst through the door into the atrium, several workmen jumped, nearly knocking over a new statue of a nymph that had just been delivered.

"Fulvia!" Gaius shouted, ignoring the staring workmen. "Fulvia?"

"Master?" Pugio came running out of the kitchen with Nisica behind him. Ludo came from the other end of the peristylium with Calista.

"Yes, husband?" Fulvia appeared at the top of the stairs to the second level with the girls on either side of her, and Daxos lurking behind them.

Gaius calmed down. "There is panic in the streets. Three legions have been slaughtered in Germania." Some of the workers gasped, others shrugged their shoulders. "You should all return to your homes at once," he said.

"You heard the master. Everyone out!" Ludo took control while Gaius raced upstairs to see his wife and children.

"Are we safe in our home, Papa?" Aemilia asked, astute as ever.

"Yes, my girl. Not to worry." Gaius turned to Pugio at the bottom of the stairs. "Make sure you're armed, and don't let anyone in without consulting me."

"Yes, Master." Pugio went to gather his weapons with Nisica trailing after him.

"Need we worry, Gaius?" Fulvia asked. "Germania is so far away."

"We'll see, my love… We'll see," Gaius soothed, trying with all his might to drown the laughter at the back of his mind.

The Caelian Hill escaped the violence that did occur that night, but other neighbourhoods were less fortunate. The Aventine and Suburan districts were struck by panic, fires, and looting. The Vigiles had a busy night.

While Fulvia and the girls slept soundly in their beds, Gaius sat up, his gladius and pugio near to hand. His mind raced over the news from Germania, and all the while laughter and the name 'Arminius' harried his thoughts.

But we sent messengers!

He remembered Commander Maximus sending riders down the frontier lines to warn of the possibility of attack.

As Gaius stood to stretch, a shadow passed before the door to his cubiculum. He grabbed his gladius and padded barefoot into the corridor, leaving Fulvia sleeping soundly.

Panic set in, and he went swiftly to his daughters' room, but they were safe, still and asleep.

Then, a sound like a rush of air whipped round the garden below.

Thieves? Gaius wondered.

Sword out and ready, he raced downstairs to the peristylium to find a hulking brute of a man leaning against one of the columns with his back to Gaius.

"Hold it there, thief. Or I'll run you through." Gaius stepped forward, ready for any move the intruder might make in his panic at being caught.

But he did not panic. Instead a dry, hoarse laughter wafted about the moonlit garden.

"Turn or I'll kill you. By Mithras, I will. What are you doing here?" The tip of Gaius' gladius was three inches from the man who began to turn his massive shoulders slowly.

It was a motion Gaius recognized. He gasped, and backed away as the man faced him and spoke.

"Bit hard…to kill me…" he rasped, "…when I am already dead."

"Ju…Julius," Gaius stammered, his hands suddenly shaking as he pointed his sword out. "No…it's not possible." Gaius could not help falling to his knees. "Mithras, protect us."

"He already does, Gaius…"

"I'm going mad." Gaius rubbed his eyes.

"Not yet…my friend." The apparition smiled sadly. "I am happy to see you have my gladius." He reached for it but stopped short, unable to touch it. "You will need it, Gaius. You will need it."

"Forgive me," Gaius muttered. All he could see was Julius' distorted face, the mad jaundiced eyes, and his own blade slicing through his neck. "Forgive me…" Gaius said again, his eyes burning.

"You saved me," Julius said. "Because of you, I walk in the Light. The immortui are destroyed."

Gaius stood, still shaking, his breath showing in the suddenly cold air of the garden.

"He is not finished, Gaius."

"Who?"

"He who ruled them all." Julius made a ghostly fist and pounded it silently into this other hand. "It has only just begun."

"You mean Varus' legions?"

The ghost nodded.

"So, it's true?"

"Yes. But it was not only Germans."

"Who then?"

"They are worse than the immortui…more ravenous. Because of them, thousands of our brothers walk in the darkness of the Germanic wood."

"How do you know this?" Gaius asked.

"I know. My anger stirs to boiling, even in this realm."

Gaius looked upstairs to make sure Fulvia or anyone else was not there to see.

Julius hung his grey, ghostly head.

"Your furlough is going to be cut short. You must ready yourself."

"For what?"

There was a pause, then came the laughter that made even Julius' lemur shudder.

"For lykoi, Gaius. Soon, you will be sent hunting." Julius moved away from Gaius then, toward the main door of the atrium where Pugio snoozed in a chair beside it.

Julius turned to Gaius one last time, saluted, and passed through the bronze and wood doors out into the night.

Gaius stood shaking on the spot with the moon's light soaking the ground about him.

·　·　·

"Husband?" The soft voice reached out gently to Gaius's cold thoughts, and he took notice. "Gaius? I'm here…" a soft hand, a touch upon the cheek. He blinked.

"Fulvia?" Gaius' eyes focused on his wife's worried face, and Ludo and Pugio beyond the columns. Worry was etched on everyone's features, but Fulvia stayed calm.

"It's me, Gaius. What happened? Why are you in the garden?" She glanced down at the gladius that hung limp in her husband's hand. "Pugio found you before sunrise," she added.

"I…had trouble sleeping."

"More dreams?" she asked. There was something different about him.

"Y…yes. More dreams. I need to run."

"Now? Today? After all your fretting about riots and violence in the streets?"

Gaius shook his head, remembered the previous day, the news from Germania.

"No. Of course not. You're right, my love. My place is here keeping you safe." Without another word, Gaius went upstairs to change and get cleaned up.

"Shall I put out breakfast, Mistress?" asked the kitchen slave, Calista.

"Yes. Do," Fulvia answered, her eyes focussing on the top of the stairs. "The girls and I will start." Fulvia went quietly to the triclinium to join her daughters who were already there waiting.

"How is Papa, Mama?" asked Aemilia.

"He's fine, my girl. Just a bad dream. He was worrying all night about the city."

"All the noisy people, you mean?" asked Faustina.

"Yes. But all's well today."

The girls looked relieved and went about eating their breakfast of honey, bread, and cheese.

When Gaius entered the room a few minutes later, Fulvia was relieved to see the odd look gone from his eyes. It had been the look of a frightened child, and it scared her.

"Are you feeling better?" she asked after a few minutes, her hand reaching out to touch him.

"Yes. It was a bad one, that's all. Another curse of a dream." Gaius touched the pommel of his gladius unconsciously before reaching for more bread.

"We should prepare to receive Antonius and his wife tonight," Fulvia reminded Gaius as he ate.

"Yes. I forgot."

"I'll have Calista prepare something nice for us that-"

There was a loud rapping at the front doors.

Gaius could hear Pugio protesting just before a tramp of hobnails echoed from the peristylium.

"Stay here!" Gaius said to Fulvia and the girls as he leapt from his couch, drawing his sword in a swift, smooth motion.

"Master!" Pugio called.

When Gaius arrived in the peristylium, he came face to face with three Praetorian guardsmen. He did not lower his sword.

"What's the meaning of this?" he demanded.

"Centurion Gaius Justus Vitalis?" the central Praetorian, a thick-necked centurion, addressed Gaius. He eyed the drawn sword and waved it aside.

"That's me," Gaius answered. "What's the meaning of this? Bursting into my home while I'm at breakfast with my family?"

"Orders from the Emperor, Centurion. You're to come with us to the palace."

"Why? I'm on furlough from the Legions."

"I really don't give a damn," the man spat and came close to Gaius.

"I'll come as the Emperor commands. Worry not. But if you spit or threaten me again in my home, I'll spill your guts out of that shiny uniform that doesn't seem to have seen any action. Got me?"

The man did not budge from Gaius' face, but Gaius could see doubt behind his eyes. Not all Praetorians were hardened warriors.

"Sir," said one of the other guardsmen. "We're wasting time. The Emperor is waiting."

"Why don't you wait out in the street, Centurion?" Gaius said.

"I don't think so," the man answered. "We'll just wait with your man in the atrium. Just make it quick." The Praetorians turned and stomped back to the atrium where Pugio stood watch over them.

Gaius watched them turn the corner and then ushered Fulvia and the girls upstairs.

"I want you all to stay up here until the front door is locked behind me, understand?"

"Yes." Fulvia stood behind Gaius as he began dressing in brown bracae and a clean crimson tunic. "But what does the Emperor want? Are you in trouble, Gaius?"

He could tell she was struggling to keep herself together and turned to hold her hands.

"I suspect it's about the disaster in Germania." He kissed her forehead. "Don't worry. I had no role in it, and I reported what I knew as soon as I was able. It'll be all right." Even as the words left his mouth, Gaius felt he was lying to himself. He went to a nearby table with feet in the shape of lion's claws and picked up the armilla and torc he had been awarded in Troesmis. He put them on, a silent prayer to Mithras on his lips.

Then he laced up his leather boots, strapped his pugio about his waist, and turned to Fulvia who wrapped his short brown cloak about his shoulders and fastened a silver brooch.

"Be careful, please. I have a bad feeling. Yesterday, this morning, and now this…" She held Gaius close. "Just come home."

"I will. And don't forget about Antonius' visit tonight." He smiled and she relaxed. "Now, I'd better go with those Praetorian grunts downstairs before Pugio tears them apart."

Gaius kissed the girls where they had been sitting silent the whole time, then went out of the cubiculum, leaving the three of them alone.

"Let's go!" Gaius barked as he strode through the atrium and out into the street without waiting for the guards. "Pugio, keep a watch," he called over his shoulder.

"Will do, Master."

Nobody had noticed Daxos where he had been sitting in the garden since breakfast. The boy watched Gaius disappear outside and then went back to his own cubiculum.

He too had seen things the previous night.

ROME WAS BUZZING WITH WORRY. THE PRAETORIANS AND Vigiles were everywhere as Gaius and his escorts came down off the Caelian and made their way up the Via Sacra. There was some debris, but not much. Most had been cleaned in the early hours.

Gaius wondered what the Aventine and Subura looked like.

"You boys have a busy night?" Gaius asked, trying to break the wall he had built between himself and the centurion. They must have been up all night.

"Hmph. Busy? Yes. But we've seen worse. More noise than anything, but the Emperor wanted it quiet so as not to cause panic. But when crazy whoresons run through the streets and taverns yelling 'The Germans are at the city gates!', well, people get a little fucking worked up."

The centurion stopped talking and strode ahead to meet the guards at the northern steps to the Palatine Hill and the imperial palace complex.

"I'm to take this centurion directly to the Emperor," the guard said to his Praetorian colleague at the gate.

The man eyed Gaius suspiciously, but nodded them through after the password had been whispered to him.

After two steep flights of stairs that led to the top of the hill, Gaius found himself in lush gardens heavily accented by building materials. There seemed to be works going on everywhere.

The air was sweeter on the Palatine, tinged with lemon and jasmine. Their boots crunched on the gravel pathway that led to the rear of the newly built temple of Apollo.

There were Praetorians everywhere on the hill, and each of them alert despite the previous night. Gaius found himself admiring their discipline.

The group rounded the back corner of the temple of Apollo which gleamed in white marble, to arrive at the rear entrance of the Emperor's house.

Gaius had never had an audience with Augustus, so he did not know what to expect.

"Leave your pugio with me," said one of the guards at the door. "No weapons in Caesar's presence."

"Of course." Gaius quickly unsheathed his dagger, flipped it and handed it, handle first, to the guard.

"Follow me," his escort mumbled as they filed into a plain corridor floored with brick. No one seemed to be about, though Gaius knew that must be otherwise. He did not enjoy being alone with the Praetorians, most of whom were Germans. Since the Pannonian revolts, he had grown acutely distrustful of any peoples from the other side of the Danuvius.

They passed out of the dimly lit hallways and into a large peristylium with some stone columns and a simple geometric floor of coloured marble. There were no statues in the garden between the columns, no trimmed hedges; only a couple of fruit trees and a quietly sputtering fountain. Beside the fountain was a bench where a woman was seated.

When she saw them, the woman stood up and her eyes followed them.

Gaius tried not to look, but she was tall, in a plain crimson stola with a single necklace of gold. She was older, and exuded power and intelligence. As they passed, Gaius bowed his head to her.

She nodded in return, but did not smile.

Finally, they reached a set of double doors flanked by two of the biggest Praetorians Gaius had ever seen. His nerves suddenly took hold of him. He had been so preoccupied with his surroundings that he had stopped mulling over the possible reasons for his summons.

Too late now, he thought as the doors swung open and he stepped into a large room devoid of ornamentation.

"Centurion Gaius Justus Vitalis of V Macedonica, Imperator." The Praetorian said to the back of a man staring out from a balcony at the far end of the room.

Gaius stepped forward and saluted. "Ave, Imperator!"

Augustus did not turn right away. He stared out the window, shoulders hunched, head low. In fact, the Emperor's appearance was altogether shocking. He was no longer the tall, tightly-muscled man of confidence as portrayed in his statues about the city.

When the Emperor turned, all Gaius could see was a tired man in a worn, black tunic that had been torn to reveal a part of his sagging chest.

Augustus' eyes were tired and red-rimmed, and his once golden hair had retreated to grey atop his head.

"Sire." Gaius knelt on one knee, his hands clasped.

"Centurion," Augustus muttered. "I believe you know the Legate."

Gaius turned to see several people lined up along one wall of the room. He had not noticed them, even Legate Iulus Maximus Sabino, his own commander. Gaius thought he looked tired, his face etched with worry.

"Commander," Gaius nodded to Maximus.

"Justus."

Augustus continued. You, have likely not met Tiberius, my step-son."

Gaius turned to salute Tiberius who was well-known to the men of the German legions. He was tall, well-built, and dressed in a fine toga that accented his broad shoulders.

"Centurion." Tiberius nodded.

"Sir," Gaius answered.

"And these two youths beside Tiberius are my nephews, Germanicus and Claudius."

Gaius acknowledged the two young men and turned when the doors opened to admit the woman from the garden.

"Ah, Livia." Augustus stepped forward to take the

Empress' hand and led her to a plain couch on the other side of the room.

She stopped before Gaius.

"Augusta Livia Drusilla," Gaius knelt again.

"Rise, Centurion," Livia said smoothly. "I am not your imperator."

Gaius rose and looked at all the people about him. The Emperor spoke.

"I suppose you're wondering why I summoned you, Centurion?"

"It is an honour, Sire. I do not question."

"Good. But it is not an honour that brings you here, nor your legate. It is a tragedy that brings you before me."

Gaius worried then, even more so as he saw the look upon Maximus' face.

"I heard rumours in the street, sire," Gaius offered. "News from Germania." Gaius shivered as he remembered Julius' lemur the night before.

"Rumours?" the Emperor questioned. "If only the gods willed it so. No, Centurion. What you heard about the loss of my legions is true. The seventeenth, eighteenth, and nineteenth Legions, plus all auxiliary forces, have been wiped out. Obliterated by the Germans under this…this…Cheruscian, Arminius.

Gaius stiffened at the name and the Emperor noticed. Augustus was still astute.

"I see you know the name, Centurion. It is the name you brought to your legate when you came out of your fever at Troesmis."

So it's true… Gaius thought. "Yes, sire. I remember the name." Augustus, Livia, and Tiberius' eyes all focussed on Gaius. "But Commander Maximus had immediately sent a dozen riders with emergency messages to reach Mogunti-acum and other surrounding forts. They must have received word."

"No. They did not." Augustus went to a large table where a map of the Danuvius frontier was laid out. "All the riders were intercepted along the way. It was only later that their remains were found by patrols, torn to ribbons every one of them."

"Torn?" Gaius could hear the laughter again and shook his head.

"Are you well, Centurion?" Livia asked from her couch, looking from Gaius to her son, Tiberius.

"Yes…yes…please forgive me."

Augustus studied Gaius a moment longer, a curious look in his eyes. Then he returned to the map.

"Sire," Tiberius stepped up with Maximus. Germanicus and Claudius came around by the emperor. "It must be that the enemy had infiltrated the auxiliary cavalry at Troesmis. If Arminius' men turned on Rome, it may be that other groups are a part of it. Those riders probably never intended on delivering those messages."

"Sire. My men were trusted beyond a doubt. Besides, why would they be killed if they had sided with the enemy?"

"These tribes have strange ways, Legate," Tiberius said. "Perhaps those men had served their purpose?"

"It's a bloody, hateful business, Maximus," Augustus said sadly. "If only your centurion had told you sooner."

"Sire," Maximus quelled his anger before speaking. He could feel Livia's gaze from across the room. "Centurion Justus warned our legion of an attack that would surely have wiped us out. He nearly died for it."

Everyone looked at Gaius again, his torc and armilla.

"He told me as soon as the name came to him. The medics said the trauma to his body should have killed him."

"And yet, here he stands," Augustus added.

"Mithras watched over me, sire," Gaius said.

"But not over my three legions!"

Augustus' first slammed onto the map where it showed a large region of forested hills.

"The gods are telling us Rome is not safe! Do you know what happened these last nights?" Augustus went to the window and his voice dropped noticeably. "They tell me that the temple on the Field of Mars was struck by lightning. Our own God of War brought low. Locusts have invaded the city of Rome too, and the only thing to devour them are the swallows nesting in our porticoes. Riders have informed me that the mountains of Cisalpine Gaul collapsed upon each other, sending up three massive columns of fire…one for each of *my* legions!"

Augustus paced, more angry and frantic as he began to tear more of his tunic.

"What's more is that the sky itself, I'm told, was set ablaze with several ill-omened comets. Spears come out of the sky. Bees swarm our camp altars, and a statue of Victory herself turned its back upon Germania." Augustus leaned once more upon the table, his eyes studying the map.

Gaius thought the Emperor looked a little crazed. Augustus had always been cold and calculating, but now he seemed to struggle for a grip on reality, or a desire to dismiss it altogether.

"We need to move quickly, sire," Tiberius said. He was a man of action. "I recommend that I muster all the force I can and march north to Germania."

"Who commands along the frontier now?" asked Maximus.

Augustus wheeled on the Legate.

"Please, Legate. I'm in no mood for your strategy. Were I a simpler man, I would think this all your fault."

"Now, husband," Livia rose smoothly and was at his side without a sound. "Legate Maximus sent word as soon as he had it. Signals would have been read by the enemy. Besides, Maximus' V Macedonica is among your most decorated legions."

Gaius was surprised to see Maximus remain silent, head bowed. Not many could cow the Legate.

Tiberius turned to Maximus to answer his question.

"Varus' nephew, Lucius Nonius Asprenas, was commanding two legions at Moguntiacum when the ambush was laid by Arminius. He has rushed down the Rhine to protect the winter camps."

Maximus nodded to Tiberius but said nothing.

"Caesar should send Tiberius to Germania at once with as many men as can be mustered. The more time that is wasted, the more territory you will lose." Livia knew when to insert herself, as keen as any battle commander. "If you do nothing, you will appear weak, and then Rome's gates will truly be open to the barbarians."

"Enough!" Augustus' hand smacked the table and spit from his mouth fell onto the map. "Tiberius, I want you to seek out volunteers from all men of military age within the city. If they refuse to take up arms for their Emperor, have them draw lots and tell them their property is forfeit for failing to fight for Rome."

"There will be much resistance." Tiberius stood straight, arms crossed.

"Use the Praetorians to help them decide. You can take three cohorts north with you."

A gleam entered Tiberius' eyes then.

Gaius thought he relished the idea of commanding the Emperor's guard.

"What of the other legions, Uncle?" Claudius put in, glancing at Maximus. "Surely they should be marching?"

"Claudius," Augustus waved a hand as though at a fly. "If we expose other parts of that frontier, the enemy will pour through that breach. They move quickly."

"What will Tiberius do once he arrives at the Rhine, Grandfather?" Germanicus asked then.

Gaius thought the young twenty-four year old asked the key question. What was the strategy?"

Augustus smiled.

"Ah, Germanicus. You're at the heart of the matter." Augustus looked to his step-son and Livia. "Tiberius will not cross the river."

"What?" Tiberius' voice boomed in the room. "Gods, why not? We should cross the frontier and utterly crush them. The tribes cannot be allowed to get away with this!"

"You will do as I command!" Augustus was his old self again. "You question me? What would you do? Cross the river and find yourself lost in those black forests? Would you and more legions be a second course for the barbarians? Hmm?"

"No, sire!" Tiberius clenched and unclenched his fists. "No."

"Listen, all of you. We need to hold the frontier at all costs and make sure it is not breached. We need to watch the enemy, within and without. We need to make sure they do not cross the river, Tiberius." Augustus laid his hand on Tiberius' shoulder. "I need you to strengthen that frontier. The fortresses, the men, the communications."

"I will," Tiberius acquiesced, yielding to the wisdom of Augustus' plan, however reluctant his compliance might have been.

There was always time for fighting.

"But, Grandfather," Germanicus began again, his sandy hair framing his brow. "Should we not send some smaller force into the forests to scout for any survivors, or capture any Germans we can torture for news of more attacks?"

Augustus smiled widely.

"That is one reason you are here, Germanicus."

The young man swelled with pride.

"Your ideas often echo my own." Augustus pet the young man on the shoulder and then turned to Gaius and Maximus. "And that is why the Legate and Centurion are here as well."

Germanicus frowned, but thought better of complaining.

"Sire?" Maximus spoke while Gaius stood straighter beside him.

Augustus was silent for a minute before speaking again.

"All of you, leave us," the Emperor said flatly. Everyone looked from one to another. "All of you can go now… except the Legate and Centurion Justus." He eyed all of them. "Now."

Claudius led the way, followed by Tiberius and Livia. Germanicus left last, his face red, his pace quick.

"Guards, wait outside," Augustus ordered before going back to the balcony.

Gaius and Maximus looked at each other and then followed the Emperor. Gaius could sense something, knew they had come to the main reason he was there.

"I've lost my legions…" Augustus muttered. "They're

gone. Varus was a fool, a damn fool. He befriended and trusted this Arminius. Now, thousands of Romans are dead."

"Gods give them all rest, sire," Maximus said.

Augustus turned, framed by the light beyond him.

"Will they, Maximus? Or will they send legions of immortui back against us?"

Gaius let out a gasp and gaped at the Emperor.

"Your commander has told me everything, Centurion. I know what you and the other survivors have been through."

"Sire." Gaius felt dizzy and gripped the side of the table.

"Yes. And I know that you yourself know how to deal with these creatures."

"But, sire, we don't even know what we are dealing with. What if they are not immortui but…something else?" Gaius' mind went back to the previous night and Julius' visit, his words.

The immortui are destroyed.

"Sit. Both of you." Augustus indicated two chairs beside his larger one. "Centurion, I was ready to execute Legate Maximus here when word first came. But then he came to me, and told me all that has happened; how you happened upon Arminius and this leader who commands them, the one who seems to have the real power."

Gaius began to fidget, struggle for control. He could not help it.

"What you say here, Centurion, will only be between the three of us," the Emperor's voice was low, anticipatory.

Gaius nodded. He had to choose his words carefully.

"Sire. Legate… I don't believe the immortui are a threat any longer."

"How do you know, Justus?" Maximus asked. "Did we

burn them all on the Carpathian plains? What if there are more in those mountains?"

"Sir, the gods have given me some visions of late…" *I can't say I see ghosts. Mithras light my way.* "There are words that came to me during the night. They said that the immortui were destroyed, but that a more ravenous enemy massacred Varus' legions and waits for us even now."

"Who?" the Emperor demanded, his eyes wide with fear. "Who is waiting?"

"I don't know, sire. I'm not adept at deciphering the gods' messages. All I know is that something, someone, is lurking in those German woods." Gaius found his strength then and his fists rested upon the table where he studied the map. "Thousands of my brothers lie massacred there, unable to walk in the light because of Arminius and the other."

"Are you fit to return to duties, Justus?" Maximus asked suddenly.

Gaius looked up and both men were staring at him.

"Yes, sir."

"Good, Centurion," Augustus said. "Because I have work for you and your fellow survivors."

"Sire?"

"How many of you are there, who survived the immortui attack?"

"Thirteen, sire. Including myself, my optio and a boy."

"Yes. Maximus mentioned the boy. He must stay for safety. However, I wish to create a… special unit…made up of you and the eleven others."

"What is the mission, sire?"

"You are to cross the Rhine in stealth and find out what you can about the attack, what happened to my legions. Try to find survivors if you can. Of utmost importance, I want you to try and track down Arminius and bring him back here, alive or dead. Most of all, I want you to try and apprehend this Carpathian lord who seems to have been helping Arminius with his power. Find him…and kill him."

The laughter entered Gaius' thoughts even then, mocking, daring. Gaius pictured Julius and his fallen comrades, Daxos' murdered family. He imagined the scene in that German forest and dreaded the dreams to come.

Then Gaius felt the sunlight filtering into the room to warm his back. He remembered his run from the mountains, striding beside Mithras, the god's bright laughter, defiant in the dark. Gaius turned to the Emperor and his Legate.

"I'll go and I'll find out what happened, sire. On my honour."

"And on your life, and that of your family, Centurion." Augustus face was dark and vengeful when he said the words, his eyes unblinking. This was the man who had conquered the Senate and centuries of Roman history.

"All of our lives hang on this, Justus," Maximus added cautiously. "For if this enemy crosses the river, we are all in peril."

"Yes, sir." Gaius' thoughts raced. "We…my men and I will…need special arms and armour…all black for stealth."

"Yes, of course," Augustus agreed. "You shall have everything you need. Armour, weapons, ballistas, horses. All of it."

"And none shall know of our operations?"

"None. And I'll even give you an imperial pass should you be questioned on your way."

"Thank you, sire. But, there is one more thing."

"What is it, Centurion?"

"This power we will be facing is great, and it may take time to…. I may die as I nearly did before. I ask that if we succeed in this mission, that we, myself, my men, and our families be allowed to live in peace after, retire if need be.”

“An early pension, you mean?”

“Yes, sire.”

“You are bold, Centurion.” Augustus nodded. “Yet you will need your boldness, I dare say. Very well. If you succeed in this, I will grant each of your families lands and pensions that would make the highest ranking Praetorian jealous, and see to the future of your children’s children’s children. Will that do?”

“Yes…yes, sire. You are most generous.”

“I am most eager to save the empire I have built!” Augustus slammed his hands together. “Send me proof of your progress when you have it. If your supplies run short, you may return to replenish.”

“Yes, sire.”

“Lastly, you are no longer a part of V Macedonica. You and your men are a stand-alone unit, reporting directly to me. Understood?”

Gaius glanced at Maximus who had stepped back a little.

“I understand, my Imperator.”

“Good. Now, I must get ready to receive my clients. You will leave as soon as you are ready, but do not travel with Tiberius. Use another route.”

“We shall, sire.”

“Don’t fail me, Centurion.” Augustus turned to Maximus. “See him off the Palatine, Maximus. Then return here. I would speak with you further.”

Maximus and Gaius saluted, and Augustus returned to the sunlit balcony.

As the two men left through the double doors, they could hear the Emperor yelling.

"Publius Quinctilius Varus! GIVE ME BACK MY LEGIONS!"

OUT IN THE GARDENS OF THE PALATINE HILL, UNDER THE watchful gaze of the Praetorians, Maximus stopped walking and turned to Gaius.

"I didn't know he would decide that, Justus. I've enjoyed having you under my command."

"It's been an honour serving you, Legate. V Macedonica has been my other familia for so long."

They continued down the shrub-lined path that led to the steps of Cacus.

"Are you in danger here, Legate?"

Maximus rubbed his jaw, his eyes looking from side to side ever so slightly.

"I don't know, to be honest. It doesn't look good. He hasn't mentioned taking my command, but then, he is a man of extreme moods. Especially since Varus' idiocy. I rushed here to tell the Emperor all I knew, but it seems the Fates were against me."

Gaius felt for the old bear. Maximus had always served Rome and the Emperor faithfully. His men loved him, and his colleagues admired him, or pretended to at any rate.

"Tonight, Optio Antonius and his new wife are joining us on the Caelian for dinner, sir. We'd be honoured if you joined us."

Maximus looked up at the sky and then back at the palace walls. They stopped as a peacock skittered across the path.

"Thank you, Justus. That's very kind of you. But…if I am allowed to leave the Palatine, I will go to stay with my brother. He's the only family I've got, and when it comes down to it, family is what it's all about."

"I understand, sir."

They reached the top of the steps of Cacus, and Maximus grabbed Gaius' arm in friendship, pulled him in close.

"I've put myself on the line for you, Justus. Don't let me down."

Gaius looked into the older man's worried eyes and nodded.

"We won't let you down, Legate. Count on it."

"Mithras watch over you, Justus."

"You too, sir," Gaius answered and saluted.

Maximus watched Gaius go down those steps where hundreds of years before, the monster Cacus would sit in wait to attack passers-by. Maximus felt a knot of dread form in the pit of his stomach. He wondered what other monsters Gaius and the rest of his former men would encounter in the coming months.

"To your marriage!" Gaius held his cup up to Antonius and his wife, Vera.

"May Venus and Diana bless you both," Fulvia added, her smile broad and genuine. "We're so glad you were safe on the Aventine after the other night."

"Thank you, both for having us." Antonius raised his cup in return. He squeezed his wife's hand and she blushed a colour to match her hair.

"Will you go anywhere to celebrate your marriage?" Fulvia asked.

Antonius looked to Gaius before speaking. "We were

thinking of a few days in Baiae, but now I believe it will have to wait. Is that true, Gaius?"

"I'm afraid so, my friend," Gaius said, smiling apologetically at Vera. "The Emperor has special…duties…for us."

The two men had not yet had a chance to speak privately about it except for a few brief words in the atrium after the introductions had been made.

Gaius looked at Fulvia on the couch beside him. She looked like a goddess in her deep blue stola. The thought of leaving her again, and earlier than planned, was no easy thing. She had taken the news well enough, but he could tell it upset her. The girls would be devastated when he told them.

They had enjoyed the meal Nisica had prepared. Antonius and Vera were very complimentary.

Fulvia had not wanted to overwhelm Vera, a butcher's daughter, with overly rich foods. The salads, olives, saffron millet, and roasted chicken with garum had all been a success.

The four of them now sat back, sipping their wine and enjoying fresh figs and honeyed dates.

Fulvia could see that Vera and Antonius were in love and her hand found Gaius'. She gave it a comforting squeeze. Even the slightest intimacy was a treasure to her these past months. Inside, Fulvia struggled not to curse the Emperor. Gaius had explained something of what was said when he had returned from the Palatine Hill: the lost legions, his new commission, and what they stood to gain.

But there were orders and threats under the surface. She had been an officer's wife long enough to know that.

"You have *such* a beautiful home, Lady Justa," Vera suddenly burst in upon her thoughts.

"Thank you, Vera. But please, call me Fulvia."

"Fulvia," the girl repeated.

"Would you like me to show you around?"

"Oh yes. Please."

Fulvia got up from the couch and winked at Gaius. It was his chance to speak with Antonius. Vera followed her out of the triclinium.

"We'll have to be careful not to wake the girls..." their voices faded around the corner.

When they were gone, Gaius turned to Antonius.

"You seem happy."

"I am. She's a wonderful girl, and so full of...erm...fire."

Gaius laughed. "That's good!" He shook his head. "I'm sorry to have to take you away from her."

"I won't pretend I'm happy about it, but when the Emperor calls-"

"We must obey," Gaius finished. "Come. Let's go to the tablinum so I can tell you all about it."

The two men topped up their wine and walked across the small courtyard to a room on the other side. The night air was cool and Gaius' head was enjoyably muddled, but the topic of conversation was going to sober him quickly. He motioned Antonius to a chair, lit a couple of lamps and sat at his table.

"Tell me," Antonius said straightaway.

"We're no longer a part of V Macedonica." Gaius watched Antonius as he slumped back. "As of now you, me, and the other ten survivors are to form a special unit answerable only to Augustus himself." Gaius opened a drawer, took out a scroll and handed it to Antonius. "Here are your discharge papers from the legion, as well as your new commission outlining duties and benefits. All of our papers were delivered to me this afternoon by imperial messenger."

Antonius perused the new commission. "They didn't waste time, did they?"

"Urgent situations don't allow for it." Gaius sipped his wine and ran his hand over his shorn head.

"So much?" Antonius' eyes shot up from the scroll. "Really?"

"Yes." Gaius stood and went to the faintly-lit wall map behind him. "You do know what they're asking?"

"Yes…I do." Antonius gripped his hands together tightly. He had suffered from bouts of shaking since their flight from the Carpathians. He closed his eyes and regained control.

"You need to know something," Gaius turned. "I don't believe it's immortui we'll be fighting."

"What? How do you know?"

"I…I don't quite know how to tell you. You'll think me mad."

"After what we've been through, Gaius, it would take a lot to convince me of that."

"Very well," he sighed and took a deep breath. "Julius told me."

Antonius said nothing. He stared at his hands.

"The other night," Gaius continued, "I heard something in the peristylium. I came down to find someone in our garden. It was Julius' lemur. Standing right there." Gaius pointed into the garden, out the door behind Antonius.

"He doesn't walk in the Light?"

"He does. He does. But he told me, as real as I am here with you, that Varus' legions were not destroyed by barbarians or immortui. He said that it was lykoi."

"Lykoi?" Antonius repeated. "That's not possible."

"And immortui are?"

"Mithras protect us."

"Only Augustus and Legate Maximus know of the immortui and of my…vision."

"I don't know what to say. I'm…I'm terrified, Gaius. Of dying, of leaving my wife and never seeing children. I don't want to roam the woods of Germania for eternity, in the dark." Antonius made the sign against evil.

"Nor do I." Gaius came around the table. " I need your help here, Antonius. You're my optio, my friend, and a great fighter."

Antonius nodded. "And you're a great leader, favoured by Mithras himself." He stood up, the letter clutched in his hand. "We need to help our fallen brothers if we can. We need to make sure they walk in the Light."

"Yes. And once we capture this Carpathian lord, we can leave all this behind and live with our families in peace."

The two men stood facing each other, the laughter at the back of Gaius' mind like a swarm of bees.

"What are you orders, sir?" Antonius forced a smile, and Gaius clapped him on the shoulder.

"While Tiberius is drafting men of the legions before heading to Germania, we need to first gather our own. I met Vitorix the other day. We'll find him at the baths. Have you seen anyone yourself?"

"I've seen Octavius, Barna, and Sabinus at the Circus."

"Good. Find them and tell them we're to meet in three days at the Mithraeum near Albanum. I suspect there may be more of the men in the city because of the Festivals."

"Word is that Augustus has cancelled the festivals and games."

"I'm not surprised," Gaius said. "You should have seen him - torn clothes, wild eyes, talking to Varus still… I thank Mithras I walked out of there alive."

"What about Commander Maximus?"

"I don't know. It doesn't look good. It looks worse if we fail."

"Then we can't fail." Antonius went over to the map, draining his cup as he looked at the line of that northern frontier and imagined what lay beyond. "What are your plans until we meet?"

"I need to take stock of what we'll need and send an order to the arms depository at Brundisium."

"Why there?"

"There's a good armourer there who knows how to customize. Augustus has given us an imperial procurement pass and I plan on using it. Also, if we leave from there for the north, we can avoid the main legions."

"Octavius told me he's heard of a small scorpion that can be carried on a man's back. We should get a few."

"Agreed. I'll look into it. Also, I'm thinking black cuirasses instead of loricas. We don't want to be clinking through those woods, drawing attention to ourselves."

"Do you think it will be bad, Gaius?" Antonius' nerve was failing.

Gaius understood, as he tried to control his own.

"Yes. It'll be bad. If they've wiped out three legions… well…they're more numerous than the immortui were. They've got to be."

Just then a head poked around the door to the peristylium and Daxos appeared.

"Centurion Gaius?"

The boy looked terrified, and Gaius cursed himself for having neglected him the last day. How long had he been listening?

Antonius held out his hand, and Daxos entered the room.

"Daxos, I'm sorry," Gaius said. "I've been so busy lately. Can you not sleep?"

"How are you, Daxos?" Antonius asked.

"Are you leaving?" the boy asked Gaius.

"The Emperor has ordered us to march north to investigate what happened." Gaius hoped this would be enough of an explanation.

"Do not go to fight lykoi," he said, his eyes looking back into the garden. "You not survive this time."

"What do you know about lykoi, Daxos?" Gaius pressed.

"Men of my village come back from winter hunting with stories… They tell of man-wolves as strong as five Romans. Difficult to kill."

"Man-wolves?" Antonius repeated.

"Lykoi!" Daxos exclaimed. "They are not just big wolves," he whispered. "They are men turned to wolves."

"Did the men of the village tell stories of how they killed any?" Gaius looked intently at the boy now.

"Big weapons through the heart."

"I think we'll need more than a few scorpions," Gaius added.

"Please take me with you, Centurion!" Daxos begged, tugging at Gaius' tunic.

"I can't. You know that. It's safer for you here."

"Centurion Justus is right, Daxos," Antonius put in. "We don't know what we'll be walking into."

"Besides," Gaius knelt to look Daxos in the eyes. "I need you to protect Fulvia and the girls."

The boy nodded disconsolately, head hung. Without another word, he turned and went to the door. He stared at the garden a moment and then went out.

"I swore I'd not put him in danger again," Gaius said.

"He's scared," Antonius added, "but seems to have a knack for this sort of thing."

"His people were a tough lot, but not enough, it seems."

The two men were silent for a minute before the sound of the women's voices jolted them.

"There you are!" Fulvia said as she stepped into the doorframe. "Antonius, Vera says she's tired and ready to go home."

"Yes. It's late," Antonius said, standing up. "And we've imposed on your hospitality long enough."

"Nonsense," Gaius said. "We're glad you came. Both of you," he added as he saw Vera appear behind Fulvia, tired but smiling. "I'll have Pugio escort you home."

"Thank you, Gaius." Antonius went to Vera who took his arm.

"Thank you for such a lovely evening," Vera said as she stepped into the street.

The four said their goodbyes and Antonius and Vera followed Pugio down the slope of the Caelian.

"Will you come up to bed?" Fulvia ran her finger along Gaius' muscled arm. She was radiant in the moonlight that filtered into the garden.

"I have some things to finish first, my love," he said.

"All right. But I'm feeling very wanton after all the wine and watching you by lamplight."

Gaius smiled. "Then I'll have to hurry."

"Do that." Fulvia smiled, only slightly disappointed, and went upstairs.

Gaius turned to go back to his tablinum to finish making a list of needs for him and the men. He did not want to forget anything. There was not a lot of time to prepare.

After a while, Ludo came in to fill up the lamps.

"Is all well, Master?"

Gaius sighed and rubbed his eyes. "The Emperor has told me my furlough is over, Ludo. I'm to go north again in a few days."

"So soon?"

"I'm afraid so."

"I'll leave you to it then, Master." The slave turned to go but Gaius stopped him.

"Ludo?"

"Yes, Master?"

"Do watch over Daxos while I'm away. He's a good lad and…and he needs more than I can give him at the moment."

"We will take care of him, Master. All of us." Ludo bowed and made his exit.

After Ludo left, Gaius finished his lists and letters of procurement. His eyes were clouding on him and he wanted to sleep. The day had caught up with him.

But Daxos was on his mind. *Poor boy…I'm failing him.*

Gaius blew out the bronze lamps and made his way upstairs to Daxos' cubiculum. He shuddered as he eyed the garden, seeking Julius out.

"Daxos?" Gaius knocked on the door and entered. The boy had his covers pulled over his head, a muffled crying welling up from beneath. "Daxos, are you all right? What's wrong?" Gaius sat on the edge of the plain bed and pulled back the covers.

Daxos dried his eyes. "I'm afraid for you and Antonius, of not seeing you again, the way I not see my parents."

"Listen to me now," Gaius tried to sound calm. "I'll be fine. I have the toughest men. We'll have the best weapons. And Mithras watches over us. All will be well."

"Ohi!" the boy reverted to his Thracian Greek. "No it won't be well. You don't know what you go to fight."

"No. I don't. But that is our mission. To find out."

"Why? Legions are already dead. Why go?"

"Because my brothers' shades, thousands of them, roam lost. Because more will die if the Carpathian lord and Arminius are not stopped." Gaius dropped his voice. "I fight because if I do not, the Emperor will harm my family."

"What about me?" Daxos asked.

"You are a part of my family. Don't you know?"

Daxos looked down, unable to answer.

"I have been to Hades and back. You know this too. I'll come back, Daxos. I promise."

"Centurion Julius tell me I should go with you."

The words were like a sudden, unexpected sword thrust. Gaius did not know if he heard correctly.

"He told you this at Troesmis?"

"No," the boy said. "Last night."

Gaius closed his eyes. He tried not to imagine the shade of the friend he had killed, roaming his home, hovering above his sleeping family. "You saw him?"

"Yes. He scared me, but spoke nicely. He said I should go with you."

"Listen, Daxos. I know we think Julius is with us, that he has spoken to us. But he is gone and I cannot follow that order. You would not be safe were I to bring you. You're like a son to me, and I need you to stay safe."

Daxos shook his head, but remained silent. Instead, he leaned against Gaius like a son enjoying the comforting presence of a father. He soon fell asleep and Gaius laid him down, covered him with a blanket, and left the cubiculum.

When he entered his own room, he found Fulvia sleeping

soundly, her chest rising and falling. Her face was so serene that he dared not wake her. Instead, he removed his clothes and lay himself down beside her, giving way to exhausted oblivion.

GAIUS WAS STANDING ON THE JAGGED TOOTH OF A MOUNTAIN as the sun dripped red in the west. He looked about and recognized the Carpathian mountains that surrounded the valley where he had lost so many men. All had been chaos when he was last there, but now, not a sound could be heard.

The air no longer smelled of putrefaction and faeces. The scent of mountain pine and dew filled his nostrils. The air grew colder and colder as the sun disappeared, its light almost gone.

"What are you doing up here, Heliodromus?"

Gaius turned to see Mithras sitting upon a neighbouring peak. The god bit into a golden apple and smiled as he crunched away, his Phrygian cap bobbing as he chewed.

"Mithras?" Gaius tried to bow but almost lost his footing.

"Don't bow, Sun Runner. It's a long way down." He laughed.

"What am I doing here?" Gaius asked.

"You tell me." Mithras stood.

"I am at a loss, Lord."

Mithras looked far to the west and north and Gaius followed his godlike gaze along the line of the Danuvius, beyond the mountains and over dark woods that stretched for an eternity.

"You have a new mission," the god stated. Mithras tossed his apple core over the precipice where it landed on the ground far below and immediately took root and blossomed.

In the distance a chorus of howling rang out, accompanied by screams.

"Is that…" the words died on Gaius' lips.

"Yes, Sun Runner. Your brothers are dying out there."

Gaius braced himself against the rising fear and felt for that memory of warmth that Mithras had left with him all those months ago.

"That's it," Mithras encouraged him. "Do not forget the Light."

"How can I help them?" Gaius pleaded. "How can I defeat the Carpathian lord?"

Mithras' face darkened. "I cannot tell you how. Only that you must." Mithras sighed, his eyes focussed on that faraway wood. "You have to help them. You must go now to see."

"But how can we run there?"

"You will not run. You will fly!"

"But-" Gaius looked far below to the rocks and crevices that would tear his body limb from limb if he jumped. Then that dark laughter mocked his cowardice, his loyalty to the Light.

"Look at me!" Mithras faced him now, his voice intense, his eyes afire. "He seeks to strike you with fear, of his savagery, of his dark arts, and of himself. But you, Heliodromus, are protected. Your worst enemy is only yourself. Now fly, and see what has come to pass."

Gaius let his cloak fall and the cold wind carried it away like a wraith's shadow. He looked to Mithras one more time.

The god nodded and smiled.

Gaius knelt like a runner at a starting line.

Now! Mithras' voice rang clear in his head.

Gaius launched himself from that deadly peak and with a terrible lurch in his guts, he was arching across the night sky, over rivers, and mountains, and fields. His ears told him of laughter and cries, of life and death, the crack of ice, and crackle of fire as he was swept headlong over land to the edge of the great forest.

His feet sank deep in the moss of a forest bog when he landed at the edge of a clearing. Mithras had not followed him this time. Gaius peered through the foliage to see a fire with many men gathered about it. In the middle stood a man in Roman armour that Gaius recognized as the traitor, Arminius.

He reached for his sword, thinking if only he could just kill Arminius then and there, the massacre could be avoided.

He burst from the fern undergrowth and reached the German in three strides. His gladius went straight through Arminius' heart.

And so did Gaius.

He had passed through several men without being noticed. Arminius continued to rally the warriors about him.

"The Carpathian lord says it is time!" Arminius said. "The lykoi are waiting for us to launch the attach on Varus. The time to avenge ourselves on Rome is now!"

"I want no part of these dark arts, Arminius!" one man said, facing the big leader. "You've gone too far in dealing with this one. The gods will curse you for it."

Arminius laughed. "Then run back home, Segimarus, and continue to bend over for the Emperor. I will lead our people to freedom."

"No, you won't," the man answered. "You shall enslave and curse them forever more." Segimarus stamped off.

Arminius turned to the rest. "Are you ready for freedom?"

"Yes!" they all roared.

The clearing was suddenly empty and Gaius was alone.

Where did they go? Gaius searched with his eyes and ears,

and picked up a sound of clanging steel and battle cries, screams, and snarls.

He began to run through the wood.

Trees, vines and lichen-covered boulders passed in a blur as Gaius followed the sounds of battle. Soon, he came to what had been the rear-guard of the marching column. All that remained were mangled bodies caked with blood and a river of scattered weapons and armour.

Not a Roman soul was left alive.

Gaius kept running as the cries grew more intense, more chaotic. As he ran, it seemed to him that day turned to night, and day again, until he arrived at a spot where several centuries of Romans had formed up behind a shield wall. Rain poured from the heavens, clanging on their armour, and Gaius could hear the call of commands faintly behind the din.

From the edges of the forest surrounding the broad field where the Romans stood about their banners, there emerged thousands of barbarian men. Their dark silhouettes were accented with sickle, sword, and spear. They were in their bloodlust now, not to be turned from the massacre.

Yet they did not charge.

The Germans seemed to enjoy baiting the Romans like a wounded bear, too tired from days of fighting.

Gaius ran across the field to where the Roman officers were gathered about the standards.

Attack them while they're hesitating, you fools! Cut a way out!

But his ghostly warning went unheeded. Then the black and weeping clouds split apart in the night sky and the light of a full moon flooded the field.

A great howling rent the air and Gaius turned to look at

the tree line where half of the enemy stepped forward and threw their weapons down.

They're surrendering? Gaius wondered.

Then the enemy soldiers ripped the clothes from their bodies, and in that silver glow, they screamed and agonized for a moment, some vomiting, others clawing at the sodden earth.

Then, it happened. They changed.

Men who had, moments before, been men, now transformed into lykoi. Their bones cracked and their skin stretched over a bulging musculature as the darkness overcame them.

Wolves bigger than any hound Gaius had ever seen. *Mithras watch over us.*

The lykoi charged and the remaining barbarians held back to watch the imminent slaughter. Here and there, wolves fell with a pilum through the chest, but most came at the Romans full force. They crashed through shield walls like forest brush, and began to tear at the Romans.

The night was filled with a chorus of slaughter and blood-choked cries.

Gaius swung his gladius, helpless in his state. He cursed the lykoi as they pulled intestines from men's bellies and fought over their kills.

Then a big burly German began to run at Gaius from the trees, ripping away his clothes as he came. Gaius took up a defensive stance to meet the attack. A scream spilled from his mouth as massive jaws and razor teeth lunged for him before sending him to darkness.

. . .

"AHH!" Gaius shot up from the sweaty sheets, his pugio clutched tightly in his hand.

The room was a spinning blur until his eyes focussed on Fulvia's face and his ears finally heard the words her lips had been mouthing.

"Gaius…Gaius? I'm here…with you…Gaius?"

The clang of the pugio upon the marble floor snapped him out of his hysteric state and he felt his wife's hands on his cheeks, her hair against his neck.

"Fulvia?" he managed.

"Yes. I'm here," she soothed. "I'm here…"

He realized his face was wet with tears. "I saw them… Varus' men. They were slaughtered by…torn to shreds."

"It was a dream, Gaius. Nothing more. Please," she stroked his arm. "Come back to me."

Gaius fell back onto the bed, his forearms crossed over his eyes. *How can it be?*

Fulvia held his face again, his eyes in hers. "You're here with me, by the Gods, Gaius. Nothing shall take you from me." She knelt over him, kissing his damp brow, his pulsing temples.

"I love you," he said, pulling her close. "I love you…"

Gaius let Fulvia, her touch, her scent and taste, her voice, overwhelm the darkness that clawed at him then, and for a short while, he felt whole again. He pulled her in desperately, and she clung to him, held him inside her as though she would never let go, as though together they were a whole shield against the darkness that bayed outside the reach of their fiery light.

Then they slept, entwined, seemingly safe, protected.

·   ·   ·

"Mithras! Mithras! Mithras!" the Heliodromus' voice reverberated within the sacred wall of the Mithraeum, answered by the Miles who all bowed in the darkness, their eyes focussed on the dimly-lit image of the Tauroctony at the front.

"Mithras! Mithras! Mithras!" they repeated.

"Hear us, Lord of Light," the Heliodromus said. "Accept our offering and watch over us as we go into the dark to free our brothers."

"May they walk in the Light!" the Miles chanted.

When they had finished saying the words of invocation and pleading, the Heliodromus took an unbloodied pugio concealed within his white sleeve.

Two men brought a white ram forward and held it upon the altar.

The Heliodromus stepped up and with a motion as deft as any surgeon, he sliced the beast's neck from one side to the other, holding it for a few moments until it lay itself down to sleep upon the stone slab of the altar. Then he turned to face the Miles.

"Where are we going?" he asked.

"Into darkness," they answered.

"What are you?"

"The Light! The Light! The Light!"

"Who are you?"

"Mithras! Mithras! Mithras!"

"Mithras," he whispered to himself, to the god he could see smiling at the mouth of the cave for the briefest of moments.

. . .

Gaius walked up the aisle as Antonius lit more torches. He wiped the blood from his hands and waited a moment for the rush of power to flow out of his mind before speaking to the eleven men there present.

"I'm glad you could make it," Gaius began. "Optio Antonius has informed you all of our new positions and…assignment?"

The men nodded and looked back at Gaius. He knew they were all good fighters, but this would test each man's metal.

Antonius, Octavius, Vitorix, and Barna were there, along with Demetrios, the medicus, Tertius, Sabinus, Caelius, Saguntus, Leonidas, and Calgacus. They were all present, as if by Mithras' will, in Rome when the time had come. Antonius and Vitorix had found them all.

As the torchlight filled the sacred speleum, Gaius took the commissions from the satchel he had brought, and handed each man his scroll.

The sound of unfurling papyrus echoed about them. Those who could read did so. Those who could not, left it for later. They had already been told what was expected. The commissions were a formality.

Gaius looked at the gathered men and saw the changes their battle with the immortui had wrought.

Vitorix, he knew, could not sleep - the black circles beneath his eyes betrayed it.

Barna's eyes were red from weeping, and Tertius' face was an agglomeration of cuts and bruises from his incessant brawling.

As soon as the ceremony was over, Sabinus had set to his obsessive sharpening of his gladius which was wearing thin as a result.

Caelius cycled through a series of charms about his neck again, and again, and again.

Saguntus was always whispering prayers, and Leonidas had become quiet and sullen.

Calgacus spoke of nothing else than getting into battle.

Gaius hoped the latter's death wish would not be the end of them.

Each man's physical wounds had healed long ago, but it was the inner fear and paranoia that Gaius worried about.

Only Mithras can bring us through this.

"Tell us when we fight, sir!" Calgacus blurted out, breaking the silence.

"Are you so eager to die?" Caelius said. "Three whole legions have been wiped out."

"That's more than our measly century used to be," added Saguntus before going back to his prayers.

"Thank you for the arithmetic lesson," Octavius said, holding back the vomit that rose in his throat.

"Enough. All of you," Gaius' voice doused the fire that threatened to spread among them. *This isn't going to be easy,* he thought. "I know you're all scared. I am too." Gaius stood where he could face them. "I won't lie to you, my brothers. This will be more dangerous than before. We are now a special unit reporting directly to Augustus with the sole purpose of finding out what happened to Varus' legions, hunting down and bringing in the traitor, Arminius, and this Carpathian lord who seems to wield all the power."

"What else?" Sabinus asked as the edge of his sharpening stone slid off the end of his blade. "There's more, isn't there?"

All of the men looked at Gaius.

"Very well," Gaius saw Antonius shake his head slightly, but he continued. "We won't be fighting immortui this time."

There was an audible sigh of relief. "My…ah…sources…tell me that massive packs of wild wolves are partly responsible for the loss of our legions."

"Wolves?" Vitorix looked shocked. "Romans killed by wolves? Impossible! I used to hunt wolves by myself!"

"These aren't normal wolves, Vitorix. They're…lykoi."

"That's a legend made up by the German barbarians to scare children," Barna said.

But Vitorix was quiet. The big man stood and leaned his head against the cave wall.

"Lykoi are no stories," he said. "The elders of my clan spoke of their enemies across the rivers, of men who, when the moon was right, transformed into powerful wolves. Nothing could stand against them."

"Everything has a weakness," Calgacus said. "Let's find out what theirs is and use it."

"And what if there are tens of thousands of lykoi?" Antonius was speaking now. "We can't win in a head-on fight."

"No. We can't," Gaius continued. "We must find out what happened and then get at the source of this dark magic: the Carpathian lord."

"We know nothing about him, sir," Demetrios finally spoke. "In my village in Macedonia, people always spoke of dark powers hidden in the Carpathian mountains."

Leonidas slapped his knee in agreement.

"That's fine," said Caelius," But the Carpathians are a long way from the German forests where Varus and his men were slaughtered."

"This isn't going to be a short assignment." Gaius felt his patience thinning. "This is going to be our last mission, and it will take time. The Emperor has given us the means, but we need to stick together in this if we want to come through it alive. If we do, I promise you, we'll all live like the richest of senators. Augustus has promised us each a fortune if we succeed."

"And if we don't?" asked Saguntus.

"Then we need to disappear beyond the Empire's borders, along with our families."

"Some choice," Saguntus added.

"A Roman choice!" Vitorix spat.

All the men were silent for a few moments, even the Romans among them.

He's right, Gaius thought. *It isn't a choice at all. I may be leading all of us to our deaths.* Gaius thought he could hear the laughter again, beyond the cave's mouth. *The Emperor has left us no choice in this.* Gaius felt the true weight of his command then.

"When do we leave?" The question was finally asked by Vitorix who, minutes before, had registered terror at the mention of the lykoi. He looked around the group. "What? We need to know, right?" And the longer we wait, the longer our brothers remain in darkness. Thousands of them lie dead in that German forest and I'll be damned to Hades if I let a few fucking wolves get in the way of our revenge." The big Gaul crossed his arms and waited for an answer.

"Well said, Vitorix." Gaius laid hand on the man's shoulder. "We leave in seven days."

"Why wait?" Calgacus asked.

"Because the armourers in Brundisium won't be finished before then."

"Brundisium?"

"Yes, Caelius," Gaius answered. "I've ordered some special equipment for all of us, and the armourer there is the best. We'll be taking ship from there to Aquileia. Then we'll march north to Germania."

"Tiberius and his new legions are setting out tomorrow," Antonius added. "Apparently he had to press a couple thousand into service."

"Civilian cowards!" Sabinus said.

"Our orders were to avoid contact with the army as much as possible." Gaius informed them. "We're to be discreet. To the rest of the world, we don't exist."

"There it is, then." Saguntus stood and pushed back his black hair.

"We'll meet here at the sixth hour of daylight in seven days time. Understood?"

"Yes, sir!" the men all stood and began to file out of the cave.

Gaius remained a minute in the cave to extinguish the torches. His eye lingered on the image of Mithras. He regretted not telling them everything, about Julius and the shades that he had said roamed the dark of that northern forest. But how could he lead them if they thought he was mad? He knew not all of them would take it as well as Antonius had.

When the final torch was doused, Gaius made for the cave mouth and the late afternoon light. The brightness washed over him and it took his eyes a moment to adjust. He looked down the rocky green slope of the mountain where it fell steeply away to the lake. The deep blue water looked inviting, sparkling as it did like a sun-kissed sapphire set in the land.

Breathe Gaius. Breathe, he told himself. He thought of the seven days he had left. It was time enough to prepare, but no amount of time would be enough for him to spend with Fulvia, Aemilia, and Faustina.

"Ready?" Antonius spoke from around the large boulder where their two horses had been tethered.

"Yes."

They mounted up and set off down the zigzagging path to the road below.

"Do you know your letters well, Antonius?" Gaius asked as they went.

"Ha. Yes!" the younger man laughed. "My mother wanted me to be a lawyer."

"Good. I want you to go to the library to find out all you can about German and Gaulish traditions relating to wolves. Anything that might be related to lykoi: how to hunt them, track them, kill them. Their own behaviours, if such a thing has been written in the histories."

"I'll do my best."

"Meanwhile, I'll speak with Daxos and see if he remembers anything that his father might have told him."

"Think he'll be able to help?"

"He's been more than helpful before," Gaius said. "I think I've underestimated him. Besides, he was terrified when he found out about our mission."

IT WAS DARK BY THE TIME GAIUS REACHED HOME. IT FELT much faster when he ran the distance to Albanum.

After cleaning up, he joined Fulvia, the girls, and Daxos in the triclinium. His wife eyed him when he came in.

"I was getting worried."

"All's well," he answered, smiling at the children.

"Did you have a nice ride in the country today, Papa?" Aemilia asked.

She seemed to have matured in the last few days. Gaius smiled at his eldest girl.

"Yes, love. But it was not for pleasure that I went."

"Why did you leave us then?" Faustina came into the conversation, her words straight to the point, as ever.

"I didn't want to." He swallowed a cup of wine, as subtly as possible, and decided to tell them. "I suppose you're all big enough to know." He eyed Daxos who kept his head down, eyes hidden behind his fringe of black hair. "I must leave again in seven days."

Fulvia swirled her cup of wine with one hand, her other squeezing Gaius'.

"Today I went to the Mithraeum at Albanum with eleven brave men who will be going with me. We must always pay our respects to the gods who watch over us, children. Today, that is what I was doing."

"But where are you going? Is it far?" Faustina persisted.

"It is. Very far. I'm going to a forest far to the north."

"Why?" the little one asked, her eyes boring into her father.

"Because some Romans were hurt there, and I've been asked by the Emperor to go and see what happened."

"Papa, will your soldier god be able to see you so far away?"

Gaius smiled. "Yes, Aemilia. Mithras sees me, is with me, and helps me wherever I am in this world. He has protected me everywhere I have gone."

"That's good," Faustina said.

"Listen to me, all of you," Gaius looked at each of them. "While I'm away, you need not worry. I'll be fine. But I'm going to be gone for a long time and I'll need you to take care of each other. You must be brave, help your mother, and pray to the gods that our family will always be safe and strong. Do you understand?"

"Yes, Papa," the girls said in unison.

How I'll miss their sweet voices... "Good. Now, it's late and you should be in bed." The girls went to their father, and each in turn wrapped her little arms about him. "I'm happy you were awake to see me," he whispered to them.

"I'll go up with them and come back," Fulvia said.

Gaius smiled and turned to Daxos who was just getting up to go.

"You stay, Daxos. You're older, and I need your help."

The young Thracian sat back down and Gaius poured him some watered wine.

"I'm sorry I didn't take you with me today. I wanted to see what the rest of the men were like."

"And?" the boy asked, his eyes meeting Gaius'.

"Not good."

"They will be worse," the boy said evenly.

Gaius held the boy's gaze before Daxos looked away, sipping at his wine. Gaius rolled up the sleeve of his tunic, and observed the criss-crossing of scars up his forearms. He'd been through much. *I must get through this alive.*

But he needed more information to be able to do that.

"Daxos. I need you to think very hard for me." The boy did not look up. "I know you said you couldn't remember much about lykoi, but your father must have spoken to you at some point. You were his eldest, only son, and as a Thracian he would have been training you."

"Stamata! Stop!" Daxos began shaking his head, eyes screwed tight. "No speak of my father. Why you ask these things?" His young, weary eyes pleaded.

"Because, Daxos. I don't want to die."

Many soldiers laugh in death's hoary face. They are constant bedfellows on campaign, in the lives they lead. Gaius had always believed himself unafraid of death, of the world beyond. And he was. Just then, with Daxos looking at him, missing his own father, Gaius realized that he feared not death, but what death meant. If he died, he might not ever see his wife and children again. He might not hold them, hear them, speak with them.

If I die…what happens to my family?

Lost as he was in that haunting thought, it was a minute before Gaius realized Daxos was staring at him, holding up a pendant he had never seen before.

"What is that?" Gaius stared at the silver image of a circle of hunters about a great wolf. It was large, and Gaius wondered how Daxos had managed to keep it hidden for so long.

"It was my father's," the boy said. "I took it from his bones before we burned him and my mother."

Gaius said nothing. He remembered the boy Daxos had been, how much he had, piece by gruesome piece, laid the bones of his parents upon the pyre back in his village.

"My father used to wear this all the time, especially when hunting."

"Hunting wolves?"

"Lykoi." The boy looked guilty a moment then stood to face Gaius. "I remember."

"Tell me. Please."

"The men of my village were great hunters. They hunt the lykoi at the end of each moon, when they come out the most. Before immortui, lykoi were our greatest danger. Until my father and the men killed the leader of the lykoi." He held up the pendant for Gaius to hold.

It was heavy. Heavier than it should have been.

"My father say that this protect him and that some day, it be mine."

"How did your father kill the lykoi?" Gaius needed practical information. His eyes were drawn to the image of the circle of men about the lykos.

"Swords and arrows not enough. Lykoi would kill you before you take their heads. Immortui easy."

"Then how?" Gaius rubbed his head, frustrated by his ignorance.

"I don't know. Sorry, Centurion."

"You must remember something."

The boy shrugged. "All I remember is my father, after being made head hunter, began to trade with other friendly villages for all their silver."

"Silver? For what? To buy weapons?"

"No. To make them."

"Silver is too soft for a blade."

"Not swords. Arrows, Centurion Gaius. Arrows."

Now Gaius' mind was working hard. He had drunk too much and now regretted it.

"Did the silver arrows work?"

"I don't know. I never see. But I do know that the lykoi stopped attacking our villages."

"Thank you, Daxos. You have helped me." Gaius' voice was absent and he barely noticed Daxos take back the amulet and go out of the triclinium.

When he came out of his thoughts, Gaius raced to his tablinum and wrote a hurried note. Then he went to the atrium.

"Ludo!" he called for his steward.

"Yes, Master? Is something the matter?"

"I need this letter sent by express messenger to Brundisium. Tonight."

"Yes, Master. Right away." Ludo took the note, donned his cloak and went out immediately.

FOR A SHORT WHILE, GAIUS STOOD IN THE PERISTYLIUM garden of his home. His thoughts were slow and dark now, like the sea at night. Part of him hoped Julius' shade would come back so that he could confirm some of the things Daxos had said.

Does a shade gain knowledge after death? he wondered.

The rustle of silk and scent of perfume preceded his wife's arm over his and her head upon his shoulder.

"I worry to ask you your thoughts," she said sadly. "How long have you been standing here, my love?"

Gaius turned to look at her, pale in the silver moonlight that filtered down to wrap them both. Even in his state of mind, Fulvia managed to stir him, remind him of his true life.

"I have trouble with time now," he answered. "It all seems to pass unnaturally quick."

"It does that," she sighed.

"All I'm aware of now are the next seven days left to us."

"You speak as if you will not be returning."

He did not answer.

"You've never lied to me, Gaius."

"No."

"Then don't start." She stepped back, the fear full in her eyes. "I couldn't bear it. Not from you."

"I won't. But I can't tell you everything."

"About what? Who? Mithras, immortui, or lykoi? The walls of our home are not as thick as all that." She stepped into the middle of the garden, onto the new circular mosaic, and turned once. "I won't press for details. Just make sure you come back to us."

"It is my only thought."

"No!" she snapped. "You must also think of killing whatever, or whomever, you are being sent to kill."

"You're a centurion now?"

Fulvia turned away quickly and put a hand to her eyes to wipe the tears that burst forward. "Don't mock me, Gaius."

"I'm not." He moved to hold her and she let him do so. "I'm sorry. I didn't mean-"

"I know. The Gods are stealing time from us and it terrifies me."

"Me too, my love. Me too."

"Don't try to be a hero," Fulvia added, her eyes intense with emotion. You are mine - not the Emperor's, your men's, or even your god's! You are mine, and always will be." She held him fast. "Just come back to me, victorious or not. If *not*, then we'll be ready to fly to the ends of the Earth with you."

Gaius held her tightly, buried his face in her hair, and breathed her in.

Mithras, watch over me so that I can come back to my family after this ordeal.

THE NEXT SEVEN DAYS DID INDEED RUN LIKE A SPRING RIVER rushing to the sea. Time stops for no man, even those loved by the gods.

Gaius intentionally avoided any other interactions with his men until the day of their assigned meeting time. Instead, he spent every waking moment with his family and Daxos. For a time, the laughter at the back of his mind was blocked out, the nightmares pushed into the shadows.

They ate every meal together, went to the theatre of Pompey, the markets and the seaside. Gaius watched Aemilia and Faustina splash about in the turquoise water, their bubbling laughter drawing him in to splash with them. He could not remember the last time he had felt so joyous.

Fulvia laughed as she watched, preferring to take in the scene from the pebbled shore.

Daxos, who had an aversion to the sea, remained beside Fulvia, and Gaius was pleased to see them deep in conversation, that Fulvia had warmed to the young Thracian.

BEFORE DAYLIGHT ON THE MORNING OF HIS DREADED departure, Gaius knelt in the darkness of the family shrine. He wore his travelling clothes, a brown tunic, bracae, riding boots, and a thick black cloak. His gladius, Julius' own blade, and pugio lay upon the altar.

Gaius bowed his head and held his hands out, palms up, in supplication to Jupiter, Juno, Minerva, Venus, Mars, and Mithras. The gods' rough images danced in the light of a single lamp as if leaning in to hear his whispers.

After Gaius had lit a chunk of incense and placed it in a bronze bowl, he spoke.

"Gods of my ancestors, protectors of my family… I've dreaded this day more than any other campaign. I don't know what I am walking into…only that Death lurks there, in the shadows of that northern forest. Gods, do not desert me, I beg you. Give me strength and cunning, and speed that I may carry out this mission and survive to return to my family. Please watch over them - Fulvia, Aemilia, Faustina, and Daxos. If I fail, I ask you to bring them to safety far away from danger. Please light my way on this path. Please help me to lead and…"

Here Gaius took his pugio and held it above his gladius on the altar. He sliced his hand and let the rivulets run on to the gleaming blade.

"Help me to kill my enemies so that they can do us no harm." The image of Daxos' pendant came to his mind then, and he thought a faint howling echoed in the air. Then he felt cold wrap itself about him.

Gaius had not noticed Julius kneeling beside him, the shade of his bald head bent in prayer, turning toward Gaius.

"Time to go, Centurion," it said.

Gaius felt his hands begin to shake, but quelled his fear.

"Time to go," Gaius repeated, his eyes closed. "Gods of my ancestors, protect us as we go into the darkness."

Gaius rose, sheathed his weapons and gazed at the gods a moment longer. The shade had gone.

In the atrium, Fulvia, Aemilia and Faustina stood beside Gaius' satchels with the servants lined up along the wall. Gaius addressed the latter first.

"Stay alert at all times, and watch over my family. If I don't succeed, you will all need to be ready to flee. Understood?"

"We understand, Master," Ludo answered for all of them. "We honour the familia and will serve faithfully."

Gaius nodded to them and turned to his daughters.

Faustina, the younger, walked up to him with her arms raised so that he could pick her up.

"I love you," he said.

"I love you, Papa." Her little hands reached out and held

his face. "Don't die. You still have to show me how to ride a horse."

"I will show you. I promise," he answered.

She smiled and kissed his cheek.

Then Gaius knelt in front of Aemilia. *She's grown so tall.* His eldest, ever the more sensitive, struggled to hold her tears. Gaius held her head gently, and smiled as he looked into her beautiful eyes. "I'll be back. I love you, my girl."

"And I love you, Papa." Aemilia wrapped her lanky arms about his neck, tight as a vice. "I'll pray and make offerings for you every day." After a few more moments, she released her grip and stepped back to hold her sister's hand.

Fulvia followed Gaius to the door where Pugio was strapping the satchels to one of the two black stallions he had procured for himself at the Emperor's expense.

"Where is Daxos?" Gaius asked.

"Hiding, I think," Fulvia answered quickly. "He's upset you're leaving him behind. He's scared."

Gaius was silent a moment.

"Tell him I'll be back. Take care of him."

"I will." Fulvia held both of her husband's hands, kissed them, and took a long last look at him.

"Time to go," he said.

"Yes." She felt the slick blood from his cut on her hand and looked at it. Then, she smeared a crimson streak across his forehead, and another across her own. "I am yours."

"And you are mine," he finished and held her close. He kissed her lips for a few last lingering heartbeats, despite the presence of the servants. "I'll be back, my love," Gaius reassured her. He reached inside for that Mithraic light and felt stronger then.

Fulvia smiled bravely and placed her hand upon his chest. "We'll be waiting," she answered before a last kiss.

Gaius turned away and mounted his horse, his legs snug between the saddle horns. He nodded to Pugio, who backed away. Then, he spurred the two mounts into the shadows of Rome's early morning streets toward the Via Appia.

Gaius would rather have run all the way to Albanum, where he was meeting the men, and then on to Brundisium. There was a tightness in his chest that only got worse and worse with each mile he rode away from Rome and his family.

Running like the wind would have helped to clear his head of some of the pain and sadness he now struggled so desperately to push back.

When he arrived at the Mithraeum, Gaius found all of the men assembled and waiting in the sunlight that was beating down on the hillside. Many of them had remained in Albanum for the week rather than travel to Rome and back.

"Besides," Vitorix said. "All you need is a taberna, and here there are three." The big Gaul laughed and clapped Saguntus on the shoulder as he prayed.

"Let's make the sacrifice, Miles, and get on our way to Brundisium. We've got an appointment with the armourer." Gaius looked at Antonius who had also left his wife behind, and went into the cave without smiling.

The men looked around and followed him in.

The sacrifice had been quick, the prayers short. Soon, the twelve men were riding toward the coast.

Three days later, the port city's outskirts came into view with the blue sea beyond. The salt-tinged air of the Mare Adriaticum reached their noses. It was fresh, the breeze working its way up the Via Appia from the inner harbour.

Brundisium was large and busy. Smoke from the tabernae, smithies, brothels, and hearths of its hundred-thousand residents mingled and swirled in the air.

As they entered the city, Gaius looked for signs of the siege Antony had laid against Augustus in this very place over forty years before. Gaius' grandfather had been in Antony's forces then, during his descent to eventual defeat. Augustus had removed all signs of the engagement. Now, statues of the Emperor graced the squares and forum.

Gaius hoped his grandfather's shade would not be angered by his allegiances. *A different age,* he thought.

When the party reached the two soaring columns marking the end of the Via Appia, they dismounted and began their circuit of the city to reach the warehouse at the far end of the inner harbour where the smith dubbed 'Vulcan's Bastard' had his workshop.

"Are you sure about this smith, sir?" Antonius asked. "*Vulcan's Bastard* doesn't sound like a reputable armourer."

"He's supposed to be one of the best, Optio," Gaius answered. "He has a private palaestra where we can test the gear." Gaius strode down the street, leading his two horses by their bridles.

"Oh, if only we could stop," Barna said to Caelius as they passed a brothel with the women and a few boys hanging out the windows, beckoning them inside.

"We're on duty, soldier!" Antonius barked back.

The train of warriors marched past the cooing women, their laughter dying as they entered the stench of the dock warehouses. At the end of a row of anchored merchant ships stood a long low building with a black roof. Before it, moored to the quay, was a black-hulled trireme.

"That's it," Gaius said, pointing out the building to Antonius and the others. And that's our ship."

Gaius tethered the horses to a nearby post and the others followed suit. Before Gaius reached the smithy door, a dark bulky shadow appeared.

"Centurion Justus?" the shadow asked.

"Yes," Gaius answered, flanked by Vitorix and Calgacus.

"Let me see it before you take one step closer."

"Are you Vulcan's Bastard?" Gaius asked, annoyed at the sniggers behind him.

"Yes. I am." The giant shadow stepped out of the darkness into the daylight. "Show me the Emperor's seal, before you get anywhere near my work."

Gaius raised the sealed scroll form his saddlebag.

"The Emperor wants no delays, smith," Gaius said. "All better be complete."

The man's soot-blotched eyes looked down on Gaius. "Aye, the order's complete. My boys and I been working day and night for a week. Then with that last-minute order you placed, you had us spinning."

"An essential addition to the order," Gaius answered. "May we come in to see what the Emperor's gold and silver have got us?"

Without another word, Vulcan's Bastard turned back into the dark of his workshop.

Gaius and the others followed. They were led through the workshops first, where the heat was thick and the tang of molten metals hung in the air.

Then the smith opened a set of solid double doors to

reveal a covered palaestra with a hard-packed dirt floor. Two assistants ran along the walls with firebrands to light the torches that rimmed the large hall.

When his eyes finally adjusted, Gaius smiled. The others gasped.

All along the left wall were stacks of gladii, hooked boar spears, javelins, compact bows, pugionis, and batches of arrows whose tips gleamed in the dark. There were even three portable scorpions that could be transported on a man or horse's back.

Gaius walked past the silent men to twelve sets of armour, all made of hardened bull's hide. Each set was displayed on a wooden dummy, a metal helmet with each. Every set of armour also had a scutum, with matching tunics, bracae, and cloaks.

"It's all black?" Sabinus wondered.

Gaius turned to the row of men as Vulcan's Bastard looked on, waiting for awe to set in.

"That's right," Gaius answered. "Everything is black. We're going to be wraiths to our enemies. We'll be what they fear. We'll be unseen. No plate armour or decorations to clang about. Our only ornament is this…"

Gaius went to one of the breastplates and ran his hand over the sign of an eagle with a sun rising over its outspread wings.

"Rome's eagle and Mithras' sun are our banners. Here…" Gaius touched the breastplate, "and there," then pointed at one of the scuta which had the same image.

The smith then came to Gaius and handed him two leather satchels. The centurion opened one and pulled out a brilliant barbed arrowhead wrought out of silver, admiring the keen edge in the torchlight.

"They're as I described?" Gaius asked the smith.

"Yes. Iron coated in pure silver. Same as the pugionis blades."

Antonius went and drew a pugio from its sheath to reveal a gleaming blade.

"I could buy my wife a farm with what's in that one bag," Saguntus whispered to Calgacus, nodding at the bag of arrowheads.

"Those are not for buying farms or trading," Gaius turned. "They're for killing."

"Well, don't just stand there all stupid," Vulcan's Bastard blurted. "Try your kit on and test the weapons. That's what we're here for, isn't it?"

"Each of you grab a set and test the fit," Gaius ordered. "Our smith will make any adjustments."

Each man moved to a set of clothing and armour and began to try things on. Gaius had approximated sizes for the smith but still, some adjustments were needed.

"What'll I do without my lucky red cloak now?" Caelius complained.

"You can wipe your ass with it!" Vitorix said.

"Unless you want to be the first spotted by the enemy," Gaius said, "you'll make the black cloak your new lucky one." Gaius placed his helmet on his head, the only one with a black crest, and waved his arms, kicked his legs, testing the sound and mobility. "Good…good," he muttered. The boots were comfortable and solid, the armour and pteruges the same. "You've lived up to your reputation, smith," Gaius said to Vulcan's Bastard.

The man grunted.

"What about the blades though?" asked Leonidas. "Will they crumple or dent?"

"There's targets at the other end of the palaestra to test your javelins, bows, and the scorpions. And over here are some training dummies. You tell me, little miss, if my blades dent or not."

Leonidas flushed, but Gaius stepped in.

"Let's get to it! Test them out!"

The men immediately tested the pila and bows, easily hoisting them and hitting their marks, the silver tips remaining intact. The clang of gladii filled the air and each man checked for nicks or dents, but Vulcan's Bastard knew his work. The scuta were light and strong, and the armour could take a heavy blow from one of the battle axes.

The men laughed like children with gifts at Saturnalia, and praised the reluctant smith.

"Barna!" Gaius called. "Test the scorpions!"

"Yes, sir!" Barna, in a minute, had one of the mobile artillery weapons set up and loaded with a silver-tipped bolt.

"Iacite!" Gaius shouted.

Barna fired the bolt and it sped the entire length of the palaestra to crash through the wooden target and embed itself in the plaster of the far wall. "Woooo!" Barna yipped.

Gaius nodded and smiled at the smith.

"Seems like a shame to waste a fortune in silver, Centurion. What are you men hunting for the Emperor?"

"You were told to ask no questions, right?" Gaius stared at the smith. "Now. You've made a fortune with this one job, and I suspect we'll need re-equipping before the end. Which means another fortune. But, if you go telling people about this, shooting your mouth off in the tabernae, you'll have a century of Praetorians down here to shake things up. Do you want that?"

The big smith struggled to hold his rage and managed, barely.

"Fine. Just give me more notice of your needs. Me and my sons worked all hours this last week."

"I will." Gaius clapped him on the shoulder. "For now, just keep making us a back supply of the same items. I'll send you a delivery location in Aquileia when I have it."

"Get in there!" The sudden shout from the workshop door stopped every man there. One of the smith's sons was pulling a dirty boy across the floor and threw him at the feet of Vulcan's Bastard and Gaius. "I caught him snooping around their horses, taking food."

The boy looked up and through the grime and bloody nose, Gaius spotted him.

"Daxos?"

"Mithras has sent him to us," Saguntus blurted out, his eyes suddenly closed in prayer.

"Shut up!" Gaius bellowed before turning and pointing his gladius at the smith's son. "You touch him again, you'll pay for it," he said through gritted teeth.

Antonius had helped Daxos up and was looking him over. "His nose is broken."

"Come with me." Gaius took Daxos roughly by the arm and led him back through the workshop and outside where he sat him down on a bench beside the horse trough.

They were both silent as Gaius paced in the sunlight beyond the shadows of the awning.

"What, in the name of all the gods, are you doing here, Daxos? I left you in Rome to watch over my family!"

"I need to watch over you, Centurion," the boy said in his

thick Thracian accent; it always became more apparent when he was in distress.

"I don't need you to watch over me. I've got eleven of the strongest men from the legions with me."

Daxos was unperturbed. "Centurion Julius told me to follow you."

"Julius is dead, Daxos."

"He no let me sleep until I sneak out of Rome to meet you." Daxos held the amulet about his neck as he spoke.

"And what of my wife? She'll be worried about you."

"Lady Fulvia knows I am here, Centurion."

That stopped Gaius. "What?"

"She knows. She catch me trying to leave and asked me where I was going. She asked me why."

"And what did you tell her?"

"Truth."

"What?"

"I tell her I have secret weapon to give you that will help you against the enemy."

"Daxos. An amulet is not a weapon. It's a charm. It can't kill."

"It helps. And me too."

"Gods, I don't believe this!" Gaius kicked the trough. He looked at Daxos and the blood pouring out of his broken nose. Then he removed the cloth that was about his neck and dipped it in the water. "Hold still," he said as he wiped the caked and fresh blood away. "I can't believe she let you go," he muttered, more to himself.

"Do not be angry with Lady Fulvia. I tell her I would come to you no matter what."

"Did you tell her what the enemy was?"

"No. But I think she knows it's not just Germans. She is

smart lady." Daxos smiled and winced when he felt it in his nose.

"She is a smart lady," Gaius agreed, taking a quick hold of Daxos' nose and squeezing.

"Ow!" the boy cried.

"You're lucky that's all those little bastards did to you."

Daxos looked rough and dirty still, but at least the blood was gone, the leaking stanched.

"Come. Let's go back inside. I haven't decided what to do with you yet, but either way, you'll need a tunic, boots and a pugio." Gaius went back into the workshop with Daxos following. "Smith! I have another order!"

That night, as the men lay in wine-soaked slumber on the floor of the palaestra, Gaius and Antonius spoke about Daxos who lay still and asleep beside them.

All of the weapons and armour had been packed up, ready to be loaded onto the black ship moored outside. The captain, a Greek named Pylos, had told them they could load everything that night so they could get an early start, but Gaius did not want to let the expensive equipment out of his sight.

"I'm thinking of sending him with you back to Rome," Gaius said to Antonius where they spoke beneath a spluttering torch. "You're the only one I trust with him. Plus, you can see your wife again."

"Much as I would like to see Vera again, I don't think she could handle another goodbye. Besides," Antonius looked at Daxos, "I think we should bring him. There's got to be something to all that stuff about his father being the head wolf-hunter."

"Even if he's just a boy, Antonius? Would you have me sacrifice him? The lykoi would tear him apart."

"We'll all protect him, and…he'll give strength to the men. Where's your faith, Heliodromus?"

"My faith is intact. It's my fear of Daxos getting killed that's bothering me."

"You said before you always underestimate him. And yet," Antonius smiled," he managed to follow us all the way here safely, on his own. The Via Appia is not the safest road in Italy."

"There aren't lykoi on the Via Appia." Gaius looked at Daxos sleeping and wondered what the boy's father would have said or done. As his lids grew heavy and closed, Gaius wondered what the chief of a Thracian mountain tribe would want for his son: to stay in Rome with the women, safe and sound? Or to go into Germania to hunt lykoi?

THE MEN WOKE TO THE SOUND OF HAMMERING. THE workshop door was ajar and Gaius, who stood up, could hear Vulcan's Bastard yelling at his sons.

All the men awoke, except Daxos who slept soundly, his face swollen and bruised.

"Daxos?" Gaius laid his hand on the boy's shoulder.

Daxos winced when he stirred, and looked up. "Please don't send me back to Rome with Antonius," he said.

"I'm not. You're coming with us. Here," Gaius handed him a pair of black bracae and a black tunic and cloak. "There are a few pairs of boots over by the wall. Find some that fit."

"I come with you, Centurion?"

"Yes." Gaius stood. "It's what your father would have wanted." Then he took a silver-bladed pugio from a nearby bench, flipped it, and caught it by the handle. "You'll also need this." Gaius handed Daxos the blade, gave him a sad smile, and went off to see to preparations for the sea voyage north to Aquileia.

By mid-morning, Captain Pylos' black-hulled ship was cutting through the waves with dolphins speeding alongside and leaping across the bow.

"My grandmother used to tell me that dolphins guide the dead safely to Hades," Leonidas said to Gaius and Caelius where they all stood with Daxos on the prow.

"Shut up, Leo!" Caelius barked, fingering his length of talismans. "Sorry, Centurion," he added.

"They're just dolphins, Caelius. They follow every ship in the Adriaticum." Gaius wished he fully believed that, but the terrified look on Leonidas' face sent dread up his spine. Laughter seemed to come at them from out of the north.

Guides of the dead to the Underworld? We just might make it there...

Gaius put his hands on Daxos' shoulders and tried to enjoy watching those sleek creatures fly, flip and roll ahead of the ship.

AFTER SOME QUIET DAYS AT SEA, THE SHIP, LOADED WITH ALL twelve men, their new arms, armour, and horses, came to Aquileia. The town lay nestled like a jewel at the head of the Adriaticum, a cluster of terracotta rooftops visible just beyond the blue-green expanse of lagoons.

"Do you think the safehouse will be ready?" Antonius asked Gaius as they watched the flow of ships and skiffs in and out of the port.

"I hope so. We'll see how powerful the Emperor's command really is.

"I suppose commanding soldiers is one thing. Commanding workmen to finish on schedule is quite another."

The two men laughed. They had debated using Vindobona on the frontier, or Aquileia itself, as a base. The latter won out because of the ease of resupply by water. Also, they did not want the legion too aware of their activities. Augustus' orders. The Emperor did not want to risk further panic.

Aquileia had once been a small outpost, but had grown into a busy commercial centre over the years. In addition to Romans and Gauls, there were now other Celtic tribes, Illyrians, Greeks, Jews, Egyptians, and Syrians, especially in the harbour. The town was busy, day and night.

On some old military maps of the region, Gaius had seen that north of the town was a former mile castle. When he asked for it as a base of operations, his request was granted. It needed repairs, he was told, as it had fallen into disuse.

"That's the last of it, Centurion," Captain Pylos said to Gaius as the final bundles of arms were loaded into the wagons they had hired. "Do you want me to wait a few days here, in case you need to hire me again?"

"No, Captain. We may be gone for some time."

"Well, if you need me, leave a message with the harbour master. He's an old friend."

"Will do, Captain," Gaius turned from the old sea dog and led Daxos to his spot on the wagon. "You all right?"

"Yes, Centurion."

"You sure you still want to come? I can send you back with Pylos if you want."

Daxos looked at the black ship bobbing gently on the murky water, the sea glinting out in the distance. Then he turned to look north, to the mountains and forests of Noricum.

"I stay with you."

Gaius felt happy at that. For some reason, it gave him comfort. "Very well. Keep your head down and stay close to me. All right?"

"Yes."

Gaius turned and mounted one of his black stallions.

None of the men were used to riding on campaign, but Gaius knew horseback would get them to where they needed to go much faster, especially with the scorpions and other special gear they carried, including a supply of naptha.

"Move out!" Gaius called as he cantered to the head of the column.

The wagon driven by the medicus, Demetrios, groaned and rolled into motion, followed by all twelve men with two horses each. Passersby stopped to gawk, but none spoke, none recognized the armour or insignia of the group.

People recognized men of war when they saw them however, and kept a safe distance.

It took the group two slow hours to get through the crowded streets of Aquileia and out of the north gate. From there, it was another hour to the mile castle. Clouds hung low as they moved farther north.

In the centre of a broad green plain where the road headed north-east toward Emona, Gaius and the group turned to the west. They travelled on that lesser road for half a mile before they spotted the mile castle.

"Hold!" Gaius held up his hand and stared into the gloom of the valley. "There it is," he called back before coaxing his mount forward.

The mile castle had a simple square plan with one gate and battlements protecting the entire walkway. Gaius smelled burning and looked more closely to see debris scattered all about the place. He and Antonius rode ahead.

Construction materials lay scattered about the grounds, timber, barrels of lyme, shovels and sand. Just as the two men reined up before the open gate, an older, thickset man in a leather apron came whistling out of the fort.

"Who are you?" Gaius demanded.

The old man stopped and crossed his arms defiantly. "I'm Helvius, the foreman. You boys must be the new residents of this shit hole."

"You're addressing a centurion with special orders from-"

"That's enough, Antonius," Gaius stopped him from revealing anything more.

"I know you come from Rome," the man answered. "Don't worry, we've finished the work as ordered."

"That's good to hear," Gaius said.

"I also lost two good builders in the rush to get it all done."

"I'm sorry to hear that."

"They're not dead," the man clarified. "Just ran off with their whores cause they couldn't handle the pace. But we did it. The place is solid and secure." The man tossed an iron key ring to Gaius. "It's all yours!" he said as he picked up a satchel and began to walk away. "I'm going home now," he said as he walked away.

When the man was gone, Gaius pushed the gates fully open to allow the wagons and horses through to the courtyard. Debris lay everywhere, but the structure was indeed finished, the fresh lyme mortar still wet in wooden buckets, the bellows fire still hot.

"I hope this place doesn't fall on our fucking heads while we sleep," Tertius grumbled as he and the others walked about.

"It'll hold," Vitorix said as he slammed a fist into some of the new stonework.

The thought of sleep tempted all of them, but Gaius broke their reverie.

"Before we sleep, we need to get this mess cleaned up. Everyone pitch in and start piling debris and building materials in the south-west corner of the courtyard." He turned to Daxos and Demetrios. "You two get some cooking fires going. Antonius and I will survey the place."

Everyone got to work with ease - it was not as if they had to dig a ditch and stockade.

There were large rooms that could be used for storage and a barracks. They could be locked with the keys Gaius had been given. With all the extra equipment and silver they had, Gaius was happy to have a strong house.

"It'll be fine," he said to Antonius as he leaned on the repaired battlements of the north wall.

"How long will we stay here?" Antonius asked as the wind whipped around them. He shivered and pulled his cloak more tightly about himself.

"Not long." Gaius stared north beyond the mountains and imagined what they might find out there, on the other side of the frontier. "We need to keep moving, Antonius. The more we stand still…the more I think of home."

"Me too. I miss Vera. I know that's not very Roman of me, sir."

"Please. I understand. I would rather give in to Venus than go off on a hunt for lykoi."

"Why didn't you then? You could have taken your family to the Caucasus, or even to Mauretania, and no one would have found you. Didn't you consider it?"

Gaius sighed and tried to shut out the laughter that then seemed to come on the cold wind. "I thought about it several times," he admitted. "But Rome is where I belong, and I want my children to hold their heads high as they walk through the Forum. If I ran, what life would they have?"

"If you die, what life will they have?" Antonius looked down as he uttered the words, but Gaius smiled.

"Well then, we'd better not die." He slapped his optio on the back. "You'd better unload and distribute the wolf pelts to everyone. The weather is about to turn."

ALL OF THE MEN SLEPT SOUNDLY THAT NIGHT. THEY WERE safe within the walls, not yet near the Danuvius frontier.

Only Daxos lay awake. His young mind turned over the faint memories of his father's talk of lykoi. It saddened him to think that the farther time moved from his family's death, the harder it was to remember them, their smell, the feel of their embrace, or the deep resonance of Thracian voices. Daxos rose from his sleeping mat and wrapped himself in the thick wolf pelt cloak that Antonius had given him.

With the barracks door shut gently behind him, Daxos walked up the wooden stairs to the wall walk.

Stars pocked the sky in the cold air, and only a sliver of moon arched among them.

"Going to be cold out there."

Daxos turned from where he leaned on the parapet to see the pale image of Julius. But the boy was unafraid.

"Centurion Julius."

The apparition smiled. "Gaius needs to move more quickly."

"We are leaving tomorrow."

"The lykoi are breeding. You must be quick on the march."

"Yes, Centurion."

"Good lad." The apparition reached out to him but faded away as it did so.

Daxos opened his eyes and fingered the silver amulet about his neck.

"Father...I wish you could speak to me. Why do you not come? Father? Mother?"

"Who are you talking to?" Gaius came up beside Daxos, his face surrounded by wolf fur.

"I...I was praying." Daxos replaced the medallion inside his tunic and looked out.

"We'll need the gods' help," Gaius said, then closed his eyes and filled his lungs with the crisp air. *Mithras, watch over your Heliodromus and Miles on their journey. We need you.*

"Centurion Julius says we must move quickly. He says the lykoi are breeding."

Gaius stared at Daxos a moment and knew the boy had little reason to lie. He realized he wished Julius had visited him again too.

"The centurion was here?"

"Yes. He speak to me."

Gaius said nothing. He put a protective arm about the boy

and listened. It was quiet then, no howling, no laughter.

Fulvia, I love you. I'll come back.

He turned Daxos toward the stairs and led him back to the barracks.

"We have an early start tomorrow. Let's rest while we can."

When day broke over the mile castle, the gates were already solidly barred, the extra supplies locked away, and the train of men, horses, and wagons already three miles down the road to Emona with the snow-capped mountains to the north-west.

They kept a steady pace on the road until they reached the frontier base at Vindobona.

Every night, they camped away from the road in tents surrounded by stakes and ditches. Taverns and inns were too busy, and they wanted to reduce the risk of word of their mission getting across the river before they did. The black-armoured men were so determined-looking that most steered clear of them, no questions.

Until they passed Virunum a week later.

A marching column of legionaries, who were making their way to Vindobona after a week's furlough, came upon the group as they were rejoining the road one morning.

"State your business, you," the senior centurion barked as he came up to Gaius at the head of his column. The man studied Gaius' black armour and the insignia of the eagle and sun upon their banner. "What's all this about then?" the man asked.

Gaius rode forward but did not dismount. "We're heading north under orders, Centurion."

"Whose orders?"

"That's our affair."

"We're about Rome's business," Antonius added.

"Ha. We're all about Rome's business, aren't we? Why else would we be freezing our balls off up here when there are warmer places with lots of women?"

Gaius did not have the patience for this, but he needed to keep his temper in check. A fight would serve nothing. He dismounted, removed a sealed scroll from his satchel and moved to the side of the road.

The centurion followed. "What's that, then?"

"This," Gaius answered, "is a seal. Do you recognize it?" Gaius showed him the imperial seal of Augustus and heard the man gulp.

"Aye. I see it."

"Good," Gaius whispered. "I would hate to be delayed. Especially as I've been granted special disciplinary privileges to be used when our work is compromised."

"Are you threatening me?"

"Yes," Gaius stated flatly. "I'm sure the Emperor won't mind if I tell him that I had to crucify a few hinderances."

"Well..." The centurion backed away a little. "If it's for the Emperor." He glanced nervously at the scroll in Gaius' hand.

"Good. And make sure you don't go telling everyone."

"Right. Well, you boys better move on ahead of us." The man seemed deflated of his bravado.

Without another word, Gaius mounted up and their dark train continued north into the early morning mist with the legionaries watching them go.

"Something's not right about that bunch," the centurion said as he watched them go.

· · ·

THE NIGHTS WERE COLD ON THE ROAD WHERE THE MEN camped beneath a canopy of mountain pines and birch.

One night into the third week of their journey, Gaius ordered that they should spend the night in a cave that sat upon a small hillock in the forest. Apart from a few bones, it was deserted, and so, after performing the cleansing incantations, they honoured Mithras with a calf they had purchased at a small village the day before.

In the dim firelight, with dusk falling outside, Gaius led the men through the prayers and sacrifice.

"What am I?" the Heliodromus asked.

"The Light! The Light! The Light!" the Miles answered.

"Mithras, Lord of Light and Truth. Guard us as we march into the darkness." Gaius slit the calf's throat, and held it tightly until its kicking stopped and the blood pooled on the rock at his feet.

That night, Gaius took his turn at the watch. While the men and Daxos slept with bellies full of sacrificial meat, he stood at the mouth of the cave watching sharp wisps of cloud pass before the slim moon.

The wind howled and Gaius wrapped himself more tightly in his wolf pelt cloak. The irony of what he was wearing was not lost on him. He felt the past weeks of marching wearing on him and knew they had to hold out. They would need all of their strength.

He closed his eyes and sighed, and when he opened them, he started at what he saw.

Mithras was striding up the path toward the cave. The god smiled as he ate what appeared to be a joint of beef.

"Mithras," Gaius whispered and bowed his head.

"Yes, Heliodromus." Mithras nodded. "I see you are resting."

"The men are tired, Lord. I can't risk breaking them before the battle even begins."

"No. But *you* should not be tired." Mithras seemed almost disappointed in Gaius. "I filled your limbs with light, and that cannot fade."

"It is not my body that is tired, Lord. My mind and heart are heavy."

Mithras was silent. Then he tossed the joint into the brush and walked up to Gaius.

Gaius fell to his knees and felt Mithras' hand upon his head. Heat radiated and soothed, and Gaius felt himself relax, heard the whimper that escaped his throat.

"Lord, thank you," Gaius said. "I remain your Sun Runner, always."

"Good. Now, stay here," Mithras said before entering the cave where he touched each and every man's head while they slept. When he came to Daxos who slept with the medallion of his father in hand, Mithras smiled. "Good youth," the god said. "Your time is coming, and you shall shine." Mithras laid his hands upon Daxos' head and sternum, and then slipped from the cave.

"I have given your men strength, Heliodromus. They shall be swift and tireless." He smiled and began making his way back into the forest. "One more thing," Mithras looked back to Gaius where he stood before the cave. "Keep the boy close…and keep moving."

With that, he was gone.

The next morning, all of the men and Daxos seemed more alive, and wondered at their rejuvenation.

"Nothing like good meat and wine to lift the spirits!"

Vitorix said as he strapped his satchel to his spare mount and swung up into the saddle like he was twenty years old again. "Gods, I feel good!"

"I don't know what's got into us," Antonius commented to Gaius and Daxos, who finally smiled.

"I have no idea…" Gaius answered, winking at Daxos. "Whatever it is, we should take advantage of it. Everyone ready to move out in two minutes!" he yelled.

Before long they were all mounted and riding back down the hill in the direction of the road.

Four days later, they arrived at Vindobona and the Danuvius frontier.

"A special unit you say?" The hulking primus pilus of Vindobona's garrison eyed Gaius and his men doubtfully.

"That's right. We have special orders and need to commandeer three barges to take us and our horses and wagon across the river."

Gaius had gone over this with an optio, a lower grade centurion, a thin-striped tribune, and now the primus pilus, the top centurion. He was tired of arguing. All bridges along the Danuvius had either been destroyed or permanently barricaded. They had been forced to ask for the transports and an hour of arguing in the rain is what it had got them.

"You know that the entire frontier is on high alert. We've just lost three legions over across the water, and you tell me you want to go over there, into Hades, with a dozen grunts and a boy?"

Gaius worked his jaw and held out the scroll with the Imperial seal for the fourth time.

"That's right, Centurion. And I wouldn't question these orders if I were you."

The man read the scroll, his face stony, still beneath his horizontal crest. When he finished, he handed it back.

"I'm assuming no questions and not a word is to be spoken?"

"That's correct."

The centurion pointed a muscled arm at the wide, swift current of the river.

"Make no mistake, you lot," he said to all of them. "That river's the Styx, not the Danuvius. Not now."

Gaius nodded and spoke low to the man. "Believe me, we don't want to cross. We have to."

The centurion nodded and called to someone inside the fortress gate house. "Cassius! Tell the camp prefect we need the barges made ready for the morrow."

"Erm. We need them now," Gaius added.

"Don't you want to sleep under a roof tonight, get clean and eat?"

"We can't." It pained Gaius to decline, but they had to keep moving.

"Suit yourselves," the primus pilus said. "Cassius, we need them ready in one hour!"

"Yes, sir!" the man replied and then rushed off.

"There are some shelters down by the riverside if you and your men want to wait there. I'll send fresh hay and oats for the horses."

"There's no need."

"You may not want food, but your horses will." The centurion turned and went back into the base.

Gaius and the men wound their way around the walls and down to the river to await the barges.

The Danuvius flowed quick and dark, and its broad depths stretched into the distance on either side of the fortress.

Atop the walls, legionaries on guard duty looked over the battlements at the force of black-clad warriors who had cowed their primus pilus into agreement.

"So much for secrecy," Barna said, his red eyes gazing up at the walls.

"The centurion will keep quiet," Gaius reassured them. "All that the legion will know is that a group of mad men and a boy crossed the river."

"Mad is right," Caelius added.

Gaius walked to where Daxos stood looking out over the water. He remembered when he found the boy washed up and terrified at Troesmis, plucked from that very river.

Now they were going back across to hunt lykoi.

"Is that where we go, Centurion Gaius?" Daxos pointed straight ahead to some low, lightly forested hills.

"No. Those are Quadi and Marcomani lands. The Cherusci are far over there, to the north-west." Gaius pointed and all of the men came up to look at the black mass of forest that was their destination.

Crossing the Danuvius took much longer than Gaius would have liked.

Half a day was lost getting onto the barges and negotiating the currents and sandbanks all the way to the other side. It was a vast body of water and disembarking on the opposite shore was made more precarious by the marshy banks.

Luckily the helmsman knew his way to a small inlet that led to a dirt track that was solid and only just wide enough to accommodate the wagon.

The barges pushed off the bank with archers ready, bows drawn and aimed at the low foliage beyond Gaius and his men.

Caelius turned around and kissed the amulets about his neck.

Sabinus began sharpening his gladius again, and Calgacus walked up the path a distance to scout things out.

"Anything?" Gaius asked when the Briton returned.

"Nothing. No tracks, or broken branches. No one around for now."

"Well, let's not wait around to be buggered," Vitorix burst out.

"He's right," Gaius answered. "We should find a secure place for the night."

"I thought we were going to travel by night?" Antonius asked.

"Not yet," Gaius said as he hoisted Daxos into the wagon beside Demetrios. "You all right?" he asked the boy.

Daxos nodded, but his eyes searched the forest.

"Remember this," Gaius tapped the boy's pugio. "You said the lykoi only went out at night, right?"

"Yes."

"Then we're all right for now."

"Yes, Centurion Gaius."

Behind Gaius a few paces, Octavius vomited.

"Octavius isn't all right, Centurion!" Tertius laughed. "Not again, man!"

Octavius wiped his mouth, and stood straight again. "I don't like boats," he said.

"You're from a fucking island," Saguntus chided him.

"Yeah. Inland."

Everyone laughed.

"That's enough," Gaius placed his helmet on his head and hoisted his covered scutum. "Move out!"

Gaius, Antonius, and Calgacus went ahead with the wagon groaning after them. The rest of the men and their horses followed.

FOR THREE DAYS, THEY FOLLOWED THE RIVER, WENDING THEIR way up and down the forested hills, trying to avoid open fields. The rain had ceased and their progress was surprisingly good.

Something in Gaius' gut told him an attack was coming, that they were being tracked. Calgacus and Vitorix scouted wide of the party, but there were never signs of the enemy; the Quadi, the Marcomani, and the Naristi were just not there.

"This doesn't make sense," Antonius said on their fourth night. "We can't be the only humans north of the river. And we're not a big force of men. If anything, our extra horses should welcome an attack by the barbarians."

"I agree," Gaius said, covering Daxos with his fur cloak. "Maybe all the tribes have joined? Maybe..." he shuddered to think it, "...maybe they've all turned to lykoi?"

Saguntus swore and muttered in his Iberian dialect.

"I hope you're wrong," Antonius said.

"Me too." Gaius looked at the nearly full moon that glowed through the trees, above the mountains that surrounded them.

They marched on slowly over the next few days, and still there was no sign of the barbarians.

"I don't like it," Vitorix told Gaius as they rode side by side. "These people should be drunk on their victory over the legions. They should be hounding and teasing us from every rocky outcrop, challenging us to battle."

"You think they're letting us through?" Gaius asked.

"No," the Gaul said. "They're nowhere near disciplined enough to stay so hidden when such a rich Roman group walks through their lands."

"Maybe they're afraid of something?" Daxos said from the wagon behind them.

It was plausible.

"Are the lykoi so ferocious?" Vitorix asked Daxos.

The boy shrugged his shoulders.

"Maybe not the lykoi…" Gaius added.

"Well, whoever or whatever has these bastards scared, I've got a little something for them." Vitorix drew his Celtic longsword from beneath his leg and swung it in the air.

"I ordered that we bring only the special weapons Vulcan's Bastard made for us. Why did you bring that?" Gaius stared at Vitorix.

"I never leave without my father's sword, sir."

"Put that away. If lykoi show up, I want each man to have his silver blade. Understood?"

"Yes, sir." The Gaul sheathed his sword and remained silent.

It was three days later on the border of the Chatti and Hermunduri lands that the first attack came. It was dusk, and the men had been resting on the banks of a wide stream where the water rippled over rocks, carrying yellow leaves downstream.

The water was fresh and clean, and Gaius ordered their skins filled and the horses watered. While the men did this, Barna went downstream to relieve himself. While doing so, the Carthaginian was dismayed to see three barbarians coming toward him, the sound of their steps hidden by the rush of water over rocks.

They were filthy and hard-looking, but Barna was more concerned with the jagged and rusty blades they levelled as they charged him. He took one out with a thrown pugio and met the other two blade to blade.

"Attack!" he yelled upstream.

The horses balked and Gaius turned just in time to dodge the blade that whistled toward his head. Just then, he heard Barna's voice.

"Attack!" Gaius repeated.

Immediately all the men raised their scuta to meet the rush of attackers.

The enemy came from every side, twenty-five of them.

"Watch out for lykoi!" Antonius yelled.

The words gave pause to his attacker and the optio took the chance to run him through.

Just then, Gaius saw Demetrios fall from the wagon as a barbarian grabbed the reins.

"Daxos!" Gaius sliced at an attacker's face and pushed past to pursue the wagon as it plunged down the forest road.

The wagon careened over fallen logs, bouncing into the air and landing with a bone-jarring crash before speeding on. Inside, Daxos huddled under the furs, gripping his pugio. Then they hit another log and the rear wheels exploded. With a cry, Daxos fell back.

The driver heard him and looked back. With the horses still charging, the barbarian stood and stepped to the back, his blade over his head to strike.

Daxos sprung up with the dagger and caught the man's knee.

The barbarian howled with rage and leaned in to strike Daxos just as a pilum broke into his sternum and sent him flying to the front of the wagon.

Gaius came running up the road and leapt onto the wagon where he grabbed the reins and pulled hard on the spooked team.

"Daxos! You hurt?" Gaius threw the furs aside to find the boy still gripping the edge of the wagon. "There, there. You did well. I'm here now." Gaius pried the boy's fingers off the blacked wood and put the dagger aside. "I've got you."

"I got him!" Daxos nodded to the impaled barbarian.

Gaius laughed. "Yes. You did."

When Gaius and Daxos arrived back at the stream, the horses blown from dragging the broken wagon, they found the men laughing and washing the blood from their hands and weapons. Antonius rushed over.

"Damage?" Gaius asked immediately.

"Everyone's alive, though the medicus was stabbed in the shoulder. He says he's fine. Two barbarians got away with two horses. The rest we killed."

"Could've been worse."

"That was good practice!" Vitorix laughed.

Gaius turned on him but noticed the others smiling and laughing too. In fact, they looked like they had all been out for a gentle stroll, not a battle.

The cave and Mithras came to Gaius' mind, and he decided not to discipline them. He hoped their confidence would hold. His own fear at having almost lost Daxos had him more angry than anything.

"I'm guessing those were not lykoi, sir." Saguntus said.

"No. They weren't. Those were peasants with rusty farming tools."

"Hermunduri?" Antonius asked.

"I don't know. Maybe Chatti." Gaius said. "I remember that wild garlic smell on them from the rebellion. Anyway, things are going to get tougher now, and the full moon is coming." Gaius looked to the sky and the sharp clouds drifting across it. "The wagon is finished." He pointed to it. "Sabinus, Caelius, and Leonidas, unhitch the horses and get everything onto the backs of all the spare mounts. We'll be in the thicker woods soon. Oh, and be careful with the pots of naphtha, keep them upright." Gaius turned and went to check on the medicus. If they lost Demetrios, they would be in trouble.

IT HAD BEEN FOUR DAYS SINCE THE ATTACK. IT RAINED THE whole time. It was cold and impossible to hear any sign of the enemy they hunted, or who hunted them.

"We don't even know what these lykoi look like. How are we supposed to know?" Tertius said to Calgacus who rode beside him.

"Just kill any wolf or barbarian that comes close. They'll want to kill you anyway."

"What if it's a woman?"

"Don't matter. Do it. Don't think. Otherwise, she'll have your balls off before you can say 'Fu-'"

"Erm," Gaius gave the men a look from where he turned in his saddle and nodded to Daxos whose eyes were wide open and staring at them.

"Sorry, sir," Calgacus said.

Gaius scanned the woods about them, his eyes searching

for any abnormality. It was getting dark, but something told Gaius they should keep moving.

The thin line of horses and riders snaked its way down the pathway. On either side, dead and dying foliage of many colours seemed to encroach, even as the men watched. Lichen-covered boulders bubbled out of the black earth, and an oppressive feeling came upon each man.

"This must be the woods. Have we come so far?" Antonius asked.

Gaius pulled the papyrus map from the fold of his cloak. "Seems so. Keep a lookout for any remains!" he called to everyone.

The path continued for another mile before it broke into a clearing. There, in the middle, was a Roman marching camp.

"Well, there's something!" Vitorix said as they came to a halt.

"It shouldn't look like that," Caelius pointed out.

Gaius nudged his horse forward, over the defensive ditch, between the sharpened stakes and among the broken tents that filled the confines.

"They left it intact. Why?" Barna asked as he rode over the ditch.

Gaius dismounted and walked over to the palisade. Normally, a marching camp would be fully dismantled and the ditches filled in so it could not be used again by the enemy.

"Seems like they left in a hurry," Antonius said as he came beside Gaius.

"How did they fit three legions and camp followers in this area?" Saguntus asked. "It's not possible."

Leonidas pointed around the interior of the camp and everyone noticed how tightly packed the tents were. No orderly rows.

"It's all just torn tents and broken bits of pot." Calgacus kicked a broken clay jar into a heap of debris.

"They obviously didn't have time to tear down." Gaius knelt to look at a puddle of rain water at the base of a palisade spike. The water was faintly bloody.

He churned it with the tip of his gladius and a finger with an iron citizen's ring bobbed to the surface. It was not cut cleanly by a blade. It seemed to have been torn away.

"They were definitely attacked here." Gaius stood, running his hand along the spike, feeling sword marks and other dents in the wood. "Check for bodies, all of you!"

The men began walking about the broken camp, lifting sodden tent leather and prodding the water-filled ditch surrounding the camp.

Nothing.

"No bodies, sir!" Barna yelled.

"There've got to be bodies," Antonius said, his complexion getting whiter. "We didn't see any on the road here, either."

Gaius turned to the group. "Maybe this is where the first attack came?" he suggested.

"Aye, but where'd they go from here?" Vitorix asked. "Sure the troops could have escaped, but some of the camp followers had to have been killed."

A raven croaked from a tree top and startled everyone.

Gaius looked up and noticed the sun had fully disappeared.

"It's going to be dark soon. I don't fancy staying in the open tonight."

"Which way, sir?" Antonius asked. "There are three paths out of here."

"I..." Gaius stopped. "Daxos! Come back!" Gaius ran

from the group to see who Daxos was speaking with. "Daxos!" He drew his gladius as he plodded through the mud.

"What's he on about?" Vitorix asked Antonius who shrugged.

WHEN GAIUS REACHED DAXOS' SIDE, HE SAW THE WOMAN the boy was speaking with.

Her face was tired and white with terror, and a horrible gash cut along the side of her head. Blood stained her shoulder and the area around her groin. She was not a barbarian.

"Who are you? What happened?" Gaius went to grab her arm but something held him back.

The woman mouthed words, but there was no sound. All she could do was move her mouth and point.

"What's she saying?"

"She say that the army go down this road." Daxos pointed in the same direction as the woman.

Gaius looked at her and back to Antonius and the others who were coming with all the horses.

"What is it, sir?" the optio asked. "What do you see?"

Gaius looked from them to the woman and back again. "You don't see her?" he asked.

The men looked at each other and back at Gaius. Caelius fingered his talismans, and Saguntus began mumbling his prayers.

They don't see her, Gaius thought. *Mithras, guide me. Is this a trap?*

The woman looked to Gaius and shook her head, tears flowing down to evaporate.

"It - I mean," Gaius recovered. "Don't you see it?" He

said to his men, pointing to the path. "Tracks and churned mud, mostly down here. We'll take this path and hopefully find a strong point for the night."

Gaius mounted up and waited beside Daxos. He had seen dead in their thousands before after a battle, but this unnerved him deeply. He wondered if there would be others like her.

"Calgacus and Vitorix. See if you can follow the trail."

"Yes, sir." The two men went first, followed by the others, Gaius and Daxos.

The latter two looked back to see the woman sitting in the mud, rocking back and forth, and wailing silently.

Then they headed into the thicket.

It was no ordinary wood into which they rode. The path was not more than a deer track. Gnarled oak and chestnut stood sentinel from among the rocks which came out of the ground like teeth.

Gaius could hear his men's breathing change. The moon came out, and silver light broke through the aged arms of the canopy.

"Daxos," Gaius called to the boy as they rode. "The woman…were you not afraid of her?"

The boy looked at Gaius. "I not afraid of the dead. It is the living I am afraid of."

The woman's face still haunted Gaius. He shook his head. Daxos was right. *Worry about the living, Gaius,* he told himself. "Antonius," Gaius called up. "Any sign of shelter?"

"Don't know, sir. Can't see a thing past the first trees."

"Clearing up ahead!" Vitorix yelled out, louder than Gaius would have liked.

The path broke onto a small clearing with a monolith in the centre.

Before he reached the open with Daxos, Gaius could hear the exclamations of his men. An odour of decay reached his nostrils and the bile immediately rose in his throat.

"Daxos," he said. "Cover your mouth and nose with your cloak. Draw your pugio and stay close."

The boy fumbled a bit but complied. He had learned that it was a good idea to listen when Gaius became alert.

Gaius heard the slither of his men's swords as they emerged from the shadows into the clearing. Corpses riddled the area about the central rock - soldiers, women, horses and dogs. The bodies were rotten, the skin, and fur, and hair limp in the mud, while white bone jutted out of the mess.

Roman standards and armour littered the ground. Octavius vomited where he stood.

"Sir, look!" Caelius hissed and pointed at three figures standing on the other side of the clearing. They appeared to be wearing Roman armour. From their silhouettes, though it appeared to be broken, sitting askew.

"Survivors?" Antonius guessed. It was too dark to tell with the moon behind black clouds. The clearing began to change as the clouds moved on and black turned slowly to silver.

"Selene is full," Daxos said, pointing at the moon. "Centurion?"

"Hold there!" Vitorix challenged as the three men mounted the monolith. "Are you men of the legions?" he said in Latin. "We're here to help."

Nothing.

The three men, who had been still and silent before, now

threw their armour to the ground and gazed up at the full face of the moon.

"They aren't Romans!" Gaius called out.

The middle man howled then, the other two joining him.

At first, the chorus seemed absurd, and Calgacus heaved a great laugh. But comedy turned to terror in a matter of seconds.

The men's horses screamed as human howls turned to deep, blood-curdling cries. All three barbarians lurched forward as if to vomit. A loud cracking of bone filled the clearing as the men's countenance morphed into something imagined only in nightmares. Their faces struck out, unnaturally elongated, and great fangs curled beside their black lips.

"Mithras, protect us," Sabinus said.

Each man was frozen in the face of what they had just witnessed.

"Kill them!" Daxos yelled. "Centurion, kill them now!"

But it was too late. The barbarians' white bodies went grey, and black fur sprouted from beneath their skin. Muscles bubbled to triple the size of each, and before the Romans knew it, they were facing three massive lykoi.

The red eyes seethed with hunger and hatred, and then a howl to break any warrior's resolve rang out. Everyone instinctively covered his ears and it was then that the lykoi unleashed their savage attack in three directions.

"Watch your flank!" Gaius yelled as he turned his horse to the right, staying in front of Daxos. He let his black pilum fly and it grazed one lykos, extracting an angry, pained yelp.

In the centre, Vitorix had jumped to the ground and rushed the middle lykos. His scutum was up as he slashed with his father's longsword into the flank of another lykos.

The beast faltered but then turned on its hind legs and

struck the big Gaul with a muscled forearm. Vitorix went down and the lykos pounced.

Calgacus and Sabinus closed with their scuta locked and slammed into the beast. Both their gladii plunged into the animal's stomach and throat.

On the left, Octavius, Barna, and Tertius had their lykos surrounded. Their sword arms shook as they observed the razor-like teeth up close and struggled to close their ears to the unnatural snarling.

"Somebody get a pilum in here!" Barna yelled.

Antonius rushed in and plunged the silver-capped pilum head into the flank. The animal slipped but recovered and reared two full heads above the men.

The jaws came down onto Tertius' scutum, knocking him to the ground. The man screamed as he sank into the churned mud.

Octavius hacked at the animal's other flank and Barna plunged a silver spike from his waist into the top of the lykos' skull.

"Over here!" The men heard Gaius yell. "He's trying to run!"

Gaius, Demetrios, and Leonidas had the other animal surrounded. Gaius crouched with his gladius pointing from the side of his scutum. Leonidas tried getting in for quick slashes, but the lykos whirled quickly. It tripped Leonidas and in an instant had hold of his arm.

Leonidas yelled out and with his other arm tried to stab with his blade, but the lykos was shaking him too violently.

"Take me!" Gaius yelled, fixing on the red eyes. His terrified horse bucked and Gaius toppled over the saddle horns into the mud below.

Daxos' horse burst between the wolf and centurion. The

beast was about to lunge when it stopped, and sniffed the air about Daxos. It let out a terrible howl and then bolted with Leonidas' arm still in its mouth.

"Get it! It'll bring more! Shoot!" Gaius yelled.

Calgacus and Saguntus had their bows out and fired into the dark of the forest.

Gaius began to run but Leonidas' cries stopped him. "Gather the horses and secure the area," he ordered as he ran to where Daxos and Demetrios knelt beside Leonidas.

Vitorix brought himself out of the mud and looked at his sword. "Did you see that?" he asked Calgacus.

"Put that fucking thing away, you Fortuna-kissed bastard."

"At least we know what the silver is good for," Sabinus said.

"Leonidas! Look at me, brother!" Gaius held the man's face as he spasmed in the mud. "Stay with me! Demetrios?" Gaius turned to the medicus. "Is he becoming one of them?"

The medicus shook his head. "No, I don't think so. Too soon to tell. It isn't the same as an immortui bite or scratch, but he has suffered a great wound." He hurried about stanching the bleeding and wrapping the stub of Leonidas' arm. "It's like a poison is taking hold of his body. He's in shock."

Gaius pounded the ground and stood. "Everyone else accounted for?"

"Yes, sir!" Antonius answered.

"Daxos." Gaius leaned on the boy's horse. "You saved me again, my boy. Why did the beast not attack you?"

Daxos shook his head wildly, fighting his fear and clenching the silver medallion.

Gaius pat his leg and turned to Demetrios. "We need to get

to safety. Vitorix, Caelius, help the medicus get Leonidas tied to a saddle."

Howls erupted from the woods all about them and the horses reared.

"We need to get out of here. Now! We ride!" Gaius mounted his big black. "Light torches!" Gaius ordered. "They already know we're here."

A minute later, they were charging down the forest path into the night.

IIT WAS A RIDE OF TERROR.

The lykoi pursued the Romans as they charged into the darkness of the German forest. Howling rent the air everywhere, and yet it was only occasionally that they would spot red eyes dashing among the trees above the small track.

The torches did little to help light the way, but Gaius did catch glimpses of debris every so often. Roman helmets and body armour caught the light everywhere, and sometimes the sockets of a skull.

"They came this way!" Antonius yelled back to Gaius.

Then the lykoi became bold and attacked on the left and right as the horses pounded past. The Romans slashed on both sides, repelling the attacks, but the horses were exhausted and slowing despite their terror.

Mithras, bring the day! Gaius prayed as black jaws snapped out of the dark and seized his mount's flank.

A pilum immediately pierced the attacking head as Calgacus charged up the line on the right.

They took a path that led up and away from the main track, crashing through the bracken, branches whipping their faces and the leather of their dark armour.

Suddenly, Vitorix, who had reached the top first, skidded to a halt and yelled. "Stop! Cliff!"

The men pulled hard on their reins and turned to meet the attack.

But it did not come.

There was screaming in the woods below.

"Where are Demetrios and Leonidas?" Gaius asked.

"They were in the rear," Saguntus answered.

"God help them," Caelius whispered.

"I'm going back." Gaius checked his scutum and gladius.

"I'm coming too," Vitorix said, holding one of the massive axes.

"Me too," Calgacus stepped up.

"The rest of you stay here, no matter what," Gaius ordered. "Antonius, watch over Daxos." He looked at the boy, smiled grimly, and plunged toward the direction of the screams.

"Don't worry," Antonius soothed unconvincingly to Daxos. "The sun will be up soon." He pointed to a grey light in the east.

The rest of the men dismounted, tied their horses, and stared down into the dark of the forest from their rocky perch above the valley.

Daxos slept uneasily while they waited, but the men paced and fretted, fighting the urge to go after their centurion and brothers.

Morning mist shrouded the forest. The accursed howling had long stopped, but still no one returned.

"Ahh!" Daxos awoke with a start, his eyes wet with tears.

"It's all right, boy," Barna muttered. "I think we'll all have our share of nightmares after this."

But it was not a nightmare that had roused Daxos from his sleep. It was the whispering wraith he had taken for Gaius who sat behind Barna.

The lemur was a soldier. Roman.

You'll never get out, Daxos heard in his head. *You're already dead, boy.* The soldier shook his head, stood and then plunged over the cliff to the forest below.

Then a horse neighed down the path, and all the men jumped up.

"We're not fucking wolves, if that's what you're worried about," Vitorix said as he came to the top, leading one of the horses. "Bad news, friends," the Gaul said as he turned the horse sideways to reveal two torsos. "We found them."

Across the back of one of the horses were slung the bloody remains of Leonidas and Demetrios. Their limbs had been ripped off and the medicus' head was missing. Blood stained the haunches of the horse carrying them and the animal's eyes were wide and wild.

"We were too late," Calgacus stepped out of the woods then. "There was nothing we could do."

"We killed about six of the beasts, but they had already ripped them apart." Vitorix looked at Daxos who had come running to the front.

"Where is Centurion Gaius?" the boy's voice cracked.

"I'm here, lad," the familiar voice said. "I'm here."

Gaius emerged into the grey light of day, his scutum cracked, and his sword and armour crusted in blood.

Daxos plunged into his arms.

"We've lost two of our brothers this day…" Gaius looked at the bloody remains and turned to vomit. When he had finished, he turned to the others. "Prepare a pyre. I'll not leave them in this place without ceremony. Everyone to it. I want two men watching the path. Daxos, you feed the horses if we have any oats left." Gaius looked out at the never ending wood in the valley below. "I need to think."

As the men gathered kindling and dead logs for a pyre, Gaius tried to regroup. He knew he had lost sight of his plan, if he had had one.

Two men were dead, and they now barely had enough horses for the rest of them. What had been Leonidas' horse was spooked to insanity, and Demetrios' had been taken by the lykoi.

I've focussed too much on fighting the lykoi, Gaius chided himself. *What were our orders? How do we get out of here and back to Rome?* Gaius put his head in his hands and allowed his eyes to close.

You must come back to me, Fulvia had said.

He wanted to give into his thoughts of home, and Rome, and laying down beside his wife in their bed. But he owed it to his family and his men to keep going. *Fulfill your orders, Gaius,* he told himself.

"You're almost there, Heliodromus."

Gaius looked beside himself to see Mithras sitting there, his white trousers and brown boots dangling over the rock ledge.

"They can't see me now. Just you." The god smiled. "And the boy." Mithras looked at Daxos who quickly turned away. Then he laughed playfully.

Lord, Gaius pleaded. *I do not know what else to do. By nightfall, they will be hunting us again.*

"You must run, of course. Run farther into the wood, into their territory. See what became of the legions."

Then what?

"Then you must kill their leader." Mithras hung his head. "Their leader is the root of the evil. Sever the root and the rest of the plant will wither."

Gaius nodded, his eyes closed. *How do I know which is the leader?*

But Mithras was gone.

Daxos was now sitting in his place. "I don't think that man was dead," the boy said.

"No, Daxos. He is ever living. He is the Light, and he came to help us."

"What did he say?" Daxos looked down where the ghostly soldier had plunged.

"He said we are to kill the leader, and that will end it."

Daxos nodded and flipped the silver medallion over in his hand.

"Ready, sir!" Antonius stood beside the pyre on which the remains of their fallen brothers had been placed.

Gaius stood and walked over to accept the torch from his optio with the men forming a circle about the pyre.

"We have travelled far, my brothers, from the Light into the Dark. We are in the land of death, make no mistake. The shades of thousands of our brothers walk here. To honour them, we must, as always, hold our courage and run with the Light which is ever with us."

Gaius saw Mithras through the smoke of the torch, staring at the bodies of his fallen miles. A tear ran down the god's cheek.

Then others emerged from the trees. Men whose bones protruded, and whose skin was bloody and peeling. Dead

Romans surrounded the living then, each staring at the flames, the Light before them.

"Mithras, Lord of Light!" Gaius continued, conscious of the presence. "Please welcome our brave brothers into the brightness of your afterlife. Let them not drift in darkness. Take them and know they were ever loyal."

Gaius plunged the torch into the bottom of the pyre where it smoked thickly before finally catching. The flames curled and crackled, and finally began to take the two bodies.

"What am I?" Gaius asked.

"The Light! The Light! The Light!" the men answered.

"Who am I?"

"Mithras! Mithras! Mithras!"

They all waited a while as the fiery consumption took place. When at last their brothers' remains were gone, Mithras himself disappeared.

Gaius waited a moment, then turned and took the reins of his horse. "Let's go find out what happened to our legions. And kill the bastard who did it!"

They then made their way back into the forest, shields ready, and swords up to meet the lykoi.

If there had been any doubt that the group was going the wrong way, that doubt was dispelled when they reached the forest floor once more.

Dim daylight revealed a trail of Roman dead - pieces of broken bones, armour, torn scraps of red standards, pila, and the corpses of pack horses.

Gaius had the men move on foot through the detritus of three legions. The torn and scattered remains of men was more than he had seen on any campaign.

"We should bury them, Centurion," Caelius whispered when they stopped.

"No time," Gaius answered, as much as he felt the urge to do just that. "We have to find Varus and the rest of the legions' officers."

Tertius picked up a helmet with a head still in it and dropped it when maggots writhed out at the edges.

"Some of this was done with a blade, sir." Vitorix said, pointing to a grouping of cleanly severed bodies. "Not all lykoi…which means-"

"They'll be out in daylight," Calgacus finished.

Everyone looked to the trees, their shields at the ready.

Gaius noticed several scuta with their leather covers still on. "Ambushes," he said. "The whole way. They didn't even have time to uncover their scuta."

"These would have been un-liftable with the leather soaked through with rain," Antonius added.

Daxos tugged on Gaius' cloak and pointed to the shade of an optio whose ribs splayed open from his bloody chest.

The wraith was screaming and pointing down the path.

Gaius and Daxos could not hear what the man was saying, but he pointed emphatically down a path deeper into the forest.

"Let's keep moving," Gaius ordered, and pulled on his horse's bridle. "Daxos, keep your helmet on, and your pugio drawn."

The boy drew his blade as they passed between two tall boulders and on into the woods. The men had all been training him sporadically but he still felt nervous holding the Roman blade.

The forest was silent.

Gaius tried to plan for darkness. He knew now that they

could not move at night, as that would risk them being hunted by the lykoi. They needed an advantage and perhaps Daxos was somehow a key to that advantage; the lykoi had left him alone, after all.

There was a sudden whistling sound, as though the air had been cut.

Gaius felt his head spinning and struggled to rise. He saw Daxos mouthing frantic words, but the boy sounded like he was under water. Then Gaius' horse reared and a spear protruded from its belly.

"Centurion!" Daxos yelled more clearly. "Attack!"

Gaius scanned around to see barbarians rushing from the foliage and undergrowth, their faces muddy and howling.

"Shield wall!" Gaius ordered and his men surrounded him. Two, then three more horses went down.

Vitorix clung to the reins of the two horses carrying the scorpions and spare bolts and arrows, while Saguntus held onto the two carrying the naphtha jars.

"How many?" Gaius shook his head as he stared at Antonius.

"Fifteen maybe."

"Yeah!" They heard Calgacus cry out.

"Make that fourteen," Antonius corrected.

Now that the Romans had overcome the initial surprise, the Germans held back among the trees launching spears and sling stones.

"Largest cluster of them thirty yards to the west," Barna yelled.

"All right. On three, we rush the bigger group. Vitorix, Saguntus, and Calgacus, hang back to slow the others."

"Yes, sir!" they answered.

"Daxos, stay with me. One…two…three…GO!"

The Roman shield wall rushed at the Germans who in turn charged to slam into the black scuta.

Gaius' sword shot up into the belly of a man who had jumped over him, and Barna swung an axe and cleaved two of the enemy in one blow.

The Germans made to surround the Romans but Vitorix, Saguntus, and Calgacus hacked away at the flankers. Vitorix howled as a spear cut a swathe from the side of his calf, and the big Gaul rushed the man in a fury, cracking him against a tree.

The horses reared, clearly spooked, but stayed where they were near to the regrouping Romans who now formed a tight circle, facing off against the remaining ten barbarians.

"Are you lykoi? Come and fight!" Calgacus taunted them.

The Germans began backing away, realizing they were too few.

"Don't let them get away!" Gaius yelled. "They'll warn others!" One German turned and bolted the way the wraith had pointed. "Sabinus, your bow!"

The twang of the string sounded and the German fell. Two more arrows brought down others before the Romans attacked the remainder. Gladii and axes stabbed and swung and it seemed they had finished them off.

"Everyone all right?" Gaius looked around. "Daxos? No." Gaius rushed to where the boy was pinned beneath a German.

"Help me, Centurion," the boy whispered, the air pressed out of his lungs. Blood covered his face and neck.

"Antonius, help!" The two men lifted the dead barbarian off and with the body came Daxos' pugio, stuck in the German's heart.

But Daxos did not move. He could not rise, but for the

short sword that had been driven through the skin of his left side.

"Gods," Antonius whispered.

"Daxos, you're all right," Gaius reassured. "But I need to take the blade out, clean and cauterize your wound to stop the bleeding."

The boy nodded, his eyes rolling back.

"Stay with me, Daxos!"

The eyes opened and a hand rose to grip the medallion about his neck.

"Caelius, get me the medicus' box of supplies and a wine skin! Sabinus, start a fire."

"Yes, sir!"

Gaius took hold of the sword as Vitorix and Antonius held Daxos down. Caelius arrived and handed Gaius the wine.

"Daxos, you ready?"

The boy nodded again, his eyes fearful.

"You can yell if you have to, but they might hear you. One…two…three!" Gaius slid the blade out as straight as he possibly could, and blood began to leak out. "Wine!" He poured the wine over the wound.

Daxos' body recurved from the pain and even Vitorix and Antonius fought to hold him steady.

But he did not yell out.

"Your father would be proud." Gaius smiled. He pressed hard on the wound with linen from the medical supplies and waited for the fire to get going.

Finally, Sabinus came up with a sizzling blade and gave it to Gaius.

"Deep breath," Gaius said before pressing it to the skin.

Daxos whimpered.

"Second blade!"

Sabinus handed him another and Gaius repeated for the exit wound.

Daxos struggled but eventually calmed down, his breathing ragged.

"Finished, lad," Gaius said. *Mithras, help him.*

THEY HAD LOST A LOT OF TIME WITH THE SKIRMISH, AND Daxos' wound. The sun was dipping again and Gaius wanted to press on.

There seemed to be no safe place. Roman debris and dead decorated the forest floor like a grisly mosaic. To make matters worse, Gaius caught frequent glimpses of wraiths among the trees. At first he took them for barbarians, but after two false sightings he began to hold his tongue. So many dead roamed that wood.

Darkness fell, and with it a thick mist. It was impossible to see more than twenty feet away, and so Gaius ordered a rest.

"Four men on perimeter watch at a time. Caelius, Barna, Vitorix, and Antonius will go first. One hour shifts," he whispered the orders.

The horses were tied, and the rest of the men and Daxos slept about a gnarled oak.

Gaius felt Daxos' head. He was slightly feverish. The centurion had done his share of emergency medical treatment on his men in the field, but his skills were not equal to a medicus. He had only patched men up and sent them back into battle. The boy before him was different, someone he cared about as family. He felt he owed it to Daxos' father to keep him safe. *Mithras, bring him through this. Help me to keep him safe...* Gaius prayed.

A wolf howled then. A deep, grating noise, not the sad

lonesome whine familiar to frontier troops.

Gaius stood up and cocked his ear into the thick white wall that pervaded the forest.

A second raging howl rang out, and a third.

The lykoi were out.

None of the men slept after that. Gaius paced around Daxos, his scutum close and his two pila sticking out of the ground for easy reach. His gladius hung ready in his hand as he listened.

All about, Gaius could see the black outlines of his remaining men at ten foot intervals.

Branches cracked, and then more, and more, until the discernible sound of marching men sounded in the wood to the north-west. They made no effort to hide themselves or be quiet.

Might as well be a pack of bleeding elephants, said the familiar voice of Julius.

Gaius looked up and the lemur laughed quietly.

Bloody Germans never could be stealthy.

Gaius closed his eyes, his hand reaching protectively for Daxos.

But Julius continued to speak. *Still not used to me. I know. But hear me, Gaius Justus Vitalis.*

Gaius dared a look at those intense eyes and felt cold creep hard upon him.

You'll want to follow that group. Arminius is with them.

Gaius looked at the lemur of his friend. It nodded. Mithras had said he needed to kill the leader, and here was Arminius marching right past. Gaius waved everyone over to the tree.

"We need to follow that group marching through the wood," he whispered. "I'll take three men - Calgacus, Tertius, and Saguntus."

"What about there rest of us?" Vitorix demanded.

"Stay here and hold this position," Gaius answered. "Vitorix, I need you to watch over Daxos for me."

The Gaul nodded and looked at the boy whose skin was ashen in the dim light.

"Don't be too long," Antonius whispered. We're stronger together."

"We're just going to see where they're headed." Gaius turned to the three men he had chosen. "Ready?"

They nodded.

"I'll be back," Gaius said to Daxos who shuddered. The centurion crept into the dark mist of the wood with the others following.

"I hope he knows what he's doing," Barna said as more howls echoed in the distance. "Can lykoi climb trees?" the Numidian asked.

They all looked up.

"I'd rather find out from up there than down here," Antonius answered. "Vitorix, think you can hoist Daxos carefully enough to the first branch?"

"I'm not going to leave the lad down here, am I?"

It was not difficult for Gaius and the others to follow the Germans. The enemy were noisy as they cut through the forest. The difficulty lay in remembering their way back to the others, and avoiding lykoi who could have been anywhere.

The black of their clothes, weapons, and armour kept them hidden in the shadows as they followed the German torches deeper and deeper into the forest.

The Romans were often face to face with their dead brothers' bones as they crawled along, closing in on the enemy. Skulls, the flesh of which had decomposed, lay in irreverent piles atop their accompanying bones. The forest, and the lykoi, had done their work.

Gaius held back the bile that had risen in his mouth as his hand gripped a legionary's rib cage. Then an officer's pelvis, though they were invisible to him in the dark. Death had no regard for rank, all men being dust in the end, especially if they were kept from the Light. Gaius wondered what they would find at the end of this.

"Wait!" Calgacus hissed. They had reached the edge of a vast field from the faint silhouette of the treeline in the distance. "Look," he said and pointed to the centre.

Torches burned around the edges of what looked to be a square enclosure.

"It's a marching camp," Gaius squinted. "Varus must have ordered one built as they went."

"As they ran, you mean," Tertius said, taking in the poor defences and crookedness of the ramparts.

"If lykoi were chasing you, you wouldn't bother with a perfect square," Saguntus answered.

"Shh, both of you!" Gaius listened and above the drunken cheers of Germans, screaming cracked the sky.

"They've got someone," Calgacus said.

"One of ours?" Tertius leaned close.

"Yes," Gaius answered. He knew it in the pit of his stomach. A roar rent the night and chills stabbed at Gaius' bones. "Lykoi," he said.

The screaming of the prisoner intensified, became choked, and was finally cut off before more cheers from the Germans.

"We've got to save those men if we can," Gaius said. "Calgacus, you up to a bit of stealthy scouting?"

"Can I sneak up on a woman?" The Celt smiled and nodded before running into the field, crouching low as he went.

While they waited, there was more screaming and howling from the wood. The wait was intolerable, but soon after, Calgacus returned short of breath, his eyes full of fury.

"I killed two sentries and got close enough to see inside." He spit. "They've got about twenty Romans in a pen and are either feeding them to a big chained lykos, or smashing their skulls on a rock altar at the centre."

"See any banners or officers?" Gaius asked.

"Nothing. All I know is that those Romans won't last the night."

"How many barbarians?" Tertius asked.

"Fifty to sixty. All drunk except for the biggest one."

"Arminius?" Gaius' face lit up fiercely.

"Might be."

"Any more lykoi?" Saguntus asked.

"I only see the one chained near the prisoners."

"Odd. There should be thousands…" Gaius thought a moment. "They're all drunk, you say?"

"They'll be sleeping like babies soon." Calgacus smiled.

"Good. Let's get the others and be back here before it's light. I've got a wakeup to warm the bastards."

When they arrived back at the oak tree, they found one of the horses upon the ground, its stomach ripped open. The others huddled nervously. Beside it was a lykos with two arrows sticking out of its neck.

Gaius looked at the tree and spotted claw marks up and down its trunk. For a moment he feared the worst, but Caelius dropped out of the branches and signalled them to come over, his eyes scanning the forest wildly.

"What happened?" Gaius asked.

Antonius dropped down. "I ordered everyone up into the tree, and not long after, this bastard came wandering out of the woods with another. They howled and changed into lykoi right in front of us." Antonius shuddered. "We killed this one when he set on the horse and grazed the second; he took off into the forest."

"Is Daxos all right?" Gaius watched the boy being lowered by Vitorix and Barna.

"He's burning up, Gaius. His wound might be festering. We need to get him to Castra Vetera on the frontier if his fever doesn't break."

Gaius knelt beside Daxos. He knew how resilient the young Thracian was, but if he did not get better treatment, he was done. The Roman prisoners needed his help too, and if Arminius, their leader, was there…perhaps it could be ended?

"Do we still have the naphtha jars?" Gaius asked Antonius.

"Yes. That horse is still with us. How many do you want?"

"Most of them."

An hour later, they were back at the edge of the field where the marching camp was. It was quiet then, the Germans having drunk themselves into oblivion.

In hushed tones, Gaius explained his plan, as weak as it was. But it was their only option. Dawn was approaching.

"We're going to take the camp back, but first I want to set it on fire. Each of you is going to take a jar of the naphtha and spread it around a portion of the palisades. We want to drive the Germans that we don't burn out of the north gate where we'll light another patch of earth and send them to Hades.

When they come out, as men or lykoi, our two scorpions will be pointed right at them."

"What about Daxos and the horses?" Saguntus asked. "Someone needs to watch over the boy."

"Will you do it?" Gaius asked in return.

"Yes, sir. I'll watch over him."

"Good. Caelius and Tertius, I want you both to man the scorpions as soon as the fire is lit. Understood?"

"Yes, sir," they answered together.

"The rest of us will spread the naphtha and set it alight. If you get close to any German sentries, kill them quietly."

"The odds aren't in our favour on this one," said Tertius.

"When have the odds been in our favour?" Vitorix retorted.

"They're all drunk, so will be slow to rise. That's when we need to hit them," Gaius instructed. "There are about twenty Roman prisoners in there and Varus might be among them. It's our duty to free those men and keep the naphtha away from them."

All the men nodded. They were ready.

Daxos was placed beneath some wolf pelts under a briar to keep him protected until they held the fort. Saguntus drew his sword, lined up a few pila, and took up a position in front of the prostrate boy.

Burn them, kill them, free the prisoners and hold the fort, Gaius tried to stay focussed. *Mithras, help us.*

The men took jars of naphtha, careful not to spill any on themselves and snuck out to their assigned positions in the dark verges about the sleeping Germans.

They emptied the sticky black contents sparingly so that it touched wood and tent, and any Germans who dozed in their own vomit. Several sentries were killed with cold efficiency and the killing zone before the gate was soaked.

All the while, the darkness covered them. As Gaius turned to signal the scorpions to get ready, a warning rent the night on the south side of the camp. Then a whooshing sound could be heard as the naphtha was ignited and the sky lit up with an orange glow.

Screams in the barbarians' tongue came from every quarter and as the first Germans ran out of the gate, they were swarmed by putrid flames that no amount of water or rolling could extinguish.

Several barbarians toppled bits of the palisade, and plunged to the grass below, but most were met by Roman arrows, pila, or gladii.

But it was the fire that did most of the work.

A group of German horsemen charged out through the fire to be met by scorpion bolts that shattered their horses' breastbones or ripped the men from their fur saddles.

Gaius could hear the Roman prisoners yelling now and rushed to where the naphtha was burning away, hoping to get into the camp.

Vitorix, Calgacus, and Sabinus followed him in.

The naphtha had worked fast. Smouldering bodies lay everywhere the fire had spread from one crazed person to the next.

The four Romans moved forward, their scuta before them as they scanned the area. Moans and faint screams could be heard.

"To the right!" Gaius yelled and wheeled as a group of six barbarians charged them. They looked like immortui where their skin had melted.

The pila took care of three of them, and then they engaged

the others, stunning them with their scuta before stabbing.

"Drunken bastards!" Sabinus mocked.

"There must be more," Gaius muttered.

"There!" Vitorix pointed to the central area of the camp. Several spikes had been erected with Romans impaled upon them, the ground beneath a litter of bones from previous kills.

The big lykos stood chained near a massive German and five other warriors, each tattooed with whorls, each breathing heavily, hatred in their eyes.

"Arminius!" Gaius called to the leader. "Traitor!"

The German laughed.

"You've come to the wrong place, Centurion," Arminius answered in Latin. "Long way to come just to die."

"Not to die. Just to take Augustus your head."

Arminius rose to his full height and pointed his battle axe at Gaius and the others.

"Rome's reach does not extend beyond the Danuvius, fool. And it never will. When I cut out your heart, you can pray in your silly cave for all eternity."

"Vitorix," Gaius whispered. "Now!"

The big Gaul broke from the group and wheeled his battle axe so that it scythed into the Germans, killing two but missing Arminius.

The Germans roared defiance. One ran to the prisoners and began stabbing wildly through the bars while Arminius raised his own axe and broke the lykos' chain.

The beast reared up to charge, but Calgacus' pilum was already in flight.

Arminius and his three warriors howled and broke into a run toward the opposite end of the fort, away from Gaius.

"After him!" Gaius yelled.

They raced over the churned ground of mud, blood and

bone, past the wailing prisoners to the south end of the camp where they met Antonius and the others.

"Where are they?" Gaius asked.

"I've never seen men run like that," Antonius said. "They outran our thrown pila."

"Gods!" Gaius looked around. "We almost had him."

Light began to break through the distant clouds.

"We'd better let that lot out," Vitorix said, pointing to the prisoners.

"Yes. Antonius, you, Vitorix, and Sabinus release the prisoners and find out who they are. If they're not mad, arm them. I'm going to get Saguntus and Daxos. The rest of you check the camp for anything useful - weapons, armour, stakes, food, anything. We've got a few hours to fortify this place again."

Within the hour, Gaius had all his men in the fort. Daxos' fever had broken and the boy now slept beside a small fire with Saguntus watching over him.

Of the twenty prisoners, the Germans had caged, thirteen were left, and of those, two were mad. One man immediately ran for the woods, and the other grabbed a German blade from a pile of weapons and plunged it into his gut at the sight of the dead lykos, sputtering that it was not really dead.

According to an optio named Junius, the spokesman for the group, they were all that remained of the three legions. They had watched their comrades being tortured for days.

"The worst was watching those beasts rip 'em apart, sir," Junius said, trying to hide his shaking hands. "They'd just tear men apart and crack their bones in their jaws."

"What about Varus and the rest of the officers?" Gaius asked. "Did Arminius take them as hostages?"

"No, sir. Legate Commander Varus fell on his sword when we saw the lykoi surround us here in the fort. The other officers were the first to be killed by the Germans. That's them over there." Junius pointed to a tangled mess of bones and skulls about a rough rock altar.

Gaius walked over to the bones and wondered if he had known any of the men. *Varus was the lucky one.* Gaius turned to the survivors. "Are you men able to fight again?" he asked.

Some of them looked uncertain, but with all they had seen that was understandable.

"The Emperor sent us to gather proof of what happened, and Arminius' head, if I can get it. We're not leaving until then."

"We'll stay, sir. Of course." Junius looked at his comrades. "But if you have some food on your pack horses, we're all starving, sir."

"We do," Gaius said. "Antonius, see them fed. Sparingly, mind you." He turned back to Junius. "Do you know where the Germans might have a camp in the woods, a village?"

"Oh, we don't have to go finding them, sir. They'll be back. All of them."

THE NEXT HOURS WERE SPENT REFORTIFYING THE CAMP WHERE the survivors of Varus' legions had made their last stand. In that time, five of the thirteen survivors had deserted. Only Junius and seven others remained. Gaius had to threaten the others with execution if they did the same, but he need not have worried. The remainder had nursed their anger and hatred during their imprisonment, and were all near nihilistic.

"Not an ideal lot," Gaius confided to Antonius, "but they'll serve."

"What's your plan, sir.?" Antonius asked. There was fear in his eyes.

"I know it feels like I'm just keeping us here to die, but…well…"

Antonius worried now at Gaius' uncertainty. He had never seen him like that.

Gaius found his thoughts. "Daxos is not strong enough to travel, let alone run. If we leave with the lykoi still out there, we're dead before the next sunrise. We've got a position here that is now somewhat strengthened, better than the damned woods, anyway. And -"

"And?" Antonius still seemed unconvinced. It was the furthest he had ever gone in questioning Gaius. The optio stood there, arms crossed. The others watched from a distance while crows cawed from the pointed tips of sharpened stakes.

"Mithras came to me," Gaius said in a low voice. "You don't have to believe me. I know I sound mad. But I tell you that Mithras has spoken to me, his Heliodromus, and he said that if I can kill the leader, it will all end. How can I not try? How can I not avenge all our dead brothers who watch our every action from the darkness?"

Everyone was silent and, for a moment, Gaius feared there would be a mutiny. He had asked a lot of them. He knew it, knew that every man had his breaking point. The men before him had already *been* broken when he had recruited them. *Speak to them, Gaius,* he told himself.

"I know this seems insane, all of it. I'm terrified of these beasts too. But I'm more terrified of what will happen if they cross the Danuvius unchallenged. What will happen to our wives, daughters, sons, and sweethearts? What will happen to Rome if these beasts run rampant through the sacred streets and into the Temple of Jupiter itself?" Gaius stood on top of a barrel to address them all directly.

"Yes, we might all die today, and never see the light of

Mithras. All I want from you is your oath as Miles that you will fight these beasts and give me just one chance at their leader in the battle. After that, you're free of your vows to the Eagles and the Sun." Gaius pointed to the symbol on a black scutum - the eagle's wings outspread beneath a shining sun.

Vitorix stepped forward, his head down.

Gaius knew that if the big Gaul gave up, the others would too.

"My father always used to say, before he went to battle, that it was a waste of time growing old. 'You can't feed yourself, you can't wipe your ass, and you can't fuck!' Now tell me, Centurion, what in Hades would make me want to grow old? Ha?"

Gaius felt his heart swell with affection for his crass trooper.

"What?" cried Barna. "My grandfather used to say the exact same thing. He was old and full of regrets. Wouldn't stop complaining. I'm with my Gaulish friend here, Centurion."

"My mother used to tell me the same thing," Calgacus laughed, and everyone joined in.

"Then let's get ready for a fight!" Tertius yelled and slammed his sword against his shield as they cheered.

Gaius laughed and smiled until he looked at Daxos leaning on one elbow beside the fire where Mithras himself was whispering in the boy's ear.

"I SHOULD NEVER HAVE BROUGHT YOU ON THIS MISSION, Daxos," Gaius said as the two of them shared a hunk of bread and watched the scorpions being set up on a mound at the centre of the camp. "I'm so sorry."

"I want come, Centurion. I told to come."

Gaius looked askance at the young Thracian. "What did the Lord of Light say to you?" He could not resist asking.

"I cannot say."

Gaius noticed that Daxos looked peaceful, despite his wound and the circumstances in which they found themselves. The boy looked older too, the amulet about his neck no longer a family heirloom that helped him hang onto his father's memory, but a burden he had willingly assumed.

Fear clenched at Gaius' guts and he fought hard to stave it off - fear for himself, fear for Daxos, fear for his wife and daughters so far away in Rome.

"You must kill the leader, Centurion," Daxos said suddenly. "And I will help you."

"I know I must, but I will not allow you to go into the battle with me."

The boy began to protest, but Gaius cut him off.

"I almost got you killed yesterday. I'll not make that mistake again. You'll stay with Caelius and Tertius on the mound and help them to reload the scorpions."

"But I will be too far from you."

Gaius knelt down, looked into the boy's blazing blue eyes, and brushed aside his wild black hair.

"I owe it to your father to keep you safe," he said, touching the medallion about Daxos' neck.

A scream, and a howl burst out in Gaius' mind as he reached out and touched the silver with his hand. He pulled his hand away, stunned a moment.

"You feel it?" Daxos asked, his face serious.

"What was that?"

"This shows how my father hunted lykoi." He pointed to the small image of a necklace about the neck of the man killing an enormous lykos. "Like this, a circle, and then the spear of silver to the heart. I figure it out."

"Why silver? I only took a chance on that for our weapons after you told me about your village buying silver for the hunt. Did you father ever say why silver?"

"No. I think because it is clean, not eaten by the blood of the lykoi. I not sure." Daxos paused a moment. He looked uncertainly at his father's amulet and then removed it. "Please wear this in the battle." The boy held out his father's amulet to Gaius.

"I can't take this. It will protect you."

"I'll be here with the scorpions. Safe…" the last said in a quick breath.

"No, Daxos. Whatever it is, whatever power it has, you should wear it."

The woods rang with laughter and ear-tearing screams just then.

Not since the immortui had slaughtered his men in front of him had Gaius felt such terror.

"Enemy sighted to the south, sir!" Antonius called from his position, followed by Octavius on the west side, and Saguntus on the east.

They were surrounded.

"Battle positions!" Gaius ordered, gaining momentary control of his nerves. "Let's show these bastards how we do things in Rome!"

Gaius pat Daxos on the back, handed him a silver edged gladius, and sent him to the top of the mound where the boy grabbed a handful of bolts to hand to Caelius and Tertius.

Gaius mounted his remaining war horse to have a better view of the area.

Germans crowded from the woods in a thin line on all

sides.

"That's all you've got?" Calgacus called from between two palisade stakes.

A huge German with bear furs on his shoulders emerged from the wood directly facing Gaius and the fort's north gate.

"It's Arminius," Gaius said to Vitorix and Calgacus.

"You said you wanted one go at 'em, sir," Calgacus said. "We'll cut a path to him for your. You'll see. Vitorix," Calgacus laughed. "Pretend there's a barrel of beer and a wench the other side of Arminius and he won't stand in our way!"

"Wait!" Gaius stared beyond Arminius to a tall dark shape beneath the trees. It seemed to him that he recognized the form, those red eyes. The laughter whirled again in Gaius' head and he felt himself frozen, unable to move.

"Centurion!" Vitorix was beside him, slapping his thigh where he sat high on his horse.

The laughter continued and the words, like a child's nightmare, came through Gaius' muddled mind.

Now, you will die, Sun Runner, the voice mocked.

"Centurion!" Daxos voice broke through and Gaius could move again.

"Scorpions. Iacite!"

The twang from Caelius' scorpion sounded loudly in the grey light and brought a howl from two men beside Arminius.

The German chieftain raised his battle axe and howled to the darkening sky where the silver moon floated into view beyond the clouds.

But no charge came.

Instead, the German warriors broke ranks and threw down their weapons.

"What are they doing?" Vitorix asked.

"Ly…lykoi!" Junius stuttered behind them.

"Mithras, help us," Gaius said under his breath. Light the fires!"

Around the palisade, the Romans lit the mixed bunches of twigs and leftover naphtha so that the camp was engulfed in a ring of fire.

At the same time, a tremendous sound of cracking bone rippled along the whole barbarian line. Men hunched over and vomited. They screamed, and clutched at the muddy field as their bodies bulged unnaturally.

To the Romans' horror, the Germans' noses elongated into fang-lined snouts, and their misshapen bodies sprouted grey, black or brown pelts that stood on end as it would for an enraged beast.

"Mithras is with us, brothers!" Gaius yelled as his horse reared and kicked, champing at its bit. "Ready yourselves! Steady! Here they come!"

The lykoi charged and Gaius tried to keep his eye on Arminius, a brown beast of unimaginable size. Howls pierced the young night and the Romans felt as though their ears were bleeding from the sound.

Bow strings and scorpion torsions snapped as the Romans fired at the masses of lykoi that were held at bay for the moment by the flaming palisade.

Gaius knew it would not hold for long.

Two lykoi crashed over the logs blocking the main gate and were met by Calgacus and Vitorix whose axes burrowed quickly into the beasts' chests.

"Hit them before they reach the gate!" Gaius ordered as he saw the lykoi from the east, south, and west swerve to the north side and the gate.

More lykoi broke through and every man was now stuck

into the chaos of battle.

One of Junius' men got trapped in the jaws of a black beast that shook until the man's body was torn in two. Caelius buried a scorpion bolt in the animal which shuddered and died in a heap.

"There are too many!" Antonius yelled as he, Barna, and Sabinus defended the hill where Daxos and the scorpions were.

Soon, Sun Runner. Soon, my wolves will eat your heart before me and your god too, the laughing voice attacked at the flanks of Gaius consciousness, his sanity.

"No!" Gaius launched a pilum which struck a lykos just before it sprang at Vitorix's back.

It was three lykoi to every man, and more massed outside the palisade.

Soon, Gaius! Soon!

Gaius looked down to see Julius' shade looking up at him.

A lykos leapt though the apparition and slammed Gaius from atop his horse. The beast's jaws scrapped and slavered at Gaius' cuirass and he only just had time to plunge his pugio into its chest, then the face.

Up close, to Gaius' horror, the eyes of the beast shivered and changed back to a man's, though the snout, teeth, and body of the lykos remained.

Calgacus pulled Gaius up. "It's now or never, sir! We can plough through them so you can ride down the leader."

All Gaius could hear was men screaming, the lykoi snarling, and the clash of weapons on wolf's teeth.

"Daxos?" Gaius looked to see the boy loading what was left of the bolts while Caelius and Sabinus' black forms stabbed down from their position, over and over at the lapping tide of fangs.

"Gaius!" Antonius yelled from nearby after killing a lykos. "Go now! Before it's too late!"

Gaius launched himself onto his horse, took a scutum from Vitorix and nodded.

Calgacus and Vitorix hefted their scuta and axes and plunged through the fiery gate into the open field.

Gaius charged after their screaming forms into the dark with a river of lykoi pouring in behind him.

Vitorix went down, and Calgacus ran to him, the two men standing back to back as they pushed forward, trying to stay apace with Gaius.

It was the eyes that froze Gaius, red and full of hate and evil. He was as far from the Light then as he had ever been.

The ground shook and when he focussed, Gaius spotted a titanic lykos careening toward him.

"Arminius!" Gaius yelled as he launched his pilum but missed. Before he knew it, his horse's neck was snapping in the jaws of the beast.

As he was spun around, Gaius stared in horror at the one gigantic eye in the middle of the monster's blood-soaked head. When he landed several feet away, his breath had gone out of him. Gaius wondered if death had finally beat him.

But the eye approached, closer, terrifying and bewildering in what it revealed. The eye seemed to reflect the massacre of Varus' legions, the shredding of over fifteen thousand Roman troops. The Germans danced on the bones of Rome, drinking their blood, smashing their skulls, and feeding them to the lykoi who rolled in mountains of bloody offal.

The great jaws opened above Gaius' head.

Fulvia, my girls... Gaius closed his eyes, his arm reaching for his gladius.

"NO!" Daxos' voice cut through the horror.

Gaius opened his eyes to see the boy standing, chest bared, before the gaping jaws of the one-eyed lykos. The eye was as big as Daxos' head. Gaius rolled over, grabbed his gladius and stood beside Daxos as they both stared at the eye and felt the waves of darkness and despair that emanated from it.

But the beast only stared, jaws agape, teeth dripping, as the medallion about Daxos' neck began to glow red from within.

Vitorix, Calgacus, Antonius, and Sabinus arrived to surround the lykos.

"Centurion," Daxos whispered. "Kill it now."

Gaius' gladius stabbed at the massive eye, then the chest of the beast, and when it roared in pain and rage, the four other men plunged pila and gladii into its every side.

All about the field, the raging snarls ceased and were replaced by keening howls. The rest of the lykoi began to run for the trees, away from the burning fort, the Romans, and away from the dissolving body of the great lykos.

As they fled, lykoi half-changed mid-stride back into men so that their vile, deformed shapes scraped and stumbled into the darkness of the forest.

The Romans were stunned, silent. Gaius looked about to see a field of ghostly Romans, thousands of them, watching him, waiting. Among them were a cluster of vexilla and three aquilae where the torn shades of Varus and his commanders stood.

Varus was still, head down, watching the blood pour from his abdomen where he had gutted himself. But the others, men like Gaius, tribunes and centurions, torn to bloody ribbons, all lifted mangled arms to point at the treeline to the north.

Gaius looked to see Arminius and the tall dark form

beside him. He had seen the two of them in Carpathia, but now Gaius strode toward them. He felt heat and light rise up within himself. His scutum and silver-bladed gladius were weightless.

The others followed Gaius, each hungry for vengeance, made all the more eager by the thousands of whispering ghosts at their backs.

"The Eagle and the Sun have vanquished you today," Gaius told them, not twenty feet away.

Arminius spat and was about to run at them when Antonius' pilum caught his side and sent the big German reeling into the undergrowth cursing.

"So you are the one who survived…" the tall form said, red eyes blazing.

"I'll always survive," Gaius answered.

The shape rushed like a black wind-blown cloud, and before Gaius knew it, he was being held three feet off the ground with a cold grip about his neck. Red eyes, white teeth, and a stench of death fluttered about Gaius' senses as the words came.

"You know nothing. You are nothing. You shall not live to see another day, and I shall torment your wife, your daughters, and your very soul for all eternity. You shall know only pain, unimaginable and unbearable, and you will know that the suffering of all you hold dear was because you, and you alone, could not protect them. Die now -"

The voice faltered and the horrible features turned on Daxos whose pugio had sliced at the thing's leg.

"You…" A hand whipped out to rip the medallion from Daxos' neck.

Gaius was flung into his men who had all stood motionless and helpless, until he slammed into them.

"Help, Centurion!" Daxos screamed as he was engulfed in black robes.

"Daxos! No!!!" Gaius leapt for the boy but fell to the bloody ground, a mass of black moths swarming about him as he and the others lost all consciousness.

IT WAS STRANGE, THE WARMTH. IT SHOULD HAVE BEEN COLD, the water frozen, and the greenery dead.

Gaius gazed into the clear spring. The water was still. A black mark ringed his neck and he could see that his hair had turned greyer. *Am I dead?* he wondered as birds chirped and sunlight warmed his back.

"No. You are dreaming, Heliodromus."

Gaius looked up to see Mithras on the other side of the spring.

The god did not smile, this time. All hints of youthful joy and daring were gone.

"What happened, Lord?" Gaius asked, his head bowed.

"The lykoi are scattered for now, but their evil remains."

"Daxos!" Gaius remembered.

Mithras shook his head, his Phrygian cap sagging. "The boy has been taken by the Carpathian."

"Taken? No." Gaius felt his heart tighten. "I was to protect him. I promised him!"

"You failed."

The words wounded. Their truth was painful. Gaius buried his face in his hands and wept.

"Despair will not help the boy, or your family," Mithras said. "He saved you again."

Gaius stopped and looked up.

"The boy knew this might happen."

"How, Lord?"

"I told him."

Gaius remembered seeing Mithras whisper to Daxos. "How can I get him back?" he asked. His vision of Mithras, the spring, the warmth, and light began to waver.

"The Carpathian is of an evil more ancient than I, Heliodromus. He lives far to the east of here, in the very mountains for which he is named."

"Daxos is there? But that's impossible!"

"As are those who turn to wolves, and men who devour other men... You must wake up, Heliodromus. Gather the survivors of your group and continue your journey."

The image began to fade to nothing.

"Don't leave me here, Lord," Gaius pleaded.

"I must." Mithras turned, a smile playing at the corners of his mouth. "And don't forget the boy's amulet."

"What about it?"

"The blood of the first lykos is in it. That is why they would not attack. That is why the Carpathian took Daxos. The boy will be made to suffer for the strength of his people, for the evil blood they spilled...and the secrets they possessed..."

THE TASTE OF IRON WAS WHAT WOKE GAIUS. THE HEAT WAS gone, replaced by bone-chilling cold. He was pressed into the mud of the killing field, the bodies of his men about him. With great effort, Gaius pushed himself up out of the sucking mud, and spat to clear his mouth of blood.

He stood and looked at the pool of black bile where he and the others had killed the great lykos. Scared now, Gaius went to the side of Vitorix who was still clutching his battle axe, and Calgacus beside him. Both men were badly scratched, as were Antonius and Sabinus.

The Gaul moaned and opened his eyes, squinting at the brilliance of the first rays of sunlight that highlighted the slaughter about them.

"Vitorix, get up." Gaius shook him.

"Wha…what happened?"

Gaius did not answer, but went straight to Calgacus who also moaned in pain, as did Antonius and Sabinus.

It took them all several minutes to realize they were not dead. When they finally stood, the carnage made them weep and rage. All about the field, lykoi corpses polluted the ground, many of them half-changed, others wolves that had been slain by the other Romans who had made the ultimate sacrifice.

Barna, Octavius, Tertius, Caelius, Saguntus, Junius and all of his men lay dead upon the field, torn to pieces or leaning against whatever stake or other object they had used for their last stand.

The horses were dead too, torn, their bellies ripped open by the lykoi who had devoured their guts.

"Gaius?" Antonius limped over. "Where's Daxos?" The optio was confused, unsure of what had happened. "I couldn't move, Gaius. I couldn't help him."

"I know," Gaius finally answered. "Daxos is gone," Those burning tears again. "I couldn't save him. It's all my fault." Gaius reached down where something glittered in the mud. He pulled on it and up came Daxos' medallion. He looked at the image and remembered it glowing red with the blood of the first lykos. Gaius cleaned the mud away from the image and tucked it into the scrip at his waist.

"I failed him, Antonius," Gaius said, fighting his despair.

"I've failed my family."

Antonius was silent, confused. He thought of his wife, Vera, the family he wanted to have with her. He watched Gaius stride over to one of the dead lykoi who had half-changed back to a man.

The beast was abhorrent. It had the snout and fangs of a lykos, but the wide open eyes, ears, and torso had reverted to a man's. The eyes suddenly moved and focussed on Gaius, pleaded with the Roman. The body was broken and stinking, but the eyes…the eyes…

"Vitorix!" Gaius called, anger taking hold of him. "Give me your battle axe."

The Gaul walked over and handed Gaius the axe.

As soon as the iron haft was in his palm, Gaius fired out and slammed the heavy blade into the lykos' chest. He hacked and hacked until black blood spread upon the icy mud and the upper half of the lykos separated. Then Gaius whirled on Antonius.

"You are going to take that thing to Rome and lay it at the feet of Augustus himself. Tell him that's what happened to his fucking legions, and that while his men fought to the last, Publius Quinctilius Varus fell on his sword. Tell him!"

All of them stared at Gaius who stood above the bloody corpse, tears running down his cheeks.

"Mithras! Lord of Light! Admit our brothers into your realm that they may walk in the Light as your loyal Miles."

Gaius stepped up to the pyre of palisade stakes, pine needles, and fern, and lit it with a small firebrand dipped in some unburned naphtha.

The fire took and thick smoke fumed around the bodies of Gaius' fallen men, those who had followed him into darkness.

As their remains blackened, and the faces of the brothers he had fought beside faded, Gaius raised his arms to the sun beyond the clouds.

"What am I?" he asked.

"The Light! The Light! The Light!" the living answered.

"Who am I?"

"Mithras! Mithras! Mithras!"

THE HORSE WAS SPOOKED BEYOND IMAGINING. IT HAD tangled itself in the branches of thick forest at the edge of the bogs where it had run to escape the lykoi.

Calgacus had found the animal, cut it free, and pulled it back onto the field.

Tightly wrapped in tent leather, Gaius finished securing the lykos' torso to the back of the animal while the others gathered all of the scuta and weapons that were still functional.

"Take this." Gaius handed Antonius a thick bag of silver. "And this." From out of his satchel, he produced the Emperor's pass that would get Antonius and Sabinus everywhere, and anything.

"But you'll need these," Antonius protested.

"No. I won't."

"You need to return to the fortlet to resupply."

"No time, my friend. I'm going after Daxos. I won't be crossing back over the Danuvius."

Antonius breathed deeply and handed the money to Sabinus to pack.

Gaius held his optio fast by the shoulders. "You must do

this for me, for my family," he insisted. "If the Emperor doesn't hear anything of our mission, our families will be in danger. I need you to take that corpse to Rome and show it to Augustus himself."

"What do I tell him about you when he asks?"

"Don't mention Daxos. But tell the Emperor about all of this." Gaius motioned to the smouldering pyre, and to Varus' fortifications. "Tell him that I've gone after Arminius and the Carpathian."

"He won't believe me, Gaius."

"He will when he sees *that*." Gaius pointed to the wrapped remnants of lykos on the horse's back. He then walked a few paces and stared at the sky to the south. "Tell Fulvia and my girls that I love them and that… I'll see them again. Will you do that for me?"

"Of course," Antonius answered.

"We're ready," Vitorix came up to the two men. "We'd better get moving, sir."

"Yes." Gaius looked over Calgacus and Vitorix. Each had an axe, and a pilum, a scutum, two gladii, and a pugio. Some of the silver spikes remained, and the armour and helmets were intact if not battered. The same weapons remained for Gaius except the axe. He turned to Antonius and Sabinus.

"Go west and you should hit the Danuvius at Castra Vetera in Germania Inferior. Tiberius' legions will be there. Use the imperial pass. Don't show anyone the body. From there, you can head south to Italy. Understood?"

The men nodded.

"I'm counting on you."

"We'll do it, sir." Sabinus saluted.

"Good luck, Centurion." Antonius smiled, saluted, and gripped Gaius' forearm.

Gaius and the others watched as the two men entered the woods.

Antonius turned and waved one last time before disappearing into the darkness.

"Just us now," Gaius said to Vitorix and Calgacus.

The Gaul and the Briton smiled.

"We're with you to the end, sir." Calgacus said.

"Let's go get our lad back," Vitorix added. "And while we're at it, I've got an axe for that Carpathian bastard."

Gaius felt his neck where it was blackened by the evil grip. Laughter rang again in his ears, but also the weeping of a young voice.

The centurion put his black helmet on his head, hoisted his scutum and satchel, and nodded to his brothers.

"Let's go." *Mithras watch over us.*

They set off at a jog, away from the slaughter of that field, toward the south-east and distant Carpathia. Behind them, the shades of fallen Romans lingered, still weeping and tearing at their ghostly flesh. The dead mouthed words of vengeance and destruction that were lost on the howling winds of that dark forest.

WEEKS LATER, TWO SOLDIERS DRESSED IN BLACK ROLLED INTO Rome with a wagon carrying a mysterious trunk. It was locked and ringed with iron strips. Dogs cowered when their wagon passed, and flies swarmed in its wake. Whenever troops would try to halt the wagon's passage, the soldiers would show the Emperor's pass and they would be let through.

Now they stood in the Emperor's throne room on the Palatine Hill, flanking their fetid cargo.

Augustus and Livia stood before them with the young Germanicus and Claudius nearby.

"How dare you come to your Emperor in such a state!" Livia hissed at the two men.

"Forgive me, sire. Our orders were to come directly to you from Germania."

"Germania?" Augustus asked.

"Did Tiberius send you?" Livia asked.

"No, my Empress." Antonius bowed his head, unsure. "We were sent by Centurion Gaius Justus Vitalis."

"A mere centurion!" Livia began, but Augustus stopped her.

"Leave us," he said flatly.

"But -"

"Now!" The Emperor's voice echoed in the vast marble room.

Livia pursed her lips and swept out in a rustle of silk, with Germanicus and Claudius in her wake.

"Guards!" Augustus called. "Bring Legate Maximus in here now." Augustus stood staring at the box, Antonius and Sabinus, until the clink of chains came through the door.

The guards brought Maximus in with shackles fastened to his hands and ankles.

"Commander?" Antonius said, and saluted.

"He is *not* your commander," Augustus pronounced. "I called him here to witness the stories your centurion told when he was here."

Antonius stepped forward, a glance at the pale reflection of his former Legate beside them. "Sire," he began. "Centurion Vitalis spoke true. We discovered what happened to your legions."

"What? Tell me now!" Augustus sprang forward, more agile than he had been in a long while.

"They were massacred by Arminius and the lykoi…"

Antonius went on to relate all they had seen, the dead remnants of three legions. He told of their pursuit of the lykoi, the battle, the Carpathian, and Gaius' pursuit. Everything.

"Impossible," the Emperor stated. "Men do not change to wolves. It is a legend to frighten children."

"Sire, may I?" Antonius knelt in front of the chest he had purchased with Augustus' silver, and unlocked it.

A stench unlike anything else, fouler than the aftermath of any battlefield, poured out of the box and one of the guards holding Maximus' chains vomited.

Antonius held his breath and uncovered the lykos corpse.

The Emperor reached in and pulled the head up to reveal the fangs, the snout, and the human eyes and shoulders.

"Gods help us…"

On a snowy windswept mountain peak far to the north, three warriors covered in black pelts looked down from their eyrie onto the valley of the river Tisia.

Their swords were freshly bloodied after a fight with Iazyges tribesmen whose bodies they left for the mountain carrion birds. Their target lay ahead, beyond the lands of the Dacians.

As they began their descent into the river valley, Mithras, their Lord of Light, smiled with pride at their determination.

"Keep running, Heliodromus," the god said.

I'm coming, Daxos, Gaius thought as he led the way. *I'm coming…*

PART III

THANATOS

M

esopotamia, 6000 B.C.

The blood moon was high and full above the dry desert plains, north of the land of two rivers. Its light, like the leaching of sacrifice, poured over sand, and rock, and life, to swallow up and fill every crack and crevice.

It was the night of the great slaughter, the time before the Light.

The sacred cattle herds of the Yazads roamed unknowingly beneath the choked stars, their lowing calm and ignorant of what was about to happen.

Behind a boulder crouched an Usij, one of the false priests who served the Daevas, those wicked and uncaring gods whom Usiji were bound to serve, to feed, and to cower to in the darkness of the long nights.

This priest, however, had never cowered, and he spat upon his brethren of the blackened cloth. Instead, he watched the silhouette of his offering in the middle of the plain, an unthinkable mound of chopped limbs and offal, of faeces and decay.

The Daevas would never be able to resist it, the Usij knew. They would gather and gorge themselves until the rising of the Sun, escaping before the Yazad came upon them with fire and the crush of his god-made weapon.

The Usij smiled as he turned his own weapons over in his hand, those sacred relics stolen from the temple at the top of the world. He had almost perished in getting them, his very soul burnt to the fringes.

But I survived, he thought, gazing at the ancient blade

carved from a stone out of the stars themselves. In his other hand, he held the unbreakable chains, forged at the creation of the world. They were heavy, but the Dark gave him strength and speed. *After tonight, I shall live to torment them eternally.* He smiled a moment, imagining what it would be like to devour their essence. He had stolen the incantations that would allow him to do so.

There was a murmur in the earth beneath him, a throbbing, hungry chant in the bowels of the Underworld.

The Usij crouched, and watched the gory feast he had laid out.

They had come.

The nervous cattle bellowed loudly, the earth shook, and a sound of cracking rock rent the air, leaving enormous gaps to be flooded with the blood moon's light.

The Daevas came down from the mountains, and from out of the rocks. They climbed out of the ground itself, their enormous, clawed hands digging in to pull themselves up.

At first, the curving horns of their heads appeared, then the pointed features. The Daevas' forked tongues licked at the air and the stench that drew them away from the cattle. Their green, black, and brown skins were red in the moonlight. They groaned and slavered, taking great strides toward the offering, making horrible sniffing sounds.

The Usij watched the Daevas of both sexes come forth, their fangs glistening as they ate.

A great crunching of bones could be heard as they devoured the bait. Blood spattered their legs and arms, chests and breasts until they were dripping with gore.

Some of the Daevas coupled on the slick ground, roaring and groaning as they entered each other. At their centre, a female with horns like an ox, and a quick strong body sucked on a long piece of intestine, savaging any others who dared to approach her. Her own bloody hands rubbed between her legs, and her enormous eyes gazed up at the moon.

She's the one... the Usij told himself. He crouched low and held his hands over the pitch-soaked torch, leaning against the rocks, and saying the word, *Tanunapat*, it burst into flame. He picked it up, and stood.

I am death.

With three long strides, the Usij hurled the firebrand at the gathered Daevas. It landed on the great circle of pitch he had surrounded the offering with.

Immediately, a wall of fire exploded in a great circle to trap the Daevas who screamed, and raged, and shook the earth with their fear of fire. Voices that sounded like coarse stone grinding on stone cried out. Some of the Daevas peered through the flames, searching for the culprit.

The Usij stepped out from his hiding place and laughed.

The female Daeva at the centre looked at him amid the panic, and pointed a long, clawed finger at the false priest.

"Usij!" she said, her red eyes fixed on him.

The Usij spat. "I am no longer your Usij," he said as a growing wind whipped his long black hair about his handsome face. "I am Death!"

The Daevas roared with rage, and a moment later, two of them were hurled out of the ring of fire by their fellows to land with a rumble on the rock and sand.

They charged.

And the Usij ran at them.

When the three clashed, a cry of divine pain rushed over the land like a sandstorm.

As the dust settled, the larger group of Daevas looked to see the Usij standing above the bodies of the slain Daevas, their blood pooling like liquid fire about his feet, dripping from the ancient weapon he held in his right hand, and the heavy chain in his left.

The big female Daeva cried out, but the Usij smiled and knelt down to cup a handful of the blood.

"Anazvara…Panipatra…Rakta…" he chanted before drinking.

The Usij closed his eyes and felt the divine fire flow through his veins.

It should have killed him, but he had discovered the words. He had unearthed the ancient spells that would allow him to take their essence.

"Ahh!" the Usij cried out as the power engulfed his person. His muscles bulged, and he became taller and more powerful than any other mortal. Mighty horns curled out from the side of his head, and he screamed and crouched as if to pounce on prey. His red eyes, peering out from the thick locks of his streaming hair, locked onto the female Daeva who roared defiance and challenge.

The Usij smiled, and fangs erupted from his mouth in excitement.

Then, it happened. That moment the rest of the world waits for.

Far to the East, light cracked over the horizon. With it came a sound of pure song, a heavenly humming that made the Daevas cover their ears and double over.

As the first rays of sun swept over the land of the two rivers, there was a great inhalation, and then a massive exhalation of sound as something landed between the Usij and the Daevas.

The shockwaves, as if a titanic stone had crashed out of the sky into the sandy seas, extinguished the fires and threw the Daevas and Usij back a distance. Dust choked the dawn, and the Daevas began fleeing.

"Yazad!" they cried, running, fleeing the brilliance of the god that had landed in their midst.

The Lord of Light shone among the wicked detritus, turning many away with his brilliance. He breathed calmly, his auburn hair falling over his shoulders from beneath his cap, his white tunic and doe skin boots were soft upon the land.

Mithras of the wide pastures, of the myriad eyes, the lofty and everlasting ruler of the provinces of men and gods, Mithras, the holy Lord of Light, had come upon the scene, a gold and adamant spear was in his hand, and a matching dagger in his belt.

"Leave now, uncaring gods of the night!" he commanded.

Some of the Daevas laughed and hurtled toward him, but the spear of light shredded their bodies before they had gone three steps.

"Mithras!" the Usij called, emerging from the dust, fearful that all his scheming and pain would be for naught. "Leave!"

"Leave?" Mithras laughed, feeling pity for the false priest. "You should beg for my help, Usij, for you have doomed yourself for eternity."

The female Daeva approached them, and the triad of enemies faced each other on the plain. She roared at the god and levelled her horns.

Mithras shook his head, and levelled his spear.

The Usij thrust out his hands and a chorus of tortured screams erupted from the sacred herd of cattle to the South as they all burst into flame.

"No!" Mithras cried as he watched.

The Usij ran then, the links of his mighty chain flying

through the air to wrap about the female Daeva who crashed to the dirt.

"Vismarana!" the Usij said as he pounced upon her. *Oblivion...*

Mithras spun, his spear seeking their dual deaths for all they had wrought, but they had vanished from the light of day. The spear struck deep into the earth where it took root and sprouted into a tree of golden apples.

The Lord of Light stood there watching the sacred herd burn to death, and knew that their cries would haunt him, as would the cries of others in the coming ages, after that dark night.

3

THANATOS

Rome, A.D. 9

Sunlight angled into the top room of a tenement on the Aventine Hill on a cool December day. Dust motes danced in the rays of light, giving an appearance of being beneath the surface of a dirty, sun-lit sea.

The apartment was a simple one of wood and plaster, with inexpensive curtains hung carefully as room dividers. On the bed at the far end of the room, Antonius slept beside his wife, Vera, who curled up beside him, trying to stay close even as he tossed and turned.

Sweat beaded on the Roman optio's forehead, and he shook for the nightmares that continued to haunt him – mountains like fangs, screaming, jaundiced eyes, and snapping jaws that tore men apart. Howls and dark laughter wrapped him in anguish as men morphed into lykoi who turned their gore-covered snouts up to bay at a full red moon.

The forest trees leaned in on him, their limbs reaching until Antonius saw three figures dangling from the dark branches, three bearded men hanging from lengths of their own intestines.

Antonius turned to vomit on the bone-strewn earth. Then he felt something brush his head and whipped to see the man in the centre.

Antonius... he said. *Help...* The eyes opened and the man choked on blood, his eyes wide and full of shock as he reached out.

Antonius looked closer, and fear seized him, so much that he felt like weeping.

"G...Gai... Gaius? No!!!"

VERA SHRIEKED WHEN HER EYES OPENED AND SHE SAW HER husband crouched in a corner before the black armour bearing an eagle and sun on the chest.

Antonius was holding out his silver-bladed gladius, but his limbs shook so much she thought he was consumed with the falling sickness.

"Antonius? Husband?" she cried. "Please, my love. You're home... You...are...home," she sobbed.

Antonius shook his head, and his eyes awoke to register the bed and his crying wife staring at him with horror and fear. He dropped the blade with a clang, and fell to the floor.

"I'm sorry..." he mumbled. "I'm so sorry... Mithras forgive me..."

Vera, having regained her wits, grabbed a blanket and went to cover his shaking, scarred body. "I'm here, my husband." She stroked his wet brow until his shaking stopped. "You're safe."

LATER THAT DAY, ANTONIUS AND VERA SAT AT THE SMALL table in their apartment, two bowls of bean soup laid out.

Antonius' was untouched. He stared into the bowl of steaming food, lost in dark thoughts.

"What was the dream about this time?" she asked, though the answer terrified her.

He clenched and unclenched his fists as they lay on the stained, wooden table, but he continued to stare at his food.

"I'm stronger than you think I am," she said, her eyes trying to lock onto his.

He could tell she was scared, but could also see she was indeed digging deep for her courage. The truth was that he was terrified himself.

"I saw Gaius, Calgacus, and Vitorix… They were hanging from trees in a wood."

"Were there wolves?" Vera asked. She had begged Antonius to tell her what he had seen when he returned from Germania.

Antonius had wanted to remain silent, but the need to speak to someone about the horrors he had witnessed had been too great.

"I could hear the wolves, yes. But they were not an immediate danger." He shook his head, trying to dismiss the image of Gaius' choked and pleading face. "Gaius needs help."

"But…but you don't even know where he is," Vera said.

"No, I don't."

"You can't leave me. You promised."

"I can't keep that promise, Vera. It was made in terror of what I had been through. I need to help my brothers."

"You need to stay with me, with us." Vera stroked her flat tummy.

"You don't even know if you're with child yet."

"I am. I can feel it. Don't you want your child to have a father?" Vera's freckled face was growing redder, sad and despairing.

"Vera… What if it was me out there beyond the frontier, in the forests of Germania? Wouldn't you want Gaius to try and help me?"

"Yes, but-"

"And what about his family?"

Vera hung her head, a little ashamed at the answer she had almost spoken. *To Hades with anyone else!*

"Not even a thousand lykoi would keep me from returning to you, my love."

"But what if Gaius and the others are perfectly fine and manage to get back to Rome without you?"

"I have to try. By Mithras, they're my brothers-in-arms!"

"And I am your wife!" she said, finally catching his eyes. "I'm…I'm afraid you'll forget me."

Antonius' face softened. "I could never forget you…you are my life, Vera."

She smiled, but sadly.

"I would be a man of honour, worthy of you and our unborn children. That's why I must go. I couldn't live with myself otherwise."

She nodded, fighting any tears that threatened to fall.

"Well, at least stay until Saturnalia is over. This is our first together."

"Yes. Of course. I need to prepare anyway."

Antonius realized he had finally made up his mind to go after Gaius and the others. It surprised him. Before, he had convinced himself he did not need to, that Gaius would have told him to stay in Rome and live his life with Vera.

"Here," Vera said, sliding a piece of folded cloth toward Antonius. "Happy Saturnalia." She was going to wait, but now everything had an air of urgency.

Antonius smiled, and unfolded the cloth to reveal a thick copper bracelet engraved with rough-looking suns and stars.

"It's beautiful," he said, sliding it over his left hand to admire. "Thank you, my love."

"Do you really like it?"

"Yes. I love it." Antonius smiled. It meant more to him than any armilla or torc the legions had awarded him. "Oh!" He jumped, scaring her a little. "I have something for you!" Antonius went to his armour and lifted the black cuirass to reveal a small wooden box. He took the box and rushed back to her. "Here."

Vera admired the box and looked excitedly at him before opening it. "Oh-"

Inside, her fingers reached for a silver chain which she lifted out to reveal a red intaglio with a goddess upon it.

"It's Juno," he said. "She will keep you safe while I'm away."

Vera's smile faded slightly, but returned. "Can you put it on me?"

Antonius got up, took the necklace and dropped it around her neck to fasten it at the back, his fingers stroking her pale neck.

"Happy Saturnalia, Vera," he whispered in her ear.

Vera looked up, her eyes wet with tears, pulled him down, and kissed him.

The two of them embraced tightly, their breathing desperate and worried as he carried her back to the bed.

"We'll be late for dinner with Fulvia," Vera muttered.

"We must live for each other, my love. There's time," Antonius said, as he removed the last of his clothing and fell on top of her.

Vera pulled him in and held her husband tightly, a swift prayer of protection to Juno for her family-to-be.

THAT SAME MORNING, IN THE JUSTUS DOMUS, DAWN BROKE into the peristyle courtyard of a silent home. Birds flitted in the garden, and a few dried leaves scraped across the mosaic floor with the new winter breeze.

Usually, the slaves, Ludo, Pugio, Nisica, and Calista were already awake, carrying out their daily duties for the familia. But, it was Saturnalia, and the slaves had been given the day off, as was tradition. So, the domus was quiet as they all slept soundly into the morning.

Fulvia Justa was the only one awake. She lay in the morning sunlight that pooled on the bed of her cubiculum on the upper floor of the domus. Curled into the crook of each of her arms lay her daughters, Aemilia and Faustina, their little chests rising and falling quietly as they slept against their mother.

Fulvia stroked their hair and closed her eyes as the sunlight warmed her skin.

"I miss you, Gaius..." she whispered.

For weeks, she had not heard anything from Gaius, nothing since Antonius had come to give her the news that he was still in the wilds of Germania, pursuing the enemy who had brought Rome to her knees, and who had abducted the boy, Daxos, who had saved Gaius' life.

Fulvia blamed herself for having let Daxos go after Gaius. Now, they were both missing. Every night the thought tortured her, the feelings of helplessness so frustrating that it was a constant struggle to keep her composure and carry on with the vital rituals of daily life that maintained a degree of normalcy in her family's life.

Gaius had been gone for many months at war in the past, but this time it felt different.

This time there was something at play in the shadowed corners of her mind and imagination. Fulvia hoped that her prayers and offerings were taken favourably by the Gods, Jupiter, Juno, Minerva, and Mars. She even offered to Mithras, even though she was unsure whether the soldiers' god would hear her.

Night was the worst, not because she missed the warm touch of her husband's body against hers desperately, but because every time she tried to sleep, her mind was harassed by images of blood and death, of dark forests where the Gods held no sway.

There was also the presence that pursued her in her dreams, a dark, smooth, sonorous threat that sought to wrap itself about her, and whispered what it would do to her, her husband, and her children.

Fulvia rubbed her face, and got out from under the warmth of the bed covers to look out at the sun's rays across the tiled rooftops of the Caelian Hill. The world spun as she tried to rouse herself. She was exhausted, and the girls would not be easy to wake either, for they too had been plagued by nightmares, though of what, they would not say.

She nudged Aemilia and Faustina, and kissed them on the cheeks. "Wake up, my girls."

Aemilia, the older of the two, opened her eyes first. "Is it morning, Mama?"

"Yes, love. It is."

"Happy Saturnalia," Faustina mumbled as she too rolled over to throw an arm onto her sister.

"Happy Saturnalia." Fulvia smiled.

"Are we making the breakfast, Mama?"

"Yes. If you'll help me."

"Do we have to?" Faustina groaned, pulling the covers back over her head.

"Yes, my girl. We must honour the day, and…" Fulvia felt her throat tighten. "…and go about things as if your father were here with us."

Fulvia felt small arms wrap around her waist and looked down to see Aemilia's big eyes looking up at her.

"We'll help, Mama. Won't we, sister?" She looked over her shoulder at the bed.

"Yes. Yes, Mama. We'll help," came Faustina's muffled voice from beneath the covers.

"Then let's get dressed and give the members of our familia a wonderful day," Fulvia said as the two girls went to the wash basin and splashed their faces.

The triclinium had been decorated with thick green garlands, and a warm brazier crackled in a corner of the room.

On the couches sat Pugio and Nisica, who were always drawn to each other, and Calista and Ludo. They waited and sipped watered wine during that one time of year when they were allowed to do nothing at all. They were quiet, however, ill at ease with the prospect of their mistress working so hard when she was obviously not well.

The slaves had noticed the dark circles beneath Fulvia's eyes, but they said nothing.

"It's not right," Ludo said as he sat stiffly on the couch. "We should be doing this."

Pugio stopped feeding grapes to Nisica, and Calista put down her cup. They watched Ludo, the steward, rub his bald head.

"The mistress needs us to make things easy on her," Ludo continued. "The master's lost in the wilds of Germania with young Daxos, and we? We sit here being served by the woman who needs us most!"

"Perhaps I should go help," Nisica began to rise.

"Wait," Pugio pulled her back down. "It's tradition. We can't just do away with that."

"What rubbish!" Ludo said, getting redder by the minute. "Why not?"

"Because we must stay strong, and because you have all been of much help over the last year."

The four slaves whipped round to see Fulvia standing in the doorway with a tray laden with fresh bread, cheeses, and honey. Aemilia followed with a bowl of boiled eggs, and Faustina with some spiced apple slices.

"Forgive me, mistress," Ludo said. "I misspoke."

Fulvia smiled as she approached the table, and laid the platter down before the couches with the girls following suit.

Samian ware had been set out for them to use, but none of the slaves made a move to eat.

"Please... Eat," Fulvia said. "It may not be as good as yours, Calista, but I do hope you enjoy."

"Thank you, mistress," Pugio said as he reached for the steaming bread.

"Mistress," said Nisica, Fulvia's body slave. "We don't mind working, honest. Can't we do something today?"

"I appreciate the sentiment, but really, no." Fulvia smiled. "Besides, you will be working for the dinner tonight, no?"

"Of course, mistress!" Ludo blurted. "We wouldn't think of-"

"Well then, it's settled." Fulvia cut him off. "Enjoy your breakfast, and I'll return later with the girls to tidy up and give you all your gifts."

"Oh, mistress, no," Ludo protested.

"Ludo!" Faustina crossed her arms and scowled at the slave. "It's tradition." She wagged a finger at him, and the others smiled. Faustina broke into giggles then, unable to remain serious for long.

They all laughed as Fulvia shuffled the girls out of the triclinium.

When their mistress was gone, Ludo spoke. "Tonight, I want everything perfect for them."

They all nodded and set about eating, laughing, and presenting each other with small tokens the like of which they could afford.

IN THE KITCHEN, FULVIA TIDIED UP WITH THE GIRLS.

It was warm, the heat from the oven fire having been kindled some time before. Fulvia felt the sweat trickling down her temples, and along her spine beneath her tunic.

The girls found working in the kitchen to be a real novelty as they pushed the rubbish into a pile

"All right now, piglets," Fulvia said. "Time to wash up. Then, we'll give them their gifts."

"Piglets!" Faustina protested, with flour on her cheeks and a bit of eggshell stuck in her hair.

Aemelia giggled when she looked at her mother.

What would I do without them? Fulvia thought as she looked at the girls and smiled, despite herself.

"Mama?" Aemilia said.

"Yes, dear?"

"What about our presents?" She looked at the floor quickly and back up. "Do we have anything?"

Fulvia knelt down and took both the squirming girls in her arms. "I think that if you go to your room, you may find some very interesting items on your beds."

The girls began to run, but Fulvia stopped them. "Ah! Ah! First, clean yourselves up." She pointed to a basin of fresh water near the kitchen door.

Fulvia laughed as the girls jostled and splashed each other and raced to the upper level to their room. The squeals made Fulvia smile, a rare enough occurrence of late.

Recently, all joys were quickly extinguished by the fact that Gaius was not there, or Daxos.

Saturnalia was always more fun with her husband there to chase the girls about, bedecked in an ivy crown, and kissing Fulvia every time he passed.

As Fulvia climbed the stairs, she decided that she would ask Antonius to go after Gaius. She had to, no matter the guilt she felt.

Ludo, Calista, Nisica, and Pugio were all pleased with the gifts they received from their mistress – a new tunic, a simple stola, a necklace, and a dagger. Indeed, they were more expensive than the usual, but Fulvia felt that while Gaius was away, they had more than earned their place in the familia.

The four servants went down to the Forum Romanum to purchase what was needed for the meal that night, and to socialize with their friends among the arcades and tabernae lining the thoroughfares.

With the main doors barred, Fulvia reclined on the couch in her bedroom while the girls paraded about in their new tunics and stolas, one in orange, and the other in blue. The bronze mirrors the girls had also received were of much use to them as they paused to admire themselves. Glints of sunlight spotted the ceiling and painted the plaster as the mirrors reflected and the girls danced.

The light lulled Fulvia. She searched her mind for a happy image of Gaius, laughing or singing, playing with the girls or swimming in the sea, but each happy memory dissolved into blood and screaming in her mind.

She shut her eyes tight.

When she felt the girls snuggle up to her, she allowed herself to sleep, the long night having finally caught up with her.

"Mistress? Mistress?"

Fulvia felt a gentle nudge and opened her eyes slowly to see Nisica's freckled face looking at her.

"What is it?" Fulvia said.

"The hour is late, mistress. The optio and his wife have just arrived."

Fulvia sat up quickly, realizing she must have slept for hours.

"Do not worry, mistress," Nisica reassured. "The meal is prepared and ready. Calista has really outdone herself."

"Oh?" Fulvia was relieved. "Girls? Wake up." She nudged Aemilia and Faustina.

"I can prepare them, mistress. Let me help you first." Nisica smiled and put a hand on Fulvia's arm. "I think the red stola for tonight?"

Fulvia nodded. "Yes. That'll do fine," she said as she got up from the bed.

AS FULVIA DESCENDED THE STAIRS TO THE MAIN FLOOR, SHE felt as though she were stepping into a dream.

Orange light suffused the courtyard and peristylium from, it seemed, a hundred burning lamps. She thought that perhaps every single lamp in the domus had been brought out, every brazier lit.

Ludo stood at the bottom of the stairs wearing his new tunic and holding a tray with a silver goblet out to Fulvia.

"Mistress," he said, lowering his head and offering the cup.

"Thank you, Ludo," Fulvia replied, gasping as she took the warm cup in her hands.

"Warm wine, mistress. To drive the chill away."

"What's that delightful aroma?"

Ludo smiled. "Calista has prepared an Etruscan boar in plum sauce. If I do say, she has made every effort tonight."

Fulvia smiled. Ludo always was sparing with his praise.

"I'm sure it is a feast fit for the emperor."

"There she is!"

Out of the triclinium door came Vera, followed by Antonius. They both held their own cups of wine, and it seemed that Vera was already feeling the effects of it, a gentle red blooming upon her fair cheeks.

"Io Saturnalia!" Fulvia said as she raised her cup.

"Io Saturnalia!" Vera and Antonius replied, and they all tipped a bit of wine onto the ground before drinking.

"I'm sorry to have kept you both waiting," Fulvia said, trying to rally her joy. "I've not been sleeping well and-"

"Nor have I," Antonius interrupted. "I mean...I understand."

He does look troubled, Fulvia thought as she drank more wine, enjoying the warm relief it brought. She turned to Vera.

"The children were up early preparing breakfast for the servants."

"Of course. Today is the day! You must be exhausted?" Vera tried to sympathize, but it felt stunted. Her husband stood beside her, and Fulvia's was far away.

Fulvia began to feel her hand shake. "Forgive me," she said as she leaned on the wall.

"Perhaps we should sit?" Vera said, helping Fulvia into the triclinium to the head couch.

The room was warm and the low, central table filled with breads and fruits, salads, dates stuffed with peppered cheese, dormice, and other delicacies which did not usually grace their table.

"How have you both been?" Fulvia asked, regaining her composure.

Antonius and Vera looked at each other, and then to their hostess.

"Well enough," Antonius answered. "The nights are long."

"Yes, they are." Fulvia stared into her cup.

"Where are the children?" Vera asked.

Fulvia saw her stroke her stomach and smiled, willing herself to be happy for them.

"Here we are!" Faustina said as she danced into the room in a flurry of orange to greet their guests.

"Happy Saturnalia, little ones!" Vera laughed.

"Io Saturnalia," Aemilia answered, much more sedately, her eyes on Antonius as he sat there when her father did not.

"Let's eat!" Fulvia clapped her hands. "Calista will be very hurt indeed if we do not enjoy her hard work. Ludo?" she called.

"Yes, mistress?" Ludo said from the doorway.

"Please make sure you and the others also enjoy the meal."

"Thank you, mistress," Ludo said. "We shall set up in the atrium."

Fulvia nodded and began to join the others in filling her plate from the table.

An hour later, after everyone had eaten their fill of the magnificent meal, Fulvia lay back on her couch wishing the wine would work its way to her head more quickly than was the case. Her sober thoughts persisted in keeping the merriment from her mind.

She watched Vera play finger wars with Faustina, who seemed to be the only one not minding the gathering.

Antonius spoke only occasionally of what was happening in Rome, his in-laws butchering business, and the weather.

Fulvia felt for her guests and regretted putting them through the ordeal of eating with her, but she was more worried about Aemilia who sat sullen and quiet at a time of year when she was always a bright, joyous light among the ranks of their familia.

Aemilia stared most of the time at Antonius, her eyes on the verge of tears. Even the bit of watered wine Fulvia had allowed her did not seem to cheer or relax the young girl.

The servants' laughter echoed from the atrium where they seemed to be enjoying the occasion.

Fulvia and Antonius looked at each other a moment, and then back to their cups.

"Why are you here?" Aemilia suddenly said to Antonius, her large glassy, brown eyes accusing, her lips trembling ever-so-slightly.

"Aemilia!" Fulvia said. "Antonius, forgive my daughter. She misses her father, and I'm afraid it has put a damper on the festivities." She turned to Aemilia. "They are here because we invited them. Because they are our friends."

"Friends? What kind of friend leaves another friend in Germania, and does not go after him?"

"Stop it!" Fulvia took her daughter's arm roughly, but Antonius spoke.

"Please, Fulvia. She's right." Antonius looked Aemilia in the eyes, though it tore at his heart to do so. "What kind of friend am I? I've been asking myself that very thing since I left your father in Germania."

Vera suddenly stopped smiling, and Faustina sat with her mother.

"Your father is my best friend, my centurion, the Sun Runner of our order. How can I sit here, safe in Rome with all of you while he is out there in the darkness?"

Fulvia closed her eyes and felt Faustina whimper against her chest.

"Please stop," Vera muttered, but Antonius continued.

"I'll tell you how. I'm afraid, Aemilia, more afraid than I've ever been in all my life."

Aemilia stared at the mosaic floor then, realizing what she had done, the pain she had caused guests beneath their roof. Her mother had often spoken of 'guest-kindness'.

"But," Antonius went on, "it is only when fear is at its most intense that true bravery is possible."

Vera buried her face in her hands as Antonius sat up. Her husband reached out to stroke her thick red curls, his hand so tender as he touched her.

"I've decided," Antonius said, his hands balled into tight fists as they came away from his wife's hair. "I'm going after Gaius."

"No!" Vera shrieked, and the laughter outside ceased. "He has two other warriors with him!"

Fulvia felt guilt wash over her then, for willing one woman to be separated from her husband so that she might have hers back, but also for the fact that her seven-year-old daughter had had the courage to speak up for Gaius when she had hesitated.

"Shh, Vera. Please," Antonius soothed. "I must, or else I could never live with myself."

"But you are my husband. Mine..." she pleaded.

Fulvia stood with her cup raised. "The Gods will honour you for this, Antonius." She felt a tear run down her cheek as she stared across the table.

Antonius looked down when he felt Aemilia's arms wrap themselves about his waist, her little body sobbing in gratitude. He looked at Fulvia and raised his cup in a shaking hand.

"May Mithras guide me to Gaius so that we may both return home."

"And back into the Light," Fulvia answered.

THREE DAYS AFTER SATURNALIA, ANTONIUS STOOD IN THE doorway of his and Vera's home.

As she finished wrapping food for him, and packing it in another satchel, Antonius looked about the domus that he hoped to see again, that he hoped to share with his wife and their unborn child.

The sunlight angled in through the windows, and a breeze ruffled the curtains, but the soft sound could not muffle Vera's weeping.

"I'll be back. And then, I'm never leaving again," he said.

"Please don't promise if you can't keep it," she answered. "My heart is breaking, and you're doing it." She held out the satchel.

Antonius put it down and took her hands. "I love you, Vera. I never thought the Gods would bless me with that, but they have. And I won't throw it away. I won't throw our life away."

She kissed him, her tears running over their lips.

"Please tell me you understand why I must go," he pleaded, knowing he could not leave her like that.

She nodded. "I do, but…I don't want you to go. I can't live without you. We can't." She stroked her stomach.

"And I can't live without you. When I'm back, and Augustus keeps his word, we can go anywhere in the Empire you wish."

"And if you don't come back?"

The question hung between them, sharp, threatening, terrifying.

"I will. One way, or another, I'll come back to you…both

of you." He knelt down and kissed her stomach. "I'll be back," he whispered.

Vera held his head close to her chest, trying to memorize the moment.

After a few silent seconds, Antonius stood and hoisted his satchels. Once more, he wore the black armour and silver-edged weapons bearing the eagle and the sun.

He kissed Vera a last time, and stepped outside into the winter light.

"I love you," he said, before going down the stairs to the two horses he had tethered in the communal courtyard.

Vera watched him go, and when he was out of sight, she lay down to cry herself to sleep.

ANTONIUS RODE IN SILENCE DOWN THE VIA APPIA TOWARD Albanum. Rome soon disappeared from view behind him.

The Mithraeum would be his first stop.

I don't even know where I should be going, he thought. *This will take months.*

He had pored over maps of the lands north of the Danuvius, trying to figure out where Gaius and the others might be, but it seemed impossible. On foot in the mountains, and crossing enemy territory all the way to the Carpathians, he knew they could be anywhere.

If they're alive.

Toward the end of the day, Antonius arrived at the cave in the hill overlooking Albanum. It was quiet but for a few ravens squawking in the naked trees below. Wind howled about the mouth of the cave, and Antonius peered into the darkness.

Not long ago, they had all been there together, the survivors.

A great sadness threatened to overwhelm Antonius then, but he focussed, thought of Gaius and the others, and stopped his shaking hands to tie the horses to a nearby log, and get out his flint box.

The torches they had left inside the entrance were still soaking in their oil buckets. He removed one, and struck the flint until it sparked enough to ignite the torch.

Orange light spread about him and reached into the empty cave.

Antonius removed the saddlebags with his food and Augustus' imperial pass, and went inside.

It seemed that no one had used the cave since they had last been there. Not surprising since all troops and fresh levies had been sent to the front with Tiberius.

As Antonius went down the central aisle to the altar, his eyes fixed on the image of the Tauroctony, and he froze.

Mithras' image was youthful, confident, and brilliant, his arms pulling back the neck of the bull of evil and ignorance, his light overcoming the dark.

Antonius lit another torch, and he put the one he held in a bracket. Then, he fell forward to lean upon the blood-stained altar.

"Mithras, Lord of Light… I am going into the Dark now, alone. I don't know where to go, which path will lead me to the Heliodromus. Please guide me, oh heavenly lord," he whispered. "Show me the way that I may help Gaius defeat the evil that has claimed the lives of so many of our brothers."

The wind howled loudly then, outside in the failing light, and Antonius could hear the jingle of horse harness as they shuffled nervously. The torches seemed to burn brighter in that moment, and Antonius felt himself grow warm and light-headed. He then heard the sound of the sea, the crying of gulls, and the creak of ship's rigging, despite the fact he was nowhere near a harbour.

Brundisium... the thought came to him.

"That's it!" he suddenly said. "I'll retrace the way to the safehouse, north of Aquileia."

"Then what?"

Antonius whipped around, his gladius unsheathed quickly as he turned to face the newcomer.

"Bout fucking time, I say!" The man stepped into the cave from the darkness outside. He held a gladius and a sharpening stone which he dragged along the blade as he approached.

"Sabinus?" Antonius peered at the soldier who was also wearing the black armour of the Eagle and the Sun.

"Antonius. How come you left Rome without me?" Sabinus said, sitting down on one of the stone couches of the Mithraeum. "We're brothers. Or have you forgotten?"

"I haven't. I just didn't want you to feel obligated-"

"Obligated?" Sabinus said loudly. "I think we're beyond obligated."

"Quite, my friend." Antonius smiled sadly.

"In fact," Sabinus went on, "this life has dragged on long enough. I'm coming with you to help the Heliodromus."

"I'm happy for the company," Antonius said, grasping Sabinus' forearm. "How did you find me?"

"I couldn't stop thinking about Gaius and the others still being out there. I finally decided we should go after them, and went to your home to say as much to you. Only, when I got there, I found your wife in tears. She told me you had already left. I guessed which way you had gone." He crossed his arms. "Seems I was right."

"Praise Mithras, brother."

"Yes. Praise him." Sabinus sighed. "So, where to then? We retrace our steps from Brundisium to the safehouse. Then what? How're we going to find them?"

"I think we should head for Aquileia again, and cut north-east into Carpathia."

"You think they're there? It's a big place."

"I don't know, Sabinus. What I do know is that Daxos is trapped there. If we arrive before Gaius, maybe we can find out where the boy is, if he's alive."

"If…"

"Do you have another plan?"

"No. Yours is fine. Mithras will light our way."

"He will. We can sleep here tonight and head to Brundisium tomorrow. With any luck, Captain Pylos will be there with news, and take us onboard."

They trusted their god to watch over them that night, and slept fitfully upon the stone couches within the sacred speleum, in shadow and covered by their black cloaks.

Antonius fell asleep to the sound of Sabinus' incessant sharpening of his gladius, a habit he had developed after their battle with the immortui in the very lands to which they were returning.

Still, he thought. *Perhaps it's better than my shaking hands…*

He closed his eyes, gripping the pommels of his gladius and pugio, and thought of Vera.

Mithras, please make it so that I return to my wife and child…

. . .

When Antonius and Sabinus arrived at Brundisium, they saw that the sea was thrashing like a great beast in the harbour.

"Look for Pylos' black ship," Antonius said to Sabinus. "I'm going to find Vulcan's Bastard and see if he has more supplies for us."

Antonius left Sabinus to look for the ship, while he walked along the harbour to the warehouse where the smith Gaius had commissioned for their special equipment was located. He entered.

Slowly, the sound of hammering stopped, and when his eyes had adjusted, Antonius could see the blackened faces of several smiths staring at him.

"What are you doing here?" the booming voice of Vulcan's Bastard broke through the silence, the hammering beginning once again.

Antonius strode up to the man who appraised the wear on the armour he had made.

"Looks like you boys found a fight."

"We did. And I'm going back in," Antonius answered. "Do you have any new creations for us?"

"Hmm. Come with me." Vulcan's Bastard beckoned him over to the door that led onto the palaestra. In a corner of the large packed dirt room where they had previously tested their weapons, the smith pulled back a large canvas sail to reveal a stash of arms and armour.

There were new sets of leather cuirasses, pteruges, and boots, bows with silver-tipped arrows, and javelins in extra-large quivers. Pila were also lined along the wall, as well as some smaller, round shields similar to those used by gladiators in the arena, except these had a protruding silver spike in the middle of the boss.

"I've made a few extras for you."

"I see that," Antonius said, walking over to inspect the equipment.

"Antonius!" Sabinus' voice echoed off of the palaestra walls. "I've found Pylos! He'll take us for triple the previous price."

"He's right to," Vulcan's Bastard said as he watched Sabinus arrive. "You're sailing in a right whore-of-a-storm."

"We've got no choice," Antonius said. "Our brothers are out there."

"How many of you are here now?" the smith asked.

"Just us two."

Vulcan's Bastard stared blankly at them. He remembered the large group of toughened veterans who had showed up at his workshop and armed themselves to the teeth.

"Our centurion and three more are alive," Antonius said.

"Well, in that case, take what you need. I'll be in the forge working. But I'm not making more until I know how many more of you are alive. My time's precious too!"

Antonius walked up to the man and looked him in the soot-encircled eyes. "You don't need to make anything else."

The smith nodded, and turned to leave them alone.

"Told you I don't like him," Sabinus muttered after the hulking man had gone.

THEY SPENT THE NIGHT ON CAPTAIN PYLOS' SHIP, AND ONCE the sun was up in the sky, they set sail for Aquileia in the North.

It was one of the worst sea voyages either man had ever experienced.

As Sabinus puked over the side of the rolling ship, Antonius gripped onto the centre mast, his thoughts focussing on the uses of the new equipment they had received. Thinking of war and battle always helped him to focus. Immortui and lykoi were one thing, but a storm-tossed sea was something else.

When, a day later, they arrived in the lagoons outside of Aquileia, Antonius and Sabinus longed for their horses and the solid ground beneath their feet once more.

"Stay alive, lads!" Captain Pylos called from the deck as they rode away, leading their skittish horses north out of town.

"Nothing! No one's been here!" Sabinus cursed as the two of them explored the safehouse north of Aquileia.

"It's not surprising, is it?" Antonius said. "We've got the imperial pass. Gaius, Calgacus, and Vitorix would not have been allowed back across the Danuvius, let alone been able to travel all the way south to Aquileia."

"We should never have split up."

"Augustus needed proof."

"Fuck Augustus!" Sabinus kicked a dirty bucket across the courtyard of the deserted safehouse, the old mile castle Gaius had been granted by the emperor for their secret operations into Germania.

Antonius rubbed his temples. "We have to take only what we absolutely need," he said, ignoring Sabinus' outburst, mostly because he agreed. "Good thing I had the keys to this place."

Sabinus said nothing. He sat on an overturned crate, and began sharpening his gladius. After a few moments, calm again, he spoke.

"Where do we go from here?" He pointed the sword at Antonius' satchel. "You have a map in there too, I hope."

"Yes." Antonius opened one of the leather bags, pulled out a folded hide map, and laid it out on another crate. "If we head for Emona, and then turn east, we can travel through Pannonia to the fortress of Viminacium near the confluence of the Danuvius and Tisia rivers."

"Why there?" Sabinus stared at the map.

"I don't want to end up behind our brothers in enemy territory, but more importantly, I think the enemy will be heading for Dacia."

Sabinus looked up and shook his head, his stone moving even more swiftly along his blade.

"Who wants to live forever anyway?" he laughed.

Antonius was deadly serious. "I do."

Sabinus stopped sharpening. "You remember fighting those Dacian bastards in the campaign, right?"

"Yes."

"Seven-foot-tall whoresons with thick mangy beards, bad teeth, and those bloody curved blades they swing? You remember?"

"Yes. I remember…too well." Antonius folded up the map.

"Plus they smell like an unwashed whore's ass hole!"

"Then hold your nose, Sabinus."

"I will!" he began sharpening again.

"I told you, you didn't have to come," Antonius said.

Sabinus' grey eyes turned on him. "Of course I'm coming. Wouldn't miss it, especially since I've got nothing else to live for except getting yours and Gaius' sorry asses back to your wives, and also helping that little boy."

"Daxos."

"Weren't for him, that bleedin' cyclops lykos would have gnashed our bones back in Germania. So yes! I'm coming."

Though he did not say so, Antonius was relieved. Going into Dacia alone was one thing. Going into Dacia among the Carpathian Mountains with immortui and lykoi lurking in the shadows was quite another.

"We'd better get some rest then," Antonius said, slapping Sabinus on the shoulder and going to bar the castle gates. "We've got a long journey ahead!"

Once more, the sharpening resumed.

DACIA – A.D. 10

THE SNOW FELL SOFTLY FROM THE SKY – GREAT, BROAD, intricate flakes falling like feathers from the heavens, covering the fields and foothills from the lands of the Iazyges along the River Tisia, to the jagged peaks of the Carpathian Mountains in the distance.

It was quiet, unnaturally so. The falling snow seemed to suck the sound out of the world. It was difficult to hear or see anything, but it was also easy to remain concealed.

Gaius Justus Vitalis stood stone-still behind a snow-covered hedge, a thick layer of white covering his black armour, woolen cloak, and wolf pelts.

He felt the ice fused to his beard and the strands of his hair, but he had grown used to this, as he had to all the aspects of his animal existence over the last several weeks journeying from Germania to Dacia.

Gaius' eyes watched carefully as a column of Dacian soldiers marched in single file through the deep snow. They held two prisoners whom they dragged in iron collars and chains. Gaius strained to see who they were, but they were hidden by their torn garments and the shuffling amble with which they moved.

It's not Daxos... he told himself.

Ever since the Carpathian lord had taken Daxos with his dark magic in Germania, during their battle with the lykoi, Gaius had searched every band of barbarians for the captive boy, torturing and killing numerous enemy warriors without getting any nearer to discovering the boys' fate.

Still, he had to take down these enemies so that he could continue toward those accursed mountains. He just needed to wait for the signal.

"Oi!"

There it is! Gaius watched, his hand on the shafts of two pila, as the bulky figures of Vitorix and Calgacus stepped out in front of the Dacians. They looked like bears, thick, grizzled, and covered in pelts. Except they held double-edged battle axes.

"Dacii?" Calgacus asked the group.

Their leader came forward, his hand gripping a phalax, the two-handed scythe-like weapon favoured by the Dacians. The man mumbled something in his barbarian tongue, and Calgacus turned to Vitorix.

"Dacians," he confirmed for the big Gaul.

A second later his pugio was sticking out of the leader's throat, spraying the surrounding snow with blood.

Gaius leapt out of hiding and launched one pilum into the first man at the back, sending him face first into the snow, hands reaching for the spear shaft embedded between his shoulder blades. Gaius' second pilum found the side of the man holding the chained prisoners who fell with their captor.

Before Gaius could free them, two of the Dacians ran at him while the other six were surrounding Calgacus and Vitorix.

Gaius drew his gladius and spun into one of the Dacians, slicing him across the shoulder and sending him toppling into the other.

Bloody cries of the others came from where Vitorix had speared two with one thrust and was hacking at the other four whom Calgacus was barely holding off.

Then the man on the ground who had been holding the prisoners' chains began to scream as blood choked his barbarian cries.

Gaius began to run toward them but stopped when he saw the prisoners clawing at the man's face and guts, their faces burrowing into him. As their hoods fell back, he saw the mottled, broken skin, and his heart skipped a few beats.

"Immortui!!!" he yelled, just as the Dacian behind slammed into him, sending Gaius toppling toward the crazed, hungry, jaundiced eyes that still haunted his nightmares.

One of the immortui lunged at him, but he rolled away in the bloody snow, trying to gain his feet.

"Gaius!" Calgacus yelled as he tossed a long phalax through the air.

Gaius caught it, and scythed the blade through the fiend's neck as it bore down on him. As he stood, the shaft of a pilum cut in front of him to knock the last Dacian off his feet before his blade had reached Gaius' chest.

Gaius looked up to see Calgacus and Vitorix standing several feet away, their hands gripping their gladii as they stared at the other immortui who continued to feed on the body of one of the Dacians.

The Briton and the Gaul fought to control their shaking limbs and panicked hearts.

"I thought they were all dead back in Carpathia?" Calgacus said.

The three of them surrounded the feasting beast, staying out of the spreading pool of blood and gore which melted the snow about it.

"Fucking Dacians!" Vitorix kicked the body of one of the men he had killed.

The fiend's eyes turned on him then, and it lurched to its feet.

Just as it did so, Gaius' blade cut it down where it fell hissing, its arms working after Vitorix, despite the fact that it was now missing the lower part of its body. It took three more swings of the phalax before it would stop moving.

Gaius turned and vomited.

"First lykoi, and now these bastards?" Calgacus cursed. "How many more do you suppose the Dacians have?"

Gaius finished wiping his mouth, and spoke. "I don't know. The Carpathian must be breeding more."

"Sooner we find the bastard and kill him, the better." Vitorix spat toward the distant mountains.

Gaius agreed. The longer the Carpathian was alive, the worse things would get. They needed to intensify the hunt, he knew, but he had to wonder if the Carpathian could even be killed.

Mithras, help us.

"We have to move. This blood will attract others, including lykoi," Gaius said. "Gather the weapons and clean them carefully. Don't take any that have immortui blood on them." Gaius tossed away the phalax he held, and picked up another. "These are good for fending off immortui. Calgacus, check the Dacians' satchels for any food."

"Will do."

"There's some smoke in the distance!" Victorix was pointing to the south-east.

"Maybe we can find out something about the Carpathian?" Calgacus suggested as he removed a loaf of hard, black bread from one of the leather satchels.

"Ask the enemy where he is? You hit your head?" Vitorix said.

"It's worth a try," Gaius conceded. "Besides, it may be that not everyone is happy about the beasts that are roaming the borders of their villages." Gaius hoisted his satchel, scutum, and bow. "Let's go. Stick to the trees."

The three men dashed off through the snow, leaving the gory scene behind for the crows.

Once again, that evil laughter harassed the edges of Gaius' consciousness as he went.

I'm coming, Daxos...

IT WAS DARK BY THE TIME THEY REACHED THE VILLAGE outskirts. A silvery crescent of moon hung quietly in a black sky, its light pouring over the snow-covered fields and hills about the village where but a few lights burned in the windows of squat, rectangular homes.

A wolf howled in the hills, and some of the village dogs raised a cry for a few minutes before quieting down.

With their scuta stowed once more behind a couple of trees at the edge of the wood, Gaius, Vitorix, and Calgacus edged their way forward until they stopped on a small rise where they hid behind a log pile to observe the town.

"It's quiet," Calgacus whispered.

"I'll bet there's some warm stew in one of those homes," Vitorix said, a yearning look on his face.

"Shh," Gaius hissed, though the thought of warm food did give him pause. "We're here for information about the Carpathian. Not to pick a fight."

"We can't just stroll into a Dacian village, knock on someone's door, and ask for directions," Vitorix said.

"No, but maybe we don't have to." Calgacus pointed to what looked like a well, located in the main street.

Around the well were two dark shadows that had come across the snow from one of the lit dwellings. The large one, a man from the sound of his barking voice, was dragging the second by the hem of the person's clothing.

There was a high-pitched curse in a girl's voice, and then the sound of a loud smack, followed by the smaller person falling to the ground beside the well.

The three men watched for a moment as the man paused, laughing, to piss on the prostrate girl before going back inside, leaving her lying in the snow.

Gaius felt his anger rising, but held himself back a minute to ensure no one else came out.

"Let's go get her," he said. "But try not to scare her too much."

"Why would she talk to us?" Vitorix asked.

"I don't think she's Dacian," Gaius said. "Their women are very strong and have decent status. Nobody would treat a Dacian woman like that in her own village."

"Might be she's a bad one in need of discipline," Calgacus said.

"Or maybe a slave who hates her master?" Gaius guessed. "Either way, let's get closer."

The three men sprinted across the snowy ground until they came to two large posts topped with carved wolf heads that marked the entrance to the village.

Gaius scanned the street to see if anyone was around, and then dashed toward the girl.

She was young, perhaps fifteen, with dark hair. A welt had begun to form on her cheek where the Dacian hit her, and her hair was wet with urine.

Calgacus and Vitorix stood behind Gaius, peering through the darkness, their double-headed battle axes at the ready.

With the edge of his fur cloak, Gaius wiped the girl's face and forehead.

She groaned and then her blue eyes shot wide.

"It's all right," Gaius said, his hands up. "We won't hurt you."

The girl backed away until she was caught against the well. Her eyes went from Gaius, to Calgacus, to Vitorix quickly, scanning for an escape.

"Please," Gaius soothed, gesturing that they meant no harm.

She bolted.

Vitorix lunged for her, but the girl's fist slammed into his groin, sending the big Gaul to his knees.

Calgacus ran her down in six strides, and picked her up, his gloved hand closing over her mouth.

The girl flailed madly, but Calgacus held her firm until she stopped, her eyes on Gaius as he stood before her.

"Dacii?" he asked, pointing at her.

She spat and shook her head.

Gaius realized her traits looked a little familiar. "Ise apo Thraki?" he asked, taking a wild guess that she might be Thracian, taken from the settlements to the South.

Her eyes fixed on him.

He continued when he saw her interest. "Imaste Romanikoi," he told her.

She was obviously wary of Romans too, but she did scan the street immediately, her finger to her mouth.

"What's she trying to say?" Calgacus asked as she pointed to a storage building nearby.

"I think she wants us to come with her," Gaius said.

"Don't trust her," Vitorix said, his breath short, his voice pained as he rubbed his groin. "She'll try and trick us."

Gaius stared at the girl, saw her shiver as the cold began to set in.

Then the girl pointed at the house the Dacian had gone into, and spat, her lip trembling.

"We can trust her," Gaius finally said, nodding to her that they would follow.

The girl began to run, and the three of them followed. They came to a two-storey, wooden structure, and she disappeared inside.

"Maybe this isn't a good idea," Calgacus said.

Then the girl poked her head out and they followed her in.

Vitorix and Calgacus checked for anyone else among the barrels, sacks, and bales of hay, but they were the only ones there.

"What are you doing here?" Gaius asked the girl as he sat opposite her. "Are you a slave?"

She nodded, but held her head high.

Definitely Thracian, Gaius thought, seeing her bearing. "I am Gaius," he said, pointing at himself, and then the others. "Vitorix. Calgacus."

"Talia," she said softly, placing her hand upon her chest.

Gaius nodded. "Good." He smiled, and went on in Thracian Greek. "Talia, we are looking for someone. We could use your help."

Another wolf howled outside the village.

"Who you look for?" she asked.

Gaius took a deep breath, hoped she would know of this.

"The Carpathian Lord – O Carpathos."

The girl jumped and backed away, terror in her eyes which had been rebellious only moments before. "Ohi! Ohi!" she said, over and over. "No! No!"

"Please," Gaius said, motioning for her to be quiet. "We need to find him."

"She's not going to help us," Vitorix said. "Knock her out and let's be on our way."

Gaius shot the Gaul an angry look. He knew Vitorix's pride was more hurt than anything, but he worried what he might do. The last few months had seen them all lose much of the civility that separated them from the animals they had fought and killed along the way.

As Gaius eyed Talia, he realized she reminded him of his daughters, and of Daxos, oddly enough. If it had not been for that, perhaps he would have knocked her out and bound her as Vitorix suggested.

"No. She'll come with us," Gaius said to Calgacus and Vitorix, before turning to the girl. "We'll get you home if you help us, Talia. Home."

The girl's eyes glossed over, and she looked much younger then. Tears breached her eyelids, and she wiped them away angrily. "Oli necri…" she said.

"What?" Calgacus asked.

"She says they're all dead," Gaius translated.

"Who?" Vitorix leaned forward.

"Pios?"

"I icogenia mou. Oli necri."

"Her whole family," Gaius translated.

"Just like poor Daxos," Vitorix said, his head down.

"Daxos?" the girl whispered softly, her eyes on Vitorix.

Gaius and Calgacus looked at each other as the girl approached Vitorix.

"Daxos?"

"What about Daxos?" Gaius asked his hand reaching out for the girl's arm, harder than he meant.

"I have a cousin named Daxos," the girl said. "Athanatoi killed him, my village…"

"What'd she say, Gaius?" Calgacus asked.

Gaius felt his hands shake and a sudden hope kindle in his gut. *Mithras, thank you for leading us to her.*

"I think…by Mithras… I think she is Daxos' cousin."

"What?" Calgacus said a little too loudly.

"They do look alike," Vitorix mused, smiling at Talia for the first time as she stared back at each of them.

Gaius cleared his throat which had suddenly gone dry. He leaned toward Talia and fished the medallion with the image of Daxos' father and others encircling and hunting the chief lykoi.

The girl's eyes were full of disbelief.

"Daxos," Gaius said quickly. "Then ine necros. Daxos is alive, Talia. Alive!"

She closed her eyes and fell to her knees, reaching for the medallion about Gaius' neck. "O thios mou!" she pointed to Daxos' father on the medallion, her uncle.

Gaius nodded.

"Pou ine, o Daxos?" she asked, hoping the Roman before her could say where her cousin was.

Gaius shook his head. "O Carpathos… He has taken

Daxos prisoner. That is why we need to find him. To save Daxos."

The girl stood up and stepped back to look at them again.

Gaius thought a determination came into her eyes then.

"I help," she said. "Take me to Daxos."

"Do you know where the Carpathian is?" Gaius asked her. He could see Vitorix and Calgacus were frustrated that they could not understand what was being said.

Talia shook her head. She did not know. "But my master," she spat. "He know."

Gaius stood and explained to the others.

Vitorix stood and hefted his battle axe. "Then let's go ask the bastard," he said darkly.

THE WOODEN DOOR OF THE RECTANGULAR DWELLING CREAKED open and Talia turned to close it gently with a last glance at the night outside.

The red glow from the hearth clawed toward her across the dirty floor boards where mice nibbled at bits of food which had fallen to the floor from her drunken captor's overturned platter.

He was in his usual spot, a low frame bed before the fire, a leather flask tipped from his loose hand. He always went for her after he woke from this state, and she hated him for it.

She thought about killing him then, knew how easy it would be.

Daxos... The thought held her hand back as she gripped the handle of a rusty dagger stinking of onions.

The reek of his sweat reached her nostrils and she wanted to retch, but there was little time. The village hunters would be out soon, she knew.

Talia slapped him hard across the face, and jumped back, the dagger pointed at him.

The Dacian sat up quickly, his drunken eyes rolling a couple of times before he focussed on the girl.

"I'll kill you for that, little bitch!" He stepped forward, but Talia's hand lashed out and cut him across his bare chest. "Arr!"

"Where is…the Carpathian lord?" she asked in her broken Dacian.

"Ha! You want a new master? Hmm? I'm much kinder than him!" He made a move around the table, but she sped to the other side.

Talia's heart beat quickly, but she needed him to tell her. "Tell me where!" she said. "I'm going to kill him!"

"Hahaha!" he laughed. "Kill him? He can't be killed, stupid girl!" The Dacian licked his lips, trying to anticipate the girl's moves. "I'll tell you! It won't do you any good though, because after this, I'm going to fuck you until you're dead!"

"Where is he?" Talia said, fighting with all her might to hold her blade steady, not to cry for the fear she felt.

"He's in the Jagged Mountains, east of Sarmizegethusa."

"Have you been there?"

"No more questions, little Thracian bitch. Now you die!"

He leapt over the table with surprising agility and his fist sent her backward to crash onto the bed by the fire. He was on her then, and she was screaming.

There was a loud splintering of wood, heavy footsteps, and then his weight was ripped off of her.

Talia turned, feeling the blood pour from her cracked lip. She saw Vitorix with his knee on the Dacian's back, his fists hammering his head into the floor.

Calgacus stood beside, his battle axe poised over the Dacian.

"Stamata!" she yelled feebly.

Gaius was beside her, his fatherly hands helping her to her feet. "Ise kala?" he asked if she was all right.

"She nodded. "Xero pou ine o Carpathos."

"Where?" he asked.

"East of Sarmizegethusa…in the pointed mountains."

Gaius looked to Vitorix and Calgacus, and nodded. "We've got it," he said.

Talia took up her rusty blade and turned to the Dacian whom Vitorix and Calgacus had hauled to his feet.

The man grunted as his shoulder joints were near to breaking from their hold on him. He laughed though as Talia approached.

"These men will fuck you too," he said. "You'll see."

Talia hesitated a moment, looking from the fur-cloaked and armoured forms of Vitorix, Calgacus, and then to Gaius behind her.

She looked Gaius in the eyes a few moments, and saw the father there, the husband, the friend. But not a tormentor. She turned back to the Dacian and saw Vitorix's slight nod to her.

"Not all men are animals," she said, and a second later, her dagger plunged deep into his groin.

The Dacian screamed, his eyes incredulous.

"Shut him up!" Gaius said.

Vitorix took the man by the head and twisted so that his face looked backward with an audible crack.

The two Celts let the body slump to the floor and Talia spat upon it. She had no tears. Only relief as she began hurrying to gather bread, cheese, and dried meat into a satchel. Then, she tied her worn boots on, and wrapped a frayed wool cloak over her shoulders.

"Hey! There's stew over the fire!" Vitorix said, dipping a ladle in and tasting it. "It's good."

"What's the hurry, girl?" Calgacus asked, and Gaius translated.

"We must leave…quickly!" she answered.

"Why?" Gaius asked. "Night is not over for a while."

"They are coming!" she said urgently.

"Who, Talia? Pios?"

She stopped, ready to go, her eyes fixed on all of them. "Lykoi."

THE THREE MEN AND THE GIRL POWERED HARD UP THE SNOWY slopes of the mountain a short while later, running as quickly as they could. Each struggled in the deepening powder, but the fury of the howls at their backs harried them on.

Once they had retrieved their scuta from the edge of the forest, they had turned south-east and run for their lives.

Gaius did not know how many lykoi there were; he did not care to find out. They needed to preserve their arms, especially if they were to meet more lykoi and immortui on the way.

Talia kept up with the men, her will to be free again encouraging her legs and muscles. She had seen the Dacian lykoi tear enemies apart.

No matter how quickly they ran, no matter how steep the ground they covered, the howling and snarls of the lykoi came closer and closer.

"We can't run until they nip at our heels!" Vitorix yelled. "Let's stop and face them!"

"I agree," Calgacus said. "We can't go all the way to the Jagged Mountains like this."

Gaius stopped with Talia beside him, and looked around. "Up in the tree," he said to the girl.

She shook her head, remembering the trees she had hid in when the immortui had slaughtered her village, or when the village lykoi had torn apart some of the Iazyges.

"Talia, please! We'll be fine." Gaius cupped his hands for her and she stepped up to be flung to a high branch of oak which she caught easily and swung herself up. Gaius turned to Vitorix and Calgacus. "Spread out so we don't get flanked. Reverse chevron formation. We can fall back to this tree if we need to and back uphill, keeping the high ground."

"They're faster than us, Gaius," Calgacus said.

"Mithras is with us. The day is almost here," Gaius answered.

"They're coming!" Vitorix called as he spotted the charging, bristling fur backs. "I count six!"

"Three more!" Talia yelled from her perch where she pointed to the far left near Calgacus.

"Bows ready!" Gaius yelled, and the strain of bowstrings stretched in the moonlit wood.

The howls and the approaching eyes made Talia want to shut her eyes, but she could not. Her worry for her liberators forced her to watch.

Please don't take more people away from me... she prayed to the gods she had long since believed to have abandoned her.

The lykoi charged straight at them, three to each man.

The first flight of arrows struck home, and the lykoi stumbled, their teeth gnashing as the silver arrowheads burrowed into their chests or shoulders.

The men drew their second arrows back and loosed quickly, but only Calgacus' found its mark.

Gaius tossed his bow down, and took up his pilum which caught one Lykos in the throat as it bore down on him. He jumped aside to avoid being hit, then lunged for his scutum, but it was knocked from his grip by a third lykos.

Gaius edged away as quickly as he could while the jaws snapped at him, his hand seeking his gladius.

Talia's screams echoed in the trees, and strained grunts and curses from Vitorix reached Gaius' ears.

As Gaius caught a glimpse of Calgacus running by, the lykos attacking yelped and Gaius' blade freed itself from the sheath before he promptly drove it into the beast's skull.

The red eyes shot wide and then faded, and Gaius' silver blade hissed and smoked as he pried it loose from the skull.

Shaking his head, Gaius clambered to his feet and leapt to help the others whose battle axes were swinging in and out at the last two lykoi. He pulled a pugio from his belt and struck the rump of one who reached back to snap at him as Vitorix's axe slammed into its neck, pulling the haft from the Gaul's hands.

The three men surrounded the last lykos, their gladii biting into it on every side. The beast would not fall, but got angrier and angrier.

Then Gaius fell forward, tripped by a snow-covered root. As he fell, the medallion fell from beneath his cloak to dangle before the lykos.

The beast paused and recoiled a moment, its head low to the ground before the image of the great lykos on the medallion.

A moment later, the head tumbled onto the ground in a pool of steaming blood.

Vitorix stood above the carcass, panting, and spat on it. "Fucking wolves!"

Calgacus was bent over, taking deep breaths, and Gaius turned to the woods about them, his eyes scanning the darkness of the treed slopes. He looked up at Talia.

The girl stared at the scene below, but there was no fear in her eyes. Rather, she gazed upon Gaius and the others with a sense of hope mixed with sated anger.

Strong girl, Gaius thought as he motioned for her to come down.

"Talia, help us gather the weapons, arrows, daggers, everything."

She nodded and set about it, her onion knife poised as she approached each corpse.

"We need to find shelter to rest," Gaius said to the others.

Vitorix and Calgacus nodded.

"I hope there aren't too many more of these bastards," the big Gaul said.

"Don't get your hopes up," Calgacus said as he wiped his blade on one of the wolves' pelts.

"I think I saw a cave mouth up the mountain," Talia said to Gaius as she came up to them and dropped several arrows, a pugio, and a pilum on the ground at their feet.

"A cave?" Gaius asked.

She nodded.

"What?" Vitorix and Calgacus said.

"Mithras is guiding us," Gaius answered.

IT WAS WARM WHERE GAIUS LAY. HE HAD NOT FELT SO comfortable and soothed by sleep in a long while. His heartbeat was slow and sure, and his mind sunned itself in happy memories.

The armour no longer encased his muscled and scarred body. He lay naked on soft furs and silks from the far East.

Fulvia... he said his wife's name to the darkness.

Yes, my love? I'm here.

Gaius felt a stirring beside him, the warmth of another. Then a soft, lithesome hand ran from his hair, down over his face, along the length of his rising and falling chest to caress his groin.

My love... he moaned as his wife's touch became more urgent.

She rose up on her knees and straddled him, slid him up inside of her.

The heat opened his eyes wide as he gazed at her blue eyes, hidden like jewels among the smooth strands of her dark hair. His hand reached for her breasts, and she moaned and slid on him, back and forth.

Gaius' gripped her buttocks, pulled her to him urgently.

Her mouth opened to utter the pleasure she felt, and their eyes locked.

Gaius?

Fulvia... he answered. Faster and faster…

Help, Gaius!

His wife's face contorted, and violent pain replaced pleasure.

Fulvia!

Gaius! Please help!

Fulvia! Gaius screamed as dark hands gripped his wife's shoulders, her neck, her hair, her stomach.

She was wrenched from him, but squirmed as someone else, something, accosted her from behind.

NO! Gaius jumped to his feet, naked and exposed, to help her, but every time he stood he was lashed to the ground by fiery strands that scorched him even as he watched his wife weep for the pain she endured.

Then the crying echoed in his head…his children's terrified voices.

Baba! Help! Come home!

Gaius thrashed, but to no avail.

Then the laughter started, taunting, harrowing, and horrible.

Sun Runner, it mocked. *Your family…all you love…is mine to abuse. They will endure pain equalled only by what I will do to you.*

The laughter.

Mithras…help me… Gaius pleaded weakly. *The Light!*

A flash of brilliant sunlight exploded in the darkness, its heavenly resonance drowning out the wicked laughter and the cries of his family.

GAIUS MOANED WHERE HE LAY, FACE-DOWN ON A BED OF SOFT green moss beside a brook that gurgled playfully.

Birdsong roused him, and he turned over to see a tiny finch looking at him. Gaius knelt and found he was clothed, but in a white tunic and breeches.

"What?" He looked up to see Mithras sitting on a fallen log on the other side of the brook.

The god sat still, staring at Gaius, his eyes filled with care and compassion, and pity.

"He is trying to break you, Heliodromus," Mithras said.

Gaius sat up, his head bowed to his god. "My wife and children, are they…safe?"

Mithras looked at the ground and back to Gaius. "No. They are in danger. That is the truth."

Gaius felt a great urge to weep then, to quit his quest and run home to his family.

"Be strong, Heliodromus," Mithras said. "The Light must overcome."

"But my wife, Lord, my children…"

"They need you…the boy needs you. They need you to fight on, deep into the Darkness so that the Light can penetrate and cleanse."

"But how?" Gaius said. "I'm so…tired." Gaius felt like falling over, and swayed on his knees in the golden sunlight of the mountain wood.

Then he felt the warm, reassuring hands of his god hold him steady and raise him up.

Familiar warmth swept through Gaius, and strength flooded through him, his mind, his body, and his spirit.

Mithras smiled.

"I am with you, Heliodromus. I am with all of my Miles who walk in the dark."

"How do we find him?" Gaius asked.

"Follow the girl. She will lead you to the boy."

"Daxos?"

Mithras nodded. "He is in pain, but it shall be infinitely more if you do not get to him."

"We are only three warriors and a girl, Lord."

"No. You are not alone," Mithras said with a mysterious certainty. "But you must press on across the mountains."

"My men are tired."

"As I have before, I shall give them strength in their limbs and in their hearts to go on, to fight. But it must be you, Heliodromus, who guides them."

"Yes, Lord."

"The Carpathian knows you are coming, but he also fears your coming. He wants you to go back to Rome. You must stay strong."

Gaius nodded. "Yes, Lord," he said. "Yes... I will..."

Gaius sat up, the sweat pouring from his brow, and cast a glance about the cave.

Vitorix and Calgacus slept soundly, unusually so, and Talia whimpered a few feet away where she had kicked off her cloak.

Gaius stood, his body surprisingly limber and warm.

Thank you, Mithras.

He slung his gladius over his shoulder and stepped over their things to cover Talia with her cloak.

She stopped whimpering then, and Gaius went to the mouth of the cave where a faint, grey light lit the mountainside.

The air was cold, and Gaius shivered as he drew his blade and scanned the misty slopes. A gasp choked him and the hairs on the back of his neck stood alert.

Among the trunks of the tall trees emerged Roman troops, hundreds of them.

They stared at him from bleeding eyes, shouted from mouths that were no longer capable of speech. There was no noise to the clinking of their shattered armour and broken banners, no thump upon the hollow, rooted ground as their hobnails trampled toward him. The slither of swords was absent, as were the hollow clunks of scuta put to rest.

The Dead... Gaius lowered his sword and nodded to them, searched the faces and found some he knew, like Odysseus in

Hades. Then, a centurion's horizontal crest emerged from the throng of fallen comrades.

Julius?

The burly centurion smiled and looked back at the dead.

Gaius had felt them, seen them following all the way from Germania, but he had had no idea so many had come, nor why. He wanted to know.

"We are going father into the Darkness, Gaius," the shade of Julius said.

"You're not of this world anymore, my friend," Gaius said, trying not to let the fear show on his face.

The shade grinned and the gash where Gaius had been forced to cut into his neck opened in a horrible grimace. "We never leave a man alone, soldier," Julius said.

Gaius nodded, not willing to argue.

"Daxos is suffering…" Julius closed his ghostly eyes and sighed in a terrifying manner. "You must get to him."

"Yes. We shall bring the Light into the Darkness," Gaius said.

"Who are you talking to?"

Gaius turned quickly to see Talia at the mouth of the cave staring at him, and then out into the empty forest.

Gaius looked from her to the silent dead who were invisible to all but him and Daxos, it seemed.

"Time to move out, Heliodromus," Julius' shade said.

Gaius nodded then turned back to Talia.

"No one. I… I have nightmares since our battles with the Carpathian began. This was a bad night."

"I always have bad dreams," the girl said. "Your friends are awake, and the Jagged Mountains are far away."

As Gaius followed Talia back into the cave to eat and

prepare to leave, he looked one last time at the shade of his friend and former centurion.

Julius mouthed the name 'Daxos', and saluted before disappearing with the other Roman dead, roaming the world in Gaius' wake.

The drip of water could drive a man to madness, let alone a boy.

The dark had its power as well, and within it, oh the terrors that lurked...

Deep in the rock, beneath mountains that raked the sky like savage claws, Daxos lay shivering in the corner of a rock cell. He groaned painfully, started at every dream that came to torture him. He had no idea where he was, only that he was in the dark, with laughter in every corridor beyond the rusty iron door that imprisoned him.

"Mithras..." Daxos croaked, but the Lord of Light could not penetrate so deeply.

Daxos clung to his memories like a beggar clings to a fallen bun, or rotting apple. Things did not feel real to the boy as he paced his cell over and over until he knew every inch of it.

He thought of his slaughtered village and his dead family, of Gaius and his new family. Thoughts of immortui and lykoi assaulted his mind, and that path led to the great one-eyed lykos and how he had made it stop attacking Gaius and the others in Germania.

Am I still in Germania? he asked himself.

The last thing he could remember was a great blackness enveloping him, a scent of blood and black earth, and then a dark sleep that saw him awake in that cell.

At first, he had not been sure he had been captured. He had looked for other dead whom he might be able to speak to as he had in the forest, but there were none.

It seemed that even the shades of the dead would not go where he was.

Daxos spent his time falling in and out of terror-ridden sleep. Always, when he would awake, there waited a plate of food and a cup of water. At first he shunned the bread, cheese, and what felt like some kind of meat, for he could not see in the dark, but he eventually grew so hungry that he ate every meal, until the plate was clean and the mice no longer scurried about him.

He wondered who his captor was, but as soon as the question came to mind, he knew the answer.

The Carpathian.

Those red eyes, the darkness, the smooth voice and the terrifying laugh that would not go away.

Why doesn't he just kill me?

In the blackness before him, Daxos saw a shimmery image that wrung his heart as his head lolled against the damp rock behind him.

A cookfire, and a woman standing over it, stirring what smelled like…

"Rabbit stew?" Daxos said.

The woman turned, brushing her black hair aside and smiling at him.

"Mama?" Daxos said, sitting up. He could smell the food that had been his favourite, hear the comforting crackle of the fire kindled with mountain pine and birch.

Then a big man approached the woman, kissed her cheek, and put his arm about her. Together, they looked at Daxos.

Pride and joy radiated from their faces, and they opened their arms to him.

Daxos stood, unsteady upon his feet, his limbs shaking for the cold in his bones. He longed for the warmth promised by his parents' open arms.

If I am dead, I am happy, he thought. *We can be together again…*

As Daxos reached out, his fingers about to grasp them, his parents' eyes dissolved into blood which poured down their cheeks like horrible tears. Gashes and scratches appeared all over their bodies until they fell in pieces.

"No! No! No!" Daxos cried.

Then the wolves roamed all about him, running in and out of the scene to steal bones and fleshy chunks from his fallen family.

He wept and looked up minutes later to see Gaius lying in the mud beside Calgacus and Vitorix. Their faces were white, their eyes looking to him for help even as black arms rose out of the ground to pull their bodies down into the Underworld.

Daxos leapt to Gaius' aid, and pulled and pried at the arms in an attempt to free him. He punched, and wailed, and punched again until the image dissolved and was replaced by darkness.

He stopped, weeping, cradling the hand which he had been driving into the solid rock of the cell floor. He could feel the flaps of savaged and bleeding skin on his knuckles, and fell backward with a scream.

"I hate you!" he yelled.

Then the laughter was closer, approaching outside the

door like the immortui shuffling through the forest on a floor of dead leaves.

Then it stopped.

The bolt on the cell door slammed open and firelight burst into the room.

Daxos fell back, blinded by the light which he had not seen for weeks. He rubbed his eyes and caught glimpses of his dark world – the empty plate, the black angular walls, the stinking corner where he relieved himself.

The figure in the doorway came into focus and Daxos immediately spotted the blade in his hand.

The man's features were covered, his clothes so dark it was hard to see him, but for the glint of his blade and the firebrand in his hand.

The man approached slowly, and Daxos thought of running, but he did not know where he should run to. Nevertheless, it was too good a chance.

Daxos burst into a run, but before he got three strides, a great fist hammered into the side of his head and all was darkness once more.

His limbs and torso were tied and clear sound was beginning to return. There was light behind his closed lids, more than he could remember. He did not open his eyes, his head felt heavy and pain throbbed at his temples. Mostly he did not want to look because there was someone…something else in that room.

Daxos could hear the crackle of torches, the step of booted feet, and a gentle clinking of chains.

It was, however, the smell that caused fear to grip his heart

– a stink of age and death unlike anything he had smelled before.

There was a low, deep, weary moan then, and Daxos' heart beat so wildly with panic that he feared it would be heard.

"Open your eyes, little one," a smooth, cold voice said.

Daxos pretended to be out.

"I can hear the blood pumping through your veins. I know you are awake," the voice said, in perfect Thracian Greek.

Slowly, perhaps lulled by the lure of that voice, Daxos opened his eyes, the firelight filling them like lava flow in a fold of earth.

Standing at a table was a tall man, cloaked all in black. His back was to Daxos and his thick, black hair fell over his shoulders as he bent over the table.

Daxos saw the edge of a blade and gasped.

The man laughed, and it was an all-too-familiar laugh from the nightmares that had haunted him for well over a year.

The man turned, and it was all Daxos could do not to scream at the sight of those red eyes, the eyes from his dreams, the eyes that had been the last thing he saw before darkness had wrapped itself about him in Germania.

"Carpathos," Daxos muttered.

"Yes," the man answered, walking toward Daxos. His black robes were more like the loose robes of a priest, than those of a warrior. "I am the Carpathian, among other things."

"Thanatos," Daxos gasped, desperate to be gone.

The man smiled knowingly. "So, you are the last of that tiresome village in my mountains to the East, the one whose people have been a constant thorn in my side. And now...you are here." The man rubbed his black beard, the red of his eyes fading now to darkest brown.

Daxos refused to speak.

"It has been some time since I took you from Germania, since all of your friends, including the centurion, have died."

Daxos looked up quickly, and the Carpathian nodded.

"Oh, yes, they finished like all the others, including your parents, torn to pieces at my will by those who serve me."

"Why don't you kill me?" Daxos said suddenly, though it struck him with fear to say the words.

"Because, I can use you." The Carpathian picked up the stone knife from the table and pointed it at Daxos' heart. "You have something inside you that will serve me well for a long time to come, my little Yazad."

Daxos did not understand the word he had used, but the way he caressed that ancient-looking knife terrified him beyond words. "I can make a being serve me for ages if I like, for I can lock and unlock the Underworld's gates at my wish." He pointed to the large stone wall on Daxos' other side. "You can help me…as she does…"

Daxos turned, and screamed.

In Rome, on the Caelian Hill, it had been a quiet night for once.

Panic in the city was finally subsiding as hopeful news was sent by Tiberius from the frontier. The citizens were more at ease, the intended effect of such announcements achieved.

However, in the house of Gaius Justus Vitalis, the tortured cries of the night had rung out yet again. As people passed the domus' door, they either stared or averted their eyes and sped on their way.

The young Vestal who approached the door was allowed through by the few bystanders who gave her a wide berth so as to avoid spoiling her sanctity.

Fulvia's servant, Calista, had gone to the House of the Vestals seeking aid for her mistress, a purification that might rid her of the lemur that harassed her every night.

When Ludo opened the door, the young priestess stepped over the threshold, holding out the lantern with a part of the sacred hearth flame in it.

The priestess stopped and looked about the domus, through the atrium to the peristylium beyond.

"It was the same last night?" the Vestal asked Calista as she came out of the kitchens.

"Yes."

"How long?"

"It's been happening for three weeks."

"What happens?" The priestess spoke softly, cautiously. There was something, some spiritual detritus about the home.

"The mistress, well, she has these violent nightmares. She screams like someone is torturing her…" Calista began to shake, and it was a struggle to press on. "I've never heard such sounds. Then…every morning, she's waking up with blood between her legs…so much blood." The servant struggled to hold back her emotions, but failed to do so.

The Vestal felt her heart speed up, and then noticed two furtive little faces peeking at her from behind a column.

"Hello," she said, crouching down lower to see Aemilia and Faustina.

The girls backed away momentarily, their wide, black-encircled eyes panicked and fearful. They did not smile.

"Have you had bad dreams girls?" the Vestal asked, approaching slowly.

They nodded, and Aemilia spoke.

"Not as bad as Mama's."

"What is in your dreams?" the priestess asked.

Faustina began to cry, and Aemilia placed her arm about her.

"Darkness…" her voice quavered. "It chokes us, and laughs at us and…and shows us our father eaten by wolves."

The priestess felt her heart constrict with pity for the two girls who should have been enjoying the blooming, innocent years of their youth, making flower chains and running in the garden. Instead, Aemilia and Faustina cowered, fear burned onto their faces.

The priestess approached them. "The Goddess Vesta is here, in your home and your hearts, to warm you and protect you, children." The priestess then took a piece of incense from the scrip at her waist and lit it in the sacred fire. The purifying smoke began to billow and wrap about the girls as a shield against the dark.

When she finished and moved through every room on the ground floor, the priestess turned to Calista.

"Take me to your mistress now."

BEFORE THE DOOR OF THE CUBICULUM, THE PRIESTESS PAUSED to catch her breath; the weight of her legs as she ascended to the upper floor had shocked her.

Calista stood by, waiting, and when the priestess nodded, she opened the door.

The room was filled with sunlight. Normally, the ill rested in darkness, but the priestess could see that everything was being done to encourage the light into that painful room.

A second slave sat beside the bed, her eyes wet with tears as she gazed on the sleeping form of her mistress.

The priestess gasped.

Fulvia lay still, sunk into the bed as much as her eyes had sunk into her face. Her skin was pale, and her eyes encircled by greyish veins.

The priestess knew Fulvia well from her frequent visits to the Temple of Vesta, her prayers and offerings. She had always known Fulvia Justa as a beautiful, vibrant woman, a caring mother, and resilient matron of her domus and familia.

Now, the priestess approached a woman she hardly recognized, the lush black hair streaked with white, and sickly skin loose over her emaciated body. The Vestal wanted to weep. She could feel the goddess' sadness at the attack on this home.

"Fulvia Justa," she said softly.

Fulvia's cracked lips parted and a slight gasp escaped as she roused.

"Fulvia," the priestess said again, this time reaching out to touch the woman's forehead.

Fulvia's eyes opened slightly, rolling to mild alertness.

"You…came…" Tears began at the corners of Fulvia's eyes. "Help… Goddess…help my family…"

"Vesta is here, Fulvia," the priestess soothed, and reached for her smoking lantern, letting the light and incense wash over Fulvia. "The goddess is with you. She is protecting you and your family, your home. Vesta is the everlasting light of the family. She overwhelms the dark-"

Anger filled the room then, a sudden malevolence that made Fulvia gasp in pain and fear.

The hangings that swayed on either side of the windows suddenly swept closed to shut out the sunlight, and the lamps in the room began to gutter violently.

"Please, no…" Fulvia cried.

The priestess stood, fighting the rising panic in her breast. She focussed on the sacred flame. "Goddess Vesta, guard us with your light…" she muttered, her voice quavering.

"Mama!" Aemilia cried from the doorway, where Calista held the two girls.

"Stay away!" the priestess warned. "Vesta, guard us with your sacred light…burn away the darkness…" She cried at a sudden pain, and Nisica wept beside the bed where she gripped her mistress' hand.

"He's back!" Fulvia cried. "Get out! Hurry!"

The priestess was suddenly flung against the wall, pressed hard by the shadows so that she writhed three feet above the floor.

"Leave her alone!" Fulvia yelled, her voice hoarse and despairing, but with more strength than she had managed in a long while.

The priestess' lantern fell to the floor and guttered dangerously, almost extinguishing the sacred flame.

"Aemilia, no!" Calista yelled as the girl charged into the room to take up the lantern and hold it up, tears streaming down her face as she stared in horror at the shuddering form of the priestess.

"Let her be!" Aemilia yelled.

The priestess' body writhed in the air, her face contorted in horrible pain, her hands grabbing at her loins. Then, she screamed, a terrible inhuman sound that pulled Fulvia from her bed.

Weak, and stumbling, Fulvia went to the window and tore the curtains from their brackets so that sunlight exploded into the cubiculum. She collapsed on the ground and Aemilia ran to her, narrowly dodging the priestess' limp body as she fell to the floor in a heap.

Laughter raked the painted walls. It was everywhere, and then, it was gone.

The only sounds were of Aemilia and Faustina crying over their mother, and the whimpering of the young priestess of Vesta on the floor.

"See to her," Fulvia croaked to Calista and Nisica, who both approached the girl reluctantly.

The priestess lay on her stomach, her hair damp with sweat and fear, her skin unnaturally pale.

The two servants rolled her over so that the girl's head lay in Nisica's lap.

"Oh, Gods!" Calista cried.

Fulvia pulled herself to her feet, and bracing herself on a nearby table, looked at the priestess.

The girl's eyes were open. She cried unabashedly, her mouth muttering prayers to Vesta.

However, it was the blood between her legs that scared Fulvia, for she knew what the Lemur had done to this pure priestess of her beloved Vesta.

"We're doomed, mistress..." Calista said, panic in her voice.

Fulvia calmed her shaking hands and looked to her daughters. "Girls, go with Calista and get warm water and towels from the kitchen and bath."

"Yes, Mama," Aemilia said, putting the lantern down beside the priestess and Nisica, before pulling Faustina away.

"Shh... Shh... The goddess loves you..." Fulvia said, struggling to believe it after the horrors of the last few weeks, after the rape of the young Vestal she had just witnessed.

"They'll kill me…" the priestess shook. "My vows are broken."

"Shh. Shh. Not willingly did you break your vows," Fulvia soothed, though her heart beat wildly. "Vesta knows your heart and courage. We'll get you cleaned up and you will take a cloak and a stola of mine to return to the temple. Say that your items were…that…"

She could not think of a viable lie. Even Suburan thugs were loath to harm a Vestal Virgin. Her mind was too shaken.

The priestess nodded, fighting the tears that stung her eyes, and the pain that coursed violently inside her body.

"We will figure this out," Fulvia said. She knew they had to, for if a priestess of Vesta had been violated in her domus, the entire familia could be executed along with the priestess herself.

"You…you can't say anything," Fulvia said to the girl. "We're all dead if you do…please."

Guilt racked Fulvia for having brought this on the kind priestess, but she needed to protect her family.

Vesta, help us. Help your priestess…

The girl nodded and struggled to her knees.

"Help me, Fulvia Justa," she said.

Fulvia hugged the girl and helped her to the bed with Nisica's aid.

When Calista arrived with the water and towels, Aemilia and Faustina were sent from the room.

They helped her out of her despoiled robes and washed her.

The girl wept the whole time, her vows and her chastity destroyed in darkness not long before.

When they finished, Fulvia as tired as she was, helped the priestess out of the room and down to the peristylium for some fresh air. The girl sat still, in shock for some time, staring at the dead foliage that skittered across the winter garden.

"I could not protect you from that evil, Fulvia Justa," she finally said. "Why is it here? I can't imagine how you have all been suffering."

Fulvia felt her body begin to shake again, the hysteric panic that gripped her when she was alone, in the dark, began to come on again. Every day had been a battle to remain composed and be there for her terrified children, and the nights had become a never-ending string of nightmares in which she fought her fears, and the heaviness of her lids, for sleep led only to the assault of her body and mind. Her very psyche was bleeding from the wounds the darkness had inflicted.

"Fulvia?" the priestess said again, her lip trembling as she saw the pain in Fulvia's eyes.

"I cannot explain the suffering, or that of my girls," she wiped a stream of tears from her cheek. "My husband, he is… fighting an enemy far away, and…and I think this may be his enemy."

"How do you know?" the priestess asked.

"As the Lemur torments me in the night, he shows me Gaius torn to shreds…bloody…" She began to shake again. "He, he is often dead on some mountainside, the darkness enveloping him"

"The laughter? Do you always hear it?" the priestess asked.

Fulvia began to weep openly then. "Yes… Always… It is everywhere. My girls too…my poor girls…"

The priestess reached out and put her shaking arms about Fulvia.

"The Light will overcome darkness. We must trust in that."

Fulvia nodded and leaned on the young woman. In that moment, she understood why Vesta had chosen that girl, and not for her virginity.

"Your strength and compassion honour the goddess," Fulvia said.

The priestess squeezed her tighter then as if fighting her self-doubt.

AN HOUR LATER, THE PRIESTESS RETURNED TO THE HOUSE OF the Vestals, her lantern still lit, its light warming the paving slabs of the road as she descended the Caelian Hill.

Fulvia watched her disappear around the corner of their street, and then returned inside behind the barred door.

Goddess Vesta, let her live, Fulvia prayed before the family shrine. *Mithras, god of my husband's, please watch over him. He is my life... Help him to defeat this darkness and come home to us.*

After making her offerings, Fulvia made her way to Aemilia and Faustina's cubiculum to see them sleeping uneasily.

"I'll lie with them tonight," Fulvia said to Nisica who had been watching over them.

"Yes, mistress. I'll wait outside."

"No. You sleep, dear. Today was hard for all of us."

"Yes, mistress."

When Nisica was gone, Fulvia closed the door and lay on the bed between her daughters.

"I love you. I promise I won't let anything happen to you, my girls."

Faustina's whimpering stopped, and Aemilia's arm reached out to wrap her mother in warmth.

"YOU BOYS ARE OUT OF YOUR FUCKING MINDS!"

The hulking centurion stood with his arms crossed, his scarred face in an angry grimace to match the rushing Danuvius behind him.

An optio stood behind the centurion shaking his head in agreement at the madness of the request they had just heard.

Antonius and Sabinus stood facing the two men who were refusing to let them cross the frontier in one of the barges at Viminacium.

Sentries looked down on them from the stout Roman fortifications which stood between Dacia and the Empire.

Antonius hated dealing with these horror-forged veteran career-centurions – they never listened to those they felt were inferior, rank-be-damned. Finally, he handed the reins of his horse to Sabinus and dug in his satchel for the tattered imperial pass and procurement orders.

"You're in no position to deny us anything, Centurion." Antonius handed the papers over, and the centurion gawked at them before handing them back to his optio to read.

"Looks like you wiped your arse with it," he spat.

"Nevertheless, they are real, and if you hold us up, you'll have to answer to Augustus himself," Antonius said, his voice more angry than it had been on the journey, despite fighting mountain bandits, and teaching a lesson or two to over-zealous, green patrols from Domavia.

"You fucking threatening me?" the centurion growled, getting up into Antonius' face and poking the chest of his black cuirass with a thick finger.

"No. But the emperor is. He's given us authority to do what we need to do to rescue our brothers and apprehend an enemy.

"Antonius!" Sabinus said.

Antonius realized he had said too much, and cursed himself for it, but it was too late. Then, he saw doubt creep in on the hard-faced centurion like water pooling from a thawing snow drift.

"Brothers? Who?" the centurion asked.

"I serve the emperor," Antonius said, "But I also serve the Light."

The centurion looked at the sun and the eagle on Antonius' breastplate.

"My Heliodromus is over there, as are two more of my brothers, Miles in the ranks of the Light."

Without a word, the centurion turned his back on Antonius and walked to the riverside.

The water rushed by, dark and cold as a leviathan, writhing and threatening to pull him under.

"Why Sarmizegethusa?" he asked. "Why do you want to go into the Dacians' asshole?"

"Because we have to," Sabinus answered. "And we need to get information."

"You speak Dacian?" the optio asked.

"No," Antonius conceded. "But we can be persuasive. Besides, we don't know where our brothers are."

"Or the enemy," Sabinus added.

The centurion turned. "They're all the enemy across this Styx here," he pointed at the Danuvius. "Still...I...can't hold you back if you are to save our brothers..."

The optio stepped forward and handed the imperial pass back to Antonius.

"I'll get my strongest men to row you across," the centurion offered.

"But there are guide ropes," Sabinus said.

"Hmph! Those won't do any good in that current," the centurion said. "You'll be lucky to reach the other side without drowning."

A SHORT WHILE LATER, TWENTY LEGIONARIES SAT IN THE benches of the barge, ready to make the crossing.

In the middle, Antonius and Sabinus stood calming their horses whose hooves stomped nervously on the boards.

"Shh…shh…" Antonius soothed, his own heart pounding as the barge rocked and swung in the current.

"Sarmizegethusa's north-east of here," the centurion had said as the barge was pushed out into the current from the Roman side. "Stay in the Light, brothers!"

Antonius had nodded his thanks and immediately he almost went overboard as the current slammed into the barge and the guide ropes that led it across the river strained and stretched audibly.

The side of the transport was tilting now into the rushing water.

"Row!" the optio called out to the crew. "Row hard or we'll fall in!"

Men were shouting and cursing, and Antonius and Sabinus gripped their horses' necks and used their own body weight to hold the beasts in place.

The wind seemed to howl more aggressively, and for a moment Antonius thought he spied dark, flitting shapes in the sky above, and on the curved faces of the rushing waves.

The centurion on the Roman shore was yelling to them at

the top of his parade ground voice, but they could barely hear him.

Then, the rope snapped and the barge spun to plow backward, up river as fast as a ballista bolt.

"Row to port! Hurry!" the optio roared.

Antonius and Sabinus strained with all their strength and taut sinew to keep their two mounts from trying to turn in the boat, for they would have trampled the rowers.

The rowers on the starboard side pulled their oars harder and faster until they were pointed once more toward the Dacian shore, rushing toward it at an angle.

"Brace yourselves!" the optio screamed.

Sabinus looked to Antonius with panic and began to loosen his grip on his mount. "We have to!" he said to Antonius. "They won't survive the impact!"

Antonius nodded and at once they let go, allowing the terrified beasts to leap in their panic from the barge and into the rushing river.

Just as Antonius and Sabinus dropped into the bottom, the barge careened into the shore with a crack and grinding, sending several men into the air and snapping several of the oars on the port side.

Antonius heard the laughter on the wind and looked up to see Sabinus' ear cocked to it as well. He took a deep breath where he lay in the bottom of the barge.

"Everyone out, gods damn-it!" the optio shouted as he went to an uprooted tree trunk on which one of the legionaries had been impaled.

The trooper's body lay limp and a spear of wood jutted from out of the top of his lorica, blood pouring from the wound as if from a well faucet.

"Check the hull and make sure there are no holes!" the optio ordered, giving Antonius and Sabinus a furious look.

Antonius ignored the man, and looked to where their horses had come ashore upriver and were now trimming the grass.

"We need to go," Sabinus said, taking the reins of both mounts and pulling them toward Antonius.

"We can't just leave them like this." Antonius looked to the dead trooper and felt guilty that the man might have a young wife, as he did, whom he would not be returning to.

"Antonius," Sabinus put a hand on his shoulder. "We have to go find shelter for the night, and then help Gaius, Daxos, and the others. We need to go."

Antonius looked at Sabinus a moment, and then at the rushing Danuvius. The air was damp and cold, but nothing compared to what they were about to experience in the mountains to the northeast where the clouds hung low, impaled on the swaying pines.

"Gather our things," Antonius said. "I'll tell the optio."

Sabinus nodded and began to fasten their satchels to the horses.

"Optio!" Antonius called. "We're heading out!"

The optio approached, his face angry. "You mean to say that after we brought you over here, and trashed our transport, and lost a good man, you're just going to leave?"

"I'm sorry about your man, Optio-"

"I don't care about your fucking apologies!"

"Ready, Antonius!" Sabinus called from atop his horse where he had his gladius out and was sharpening it.

"I'm sorry," Antonius said again before turning his back on the optio, mounting his own horse, and leading the way up a path, away from the Danuvius.

They could hear the optio shouting and cursing them, but they pressed on – they had to.

We're coming Gaius... Antonius thought. *Mithras guide us.*

THE JOURNEY WAS NOT EASY.

The Carpathian lowlands became steeper and more jagged, and the closer Antonius and Sabinus came to Sarmizegethusa, the more dangerous life became.

Dacians were all over the hills, like worker ants about a great colony, moving to and from the citadel in patrol groups of hunters and warriors.

"So many," Sabinus whispered as they watched a troupe of ten from some thick undergrowth.

"Shh…" Antonius put his fingers to his lips as the last Dacian, a great bearded one holding a long sword and a staff topped with a wolf's head, stopped to listen to the wood around him.

Sabinus began to unsheathe his gladius, but Antonius shook his head.

The Dacian cocked his ear, but moved to catch up with his fellows a moment later.

"We'll never get anywhere at this rate," Sabinus said. "We've been travelling for three days, and Sarmizegethusa isn't much closer."

"I know, I know." Antonius sat up and thought for a moment. "Let's find a place to rest for the night. There must be a cave somewhere nearby in these hills."

"We still don't know what we're doing."

"No," Antonius answered. "But maybe we'll find out."

They turned away from the main road and went to get

their horses farther back in the woods. When they had climbed up the mountain, among the resinous pines and boulder-strewn ground, they eventually did find a cave, not well hidden, but far enough from the road to go unnoticed by wanderers.

When the horses were tethered, and the fire lit, the two men leaned back and stared at the fire Sabinus had just started.

Exhaustion began to set in.

"I'll take first watch," Sabinus said as he shoved a piece of hard bread into his mouth and then drank from his water skin.

"I won't say no," Antonius answered, gratitude sweeping through his tired body and mind. "Just don't sharpen your gladius outside – the sound will carry downhill."

Sabinus put his sharpening stone back in his satchel and went to the entrance of the cave. "You're on in two hours," he said before going outside.

Antonius nodded and finished his last bite of dried beef.

The small fire danced lethargically in front of him as he stared into the heart of it, his eyelids heavier by the moment.

Vera... his thoughts ranged over all the leagues he had travelled to his wife, and he wondered if her belly was growing larger even then, as he gazed into the light. *Mithras, guide us... Help us to find our Heliodromus.*

Antonius' head lolled back against the rock wall and his grip on his silver-bladed gladius slackened as he nodded off.

ANTONIUS?

The sound of a woman weeping softly echoed in the darkness.

Vera? Antonius' eyes searched but he could see nothing except firelight. In the midst of the flames a face stared at him.

Vera's tears traced steaming lines down her cheeks as her eyes looked accusingly at him, pitifully.

Why did you leave?

I had to, he said, slapping his head hard. *Mithras, Lord of Light,* he said, and the fire grew wilder. *We don't know where to go. We only wish to get to Gaius and our friends. Which way, Lord?*

A long finger of flame reached out from the fire then, shaped like a hand at the end of a muscular arm.

Antonius might have recoiled, but instead he leaned into it and felt heat and energy rush through his body and enliven his limbs.

The fiery hand then reached up and touched his forehead.

Antonius saw a vast settlement set among mountains, rows and rows of wooden buildings covered in turf. A great chieftain walked along a central road surrounded by villagers. Long swords hung from the belts of the chieftain and his men, and they shoved people to make way.

No one dared speak up. No one dared follow them as they trekked east, out of the settlement.

"You cannot leave Sarmizegethusa!" one woman yelled after the chieftain.

"What of the lykoi?" said another. "They and the immortui will devour us!"

People wept and called in vain after the chieftain and his warriors who marched off into the wilds without a word.

"They cannot stay," said a man in ragged priest's robes to the crowd of villagers. "He is bound to go, else you would all be dead."

"Go away, priest!" the people yelled. "The Gods abandoned us long ago!"

The priest looked upon the people with sadness and despair. "It's you who turned you backs on our gods," he answered. "Your hatred of Rome has consumed you. You've turned to the darkness!" he said before walking away, until he came to a quiet hill at the far end of the village.

The priest climbed the snow-covered slopes until he came to a derelict, circular enclosure.

"Gods help us… I don't know what to do. What offering would you have to come back to us?"

The priest stopped and was very still then. He began to look up, slowly, at the space above the fire.

He stared directly at Antonius.

Antonius jerked awake, his hand grabbing for his blade.

"Whoa! Easy!" Sabinus was saying. He stood back cautiously. "It's been two hours. Your turn on watch."

"Oh…ah…right. Sorry."

"Bad dreams?" Sabinus asked.

"Strange…very strange."

"Well, you figure it out while I sleep."

Antonius stood and picked up his cloak and gladius before making his way to the mouth of the cave. As he wrapped the wolf pelts about himself against the chill air, he could hear the faint sound of a sharpening stone from inside the cave.

"Mithras, what were you showing me?"

He stared into the darkness, his eyes still blinded by firelight, and stepped out a few paces to where the wind tore at his cloak and cold wrapped itself about him. The moon glowed above, casting occasional rays of silver light into the darkness of the trees.

There! Movement.

Antonius drew his gladius.

"Sabinus," he whispered hoarsely, but his comrade was already asleep.

The cave had been too small to get the horses inside, so they had penned them with dead wood and branches of cedar around the side of the cave's entrance.

Antonius walked that way, his ears picking up the sound of the mounts' shuffling hooves.

The horses were nervous.

As Antonius turned the corner, he froze.

Beyond the enclosure wall, two lykoi crouched, ready to pounce onto the horses.

"No!" Antonius yelled, running at them.

The lykoi's massive heads looked at Antonius, their eyes red and awful, threatening death. They leapt over the enclosure walls and began tearing at the horses' bellies and thrashing legs.

The horses screamed, and as Antonius made to leap over the wall, he was knocked off his feet into the trunk of a nearby tree.

The dark surroundings spun momentarily, and then he saw the hateful eyes bearing down on him, the rank breath of blood and flesh clawing its way into his senses.

He brought up his gladius in time to plunge it into the lykos' belly where it sizzled in the steaming offal.

"Ahh! Ahh!" the lykos cried out with the voice of a man, and even as he began to transform before Antonius' astonished eyes, the whistle of another blade cut the creature down mid-shift.

"The horses!" Sabinus yelled, pulling Antonius to his feet.

The two men ran toward the enclosure, but stopped when they saw one lykos glutting itself on a still-crying horse.

The other mount flailed, and kicked, and landed a good blow on the face of the third lykos, knocking the fangs from its mouth and sending it into the wall.

The horse collapsed, exhausted, but no sooner had it fallen than the other lykos stopped its feeding and lunged upon it with a terrible snarl.

Sabinus and Antonius leapt down and hacked at the lykos' thighs and side, the silver edges of their gladii searing its black pelt and flesh.

The thing turned on hind legs, but collapsed toward them, its jaws open.

Antonius stepped out of the way and brought his gladius down to pin the head to the ground. When he looked more closely, he saw his blade through the skull of a bearded Dacian, the one who had sensed them on the road earlier that day.

Antonius vomited when he saw the corpse of the gutted horse.

"She's alive," Sabinus said, pointing at the glassy eyes.

Antonius stepped toward the savaged animal, and with his blade above the heart area, ended her suffering. When he turned to Sabinus, he could hear him soothing his mount.

"Shh…shh…" Sabinus stroked his horse's neck.

Two legs were broken, and she was bleeding fluidly from slashes to her rib cage.

Before Antonius could say anything, Sabinus' sword plunged into the horse's brain behind the eye.

Sabinus rose from the clotted snow and pointed at the dead men. "How many Dacians have made this pact?"

"I don't know, but there are more than I ever imagined," Antonius answered.

"My friend, after seeing what we've seen…I… I no longer doubt anything. I expect the worst," Sabinus shuddered visibly then, and Antonius understood.

Then, Antonius remembered his dream.

"Let's get to Sarmizegethusa. We have to leave now."

"Why?" Sabinus asked.

"I believe Mithras will show us when we get there."

Sabinus looked at Antonius for a moment. "May we ever walk in His Light."

ON THE MOUNTAIN TERRAIN OF THE CARPATHIANS, ANTONIUS and Sabinus were able to move more quickly without the horses, though the visibility was hampered by fog and snow.

"Doesn't the sun ever come out in these parts?" Sabinus asked as they rested in a copse of trees. "How do the bastards live here?" he mused.

Antonius smiled but said nothing. When they had rested and eaten, they gathered their satchels, scuta, and weapons, and continued north.

"I hope we're going the right way," Sabinus said.

"Me too. Keep alert. We should reach Sarmizegethusa toward the end of the day. There'll be more Dacian patrols."

It had been three days since the lykoi had hit them, three days since Antonius' dream. As he walked, Antonius thought back to the vivid memories of his first battle, the first lives he had taken in the green spring of his life as a man of the legions.

He had killed so much and so easily since that first encounter with the immortui, that he no longer noticed the spray of blood across his face, or the slip of viscera beneath his booted feet.

At that moment, as he walked over boulders and moss-covered logs, among the pine trees, he was only aware of what he had left behind.

Vera would love the fresh pine smell in the mountains, he thought, taking a deep breath to fill his lungs.

"Wait!" Sabinus hissed, his hand out to stop Antonius getting closer. "Get down."

They crouched, their scuta protecting their backs as they peered from behind a boulder to look up the mountainside.

Antonius stared. "That's it."

"What?"

"Sarmizegethusa. We're here." He pointed at the dark line of thick stone walls among the trees, running in a quadrilateral up the slope.

"Great. Now what?" Sabinus turned to scan the trees around them for any sentries or wandering villagers.

"It's oddly quiet for the capital of Dacia," Antonius whispered. He looked up the length of the main dirt road, flanked by wooden houses with turf rooftops, and the slither of smoke from many, indicating a warm fire and hot food. The walls and fortress were much more extensive than he had imagined.

"What now, Antonius?" Sabinus asked again.

"Let's wait until nightfall. Then we wander in and see what we can find out."

"Except we don't speak fucking Dacian!" Sabinus said sarcastically.

THEY WAITED OUT THE LAST TWO HOURS OF DAYLIGHT, watching villagers move through the open gate and among the houses, carrying baskets of bread and buckets of water from a well.

They did not see many warriors about. Yes, there were young men, mostly labourers, but no men who bore swords or axes.

Antonius decided to tell Sabinus about the priest he believed Mithras had shown him some nights before in the cave.

"And you think he's up there? We haven't seen anyone like that the whole time we've been watching," Sabinus whispered.

"You don't believe me?"

"I didn't say that. Actually, I said, if you remember, that I'll believe anything now. Mithras has guided us before, why would he not guide us to our Heliodromus?"

It took some time and care for Antonius and Sabinus to ascend from their hiding place, but eventually they found themselves on the trampled snow of the road leading into the Dacian capital.

A few torches were lit along the road through Sarmizegethusa, and sounds of laughter, talk, yelling, and screwing emanated from behind the village's hide-covered windows.

"Their chieftain is away," Antonius whispered. "Must have taken his warriors with him."

"Where?"

Antonius shrugged, and with his back to the wall of one wooden house, he listened a moment before chancing a look behind the curtain.

On the floor beside a fire, a Dacian man was pumping away silently at his woman who raked his back with her nails. In a far corner, two children slept beneath a pile of furs.

Antonius shook his head and indicated they should move on.

Together, the two Romans skirted behind the houses, away from the road and up the fortress' terraces, until they came to a larger structure where several men's voices were raised in argument.

"What're they saying? Sabinus asked, so low that Antonius could barely understand.

Antonius shrugged and moved on; there were too many in that building.

Sarmizegethusa was much bigger than they had thought, and there did not seem to be anyone outside once it got dark.

The air was damp and windy, so high up on the mountain.

The two Romans were aware that if someone were watching, they would be spotted instantly from one of the six citadels spread over the five terraces of the Dacian capital.

They stuck to the shadows, like wraiths skirting the darkness behind houses, palisades and trunks of mountain pine and ash. The snow and rushing of a nearby river muted their progress as they went.

When they came to a jutting outcrop of rock, they stopped and peered around, their way blocked.

"We'll need to head back to the main road," Antonius whispered.

Sabinus listened to the increasing sound of voices spreading out around the settlement. "Their gathering must be finished," he said.

They edged along the rockface toward the main track, their pila and scuta at the ready for anything, their black armour and weapons shielding them from local eyes as they moved through the shadows. They had learned to move as shades, silently making their trespass among the enemies of Rome.

As they passed a lit window, unaware that the curtain had been hung aside, a woman screamed and the two Romans turned to see a tall blonde Dacian woman staring at them, her breasts exposed for the pleasure of the man who knelt before her.

"Sons of whores!" Sabinus said, rushing to the front of the dwelling and plunging the tip of his pilum through the man's eye and brain, killing him instantly.

The naked Dacian woman emerged shrieking from the light within, and Sabinus brought his scutum up just in time to stop her axe from burying itself in his face.

His right hand released the grip on his pilum and he slid his gladius free to plunge directly into the woman's white abdomen.

She hunched over, blood pouring from her mouth into the snow at Sabinus' feet.

The Roman stared in horror at the woman and moved only when roused by Antonius' voice and rough hands.

"Let's move!" Antonius slapped Sabinus who came to and tried pulling his pilum out of the man's skull. "Leave it! We have to-"

Howling. Distant but unmistakable.

"Lykoi!" Sabinus said.

They hurried out into and across the road, scanning up and down as they went, and discerning the running shapes of villagers in a panic.

People were screaming, and far away, at the end of the village where they had entered, the sounds of snarling and blood-choked cries erupted. Several lykoi tore into one of the unfortunate villagers.

"Now's our chance!" Antonius ran up toward the north-east end of the village, past homes, and smithies, taverns, and columns topped with ornate wolf heads. Another terrace appeared ahead of them, hidden among the trees and their legs powered up the incline, slipping occasionally on the crisp snow."Up into the grove!" Antonius called.

"We need to get inside," Sabinus said. "They'll pick us off out in the open like this!"

They attained a flat area surrounded by tall trees that contained a few small buildings, rectangular temples, and a large, round structure. A pungent smell of smoke, herbs, and charred flesh pricked at their panicked senses as they searched for a place to hide.

"In there!" Sabinus pointed to a run-down temple made of stone and wood, and ran toward it. He kicked the door open, and the two burst inside.

Two Dacians who had been standing before an older man turned, and when their eyes widened in recognition of the foreign armour, they ran at Antonius and Sabinus.

Sabinus' gladius whistled through the air to take one man in the chest, and the other was quickly pinioned to a wooden post by Antonius' pilum.

Sabinus ripped his gladius free and rushed the old man, pushing his head down and holding his bloody blade to his neck. "What now?" he said to Antonius, his breathing heavy, his iron grip making the man wince.

"I don't know! We need the priest. We'll have to go back!"

"Gods, Antonius! That'll be us, then; buggered well and good! Half of Dacia and a pack of lykoi are already on to us!"

"Mithras help us…" Antonius murmured. He noticed the

old man then, dressed in dirty, floor-length robes, staring at him from the bush of his wiry, grey beard and brows.

"Romans?" he said hesitantly.

"What?" Sabinus looked down and jerked him to his feet so that the man now stared openly at him. "You?" Antonius gasped. "It's him, Sabinus."

"The priest?"

"Yes." Antonius walked over to face the old man.

"Why are you here?" the old man said in broken Latin.

Antonius grabbed him by the robes and shook him. "I saw you! In the flames!"

"This…" The man pointed to the eagle and sun on Antonius' black cuirass. "Why you here? To kill me? To kill my people?"

"No." Antonius shook his head and loosened his grip. "We are looking for three friends. Romans…with armour like this. Have you seen them?"

"No."

"And a boy, Daxos by name," Sabinus added.

"Yes," Antonius jumped in. He was taken by the one they call the Carpathian."

The man looked up, his eyes wide, angry, and haunted.

Sabinus' blade was at his throat again. "Don't even think of calling for help."

"Your people follow him? This Carpathian?" Antonius asked.

The man swept the blade away, his face red with sudden rage. "No! Not all of us. Not the good among us."

"Your chieftain follows him?"

"Yes, though I advised him not to." The man rubbed his grey beard and tied back his long grey hair. "Long ago, the warriors of our people, those who live by violence, enjoyed the power the Carpathian gave to them in return for their service." He sat down, glancing at the barred doors as the howling outside grew closer. "But as the years passed, more was demanded of the tribes, and the chieftains gave it – more men, more lives, more battles with Rome… The Carpathian has seduced our leaders with power, so much so that many have turned their backs on our gods, and worship only Death and Darkness. The temples of Bendis, Gebeleizis, Derzelas, and Sabazios are quiet and untended. This temple of mighty Zalmoxis," he waved his arm reverently about the temple in which they stood, "now is only tended by me, and not without risking my life."

"The Carpathian has replaced your gods?" Sabinus asked.

"Not for all, but fear of the Carpathian – of his lykoi and the immortui – is deep and has been cutting out our hearts for generations now."

"Wait," Antonius put up a hand. "How long has this Carpathian lord been here? How long has he held sway?"

"For as far back as our histories go," the priest said. "For a long time, our gods were able to keep him at bay. His power has only really taken hold in the last generation, but his shadow has fallen across the land for a very long time."

The wind howled loudly outside and the temple doors shook violently, the wooden bar creaking.

Sabinus stepped into the aisle to listen and just as he did so, the door splintered and exploded.

"Look out!" Antonius yelled, leaping to his friend's side and driving his gladius into the beast's skull.

A second lykos burst in and knocked Antonius back several feet, but Sabinus' blade was quick in hacking at it as it leapt.

Together, both men drove their blades into the lykos until its teeth stopped gnashing.

The priest stared wide-eyed at the two Romans who had displayed no fear in the sudden attack, and whose weapons actually slew the beasts on contact.

"What will you say to the Carpathian when you see him? He won't listen to you."

"We're not going to talk to the bastard, old man," Sabinus growled.

"We're going to kill him," Antonius finished, helping the priest to his feet.

The old man looked at them, two tired and dirty Romans, brave and determined, and there was new hope in his eyes.

Zalmoxis, Lord, guide me in this.

"Come with me, quickly," the priest said.

"Why? So you can feed us to your fellow villagers?" Sabinus kicked one of the lykoi corpses.

"No. So that I can help save my fellow Dacians."

Antonius looked at Sabinus and back at the priest. "What's your name, priest?"

"Corax. Now hurry before more lykoi arrive."

Before they could say anything else, the priest was out the door into the cold, blowing night, more howls approaching in the distance.

The snows were up then, shielding them to unfriendly eyes as they followed the priest from the temple to a square house not far away.

"This is our guest house, for pilgrims who have the courage to seek our gods," Corax said as he shut the door. "It has been unoccupied for some time, save for myself. I use it for storage now, a place to hide the offerings I do receive."

"Offerings from whom?" Antonius asked.

"From those among us still loyal to Zalmoxis and our other gods. They are afraid to come themselves, so they give the gods' gifts to me to pass along."

"Why?" Sabinus said.

"Because the Carpathian has eyes everywhere. He sees all…knows all."

"He's not a bloody god, is he?" Sabinus asked, beginning to sharpen his gladius.

Corax stared at the two Romans and shook his head. "No. Not to me. But you cannot kill him."

"Why?" Antonius said, though he had not really thought about it. He had only been focussed on finding Gaius and the others.

"He is Death – Thanatos, as the Thracians say. And you cannot kill Death."

The Romans had no words, and the hope in Corax's aged eyes suddenly faded, swallowed by the deep lines of worry on his brow.

"The boy we seek is Thracian," Antonius began. "His father and the people of his village were lykoi hunters."

"I know the village you speak of," Corax said. "There was talk of that village when the Cheruscan, Arminius, passed through here with our chieftain."

"The entire place was wiped out by immortui over a year ago. Daxos, the boy, is the only survivor. As we said, the Carpathian took Daxos captive," Antonius said. "We need to find him."

Corax stood and rubbed his beard in thought before the glowing fire at the centre of the room. "The boy must have something the Carpathian wants. Else, why would he keep him alive?"

"We're wasting time now!" blurted Sabinus. "By Mithras,

while we talk history and intrigue, our friends are all in danger. We need to move now, Antonius!"

"Corax," Antonius said. "He's right. We need to keep moving. If you could spare some food, climbing rope and a hook, if you have one, we would be grateful."

"You are welcome to those things, and more." The old man stood more upright, as though coming to a decision. "I'm coming with you. I want to see this evil defeated as much as you do."

"With respect," Antonius said. "You're too old, and would slow us down."

"I also know the way to the Carpathian's fortress in the jagged mountains." He gazed at the two men for a moment. "Bendis, our goddess of the moon and of the hunt will see me through this as we track Death to his own door."

"You likely will not come back to Sarmizegethusa," Antonius said.

Corax shrugged. "As an old man, I have endured too much dread in this life." He smiled then, sad and resigned, but stronger for his new-found determination. "As a Dacian, I am ready for a final, wild hunt."

Antonius put out his hand and the old man took it.

"Then may our gods all guide us to the same end. We leave before dawn."

"Girl!"

The squelching became louder, something grotesque to match the scene all about them. They were breathless from the fight, their worst yet, except the girl.

The silver blade of her pugio plunged again and again into

the body of a lykos that had begun to transform back into that of a Dacian man with the first hissing cut.

When the beard and human eyes emerged from the thick pelt through the mist of evaporating evil, her blade plunged harder and faster so that now, after minutes of pommelling, all that was left was a shattered skull revealing shredded brains.

"Talia!" Gaius yelled, splitting the silence among the trees on the narrow mountain path. "Stop!"

The young Thracian looked up at him and he saw the humanity return to her eyes.

"It's all right now. You can stop. Save your strength."

She nodded, silent, and stood to stare down at her work before spitting.

Gaius breathed and wiped the blood from his check only to add more.

The pack that had been tracking them was a large one, larger by far than any of the others they had encountered. When Gaius had ordered them to make a stand instead of running along the sheer clifftops, Calgacus and Vitorix had laid several traps for their pursuers.

Eight lykoi had fallen to those traps, but another twenty had come on at the small group, hidden as they were behind boulders and up in the trees.

The Romans' strategy had worked, and they had lured the wolves into their bottleneck to lame them with pila and arrows before wading into the savage gathering of blood and gnashing fangs to finish the lykoi off by hand with gladius and battle axe.

Now, Vitorix and Calgacus stood with Gaius and Talia, staring about the slaughter, their chests heaving, and the fire in their veins leeching away.

They had all laid into the lykoi with anger and rage, so

much so that now it was hard to discern which limbs belonged to which corpses.

When Talia had dropped out of a tree to help the men finish the lykoi, she had not held back in her fury, but rushed from one flailing body to the next gaping maw, her blade ripping into flesh, fur, and bone.

Gaius heard a faint grunting sound and looked to see Vitorix hammering something with his fist.

"What's going on?" Gaius called as he ran to join them at the base of a tall pine.

Vitorix stopped, his hand bloody, his eyes wild as Calgacus watched, wiping his gladius' blade.

At the big Gaul's feet lay a man with a thick torc about his neck, and a wolf tattooed on the chest beneath his torn tunic.

"He's one of the fucking Dacian chieftains!" Vitorix said, pointing at the torc. "Won't tell us anything."

Gaius looked at the thickset man who gazed back through swelling eyes. "Talia! Come here," Gaius called.

The girl came over to them, brushing her black hair out of the way so that it stuck to the side of her gore-covered head.

"Ask him why they were hunting us?"

Talia kicked the chieftain's leg and he howled in pain, his eyes rounding fiercely on her. Then she asked the question and he spoke.

"He says they only pick up our scent recently. That they going somewhere."

"Ask him where," Gaius said, his gladius feeling lighter again in his hand as he held it.

"He says to fuck yourself."

The triangular point of Gaius' blade came up to split the Dacian's nose so that the man screamed.

"Wait!" Talia suddenly said, her hand out to stop Gaius. "I have seen this man."

"Where?" Calgacus asked.

"In the village where I was prisoner. He visited." Talia knelt to look more closely.

"Was he a visiting chieftain?" Gaius said. "Maybe from a neighbouring tribe?"

"Not a chieftain," Talia said. "Their king."

"A king of a village?" Vitorix asked.

"No. King of all Dacians. His name is Koson." Talia stood, crossing her arms and staring down in disdain on the man.

"Ask him why he sold the lives of his own people to the Carpathian," Gaius said through clenched teeth. "Is he a coward?"

When Talia finished asking, the Dacian spoke a few words before spitting again.

"He say to stop Rome. But more, because the Carpathian is all power. All tribes must join him…or die."

"Why?" Gaius asked. "Just to stop Rome?"

"No," Talia said after the Dacian answered. "Because the Carpathian is-" she stopped herself for a moment, as if gathering courage to speak the words. "Because he is Death, and Death cannot be beaten."

They were silent, but in a flash, the Dacian reached for a nearby blade, and just as he was about to slash at Talia, Vitorix's blade pinned his hand to the ground. The Dacian screamed and Gaius knelt down to speak to him.

"King Koson," he began. "We will free you from the Carpathian if you tell us where he is."

Talia translated.

"He says they were going to him, to the Jagged Mountains, and the fortress in the earth."

"Fortress in the earth? That way?" Gaius pointed down the treacherous path to the East, and the Dacian nodded. "Vitorix, take your sword out of his hand."

"Yes, sir." Vitorix smiled and pulled the blade out with a jerk.

The Dacian cried out again as the blade scraped his hand bones. Gaius helped him to his feet and saw the Dacian snarl at Talia.

"Some king," Gaius said before heaving the man into the air and throwing him over the cliff.

King Koson roared as he plummeted into the snow-white abyss, his body splintering on the rocks and trees far below.

Vitorix and Calgacus stared at Gaius, and Talia nodded, sheathing her blade.

"He's free from the Carpathian now," Gaius said.

"Aye. That he is," Vitorix smiled.

"Gather everything that's still of use," Gaius ordered. "I don't know how much time Daxos might have left."

Within ten minutes, they were once more tracing the path toward the fang-like peaks that pierced the sky in the distance.

THAT NIGHT, GAIUS CALLED A REST, THEIR STRENGTH drained from the fight earlier that day with the Dacian king's men.

They sat huddled about a small fire at the base of a cluster of tall mountain pines while the carcass of a mountain hare Talia had killed roasted slowly over the flames, the scent of it almost too much to bear with patience.

"How long must the Carpathian have had a hold on the

tribes in this area?" The question came suddenly from Gaius' mouth, though he had been mulling it over for a long time.

"Longer than is natural, for a mortal man," said Calgacus.

"But he isn't mortal, is he?" Vitorix said. "I mean, we all saw how he disappeared with Daxos."

Talia looked up at the mention of her cousin. "How he take Daxos?" she asked.

"We had a battle with the lykoi in Germania," Gaius said. "There was a giant lykos there, the biggest we ever saw. It was about to kill me when…when Daxos approached with his medallion." Gaius pulled out the silver disc with the image of Daxos' father and his men killing another great lykos. "The big lykos stopped because of Daxos, and that gave me time to kill it. That is when the Carpathian took Daxos into his cloak and vanished in a cloud of black moths."

"The dark magic," Talia whispered, her eyes closing and opening slowly.

"Gaius," Vitorix began. "You know we're with you, to the death, as always. But how are we going to fight this Carpathian? What if even these special weapons don't work on him?"

"In truth, I… I don't know. All I know is that Daxos has saved my life more than once, and I cannot repay him by leaving him to this fiend."

"You don't need to say that," Calgacus added. "You know we're in."

"I know. And I know that Mithras is with us," Gaius added, breathing in the mountain air.

The firelight danced wildly and then faded beneath the roasting hare, to be replaced by a bright light that illuminated the blackness of the forest around them. The brilliance became closer and more intense until out of the trees emerged a pair of soft doeskin boots, and a white tunic and trousers.

Gaius and the others rubbed their eyes and groped for their swords, but the light finally lessened and the urgency of their surprise was replaced with awe.

Mithras smiled at the three men and the girl, his auburn hair tied back loosely, his curved dagger glinting at his waist.

His laughter lightened their hearts, even as they feared the days to come. He stared at them all and rested his eyes on Gaius last.

"You've come far, Heliodromus."

"My Lord," Gaius fell to his knees, his arms crossed over his chest, and Calgacus and Vitorix followed suit. Talia sat still, not on her knees, but silent and still.

"Only you can hear me," Mithras said to Gaius. The god then reached out, his hand hovering over the heads of the others, one at a time, until each lay down to rest in blissful sleep. "They will be rejuvenated for the morrow."

"Lord," Gaius looked up. "What will the morrow bring? Do we go to meet Death himself?"

Mithras smiled sadly and stepped to the edge of the cliff where he could see the cold starlight of the heavens.

"I do not know. That is the truth, for I cannot see into the Carpathian's realm. My light does not penetrate so deep without being invited in by a power."

"What power?" Gaius asked reluctantly.

"It is ancient, as is the Carpathian."

"Then he is immortal?"

"No. But he is not mortal like you."

"Lord, who is he? How can we defeat him?"

"I believe he is the one I have sought for ages, a priest who turned on my ancient Daeva enemies, and usurped their power with darkness. He is an Usij. He is treachery, and pain, and darkness. And yes, he is Death, in some ways. He is destruction."

"But how can we, mere men," Gaius indicated his brothers on the ground before the fire, "defeat such a being?" Gaius' heart grew desperate.

"I cannot see into his realm, but you will be my eyes and ears. You will penetrate his realm, and if you can fight your way to the heart of his lair, you must do one thing."

Gaius looked upon the brilliant form of Mithras and felt the heat radiating off him. "What would you have me do, Lord?"

"Make him call me."

Gaius stared out at the night, his god standing there beside him, and felt dread at the limits of his psyche.

"You will see your family again, Heliodromus. But for their sakes too, this must be done. If not, the Carpathian's darkness will outlast you, Rome, the Pantheon of my divine cousins, and eventually myself."

In his mind's eye, Gaius saw the world choked by darkness, he saw rivers of fire and heard screams echo across the lands of the Middle Sea and beyond the edges of the world. All he saw and heard, all he felt in those few moments were pain and desperation covered with a storm of dark laughter.

"You see correctly," Mithras sighed, no trace of the youthful smile upon his face.

"I will bring the Light into the Darkness, my Lord," Gaius said, tears in his eyes. *Oh, my family...* "Even if it means my death."

Mithras turned to Gaius and placed both his hands upon his head.

"Walk in the Light, Heliodromus," he said, laying Gaius

down to sleep. "Rest for this great battle, my Sun Runner. Rest…"

For a while, Mithras watched over the four of them, and when the sun rose in the East, he disappeared back into the forest.

GAIUS AWOKE TO THE SOUND OF THE CRACKLING FIRE AND THE smell of freshly roasted hare. Woodsmoke crept up among the trunks of pine where sunlight filtered through at an angle to rest on the path they must take.

He smiled a moment, and a wonderful feeling of heat and strength ran through his limbs. It felt good, but his thoughts soon turned to what Mithras had told him, the task they must perform. His elation and good feeling was now at odds with the fear in his gut.

We've been through so much… Just a little farther into the Darkness so that the Light can prevail. Gaius stood and fastened the wolf pelt cloak more snuggly about his shoulders. *Fulvia, my love,* he thought, his eyes closed. *I will come back to you. I will come back.*

The mountain path along the cliffs disappeared farther ahead to his right, swallowed by bushes, and trees, and morning mist. His ear could not detect the laughter that had been hounding him for so long, but he knew the Carpathian was out there somewhere in the darkness of those mountains.

Gaius' face darkened and his hand went to the handle of his gladius. He turned to see misty shapes lurking in the morning wood. He was about to yell, but stopped when he recognized the biggest among them.

Julius.

The hair on the back of Gaius' neck prickled. The dead still followed him after so long.

The big shade nodded his centurion's helmet, and Gaius could hear his thoughts.

Keep going, Gaius, it said. *Move out.*

Gaius nodded slowly and walked back to where his three companions slept soundly. "Time to get up," he said.

Calgacus stirred first, rolling over sleepily, and then his eyes darting around for another glimpse of Mithras.

Gaius smiled at him and nodded.

The Briton stood, stretched, and breathed deeply of the mountain air which felt fresh and lively in his lungs.

"Gods I feel good!" Vitorix said as he sat up, rubbing his eyes and flexing his massive arms. He looked at Gaius and Calgacus. "Did he…I mean… Was that really him?"

"Yes," Gaius answered. "The Lord of Light did come to us last night. He blessed us. I spoke with him."

"I knew I started praying to him for a reason!" Vitorix laughed like a child and stood up. "What did he say to you?"

Gaius looked at the two men and at Talia who was now sitting up and cutting the hare for all of them.

As they ate and sharpened their weapons, Gaius told them what Mithras had said about the enemy they were about to face. When he finished, they were utterly silent.

A raven croaked from somewhere in the trees, breaking the silence.

"Well," Vitorix finally said. "I've had enough talking and waiting to take this bastard on. I'm feeling better than I've ever felt right now, so what better time for a fight?"

Gaius smiled, but the words chilled him.

Calgacus was silent and stern-faced.

Gaius turned to Talia, her bright eyes boring into his from

beneath the dirty wisps of her black hair. He could not get over her resemblance to Daxos.

"You don't have to come," he told her.

She looked up, her eyes suddenly angry, despite the strength and warmth she felt inside since waking up. "Daxos is my cousin!" She stood and sheathed the pugio she had been sharpening. "I'm going with you."

Gaius nodded to her, but felt a pang at the thought of the experiences that she had endured to make her so tough.

"We'll be glad to have you fight with us," Vitorix said, clapping Talia on the shoulder. He did not understand her Thracian Greek, but her look said it all.

"Then let's go," Gaius said, hoisting his satchel and pilum.

Calgacus kicked snow onto the flames of their cookfire as Vitorix shoved the last piece of meat into his mouth.

Talia stood beside Gaius on the path, and the two Celts joined them so that, as four, they turned to stare ahead.

"Mithras is with us. We need not fear," Gaius said, knowing he was trying to convince himself as he started forward. He gripped the shaft of his pilum tightly against the horrifying images of his wife and daughters weeping and bloody, and he hoped that what he saw was his own fear. But with each step toward the Jagged Mountains, the laughter at the back of his mind grew louder and more exuberant.

The others broke into a jog to keep up with Gaius who was disappearing ahead of them.

"We need to stay with him, Vitorix," Calgacus said as they padded along behind Talia, whose nimble legs pushed her forward without tiring.

They moved at that unrelenting pace for half the day, without any sign of lykoi, or immortui along the way. The trees became less densely packed as they went, the clouds low and grey, having succeeded in choking out the sun.

When Gaius came to an abrupt stop ahead of them, Vitorix, Calgacus, and Talia slowed until they came up beside him. He stood at a line in the earth and rock of the forest floor which ended as though scorched of all life and colour.

"What's this?" Vitorix asked as their eyes took in the grey-black landscape, devoid of trees, or scrub, or even of snow.

"There's nothing here," Calgacus said.

"It's the Carpathian's realm, his power," Gaius said, drawing a line in the ashen earth before them with the point of his pilum. "We're close."

Talia placed a tentative foot over the line and stepped onto the other side.

"Talia wait!" Gaius said loudly, but she did not turn. He stepped forward to grab her but as he did so, his ears rang with the sounds of weeping, of hunger, and thirst, and exhaustion. Gaius spun to see Calgacus and Vitorix's mouths moving quickly, but he could not hear them.

The two warriors moved forward and –

"What is this place?" Vitorix was shouting, covering his ears.

"Talia, could you not hear us yelling?" Gaius said.

She turned and shook her head, her face confused. "You spoke?"

"Yes." Gaius looked back at the line where brown, green, and white gave way suddenly to grey and black. "There must be a path," he said, not wanting to delay.

"Over there!" Calgacus ran forward and saw a trail slithering upward to disappear into a series of black peaks that rose up like fangs beside a deep canyon.

"The Jagged Mountains," Talia said, pointing into the near distance.

Before the others could say anything, she was running down the path toward those deadly peaks.

"Mithras, Lord, I hope you can hear us in this place," Gaius said as they set off after her.

Daxos could only just feel the heat from the fire several feet away. It seemed as though he had been cold forever, locked in the rock cell with the memories of his dead family, and his fear, fear that Gaius and the others were all truly dead, food for the mountain crows. And then there was the fear of his own death…

After a nightmare in which he had seen his adopted sisters and mother torn to shreds and rotting in a pool of blood, he had begun to feel like his end was near. When he had awoken, he found himself bound by a chain, before the fire where he now found himself.

Daxos tried to slip his hands free, but the ropes from before had cut deep into his skin making even the slightest movement an agony. He was numb with pain. Worst of all, however, was that he was seated directly facing the creature that had so terrified him the last time he had been in that room.

He knew she was there, but had avoided looking, trying to avert every one of his senses from the sight, sound, and smell of the Daeva, which is what the Carpathian had referred to her as.

However, the incessant, pained moaning caused Daxos to finally look up. The sight filled him with disgust, fear, and pity all at once.

The Daeva was taller than any man Daxos had ever seen. Her skin was greenish-black and hard-looking, covered in scars from her ram-horned head to her clawed feet, signs of her tortured incarceration. She wore no clothing, genitalia and wounded breasts openly visible, tied upright as she was by the adamant chains that pulled her arms and legs taught.

Daxos glanced at the table where the ancient stone dagger lay in silent menace, and then looked back to the Daeva.

The massive horned head lolled sideways to look at him, and the Daeva's green eyes met his. They were not terrifying now that Daxos looked back. He was unaware of the ages of harm the creature had done, the babies and beasts she had blissfully devoured so long ago.

All Daxos saw now in those eyes was pain and exhaustion beyond measure, and an unimaginable wish for the finality of death.

The only movement she made besides the lolling of her head was made by the torn wings that jutted from the spine at her back, where they were crushed against the rockface.

"Ti ise?" Daxos whispered, asking who she was.

The faded eyes looked at him and she opened her mouth to reveal broken fangs in a pained grimace. There was no sound.

As the Daeva tried to say something, to move just a bit more, a stream of tears leached out of the corner of one eye. She made to try again, but before she could raise her head, a shadow came across her, and her neck snapped sideways hideously.

The Carpathian stood there before her and turned to face Daxos. His long black hair framed his furious, red eyes, and it was then that Daxos felt real fear take hold of him.

"Don't pity that monster, boy. You've no idea what she has done."

The Carpathian's eyes dimmed to dark again as he moved closer to the fire to gaze into the leaping flames. He was of an average size now that Daxos took in his shape, outlined by his thick, floor length cloak of black.

"Take a good look," the Carpathian said before turning to walk slowly toward Daxos. "I'm ages old, and yet, I cannot die. I am Death. Ime Thanatos…"

He laughed slowly, deeply, the soundscape of Daxos' nightmares come to fruition.

"Why you not kill me?" Daxos asked, his voice shaking, though he tried to still it.

"Why?" the Carpathian answered. "I could have killed *her* thousands of years ago. Why? Because, to bring death, I must keep her alive. I served their kind, the Daevas," he spat, "for years. I watched them wreak havoc and chaos on the people around me. This one…" he pointed at the chained Daeva. "She devoured babies as she rolled in their parents' blood and offal. She and her ilk slaughtered people as they slaughtered the cattle of the arrogant Yazads, who did little to stop the suffering of my fellow humans."

Daxos' brow creased suddenly as he realized that he could understand the Carpathian's words. Death spoke his tongue, it seemed, as he spoke all tongues.

"But humans are weak and short-lived. I found a way to milk the strength of my enemies, and this one has kept me alive and powerful, and dealing death for ages."

"You crazy…" Daxos stuttered.

The Carpathian smiled and moved to the table to take up the ancient blade and a golden goblet. He then walked toward Daxos, but veered away to go stand before the Daeva, and with the stone blade, he cut into her thick skin as he had countless times before, this time below the left breast.

The creature groaned as he pressed the goblet to the cut to catch the blood that flowed out of the wound, hot and steaming.

The Carpathian then turned to Daxos, smiling as he held the goblet up, its gilded surface glinting in the firelight.

"I am the Night, and all Dread," he said, his eyes closed. "To the Darkness I belong. Timeless I am. I am Power, and Destruction. I command legions of undead. The gods themselves fear me… For I am Thanatos."

He smiled and drank, the blood pouring down his gullet slowly, smoothly, filling his limbs with fire and power beyond imagining. Immortal youth sprang up so that he might continue to destroy Rome, to destroy the world.

When he finished drinking, the Carpathian smiled at Daxos who had vomited on the floor.

"You madness," Daxos said. "You lie about everything."

"I do not, boy. And believe me when I tell you that I will not kill you."

"Why not?"

"Because she," he gestured to the Daeva, "is weakening. The Daevas are mortal in essence, though their bodies can live on. But I have found something better."

Daxos felt his heart beat faster with terror, his limbs shake, the veins in his head and neck pulsing.

"Yes. I have a Yazad to milk now." He pointed the dagger at Daxos. "You. Yes. Your village stood up against the Dark for ages for a reason. All others bent their knees to me."

"You are crazy. I not a god."

The Carpathian laughed again. "They hid you well for long, but when I finally found you, the immortui were able to tear up your protectors. There would never have been a safe place for you, anywhere."

"You know not what you say," Daxos said faintly, tears burning his eyes.

"No? I know more than you, boy. I know that when a Yazad lies with a mortal woman, it produces a being of strength."

He came close to Daxos then, his face so near the boy could smell decay and blood.

"The essence of a Yazad is more powerful than a Daeva's, and I shall have yours once the incantations are complete."

Daxos, despite his terror, the spinning thoughts caught in the maelstrom of his mind, managed to gather enough saliva to spit in the Carpathian's face.

"How dare you!" the Carpathian hissed, revealing the growing fangs in his mouth like those of the Daeva's. "I want you to imagine the pain she has gone through, and multiply it a hundred times. That is what I shall do to you."

He began to undress before Daxos until he was naked, his body that of a youthful man, muscled and lean.

"I shall keep the power I have milked from her..." He raised his arms and the muscles rippled, the skin hardened. "I am Death. I am a Daeva." Curved horns sprouted from his skull, and nails like iron claws erupted from his fingertips. "And soon, I shall drink of Yazad blood!"

"Monster!" Daxos cursed and spat again, his courage evanescent.

"No," the Carpathian said. "I am Death to Rome and all the world!"

He roared to shake the mountain, enormous black wings sprouting from his back, his eyes flashing fire in the darkness.

Daxos screamed as his ear drums burst, and the chained Daeva added her own chorus of pain.

Then, all was darkness, and Daxos slumped into oblivion.

"WHAT WAS THAT?" GAIUS YELLED AS THEY STOPPED AT THE foot of the first jagged peak to avoid a rush of boulders and rubble.

"Daxos!" Talia cried as she was pulled to cover by Vitorix, a giant rock crashing where she had been standing a moment before.

"We need to keep moving!" Gaius cried when the rock-slide stopped.

The four of them powered up the slope of grey rock between walls of blackness, but stopped when sets of red eyes peered at them from above.

Howls pierced the air, loud enough to drown out the incessant sounds of weeping that had been peeling through their ears since they set foot in those lands.

"Back to the open!" Calgacus turned to run, but stopped short when faced with a hundred sets of wild, jaundiced eyes and reaching arms.

"Immortui!"

FULVIA SHOT UP IN BED AND FELL TO THE FLOOR, HER HEAD ringing with screams and slaughter, her face wet with tears.

"Gaius!" she cried.

"Mama? What's wrong?" Aemilia sat up in the bed they had been sharing, nudging Faustina.

"Girls," Fulvia wrapped a cloak about her sweaty, pained body. "We must go to the lararium. Now!" She tossed two more cloaks to the girls and went out the door, down to the peristylium, and then to the family shrine.

Fulvia lit a chuck of incense in the ever-burning flame dedicated to Vesta, and put it on the altar before the statues of Jupiter, Juno, Minerva, Vesta, and others, including an image of Mithras.

Aemilia and Faustina came running in and knelt beside their mother. They all gripped hands.

"Gods and Goddesses of our ancestors, watch over our husband and father. Keep him safe in the darkness." She wept as she spoke, the panicked words pouring rapidly out of her trembling mouth, the girls barely able to echo them.

"Light Gaius' way. Lend your strength to his arm, and justice to his sword. Fill his heart with courage, and love, and will beyond measure."

She slowed, her short energy reserves exhausted.

"Gods and Goddesses, we honour you… Please…help him. Bring him back to us."

"Mithras, Lord of Light," Aemilia suddenly said, remembering the words she had heard her father utter. "Protect our father as he heads into darkness. Stand by him, and light his way. Please. Please…"

"Please, Gods," Faustina added. "Please."

Mother and daughters stayed there, huddled together in their prayers and appeals, hoping that their words would reach the Gods' ears.

"What ungodly place is this?" Antonius asked the Dacian priest, Corax, as they stood at the edge of the forest looking into the dry, colourless waste before them.

"The Jagged Mountains. This is the Carpathian's realm. I have only ever come this far."

Antonius looked across at the old man, and Sabinus looked at him with doubt.

Corax had slowed them, as they had expected, but he had shown them the way through the Dacian forests, hills, and gullies. However, the journey had taken a toll on him, and he now panted and grabbed occasionally at his chest.

It was only determination and his gods, Zalmoxis, Bendis, and Gebeleizis, that kept Corax going. His hatred of the Carpathian too had a role in his stubborn persistence.

"There are some tracks there." Sabinus pointed. "There, in the dust."

They all gazed at the sets of foot prints, not yet daring to step onto the grey earth and rock before them.

"Four sets of prints," Sabinus confirmed. "With these, and that mass of dead Dacians we saw a couple days ago, I'd say we're on the right track."

Relief swept over Antonius as he recognized the three sets of treads similar to his own black boots. "Looks like Gaius has picked up a companion," he said, pointing toward the smaller prints. "They follow that path. Let's go!"

Corax stepped across first and as soon as he crossed the line, he fell to his knees, covering his ears.

Antonius and Sabinus rushed to the old man only to be hit by the all-too-familiar sounds of raging lykoi, and ravenous immortui.

"Mithras, no!" Antonius yelled, getting to his feet and drawing his gladius.

"Come on, Corax!' Sabinus helped the priest to his feet. He then tore a strip of his cloak away and tied it about Corax's ears to muffle the sounds.

"Let's go!" Antonius yelled, trying to be heard above the sounds of chaos in the jagged rocks ahead of them.

The three men began to run, uncertain of what they would find, and if they would live out the day.

"CLIMB! UP THE ROCKFACE! CLIMB!" GAIUS YELLED AS THE lykoi rushed down the path and the immortui up it.

All they could see in the grey light were furious eyes, all they could hear were the howls, moans, and gnashing teeth of the enemies bearing down on them.

Gaius sheathed his gladius and gripped the black rock, pulling himself up, with Calgacus doing the same, his own sword slashing at a lunging lykos.

"Up you go, girl!" Vitorix yelled, all but tossing Talia high onto a small ledge before turning to behead two immortui with one swing before hoisting himself up, his bloodied battle axe slung quickly over his shoulder.

Gaius looked about to make sure they were all fine, unaware that on the ledge above him, a pair of red eyes was watching. He felt the saliva on his cheek, whirled around, and jerked back just in time to avoid the jaws. But he lost his grip.

"No!" Calgacus yelled as he watched Gaius tumble into a mass of immortui and lykoi who were tearing away at each other.

The impact when he fell on his back winded Gaius, but he rolled quickly out of the way and lunged for the rockface again, his arms burning as he pulled his body up, legs kicking at the clawing hands below.

"Gaius! I'm coming!" Vitorix yelled.

"No! I'm fine! Stay there!" Gaius heaved deep breaths of putrid air, his face pressed against the rock. He turned a few moments later to see Calgacus and Vitorix on the rockface on the opposite side of the choked path. High up, Talia had continued to climb. "I'll find you!" Gaius yelled over to them. "Stay together and try to find Daxos. Talia wait!" Gaius watched as the girl disappeared into one of the many holes that pocked the mountainside. "Go after her!" Gaius said to the other two men. "I'll find you!"

Calgacus nodded and began to climb, while Vitorix waited a moment longer, watching Gaius.

"Go!" Gaius yelled one more time to the big Gaul.

Vitorix nodded and grunted as he began climbing again.

Gaius climbed higher, his arms and legs trying to find foot and hand holds that would bear his armoured weight. It was a slow and tiring progress, but luckily he found a large ledge where he was able to rest a moment.

When he looked up, the others were gone, disappeared into what he now saw to be a series of rock-hewn tunnels in the mountainside.

Far below, the lykoi were dispersing, having torn apart most of the immortui except for those who were feasting on the entrails of one lykos they had managed to overwhelm in the chaos.

"Ha, ha, ha…." came the laugh. "Centurion…"

Gaius stopped and looked around, felt cold fear grip his heart.

"I see you, Centurion…" it mocked.

Gaius drew his gladius, the silver blade hard in the dull light.

He heard scuffling on rock and searched around, his eyes probing the darkness of the tunnels around him.

Then a lykos head poked out, snarling, then another, and another.

Gaius slashed and cut at them, their bodies falling out only to be replaced by others.

Then, on the cliff above, a mass of immortui appeared, looking down at Gaius. Their eyes sent chills up Gaius' spine, but he willed his sword to hack anything that came too near.

Then, two immortui dropped, narrowly missing him as they cracked on the rock edge where Gaius stood, almost taking him with them to the bottom of the cliff.

"Ha, ha, ha...."

Gaius shut out the laughter as best he could and scanned high up to go back down and follow the others. Then he noticed one of the tunnels near him; it had not regurgitated any lykoi or immortui. That one path seemed like his only way out and so he prepared to jump for it.

The tunnel faced onto a smaller ledge that seemed like the only quiet point all around.

Gaius lunged, his fingertips narrowly hanging on as a lykos snapped wildly at him from a few feet away. When he pulled himself up, he leaned forward into the tunnel to get away from another lykos' jaws, but got off balance and pitched himself headlong into the darkness.

He fell and fell, the sound of rock against his helmet and armour repetitive and painful until, his head spinning, Gaius hit bottom and lay there unconscious in the dark within the mountain.

"Talia!" Vitorix' voice called in the dark where only a single bit of grey light from outside penetrated. "Talia!"

"Keep your voice down," Calgacus hissed. "She's not here. We've taken the wrong tunnel."

"Gods!" Vitorix looked back the way they had come. "We've got to go back."

"We can't. We don't know which tunnel she took. Besides, we need to press on and find Daxos and Gaius too."

"Press on? How are we going to do that with no light?" Vitorix peered ahead into the pitch blackness of the mountain.

"Mithras will light our way, my friend," Calgacus said. "Whatever tunnel Talia took, she'll have pressed on to find her cousin. If we go back, we're less likely to find her." Calgacus drew his gladius and pointed into the dark.

Vitorix smiled to himself. "Aye, she's tough, I'll give her that. Fine. Let's go." Vitorix stepped past Calgacus, one hand holding his sword, the other out to touch the walls and ceiling of the tunnel.

They stumbled through the dark for what felt like hours, their breath shallow in the close, rank air.

"We might never get out of here," Vitorix muttered. "Oh, Lord Mithras, light our way."

Calgacus stopped to wipe sweat away from his brow. "What's that sound?" he said, his hand reaching out for Vitorix.

The big Gaul cocked his head and listened too. "Sounds like scraping."

"It's something. Let's move forward."

As they pressed on, they found their eyes drawn to a faint orange light up ahead. They came closer to it until they were a few yards away and the floor dropped before them.

The two men crashed onto an uneven floor where they lay stunned for a few moments, filling their lungs with air again.

Moaning, Calgacus rolled over onto his knees and stopped.

They were surrounded by eyes, near and distant, yellow

and red. There was a thrumming of sickly groans and snarling, the eyes narrowing in anger.

"Vitorix!" Calgacus shook the Gaul. "Get up now!"

"Oh, my fucking shoulder," Vitorix groaned and pushed himself up. "By Mars' hairy balls!"

"Back-to-back. Now!" Calgacus pressed his back to the Gaul's and they turned slowly, their gladii out and ready.

"Where'd they all come from?" Vitorix asked.

Then the ground, the mountain itself, began to shake, and the sound of cracking rock echoed in the chamber.

"Look out!" Vitorix pulled Calgacus away as the earth itself cracked open to reveal a fiery light that bathed the chamber in red. All around them, the lykoi and immortui were moving in, and both men feared that these were greater numbers than they had ever faced.

"Stay back-to-back," Calgacus said.

Lykoi and immortui jostled each other to close in, each uncaring of the other, just so long as they could fix their terrible eyes on the two men.

The first of the lykoi lunged, and Calgacus yelled. "Mithras!"

Both Romans' swords shot out, the silver edges glinting in the red light. They hacked and slashed, feinted and attacked again, but none of the beasts fell, nor raged more, nor showed any sign of having been weakened.

Their weapons were ineffective.

"Battle axes!" Vitorix said as they both unhitched their axes from their backs.

Their swings were heavy and deadly, and would have cut three men in half easily. However, their weapons sliced through the air, as flimsy as feathers in a fight. When the axes did not work, either, both men laid into them enemy with gloved fists, punching snouts and ripping lykoi jaws asunder in showers of blood. They punched at the flesh of immortui with a fury that surpassed the ancient battle frenzies of their ancestors, piling immortui heads and limbs about them in pools of black blood and puss.

Wave upon wave of foul creatures came at them, but they continued to fight with the fire of Mithras warming their spirits.

Then a great lykos closed its jaws around Vitorix's ankle and dragged him to a far side of the cave.

The big Gaul bellowed as pain tore through him, the wolf's teeth grinding on his bones. Then he sat up as he was being dragged and reached for the lykos' head, pressing his thumbs into the malevolent eyes.

The lykos shuddered, and its features began to turn back to those of a man.

Before the change could be completed, Vitorix hoisted the beast and slammed it against the rockface. His fists pounded in and out, sometimes missing and connecting with the rock, other times hammering flesh and bone.

"Vitorix…"

Vitorix turned but could not see Calgacus. Then he felt a pain in his stomach that sent him toppling backward. As he fell, jaws and jaundiced eyes closed in around him until he felt his face being pommeled.

"Calgacus! Help! Ahh!"

Darkness enveloped them, and the cave was silent.

"Vitor… Vitorix? Are you there?" Calgacus muttered weakly. There was no response, but he did hear frenzied breathing nearby, and a pained moan. "Vitorix?" Calgacus reached out in the dark.

"I'm here."

They lay beside each other in the dark, on the cave floor, an echo of laughter circling them like a bat in the dark.

Calgacus tried to see something, but could not. His face felt bloody and swollen. "I can't see."

"I think I've broken my hand," Vitorix muttered, shifting painfully so that he was now kneeling. "Where are our weapons?"

There was a pause.

"We're wearing them," Calgacus said, now aware that his gladius and battle axe were still strapped to himself.

"Where did the lykoi and immortui go?" Vitorix asked.

"Ah," Calgacus felt his face burning, tightening. "I don't think there were any."

"Impossible! I tore many apart. I saw you do it too. That last one that dragged me away began to change back as I beat him."

"That was me, my friend."

The laughter grew louder and louder, and Vitorix clenched his broken hand in anger. "We're going to kill you!" he shouted at the darkness.

"We need to get out of here," Calgacus said.

"That fall was real enough," Vitorix added. "We're not in the tunnel, and I can see the fire up above." He looked up to see a flicker of light.

"There's got to be a tunnel out of here," Calgacus said. "Walk to the side and we'll circle the perimeter of this chamber with our hands on the wall. I'll hold your cloak as we go. My one eye is shut."

"I'm sorry," Vitorix said, suddenly silent.

"Me too. If your rib is broken, it was probably from me kicking at you."

"Let's get out of here," Vitorix said, moving with his hands out until he found the wall. "Got it."

They shuffled along the uneven ground for a long time without finding anything. Just as they thought they were going to be trapped, Vitorix's leg slipped into the mouth of a shaft.

"Ahh!"

"What?" Calgacus said, gripping the Gaul's arm tightly.

"It's a shaft of some kind." He felt around. "Seems like our only option."

"How big? Will we fit?"

Vitorix felt the mouth of it. "Yes. At the top anyway." He felt around for a rock and then dropped it down the shaft. It tumbled down at an angle and they heard a distant crack as it hit bottom. "No water," Vitorix said gladly.

Then there was a lone growl at the bottom.

"Gaping jaws better?" Calgacus asked.

Vitorix unsheathed his gladius. "Only if they're real. Come on. No other options, right?"

"Right."

Vitorix put both his legs down the shaft. "You follow after five seconds."

"Mithras guide you. Slash at anything around you."

"One…two…three!" Vitorix plunged feet first into the shaft.

Calgacus waited, and then followed. The rocky surface tore at his cloak and armour, and he heard a yell, the swing of a blade, and then a loud yelp. He hit the ground hard and looked about with his one eye. He could hear Vitorix spitting, and smelled the tang of blood.

"Real?" Calgacus asked.

"Yes. And so is my gladius. Which way now?"

Calgacus tried to remember the upper tunnel, but they had become too turned around.

A scream suddenly pierced the darkness somewhere far away to their left.

"Talia!" Vitorix said. "We're coming!"

Calgacus drew his own gladius and followed, holding Vitorix's torn cloak as they went on blindly, guided only by the sound of screaming.

TALIA CROUCHED IN THE THIRD TUNNEL SHE HAD TAKEN SINCE losing the others. The dark was not as bad for her eyes, used as she was to hiding in the dark. She was, however, not used to being so close to one of the lykoi.

Her scream had been unintentional when the beast surprised her. That upset her.

As the red eyes and snarling jaws came closer and closer, she drew the silver blade she had been carrying, and pointed it out.

The lykos snapped, and she swung, just missing, so that the blade hit the rock and sent sparks into the air. The beast lunged again and retreated, avoiding her flailing blade.

Talia prodded and poked, as a child tries to tease a dog with naught but a stick, but she wanted the beast to come closer.

The lykos tired of the standoff, saliva dripping from its blood-hungry teeth. It lunged high for Talia's head, but she dropped and pushed up with all her strength into the soft belly.

The creature crashed into the rockface, gripped by seizures as the wound sizzled around the silver-edged steel. Then, the head rounded, and bone and muscle contorted and contracted until all that lay there was a young Dacian man, blood leaking from his grimacing mouth.

Talia spat on the corpse, and pulled her blade free, spinning in case any others were behind her.

She was alone.

"Talia!"

She heard the call, and her heart leapt a little.

"Talia!" it came again.

She moved on in the direction of the voice until she came into a wider tunnel with a high ceiling, almost the width of a road.

"Talia, there you are, my girl!"

Talia wheeled around to see her mother running toward her across the village.

"Quickly, love. You must run! They're here!"

"Mama?" Talia felt her hands shake. "Where is Baba?"

Her mother looked around the village, the central well beneath the tall trees crowded with crying children. "Run, Talia! Run, and don't stop!"

"Mama! No!!!" Talia watched as waves of immortui slammed into the cluster of villagers, tearing at the limbs of men, women, and children. They feasted beneath sprays of blood which showered their jaundiced eyes.

Then Talia's mother was knocked off her feet by a charging pair of immortui. Her screams were choked as they plunged their jagged nails into her stomach as Talia looked on in absolute horror.

Talia's whole body shook as she watched in the dark of that tunnel, but then she stopped, the handle of the pugio bringing her back.

"That already happened," she said slowly, evenly, her eyes open again, and her blade up.

The images of slaughter and death vanished and all she could hear was her breathing.

Then a familiar, drunken laughter echoed around her, and several feet away, the form of a muscled, naked man holding a drinking horn stumbled toward her.

"Come here, my Thracian bitch!" he slurred.

Talia fought the racing of her heart, and the urge to cry as he came close, the dirty, erect phallus between his legs pointing threateningly at her.

Talia forced herself to remember what it felt like when her dagger had plunged into her captor's groin, and the sounds of his screams as blood poured out of his hateful body.

"He's dead now!" she said, loud and strong, so that her voice pierced the darkness. "I killed him!"

Again, the image vanished and she felt her strength return, standing in that spot for a minute before moving on.

Talia walked on in darkness, not daring to call out anymore. She had an urge to eat and sleep, but that went away the second she heard the sound of distant sobbing, a sound so pitiful and pained, of ultimate despair, that it made her feel compassion for the first time in a long while.

"Daxos?" she said to herself, and began to run, heedless of what she ran into, so long as it brought her closer to her cousin's voice.

ANOTHER NIGHT WAS FALLING, AND THE DISTANT SOUND OF ranging lykoi came from every direction in the jagged mountains. The moon was emerging from behind clouds, seemingly giving voice to the beasts that had no doubt picked up the scent of the three men making their way in the grey light.

Sabinus stooped to look at the immortui and lykoi

corpses that littered the path into the mountain. "None of ours," he said. "But they stop here. Look, only paw prints and shuffling footsteps go beyond this point. No Roman boots."

The three men looked around, trying to see what they could in the dying light.

"Perhaps they were overwhelmed?" Corax said hesitantly. "Some of these corpses are so torn we might not be able to tell."

Antonius shot the Dacian a fiery look. "You don't know Gaius or the others. They're alive, I know it." He closed his eyes, tried to ignore the ringing in his ears.

"Look up!" Sabinus pointed with his gladius. "Tunnels. I can just make out the holes."

"They climbed," Antonius whispered.

"But which one? There are dozens," Corax said. "Even in daylight, I could not make that climb."

"Even if they did make it up there, it's too dark now," Sabinus said. "Besides, I see some eyes."

They fell silent and looked more closely at the tunnels.

Peering out from each hole were faint red eyes, watching, waiting, ready to pounce.

"Let's go," Antonius said. "Now!"

They broke into a run, continuing on the path into the mountains. As they went, howls broke from the caves and tunnels. The lykoi were moving to head them off.

"Quickly!" Sabinus said to Corax, taking the old man's satchel from him.

"There!" Antonius pointed to a dead tree that rose beside a high boulder. "Up the tree and onto the rock!"

Sabinus arrived first, throwing himself up into the branches and leaping for the top of the boulder. "Come on!"

he yelled, reaching his hand out to Corax whom Antonius had helped up.

The old Dacian struggled, but found the strength to pull himself to safety.

Antonius turned quickly, his blade slashing at the first lykos to reach him, and then heaved himself up before others arrived.

Corax covered his ears for all the baying, and Sabinus scanned the area.

There were about thirteen lykoi about the boulder now. "We're trapped!" Sabinus said.

"Just hold. We can't take them all, and we can't outrun them. Let's lie down so they can't see us. Maybe they'll go away."

The three men lay flat on the cold rock surface and stared at the sky and clouds, the strangled stars that were beginning to twinkle far above. The snarling drove them near to madness, but Antonius and Sabinus, who began sharpening his gladius again, lay back and waited, their minds searching for Mithras' light in the midst of that chaos and darkness.

Corax found his words and, as though speaking into the teeth of a gale, prayed to Zalmoxis and Bendis, Gebeleizis and Derzelas to watch over him in that land of evil.

My wolves, and the undead, will feast on your flesh soon, old man... the mocking voice pried its way into Corax's prayers and the old man shut his eyes tightly against it.

Then the wind began with a howl that tore at their ears and threatened to rip them from their rocky perch.

They pulled their cloaks on over their faces and bodies then, huddling together against the force of the wind, and against the terrors of the night.

They dozed uneasily, aware of a feeling that a thousand

pairs of eyes were on them, or perhaps just the one. The darkness was complete, and the howls of the lykoi fell away.

When morning came, dim and silent, Antonius woke with a start, nearly falling over the edge of the rock. He looked down, scanning the shadows, and noticed the lykoi were not there.

"They're gone," he said to Sabinus who was also looking around, one hand shaking Corax gently.

"The wolves are gone, but the enemy is still here," Sabinus said.

"What?" Antonius stood and peered over the opposite ledge. There, on the ground, slept three men. "They've changed back."

"Let's kill them before they wake," Sabinus urged, running his finger across his throat.

"Wait," said Corax who was pointing at a youth with long, matted hair. "I know him!"

"You can't save him, Corax," Antonius said.

The old man did not speak.

Antonius and Sabinus went first, lowering themselves as quietly as they could onto the limbs of the dead tree.

Then Corax stepped onto one of the tree branches, but lost his footing and fell hard upon it so that the branch cracked and he plummeted to the ashen ground.

Antonius and Sabinus drew their swords and went around to find two of the men still sleeping. Without hesitation, they lunged and plunged their gladii into their enemies' hearts.

The men cried out briefly before their heads fell back.

"Where's the third?" Antonius asked, but he was knocked from his feet a second later by the remaining man. They struggled on the ground, and as Sabinus rushed in, his blade flashing, the man leapt high into the air and landed away from the two Romans.

"He's going to warn others!" cried Sabinus. "Kill him!"

"Wait!" Corax said, now back on his feet and running around to face the young man, his hands out. "Gormund? It's me, Corax. Do you remember me, lad? You used to help me at the temple of Zalmoxis years ago. We are friends, no? I know your parents."

"They're dead, old man," the boy spat.

"No…"

"And I did it!" he said triumphantly. "The Carpathian is the only true god and ruler. You!" He pointed at Antonius and Sabinus. "Rome will burn, and your families will cry for the rest of their days."

"Let's just kill the little bastard already!" Sabinus grumbled.

The young man raised his arms to the mountains, a maniacal grin on his face. "Our lord is all powerful, he is Death!" Then, he looked back at Antonius and Sabinus, and his muscles bulged and his bones cracked.

"No, Gormund!" Corax cried. "Fight it!"

Gormund laughed and as the snout and fangs of a lykos began to push out, Antonius' pugio embedded itself in his stomach, just as he was falling onto all fours.

"No!" Corax yelled.

"Shut up!" Sabinus chided him. "Do you want to wake the whole fucking valley?"

But Corax ignored him, walking over to the youth who had helped him make countless offerings to their Dacian gods. He was unrecognizable but for the eyes which he had got from his mother.

"We need to move." Antonius took his pugio from the body, and pulled Corax away. "Come. Now!"

They remained in the shadows, sheer rockfaces rising up on their right, and now a deadly drop on their left. They moved faster when a group of immortui to the South, down a long defile, spotted them and began their crazed amble toward them.

Then they were face-to-face with a high black hole in the mountain, as if it were a gateway made for a giant.

"What's this?" Antonius said, his voice a croak. "Mithras help us."

Nothing could be seen within for all the darkness, but something could be heard. A snarl unlike any they had heard before.

"I don't like this," Sabinus said, his sword out.

Before they could run, a group of three lykoi emerged from the darkness. However, these were different, armed with axes and standing on their hind legs like men, despite the fact that they were wolves.

"Gods help us!" Corax said as Antonius and Sabinus rushed the new enemies.

THE FIGHTING RAGED BEFORE THE DACIAN PRIEST'S EYES, AND he remembered long ago days of youthful brawling along the green banks of mountain rivers covered in wildflowers. Then, he had fought and felt strong, invincible beneath a hot sun.

But as Corax stood there, watching the horrors of a battle with powers unknown, he found himself silent and still, frozen, despite the yells of the two Romans.

He found himself in tattered priest's robes, back in the

sacred precincts of Sarmizegethusa. The temples were dark, colourless, broken and silent. All about him, wolves slunk in and out of the shadows, around the temples of his forbears. The beasts howled, and urinated on the columns. They yelped in a ferocious frenzy as dark clouds moved in, followed by laughter as hateful as the atrocities visited upon a sacked village.

When he heard crying, and calls for help, Corax spotted some of his fellow Dacians running toward him – men, women, and children with whom he had lived and worshipped the gods.

A little boy came to the fore, the one who helped him at the temple.

"You are safe now," Corax said as he spread his arms wide to usher them all into the temple sanctuary of Zalmoxis.

The boy shook his head, reached beneath his cloak and produced a dagger.

Before Corax realized it, he felt the blade's handle protruding from his gut, the blood pouring out as the men and women heaved him up, his blood washing over them. Into the temple they went, and placed him upon the stone altar.

He could not hear a thing as they beat him, and stabbed at his body.

When they were finished, they stepped back to make way for the Carpathian, laughter upon his lips and fire in his eyes.

Corax felt the fire on his skin which began to peel and curl like burning animal hide or papyrus. All about him, the wooden images of his gods began to dissolve into clouds of ash out of which wolf eyes emerged.

"Ah!!!" Corax yelled, his ears ringing with sounds of pain and exhaustion, and the crack of metal on fangs. He raised his sword to charge to the Romans' aid, his dark reverie broken, but even as his blade caught the grey light, a snout and sharp fangs bored into his stomach, rending him with pain beyond imagining.

The pulling and tearing stopped abruptly then, and the faces of the Romans appeared above him, red and blurry through his tearing eyes.

"I am done…" Corax muttered. "Go, and may your gods protect you better than mine have…go…go. Bendis…I come…"

"He's done," Sabinus said, breathless from fighting. He pulled Antonius up from his knees beside Corax's body.

The two of them stared at the scene of slaughter, the three lykoi scattered in hacked pieces about the clotted ground.

Antonius stared at the void of the gate before them. *Mithras, I pray you can see us in there, Lord.*

"Gaius and the others are in there somewhere," Sabinus said. "Our brothers need our help."

The laughter in Antonius' head seemed to set off a chorus of more howls, but he gripped his gladius and looked at Sabinus.

"Our Heliodromus needs us," he said, "and we will bring the Light."

Sabinus nodded and looked at the pitiful remnants of Corax.

"Farewell, Dacian," Antonius said, and the two men ran into the darkness.

IT WAS NOT LONG BEFORE THEY WERE RUNNING FOR THEIR lives in the darkness, lykoi at their heels, their gladii slashing blindly on either side.

Sabinus ran ahead, sensing that Antonius was behind, but unable to turn for all the jaws snapping at him. Every sword or dagger thrust he laid out behind him seemed ineffective at the run.

Romans were not used to retreating or running from an enemy.

"Antonius! We have to turn and fight!" he yelled, but there was no answer. All Sabinus could see were red eyes in the dark, and the glimmer of fangs dripping with saliva. "Come on!" he spat at the lykoi, kicking one in the face and slashing the snout of another. "Antonius!" he yelled again, but his mind only saw a bloody, mangled shell that was his comrade, lying on the floor of a cave.

The lykoi pressed in on him, trying to flank him as he backed up slowly, his blade only just holding them off.

Sabinus felt his foot slip and went down to one knee, and that is when the lead lykos pounced. His gladius thrust up quickly, but both Sabinus and the wolf went over the edge of the void where the chase had ended in a tumble of rubble and blood.

The other lykoi howled above the black pit and turned to run another way.

"Sabinus!" Antonius yelled when the sounds of howling reached his ears. "Where are you?"

You...you...you... his voice echoed back at him where he stood, knee-high in a pile of lykoi corpses.

He stumbled out of the bloody mass, willing himself to feel light and heat as he remembered them. He felt the ground begin to rise, and followed the path for some time until he reached a sandy plateau in the mountain.

Then, he sensed it, a smell of jasmine and lemon blossom. *Perfume?*

Antonius rubbed his eyes and shook his head, moving forward cautiously. He closed his eyes again, feeling suddenly sleepy, and when he opened them, he was in a room with white-washed walls decorated with red borders and frescoes of nymphs in a wood. Firelight warmed the walls with a welcome glow.

There was a bed at the back of the room, wide and soft, and as white as a lily. The sheets shifted, and Antonius approached, his sword out.

When the sheet was pulled back, his gladius fell from his hand.

Vera sat up on the edge of the bed, her hair brilliant red, her belly full with the life of their child.

"Vera, my love. I've missed you." Antonius began to walk toward her, but she held out her hands, a pleading look on her face.

"Why did you leave me? How could you?" she said.

"I didn't want to!" he protested. "I had to –"

"Ahhh!!!" Vera cried out in horrendous pain, and doubled over, the veins bulging on the sides of her head, and over her pregnant belly. She struggled to stand, to reach out to Antonius, but as she did so, her legs spread, and a dead foetus fell to the ground, unmoving, clotted with blood and sand.

Vera screamed so that they would hear her on the dark riverbanks of Hades, hate in her eyes.

"Vera, no!" Antonius cried, his eyes burning, his limbs shaking, but his wife continued to scream as blood poured from between her legs in torrents until she dropped to the ground, dead beside their child, the white pallor of death already tainting her face and body.

"Noooo!" Antonius fell to his knees where she had lain, cradling nothing but air and darkness in his despair.

The laughter came again, but this time closer and more hateful than ever before.

"You are alone now, Roman. And you shall die alone."

Antonius groped for the blade he had dropped, despite the tendrils of fear that restrained his body, and the moment he had the pommel, he whirled around for a killing blow.

The blade was caught in a black fist as of iron, and all Antonius saw in that moment were flaming red eyes, white fangs, twisted horns, and black wings that surrounded and crushed him to shut out his consciousness.

The wind ripped through the Carpathian Mountains with a ferocity that had not been seen for an age. Storm clouds circled like a dark maelstrom, and trees in the ancient Dacian groves buckled like wheat before the farmer's scythe.

In the Jagged Mountains, lykoi and immortui ranged the borders, caves, and crevices, hunting down all things that lived and breathed and defied the darkness. Blood ran in rivulets wherever the dark beasts went, and the gods of men wept at their helplessness, their inability to pierce the dark that had taken root in those lands ages before, and was now blossoming into the terrible power they had always feared.

Alone, a sentry glimmer of golden light amidst the darkness, Mithras stood at the edge of the wood, waiting, willing his Miles and Sun Runner to fight, to live.

"Live, my sons..." he said. "Live for the children. They do not yet know who they are..."

The wind and shadows lashed at Mithras' light, but were unable, as yet, to weaken him as they weakened others, and brought them to their knees in the mountain.

"Live..."

· · ·

CURLED UP, TANGLED IN HIS CLOAK AT THE BOTTOM OF A rock chute like a pile of broken refuse, Gaius Justus Vitalis groaned, his hand going to the gash on the side of his head, beneath the dented line of his helmet.

The wind pushed him with ferocity against the rock wall, making it hard to breathe. He managed to pull his cloak over his head and turn his back to the gale.

Breathe, Gaius, he told himself. *Breathe.*

Live... he heard a faint voice. So faint.

He felt the weight of the medallion beneath his tunic.

Daxos...

Gaius pushed himself to his feet, clinging to the sharp rockface for support as he did so. His vision was blurry, and his head spun momentarily before he vomited.

When he had gathered his wits, he found his gladius and began to feel his way along the wall, his left hand never leaving the rockface.

For what seemed like hours, he walked, stumbled, and ran when he could do so, as long as his hand was on the wall and the wind was violent enough to hide the sound of his footsteps in the dark. He tripped over something in the faint light of an air shaft, and rolled away, his sword out to clang against the blade that was also pointed at him.

Gaius thought fast and twisted his blade so that the other's fell with a clang.

There was a sound of quick, panicked breaths, just discernible beneath the mountain's howl.

"Gaius? No! Please no kill me!"

"Talia?"

"Yes!"

Gaius lowered his weapon and felt the girl grab hold of him.

"I thought you dead," she said, her grip tight.

"Almost. Where are the others?"

"We separated in the tunnel. I was looking for Daxos, but I not find him."

It was the first time Gaius had heard her sound weak, and it pained him to hear it, and to hear Daxos' name spoken again by someone else.

"We need to find Daxos and the others, Talia. Are you feeling strong enough?"

He heard a determined sniff as she bent to retrieve her pugio. "Yes."

"Hold onto my cloak as I walk then. I have a feeling we are almost there. We'll find them, Talia. We will."

Together, Gaius and the young girl moved deeper into the mountain, their hands on rock and blade, their minds on their friends' need. They walked, and walked, exhaustion and disorientation harrying them like mountain skirmishers at the edges of the mind.

When they turned a last corner, there was no longer a need for them to hold to the wall.

They had stepped onto a long, wide, sandy road within the mountain. The wind swirled around them, and sand snakes surrounded them and bit at their feet as they moved forward.

Ahead, two cauldrons filled with fire shooting upwards flanked a massive arch hewn into the rock. There, standing before the maw of that gate, was the Carpathian. His arms were crossed, and his red eyes flashed beneath the black cowl of his cloak.

"We've been waiting for you, Centurion."

. . .

GAIUS' BREATH CAUGHT IN HIS CHEST, AND HE FOUGHT THE shaking in his arms and legs.

The fear and impending sense of doom that crept like ice through his veins threatened to immobilize Gaius, and did so temporarily, before he went over the words in his head, gripping Talia with his left hand, his gladius with his right.

I am the Sun Runner. I bring the Light into the Darkness.

"Then come, Sun Runner," The Carpathian scoffed. "Your friends have little time, and I want you to watch."

Gaius began to walk forward with Talia, aware of many eyes gazing at them from recesses in the rock.

"I don't know what we'll find," he whispered to Talia, "but you'll need to look for a way to get Daxos."

"What you do?" Talia asked.

"I'll distract the Carpathian."

"He is Death, Gaius… Ine Thanatos!" she hissed.

They paused between the flaming cauldrons on either side of the gateway where two giant Daemons were carved into the black rock, their visages horrible and lively in the orange light.

"Talia. Be strong like I know you are," Gaius said. "For Daxos…for your family…for your people."

"And for Good," she said, her pugio ready.

Gaius nodded and they walked through into a fire-lit hall of stone. Then, he dropped his gladius with a clang on the ground.

He had to fight for composure, harder than he had ever fought.

Before a great fire in the far wall, was the chained Daeva, a creature Gaius had never imagined existed.

She turned her massive, horned head to look directly at the

Roman, black tears running down her scaly face and scarred body.

Yet, another horror awoke Gaius and Talia from their shock.

A few feet away, Daxos stood chained in the same manner, naked but for a loincloth, his young, pale, lean-muscled limbs stretched painfully taut.

"Daxos!" Talia called, and the boy's head lolled, eyes rolling as he searched for the source of the sound.

"What have you done to him?" Gaius demanded, struggling to hold his rage.

"Nothing yet, Centurion. It is what I shall do to him, for an age and more now that you are here to witness it. But, you have missed someone else," the Carpathian laughed. "Look behind you."

Gaius turned to see Antonius chained to another wall, his arms above his head, his face swollen and fearful as he gazed at Gaius, unable to speak for the gag in his mouth. On the ground beside him, a tangled bloody mass of limbs and shredded armour told Gaius that Sabinus had perished.

"He died stupidly," the Carpathian said. "But then, that seems to be the way with Romans."

"I'll kill you," Gaius said as he approached.

"Kill me? I cannot die, Centurion. I am Death. I am your greatest fears, and the horrors of your reality. I've been watching you…and your family."

Gaius looked up.

"Ah yes. I've been enjoying your wife. She even brought me a virgin priestess." He held up a hand. "But who is this?" He looked at Talia. "Another?"

The Carpathian looked from Talia to Daxos and back again. He approached the girl and sniffed the air about her.

"You smell of the divine like your…cousin?" He smiled horribly, his white teeth framed by his long black hair.

Gaius stepped forward pulling the medallion from inside his tunic and picking up his gladius, thrust the silver blade into the Carpathian's chest as quickly as he could.

For a moment, the Carpathian looked surprised, but then he smiled, and with his left hand, pulled Gaius' blade out of his body. No injury showed.

"You disappoint me." The Carpathian reached up, grasped the medallion in his right hand, and crushed it as though he were crumpling a dead leaf. "I am no lykos," he laughed. "The blood of the first lykos, or any other, cannot harm or deflect me, fool!"

The blood that had been held captive in the hollow medallion, that had struck fear and awe into an army of lykoi, now leaked in thick rivulets down the Carpathian's forearm where he licked it and continued to laugh.

Talia screamed, and launched herself at the Carpathian, but his fist shot out, viper-quick, and sent her stumbling across the room to land unconscious at Antonius' chained feet.

Gaius rushed in, but was stopped in his attack, the Carpathian's hand hovering before his forehead.

"I know who you are…Usij," Gaius said, his teeth gritted against the invisible force that held him. "Rome will endure… and so will the Light."

The Carpathian studied Gaius closely, his now dark eyes more those of a man's, staring at the Roman.

"Rome is already falling, and so are your gods. They are weak, as are you," he laughed. "All of you."

He wrenched Gaius' head back as he laughed, his eyes straying to Daxos and Talia. "I never thought to find two Yazad offspring."

Gaius glimpsed some movement high in the ceiling above, but looked at those terrible eyes when the last was spoken.

"Of course, you don't know," the Carpathian said. "Why would your own Yazad, your god," his voice dripped with irony, "even think to share the truth with you? The Yazads and Daevas are the same, and both shall fall from their perches like slaughtered bulls once I bleed their own." He looked again at Daxos and Talia, who was still unconscious upon the ground.

"Yes," the soft voice said, sending chills through Gaius' whole person. "They are children of the Yazads, of their divine blood. Why else do you think their village survived as long against my forces? They were protected and empowered…but not enough. Now, I will bleed them of their divine essence and unseat those whose arrogance lets them believe they are true gods. Only Death is the true god and power."

The Carpathian let go of Gaius' face, but Gaius still could not move. He watched as the Carpathian took a goblet and a stone knife from a table, and walked slowly to the Daeva.

Without hesitation, he slit a deep cut in the creature's neck, and caught the blood in the cup. He then turned to Gaius with the cup upraised.

"Thanatos." The Carpathian then drank deeply.

Gaius watched as the Carpathian's body blackened and bulged. Horns curled out of his head, and great wings hatched out of his back to spread wide.

The blood-red eyes turned to Gaius in a fanged smile, and the hall disappeared.

GAIUS FELT AT PEACE FOR A MOMENT, CONTENT IN THE ATRIUM of his home on the Caelian Hill in Rome. Birds sang in the garden, and sunlight filtered through the green foliage of the fruit trees surrounding a fountain.

He heard voices and turned to see Fulvia, Aemilia, and Faustina coming toward him.

He was home at last, and he reached out to his family, tears of joy and laughter burning his lids.

His wife and daughters stopped suddenly, paralyzed, their joyous expressions morphing in a few heartbeats to sadness, and then terror as the shadow of a horned demon swept into the atrium.

Gaius watched, yelling desperately as great, clawed arms ripped his wife's clothing away, and lacerated his children's bodies. He shook with rage, fell to his knees in anguish, staring at their dead and mangled bodies where blood pooled about them on the marble floor.

Their vacant eyes stared back at him, accusing him of failure.

Gaius shut his eyes tight, and dug his fists into the earth, wanting nothing more than to die.

THE ECHOES OF GAIUS' CRIES, AND THE LAUGHTER OF THE Carpathian travelled high up to where Vitorix and Calgacus were perched at the exit of one of the mountain tunnels.

"He's going to kill them," Vitorix whispered.

Calgacus stared at the wall, looking for foot and hand-holds that would get them to the bottom safely.

Vitorix watched Gaius crying on his knees as the Carpathian took up the stone dagger and cup again, and walked slowly to where Daxos hung chained and shaking.

The boy was fully awake now, his eyes wide as he watched the blade approaching his chest.

"Hold the rope for me," Calgacus said. "I'll drop down fast...you follow using those protruding stones in the wall."

Vitorix looked and nodded, slinging his axe over his shoulder and unravelling the rope, bracing it around his back and forearms so that he could take Calgacus' weight.

"See you at the bottom, Brother," Calgacus said before jumping.

"Ohi!" Daxos cried and strained at his iron bonds. "No! No!" he screamed, as the stone blade cut into his chest.

Gaius swayed, his nightmare broken, and looked up to see the Carpathian before Daxos, filling his goblet with the boy's blood.

"No!" Gaius charged just as Calgacus landed on top of the Carpathian, knocking the cup to the sand so that the blood poured out.

The Carpathian reared, his black wings wide, his face an image of rage and vengeance as he bent to grab Calgacus.

Gaius was there, his eyes still blurry from pain, his shaking arms breaking the Carpathian's hold on Calgacus who was flung into the chained Daeva, the latter rearing in pain as the Roman slammed into her and rolled away quickly to gather his gladius.

Gaius stood before Daxos, and the Carpathian between them and Calgacus.

Calgacus spotted Talia groaning on the ground before Antonius who strained violently at his bonds.

"I shall feast on all of you," the Carpathian threatened. "Then, I will ravage the bodies of your families, your children, so that your bloodlines shall die."

"Ahhh!" Vitorix yelled as he tumbled from his last

foothold above, holding his axe, to land before Antonius. Without a word, the Gaul slammed his blade into Antonius' chains, freeing him, and handed him a gladius. He then got Talia to her feet and began moving toward the exit.

"You won't escape this hall," the Carpathian said.

"Maybe not," Vitorix said, looking sidelong at Talia and winking. "Then again…"

Vitorix tossed the battle axe to Gaius who caught it and hacked at Daxos' chains.

Daxos collapsed, and Talia ran to his side, her pugio in hand.

"The Yazad spawn are mine!" the Carpathian roared, threw Gaius aside, and descended on Daxos and Talia.

He was stopped for a moment as Vitorix' huge arms locked about his black body, wings flailing, horned head slamming back against the Gaul's face.

"Vitorix!" Calgacus yelled.

The Carpathian shrieked and fiery light welled within him as he expanded, as if willing himself to double in size.

Vitorix cried out as his skin began to smoke and burn, his eyes shut tight against the immense pain.

"No!" Gaius yelled as his brother's veins turned to fire beneath his charring skin, before bursting into flame and finally ash about the clawed feet of the Carpathian.

Gaius, Calgacus, and Antonius closed in, their battle cries harsh and horrible, their blades jabbing, slicing, and puncturing to little effect.

Behind them, Daxos crawled on the sand, trying to get to the stone dagger, and Talia still stared through her tears to where Vitorix had been standing a moment before.

Antonius felt himself lifted off the ground, the cavern

spinning as he landed in a table with Calgacus, both of them feeling their skin burning, their minds reeling.

Gaius' rage took hold, and his fists closed to slam against the Carpathian's face and ribs, but he only enraged the beast.

The Carpathian's wings closed in on Gaius as if he was falling into an inferno, but Gaius dropped and rolled, only to be pinned by the Carpathian's foot.

The cries of Calgacus and Antonius echoed in the chamber as Gaius stared up at those red eyes. He felt the life being crushed out of him in the face of that hateful laughter.

"Mithras," Gaius croaked. "Mithras…"

"You think the Yazad cares for you?" the Carpathian laughed. "You don't deserve to live, Heliodromus."

"Mithras…is great. He is the Light."

"He is nothing."

"Mithras!" Gaius shouted with the last of his strength. "Mithras!!!"

The Carpathian reared in anger at hearing the name he had hated for ages. "I will kill Mithras!"

LIGHT EXPLODED IN THE CAVERN.

Light such as was at the creation of the world, the stars, the vast expanse of the heavens.

The cavern shook with light, and sand whirled about the Carpathian and his victims. None could see, or hear, or speak, but when the dust settled, and the light dimmed, Mithras stood among them, rising from his one knee to look about the hall. He was brilliant and calm in that dark place.

"Yazad," the Carpathian sneered.

"Usij," the god answered. "You will no longer lurk in the shadows, nor harm my soldiers and children again."

"I am greater than you, or Ahura Mazda and all the Daevas combined. My power is infinite, Yazad, and soon I shall devour your divine essence too."

Mithras smiled then, almost casually, but then his eyes were drawn to the flaming hearth where the Daeva was chained, her weak, gravelly voice calling out to him.

"Yazad…" she strained at her chains, her head leaning pitifully toward Mithras. "Yazad…" she said again, her once-fearsome, wicked eyes now pleading for death. "Yazad… sajcodayati me. Thanatos," she said, straining to bare her chest, tears running down her time-worn cheeks.

"I have milked her for ages," the Carpathian laughed, and stretched, and flexed his black body, towering over Mithras.

The Lord of Light looked back to the Carpathian. He did not care anymore for his treachery of the Daevas, or the slaughter of the Cattle of the Sun on the sandy plains of the world between the sacred rivers.

Mithras cared for the lives of his soldiers, their families. He felt sadness for the loyal, brave mortals on the ground in pain about him, for the two children a few feet away who were born of his deep love for two mortal women, sisters.

Daxos and Talia had been entrusted to other loyal followers, all of whom had been slaughtered by the Usij before him, he who wanted to unseat and drain the essence of the Gods themselves.

Mithras removed his Phrygian cap, and tucked it in his belt. Strands of his auburn hair fell loose to frame his eternally-youthful face.

"There is nothing of the divine in you, Usij," Mithras said evenly. "There never was."

The Carpathian's sharp wings outstretched and fire burned within him. "I will drink of the essence of three Yazads for ages to come, and you, Mithras, will experience pain beyond the reaches of even your understanding." He took a step closer, but Mithras continued, as though the Carpathian had not spoken.

"A true god does not seek to destroy all before him," Mithras said, raising his left hand so that the palm faced upward as he stared at it. "A true god…creates."

In that moment, Mithras' palm filled with golden light, and from where he sat on his knees, Gaius watched as a delicate apple tree grew, blossomed, and bore golden fruit. It was full of life, and light, and its leaves whispered in a gentle breeze. It was the beauty of life itself.

Mithras smiled and looked at the Carpathian whose nostrils flared and smoked, the red of his evil eyes seeking death and destruction any moment.

"Wait, Usij!" Mithras commanded. "Divinity is creation in all its many forms. It is…" Mithras raised his right palm now, and from the golden burst of heavenly light, a stone spear was born, "…compassion."

The apple tree dissolved in a flash of falling leaves and fruit, and a moment later, Mithras had spun to send the spear from his hand to plunge into the breast of the chained Daeva.

The Daeva looked at Mithras, a weak smile on her face, and gratitude in her dimming eyes as she looked down to see the protruding, god-made spear.

Mithras nodded to her, and with a final sigh, her body turned to ashes.

The Carpathian roared and raged, his massive wings whipping up wind that scattered the dusty remains of the Daeva.

Mithras ignored him, helped Gaius, Antonius, and Calgacus to their feet, before walking toward Daxos and Talia.

"I can create as well, Yazad!" the Carpathian spat, extending claws like daggers. "I shall create your death!"

"I know you have created, Usij." Mithras put his hands on the children's shoulders. "But you forget that even the Gods must live with the things we create. We are what we create."

Mithras' voice echoed throughout the dark halls, and a ghostly thrumming came closer and closer out of the darkness, beyond the gate to the cavernous hall.

As the Carpathian leapt for Mithras and the children, Gaius, Calgacus, and Antonius rushed to hold him with all their strength, despite the claws tearing at their straining muscles.

The sound of drums and horns became even louder, and then the dead themselves poured into the cavern led by the shade of Gaius' long-dead friend, Julius.

Gaius, Calgacus, and Antonius fell back as the Carpathian Lord was hoisted and pommelled by the vengeful shades whom he had slaughtered with his evil.

The Carpathian's power was gone, his strength and evil sapped by the death of the Daeva.

Talia and Daxos covered their ears for all the horror of his screams, and those of the angry dead, but then Daxos spotted the stone dagger in the sand three feet away, beside his own spilt blood.

He ran, picked it up, and tossed it to Gaius.

Gaius felt strength returning to his limbs, not by divine interference, or any magical properties of the blade itself. As Gaius walked among the shades of legionaries, he felt the power of a man wanting justice for friends and brothers, his family, for Goodness itself. He stood beneath the Carpathian's writhing body, calmer than he had been in a long time, with

Calgacus and Antonius beside him, among the legions of their desecrated brothers.

Julius' shade was before him, mouthing the words, willing Gaius, as Heliodromus, to speak.

Gaius nodded.

"Where are we going?" Gaius called out.

"Into Darkness!" the living and the dead answered.

"What are you?" Gaius looked at all his brothers.

"The Light! The Light! The Light!"

"And who are you?" Gaius looked at his god, standing with Daxos and Talia, and the dead answered.

"Mithras! Mithras! Mithras!"

"Accept our offering..." Gaius finished, gripping the dagger and thrusting upward with all of his strength.

The Carpathian howled and writhed, the fire inside him burning violently for several moments as the shades of the dead raised their faces as if to a heavenly light.

Mithras himself stepped forward and with a furious wave of one hand, the charred remains of the Usij were wiped from the face of the earth in a violent gust of wind and light.

When the wind died down, Mithras stepped in among his followers, and took in each of their faces, coming to a stop before Julius' shade.

"Walk in the Light, my sons, my soldiers. Your fight is done. Be at peace in the Light..."

His voice was soft, gentle, and melodious as it uttered the words the men had longed to hear.

The Light...

. . .

THE SHADES BEGAN TO DISSIPATE, BRILLIANT AS THE SUN when it dips beneath the sea at the end of the longest day - calm, radiant, and peaceful.

"No!" Daxos cried, running over to where Gaius, Calgacus, and Antonius lay upon the sand, the sound as an echo in time.

Gaius' eyes had closed when he heard *The Light,* and his last thought was of his family, and of bright sunshine.

THE SUN RETURNED TO THE CARPATHIAN MOUNTAINS WITH the dawning of the next day. It filtered through the shattered remains of the mountain cavern's ceiling to rest on Mithras' shoulders.

The god knelt in the ashen sand beside the bodies of his three surviving warriors. He looked upon them with sadness and pity, for they were broken and exhausted beyond reckoning, their strength bled away by their battle with Darkness.

He also felt gratitude to the three mortal men, and tears formed at the edges of his lids. Mithras gripped his leather cap tightly in his fists as he sat there, his long battle with the Usij finally at an end, thanks to the courage of his Heliodromus and his Miles, his soldiers of Light.

"Can you help them?" Daxos said, choked with worry and pain.

Mithras knew how much Gaius meant to Daxos, and now Talia as well.

"Please, Lord," Talia said as she bent to hold Gaius' bloody hand, squeezing it hard as her tears fell upon his skin, the specks flashing as of liquid light.

Mithras stood and looked behind to the mountain road beyond the gate to see dozens of naked Dacians walking toward him, their eyes clear for the first time with the destruction of the evil that had imprisoned and possessed them, robbed them of their humanity.

They fell to their knees, exhausted, muttering teary thanks.

Mithras looked upon them and then drew the veil before their eyes that they might not see him and the children. He then turned and went to kneel beside Gaius, Antonius, and Calgacus.

Light within the god burst forth, a blinding sunfire that ran through his veins to gather in the palms of his divine hands.

Daxos and Talia shielded their eyes, but not before they saw the god, their divine father, place his hands upon each of the men's foreheads.

"Live in the Light of this world. Live…"

Mithras closed his eyes, and the light filled the caverns, flooded through the whole of the mountains and forests, the valleys and rivers of the Carpathians to burn away the evil that had held sway there for ages.

When Daxos and Talia opened their eyes, Mithras was gone.

THE WORLD SPUN IN GAIUS' MIND. COLOUR AND LIGHT danced, punctuated by the sounds of wind, and water, and fire, by birdsong, and wolf's howl.

And there was heat, radiating and powerful, dizzying heat. There were also voices, whispering and wandering, in and out of his consciousness.

Gaius strained to hear those of his wife and children, as if searching in an infinite crowd, before the voices died away, and all that was left was a gentle lapping of water beside a river.

He despaired in his heart. *Is death so peaceful?*

IT HURT, THE LIGHT DID, AS IT SEARED THE CRACKS OF GAIUS' eyelids when he stirred.

I'm dead... he cried inside. *Oh, Fulvia...my girls... I'm sorry.*

He had not believed such pain would be possible in Elysium, but it seemed it was.

I've failed... Oh, Mithras, Lord, watch over my family for me...

Gaius then felt a hand, two in fact, one upon his forehead and one upon his chest.

He opened his eyes, ready for the first glimpse of the Afterlife, and there he saw Daxos and Talia looking down at him, their black hair contrasted against a brilliant blue sky that matched their eyes.

"Centurion," Daxos said, his voice shaky.

I'm sorry, Daxos, Gaius tried to say.

"Gaius," Talia said next. "Ise zontanos. You alive."

It's not possible.

Daxos smiled. "Yes...we are alive," Daxos cried. "We are alive."

Gaius opened his eyes wide and pushed himself up slowly. They were beside a river, a warm fire crackling nearby. Birds sang in the reeds, and beyond in the trees. The sun was bright and warm as his senses quickened to reality.

He looked at Daxos and Talia. "Is this the Styx?" he asked.

Daxos shook his head. "No," he smiled. "It is the Danuvius."

"But how?"

"The Dacians," Talia said. "They grateful to you for freeing them. They help us to the river, to cross to Roman side."

Gaius felt his throat tighten, reached for both children, and pulled them to him tightly.

They held onto him, their hearts and minds warm and peaceful at last.

Gaius looked at them through misty eyes, unable to say anymore. He followed Daxos' gaze to the other side of the fire where Antonius and Calgacus lay breathing steadily as they began to move and open their own eyes to the wonder of the world in which they now found themselves. Gaius crawled toward his brothers, grasped their hands, and spoke.

"We're alive, brothers. We're alive."

The three men looked at each other, incredulity washing over them as the Danuvius lapped the sandy shore. In their hearts, they remembered Sabinus, Vitorix, and so many others who now walked in the Light. They hoped their fallen comrades were joyful now.

For themselves, Gaius, Antonius, and Calgacus did not know if they would ever again laugh or feel any measure of joy, with the memories of the fallen at the back of their minds.

But they were alive.

It was a start.

THE DACIANS HAD SET DOWN GAIUS AND THE OTHERS ON THE south bank of the Danuvius during the night, just downriver from the legionary fortress at Novae.

When a cavalry patrol found them, Gaius explained what he dared of their situation, and asked to be taken to the legion's legate commander.

It seemed that the Gods were indeed on their side.

Since the Carpathian's fall, skirmishes with the Dacians had ceased. Roman patrols had not been attacked in days, and the commander, a friend of Gaius' old commander, Legate Maximus, decided to give Gaius and his group fresh supplies and horses, as well as a pass that would see them safely back to Rome.

With the frontier at their backs then, Gaius, the children, Antonius, and Calgacus set off through Thrace and Moesia Superior until they reached the Mare Adriaticus.

Several weeks later, they halted on the Via Appia, just outside of Rome.

The city walls loomed large before them, and the monuments to the dead that lined the road were quiet, their inscriptions telling of the lives of hundreds of men and women who had passed from the world.

Talia sat on her horse with wide eyes as Daxos explained what she would see.

Antonius imagined Vera, her swollen belly, and prayed that she lived and would not accuse him of abandonment as she had in his nightmares.

Gaius felt nervous, sad, and grateful all at once. *Let them be alive. Let them be happy...* he prayed.

Only Calgacus stared at Rome, and felt nothing. Its bulging hills covered in marble temples, the tiled roofs of villas, and trimmed trees meant nothing to him. He sighed and turned to Gaius.

"I'm not coming with you," he said as he dismounted.

Gaius and Antonius both dismounted and walked over to the Briton.

"I can't go back there," Calgacus said, nodding in the direction of Rome.

Gaius was silent. He had been expecting it. He had seen the wandering, sad look in his friend's eyes since Novae. He knew he and Antonius had loved ones to go back to, but Calgacus? All he had were his memories of fallen friends, of darkness, and a homeland far away where Rome's reach had not yet taken hold.

"My friends, here I say farewell," Calgacus said, trying to hold his composure. "Neither Rome, nor Augustus' money will calm my heart at this point." He stared at each of them, a tremble in his lip beneath his beard. "I'll miss you. Much. But my soul cries out for the moors and crashing seas of Britannia. I... I can't –"

"We know," Gaius said, grasping his forearm. "We understand."

No explanation was needed.

"Our home is always open to you. Always. You know that, right?" Gaius said. "You're my brother."

"Aye. I know." Calgacus looked at Gaius and hugged him tightly.

As Antonius watched, his mind returned to the worry of what he would find at home after so many long months. Then Calgacus walked up to him, and Antonius embraced him too. "Farewell."

"Take care of your families, brothers. They are precious," Calgacus said, a sad smile playing about his warlike face.

It was hard to leave. It was the sort of goodbye one knew was necessary, but that one never wanted to have to make.

Calgacus turned to Daxos and Talia, and put a hand on each of their shoulders. "Take care of yourselves, and these old goats here," he said, winking playfully.

They threw their arms about him, pulling him down to one knee, and felt his arms grip them tightly as they shook.

Then he stood, wiping a stray tear away. He mounted his horse and looked down at Gaius and Antonius one more time.

"Walk in the Light, brothers," he said, before turning his mount and cantering onto the road that by-passed the city of Rome and headed north.

"Farewell, my friend," Gaius said. "Walk in the Light."

"You sure you don't want to come over?" Antonius said to Gaius as they rode through the streets of Rome. "The baby might be born by now."

"No. The homecoming should belong only to you, my friend. In a few days, I'll send word for you, Vera, and the baby to come to our home. We'll meet them then." Gaius silently hoped that Antonius would find a happy scene when he arrived home.

Antonius nodded. He was nervous about what he might find, but he understood Gaius' need to get back to his own family. "I'll be waiting," he said to Gaius.

Antonius hugged both children, and watched as Gaius led them in the direction of the Caelian Hill. He then turned and led his horse through the noisy streets to the insula where Vera was waiting.

People stared as Antonius passed, his black armour and weapons battered and broken, his face an array of healing cuts and bruises. He did not care, not about the stink of Rome, the shit in the streets, the tang of the fuller's nearby, none of it bothered him. As he walked into the insula courtyard, he sighed and looked up to the door.

Please be alive, my love.

He tied the horse to a post and removed the heavy saddle-bags. His boots echoed on the wooden steps as he climbed, his stomach in knots.

He knocked gently, three times.

"Coming!" a voice called out.

Vera!

Antonius straightened and waited, his throat tightening.

The door opened after some shuffling, and then Vera was standing before him.

Her eyes shot wide, and pooled immediately, but she was silent. Then, as a sun rising is seen for the first time after an age in darkness, she smiled at him, and threw herself into his arms, sobbing and letting loose all her dammed-up worry and sorrow.

Antonius held her tightly, inhaled the smell of her fiery hair, kissed her lips and forehead and cheeks. Then he stopped, fear upon him as he realized that her belly was flat.

Gods no!

"Come!" Vera said, wiping her eyes and pulling him inside. "Look!"

There on the bed lay two babies, both sleeping soundly, side by side.

Antonius looked at his wife, tears running down his face now, and she laughed and cried with him.

They were together, at last. Together.

"I'll never leave you again," he whispered, and she believed him.

With all her heart, she believed him.

Gaius stood at last before the door to his home on the Caelian Hill, Talia and Daxos by his side.

The street was silent, still, and he struggled to push away the flashing images of blood and pain that had stayed with him, that had threatened him the closer he got to home.

Before he could knock, the bolt slid, and Ludo opened the door.

The slave immediately stood back, but then fell to his knees. "Master? Is it you?" he said, tears coming to his eyes.

Gaius leaned to pick up the old man, who clung, desperate and shaking, to him.

"It's me, Ludo. I'm home," Gaius said. "We're home." He looked at Daxos and Talia.

Ludo grabbed Daxos into a big embrace, tears flowing down his contorted features in a display that was not like himself. "You gave us a fright, boy." He smiled now. "It is well you are home."

Talia hung back, unsure of her new world, the increasing cacophony that came from beyond the strange, shiny atrium.

"Ludo," Gaius said seriously. "Is my wife...is Fulvia within? Is she -"

He stopped, unable to speak any more. He gasped, his mind unable to form the panicked thoughts into coherent words.

"She is sleeping in the garden, Master."

Thank you Gods.

"Master, she is...not the... You will not recognize her." Ludo gripped his hands tightly before him.

"She is changed, Master," Calista said, emerging from the kitchen into the atrium. "But your return will help her beyond measure."

Without another word, Gaius strode through the atrium, around the peristylium, and to the edge of the garden.

Fulvia slept on a couch that had been laid out in the sunshine.

Gaius felt tears burn his eyes as he set them upon her emaciated, pale form. *Gods, please make it so that she is well. Please, I beg you.*

He left Daxos and Talia behind him and stepped quietly to kneel beside his wife. She was different, he could see, as he was. But behind the pale skin and whitening hair, she was still his Fulvia.

"My love…" he whispered, and kissed her forehead. "I'm home, Fulvia. I'm home."

Her eyelids flickered momentarily, tightening as if trying to shut out a horrible dream. Then Fulvia gasped, and her eyes locked onto Gaius'.

"Is this a dream?" she asked, before closing them again. "No more illusions, Gods. Please. No more!"

"It's not a dream, my love," Gaius said, his voice wavering. "I'm here, and real. As real as you are, this couch, the trees about us, or the sun shining down upon your skin. I'm home, Fulvia."

"Gaius?" She looked at him, and threw her arms about his neck as he bent over her. "Gaius!"

"I'm home," he told her, and himself. "I'm never leaving you again."

"My love…my love… Oh Vesta, thank you," Fulvia prayed, squeezing Gaius fervently, her body racked with sobs.

"Father?"

Gaius turned to see Aemilia and Faustina staring at him from beside Daxos, whose hands they grasped.

Daxos wept openly, unable to contain his joy, his relief, and Talia put a protective arm about him.

"Father!" the girls cried and ran to Gaius and Fulvia, a

flurry of white tunics and tears. "You're home!" Aemilia sobbed. "You're home!"

Gaius held both his daughters tightly. He had never thought to hold them again, to hear their laughter, their tears, to feel the welcome weight of their thin arms about his neck.

And yet, he was in his own home again, with his wife and daughters, their family huddled together in joy and gratitude which they had believed extinct from their lives.

Fulvia laughed and cried as the girls plastered their father with hugs and kisses. *Thank you Goddess Vesta. Thank you!*

Then Fulvia reached out to Daxos.

The boy approached, leading Talia, and fell into Fulvia's arms.

"Welcome home, Daxos," she said, squeezing him hard.

Gaius looked at Talia whose face betrayed her fear and reluctance. He stood and led her to the centre of the garden, beckoning the slaves, Ludo, Calista, a smiling Pugio, and Nisica, to join them.

"Everyone, this is Talia. Daxos' cousin. She will be living with us now."

The familia stared at the girl, but Fulvia turned to sit on the edge of the couch and, despite the effort, stood before Talia. She could see pain in those eyes, and sadness, but she could also see strength, and a will, things that had got her through whatever horrors she had endured.

"Welcome, Talia," she said. "You do not need to worry now, or be afraid. Your place is here." She placed a hand on Daxos' shoulder, and smiled. "Will you stay?"

Talia nodded, fighting the tears which became harder and harder to master as she had done for so long, exhausted by the maintenance of the façade of strength she had been forced to live behind.

Gaius smiled at the members of his household, and knew he was blessed. No matter for the wars that Rome continued to wage, the fortune that Augustus would no doubt pay him.

The Order of the Eagle and the Sun would be disbanded and not spoken of, and it did not matter.

Gaius Justus Vitalis was alive and among the people who filled his world with warmth and goodness.

As he sat on the edge of the couch beside Fulvia, Aemilia, and Faustina, with the servants laughing again, the children playing and talking, he was grateful beyond all imagining.

Of course there were questions in his mind about what he had learned about Daxos and Talia, and who their father actually was, but by Mithras' will, they were still with Gaius, and he was their protector. Their secret was safe, and besides, Gaius knew that some questions were not intended to be answered.

Sunlight poured into the garden from the heights of heaven, and he closed his eyes, his face to the sky.

Thank you, Mithras. Thank you... By your eternal Light, I thank you for my life.

In the back of his mind, Gaius heard the familiar, youthful voice...

Thank you, Heliodromus, for watching over them. Walk in the Light...always...

THE END

Thank you for reading!

Did you enjoy *The Carpathian Interlude*? Here is what you can do next.

If you enjoyed these adventures with Gaius Justus Vitalis and his men, and if you have a minute to spare, please post a short review on the web page where you purchased the book.

Reviews are a wonderful way for new readers to find this series of books and your help in spreading the word is greatly appreciated.

More exciting historical fantasy set in the ancient world will be coming soon, so be sure to sign-up for e-mail updates at:

https://eaglesanddragonspublishing.com/newsletter-join-the-legions/

Newsletter subscribers get a FREE BOOK, and first access to new releases, special offers, and much more!

To read more about the history, people, places, and ancient beliefs featured in this series, check out *The World of The Carpathian Interlude* blog series at:

http://eaglesanddragonspublishing.com/the-world-of-the-carpathian-interlude/

Alternate Ending

It felt like an age since the darkness of that cavern, an age since the blood and pain of battle, since the cries of the dead in his ears.

But Gaius Justus Vitalis felt strong again, grateful for the warmth that ran through him, as swift and free as when he had run on the roads outside of Rome.

He looked down at where Fulvia, at last reunited with him, rested her head, her beautiful black hair in his lap, her eyes gazing lovingly up at him.

"I never thought we would be together again. In the darkest depths of my nightmare, I never thought to have this." He looked about him, happy and admiring.

"Me neither," Fulvia said, stretching and sitting to curl in the crook of his arm, as they leaned against a blossoming apple tree.

Birds sang more heavenly than ever to their ears, a tune to match the sounds of their children's joyful play in the grass a short distance away.

Aemilia and Faustina picked brilliant wildflowers which they fashioned into crowns and placed upon each other's heads. Sunlight played about them, and the sky was a lively blue for as far as the eye could see.

"I missed you." Gaius smiled, pulled a golden apple from a branch, and gave it to Fulvia as they both got up from the soft grass.

Together, they walked barefoot, following their skipping daughters' laughter and songs, the worries of the past far behind them.

They had quite forgotten the Darkness and the Evil.

Gaius no longer felt the urge to fight, or lead, or bow to any man. His life was his now, the world he had always wanted and yearned for – Fulvia by his side, warm and beautiful as ever, his children safe and full of life. He had the stout home he had dreamed of on the hill behind the orchards where they strolled.

The sun was above them, their home, their crops, their horses. It warmed everything, Friends from the legions, and their laughing, lovely women lived all about them, everyone grateful for the peace they now enjoyed after all the long wars.

"Aemilia, Faustina, wait for us!" Fulvia called with a chuckle.

"Let them run, my love," Gaius said. "They fill their lungs with healthy, summer air."

"I know. It's just the river that worries me," Fulvia said, squeezing his hand. "It's so broad and dark."

"I'll get them." Gaius smiled, walking backwards and looking at Fulvia playfully. "You're so beautiful!" he said as he spun and ran after the girls.

When he caught up with Aemilia and Faustina, they were holding hands and spinning a few feet from the shore of the river. Gaius whooped and danced about them three times, his bare feet kicking high, his voice chiming in concert with theirs.

"Run to your mother, girls! It's time to head back to prepare for our guests."

"So soon?" Faustina asked.

"Well, perhaps we can feed some apples to the horses before we go!" Gaius said, grinning. "Run and pick some!"

"Yes, Father!" they sang.

Gaius watched them go, arms crossed, still humming the tune they had been singing. Then he turned to look at the wide, black river, and stopped singing.

Daxos and Talia stood on the desert sands, Mithras, the Lord of Light and Truth, with them, a hand on each of their shoulders. Their white robes rippled softly in the hot breeze, and sand danced about their sandalled feet where they stood, staring across the river.

Talia turned to Mithras, her blue eyes expectant, questioning as always.

"Father?"

"Yes, Daughter," Mithras answered, smiling at Talia while Daxos stared across the water. "They are happy, aren't they?" The girl's face was bright, but shadowed slightly by concern.

Mithras looked across to see Fulvia and her daughters skipping through the emerald grass toward the orchard where they would pick apples, and then he sighed, as a melancholy breeze ruffles paradise for but a heartbeat.

"Yes," he said. "They are joyous, and they are together." Mithras looked at his son sidelong, gripping his arm. "Daxos, they are happy, and healthy. They know neither pain, nor fear, nor hardship. They are well."

"Can he see us?" Daxos asked, looking at Gaius who looked fixedly across the water toward them.

"Only if we want him to, but it would disturb his peace,

my son." Mithras hung his head for he knew that even a Yazad felt pain, and loss, and for much longer. He watched as a tear fell from Daxos' eyes into the sand and there blossomed into a lithe sapling which sprouted upward in green leaf and crimson pomegranate. Mithras squeezed the boy's shoulder and gazed across the black water.

"Just this once, my son, out of gratitude to both you, and him."

Daxos, his black hair blowing about his face, gazed across at Gaius with his sad blue eyes, and slowly raised his hand.

Far on the other side, Gaius Justus Vitalis slowly raised his own hand in return.

"Just as the sun rises and sets, my children," Mithras explained, "so too does life go ever on. It rises and sets again, and again, and again, each time more brilliant than the last…"

"Thank you, Centurion," Daxos whispered before finally turning away from the river to follow Mithras and Talia into the East.

"Farewell… Farewell…" Gaius whispered as he lowered his hand, the swift-flowing river widening as the far bank fell farther away. The sounds of his family, the birds, and the neighing of his horses grew louder again in his ears, but not before an evanescent moment of sadness sprang up within his soul.

"What're you looking at, Centurion?" said a deep, jovial voice beside him.

Gaius turned to see Julius Lycus standing beside him, his bald head bright in the sunshine.

"Old friends…far away," Gaius answered solemnly before smiling. "Are you joining us tonight? Fulvia's asked the servants to make all your favourites."

"The roast duck as well?" Julius asked.

"Of course!"

"I'd be delighted!" Julius clapped Gaius on the back and they turned away from the river to walk toward the orchard. "Will the others be there?" he asked.

"Vitorix and Calgacus are hunting for boar in the forest up the mountain and will be joining us soon. Antonius and his family are at the house already."

"Can't wait!" Julius laughed as he went to greet Fulvia and lift Faustina into the air.

Gaius laughed heartily, but stopped and turned to stare back at the river one more time.

"Come, my love," Fulvia said, as she looped her arm through his. "The others will be joining us soon."

He reached up to touch her cheek gently with his fingers, and together they walked beneath the apple blossoms, petals raining down on them as they went, back toward their home and their happiness beneath the light of the sun.

Walk in the Light, the wind whispered....

THE END

AUTHOR'S NOTE

The Carpathian Interlude series started out as a bit of fun, a series of novellas in which I thought it would be cool to pit Roman soldiers against Zombies (*Immortui*), and Werewolves (*Lykoi*).

But this series turned into much more than simple historical horror or fantasy. It came to be an exploration into the greatest fears of its characters during a time of darkness and war. Through writing these novels, I have come to see Mithraism, not as a trendy exercise in faith among the men of the legions, but as Roman soldiers' greatest shield against the darkness with which they lived day in and day out.

As a mystery religion, we don't know much about Mithraism, apart from the fact that the rites were carried out in caves, or cave-like settings, that there were grades of initiates such as the *Pater* (Father), *Heliodromus* (Sun Runner), and *Miles* (Soldiers), and that the ultimate sacrifice was that of a bull, as is evident in portrayals of the *tauroctony* in which Mithras, the God of Light and Truth, is seen slaying the bull of ignorance and darkness.

Mithras himself has his roots in the Indo-European tradition. To portray this, I have opted for the Zoroastrian version. This was the religion of ancient Persia, in which Mithras and Ahura Mazda were *Yazads*, or 'good divinities'. In Zoroastrianism, the *Daevas* were wicked and uncaring gods, and enemies of the Yazads, and the *Usij* were indeed the false priests of the *Daevas* who lacked any goodness. The latter seemed to be the perfect origin for the Carpathian Lord, rather than a Vampire of sorts, which was the original idea when setting out on this literary journey.

Some of the information I used on Zoroastrianism can be found in the scriptures known as the *Yasna*, and the *Khorda Avesta*. The *Gathas*, the oldest text of Zoroastrianism, said to be written by Zoroaster himself, was also invaluable as to the nature of this belief system of which I have only scratched the surface.

I should note that any errors in interpretation are entirely my own. Suffice it to say that I can see why Roman troops would have gravitated to this religion, said by some to be a precursor to Christianity. If the possibility of death in battle is ever-present, how much more comforting would it be to know that the faithful will "Walk in the Light" once they pass from this world? This is something that most religions have in common, something that all peoples wish for – peace after the hard-fought battle of life.

It has been theorized that the defining religious theme of Good vs. Evil, Light vs. Darkness, may have originated in ancient Zoroastrianism (which still has a minority of followers today in Iran) and then been absorbed by other religions such as Judaism, Christianity, and Islam.

As for the period of these novellas, the reign of Emperor Augustus (63 B.C. – A.D. 14), I have taken some liberties with Mithraism, the cult of which had not really caught on among the troops until later, though the seeds were certainly sown.

The Varus disaster of A.D. 9 seemed like a suitably catastrophic event to serve as the backdrop for these stories. How could three legions be completely wiped out? Varus' arrogance and ineptitude were a part of the cause, but I have, as you know, opted for a darker reason. Certainly the Roman people felt that darkness was descending on the Empire. Panic set it, and even Augustus was shaken to his core.

In truth, Arminius was a brilliant tactician and astute liar who stayed in Varus' confidence until the last minute. As for the man Arminius himself, he survived, but was eventually killed by his own people years later, in A.D. 21, because he had become too powerful. Hubris was certainly not relegated to Imperial Rome.

In the years following the Varus disaster, Tiberius waged a campaign to secure the Danube and Rhine frontiers, and six years later, Germanicus, the nephew of Augustus, led a force into the Teutoberg Forest in Germania to find and bury the bones of the thousands of Roman dead who had been massacred by the Germanic tribes. The year after that, in A.D. 16, Germanicus managed to retrieve two of the three legionary eagles (*aquila*) that had been lost by Varus and his men.

I have not invented the ancient beliefs in zombies or werewolves for these stories. In truth, beliefs in the waking dead and humans who turned into wolves date as far back as ancient Babylon and Egypt, on through ancient Greece and into the Roman period. These beliefs are not the product of modern-day novelists who created fanciful villains to frighten their audiences. Zombies, Werewolves, and Demons of all sorts are products of our ancient human beliefs and fears, evils to balance the good and light within us all, and all around us.

Where there is Good, there is Evil. Where there is Light, there is Darkness. These ideas are as old as the world itself, and they are at the very foundations of storytelling.

In *The Carpathian Interlude*, I have tried to explore the theme of Light and Dark in what I hope is a unique, thought-provoking, and entertaining way. I hope you have enjoyed it, and that you have been inspired by it.

At the end of the day, I hope that we may all walk in the Light.

Thank you for reading.

Adam Alexander Haviaras
Toronto, October 2017

ACKNOWLEDGMENTS

It's a strange thing to come to the end of a book, even more so to complete a trilogy. You can't silence the voices that have been with you for so long. Nor can you shut your eyes against the images that have haunted you, that you have created. All of it is remembered and felt, like shades of the departed at your shoulder.

Nor can you forget the help of the living who have stood by your side in the creation of a work of literature. For me, there have been some who, by their kindness, support, and belief, have helped me to come through this campaign of words, thoughts, feelings and images.

Firstly, to my dear friend and fellow historian, Andrew Fenwick, whose constant enthusiasm for Roman history has always been highly educational. No historian I know has a better knowledge of Roman arms, armour, and strategy than Andy. It is through our long conversations over countless pints that I managed to absorb the details of history's most efficient army.

To Jon Stanley, my deep gratitude for his theological perspective on various aspects of ancient religion that helped me to formulate this story, but also for his friendship and compassionate ear in a time of crisis. Without his critical support, the conclusion of this series might well have languished in Purgatory without ever seeing the Light.

Thanks must, as ever, go to Laura at LLPIX for her excellent cover design skills that have helped to bring the face of this series to life. It is no easy thing to capture mood and historical period, and she has always done so with patience and perfection.

To you, my readers, I must offer thanks for all of your support over the years. Our interactions and shared love of history are one of the reasons I sit down at the keyboard everyday. Thank you to all of you for taking a chance on this slight deviation from my usual tales. To the thousands of you who have supported me and Eagles and Dragons Publishing to date, I am extremely grateful. Long may the adventures continue!

To Angelina, my own Light in the Darkness… I can never fully express my thanks for all that you have done over the course of this journey, from line editing and story advice, to help in correcting my broken Greek. Your critical eyes are as sharp as a well-honed *gladius* blade, the greatest weapons I have had in this fight. However, nothing lifts me up more than your constant support and strength, even in the darkest of times.

Finally, to my father, who passed away during the final stages of this trilogy and did not get a chance to read the conclusion. My love and gratitude to you always, *Pater*. I hope with all my heart that the world is full of wonder, wherever you are…

Adam Alexander Haviaras
Toronto, Ontario
October, 2017

GLOSSARY

aedes – a temple; sometimes a room

aedituus – a keeper of a temple

aestivus – relating to summer; a summer camp or pasture

agora – Greek word for the central gathering place of a city or settlement

ala – an auxiliary cavalry unit

amita – an aunt

amphitheatre – an oval or round arena where people enjoyed gladiatorial combat and other spectacles

anguis – a dragon, serpent or hydra; also used to refer to the 'Draco' constellation

angusticlavius – 'narrow stripe' on a tunic; Lucius Metellus Anguis is a *tribunus angusticlavius*

apodyterium – the changing room of a bath house

aquila – a legion's eagle standard which was made of gold during the Empire

aquilifer – senior standard bearer in a Roman legion who carried the legion's eagle

ara – an altar

armilla – an arm band that served as a military decoration

as - a bronze coin; 400 asses = 1 gold aureus approx.

athanatoi - Greek word for 'undead'

atrium – unroofed entrance room of a Roman house, usually containing a pool, or impluvium

augur – a priest who observes natural occurrences to determine if omens are good or bad; a soothsayer

aureus – a Roman gold coin; worth twenty-five silver *denarii*

auriga – a charioteer

ballista – an ancient missile-firing weapon that fired either heavy 'bolts' or rocks

bireme – a galley with two banks of oars on either side

bracae – knee or full-length breeches originally worn by barbarians but adopted by the Romans

caldarium – the 'hot' room of a bath house; from the Latin *calidus*

caligae – military shoes or boots with or without hobnail soles

cardo – a hinge-point or central, north-south thoroughfare in a fort or settlement, the *cardo maximus*

castrum – a Roman fort

cataphract – a heavy cavalryman; both horse and rider were armoured

cena- the principal, afternoon meal of the Romans

centurion – a Roman officer who commanded a century of 80 men; centurions were usually career soldiers

chiton – a long woollen tunic of Greek fashion

chryselephantine – ancient Greek sculptural medium using gold and ivory; used for cult statues

cingulum – a belt or harness

civica – relating to 'civic'; the civic crown was awarded to one who saved a Roman citizen in war

civitas – a settlement or commonwealth; an administrative centre in tribal areas of the Empire

clepsydra – a water clock

cognomen – the surname of a Roman which distinguished the branch of a gens

collegia – an association or guild; e.g. *collegium pontificum* means 'college of priests'

colonia – a colony; also used for a farm or estate

consul – an honorary position in the Empire; during the Republic they presided over the Senate

contubernium – a military unit of eight men within a century who shared a tent

contus – a long cavalry spear; sometimes spelled 'kontus'

corbita – a type of large hold merchant ship

cornicen – the horn blower in a legion

cornu – a curved military horn

cornucopia – the horn of plenty

corona – a crown; often used as a military decoration

cubiculum – a bedchamber

cursus honorem - the course of honour; a specific career path for upper class Roman men

curia – the Senate building in the Roman Forum

curule – refers to the chair upon which Roman magistrates would sit (e.g. *curule aedile*)

daevas - wicked and uncaring gods in Zoroastrian religion; enemies of Ahura Mazda and Mithras; similar to demons

decumanus – refers to the tenth; the *decumanus maximus* ran east to west in a Roman fort or city

denarius – A Roman silver coin; worth one hundred brass *sestertii*

dignitas – a Roman's worth, honour and reputation

domus – a home or house

draco – a military standard in the shape of a dragon's head first used by Sarmatians and adopted by Rome

draconarius – a military standard bearer who held the draco

duplicarius – trooper with special skills who receives double-pay (ex. an engineer) eques – a horseman or rider

    equites – cavalry; of the order of knights in ancient Rome

fabrica – a workshop

    fabula – an untrue or mythical story; a play or drama

    familia – a Roman's household, including slaves

    fascies – double-headed axes bound in reeds and carried by lictors who followed senior officials

    flammeum – a flame-coloured bridal veil

    forum – an open square or marketplace; also a place of public business (e.g. the *Forum Romanum*)

    fossa – a ditch or trench; a part of defensive earthworks

    frigidarium – the 'cold room' of a bath house; a cold plunge pool

    funeraticia – from *funereus* for funeral; the *collegia funeraticia* assured all received decent burial

garum – a fish sauce that was very popular in the Roman world

    gens humanum – the human race; gens means clan

    gladius – a Roman short sword

    gorgon – a terrifying visage of a woman with snakes for hair; also known as Medusa

    greaves – armoured shin and knee guards worn by high-ranking officers

    groma – a surveying instrument; used for accurately marking out towns, marching camps and forts etc.

hasta – a spear or javelin

    hastile – a staff with a large orb on one end, carried by an optio heliodromus - literally means 'Sun Runner'; a high ranking grade in Mithraic religion, just below level of 'Pater'

heptastadion – a causeway built to connect Alexandria to the island of Pharos; seven stades long

hetaira – a courtesan; different from a common prostitute, or lupa

horreum – a granary

hydraulis – a water organ

hypocaust – area beneath a floor in a home or bath house that is heated by a furnace

images – standards that bore the image of the emperor and were carried with the legionary standards

imperator – a commander or leader; commander-in-chief

impluvium – the pool in a household atrium that was open to the sky and caught rain water

insula – a block of flats leased to the poor

intervallum – the space between two palisades

itinere – a road or itinerary; the journey

lanista – a gladiator trainer

lararium - a shrine to the guardian spirits in a Roman household

lemure – a ghost

libellus – a little book or diary

lituus – the curved staff or wand of an augur; also a cavalry trumpet

lorica – body armour; can be made of mail, scales or metal strips; can also refer to a cuirass

lupa – a common prostitute; lupa literally means 'she-wolf'

lupanar – a brothel; example is the 'Great Lupanar' of Pompeii

lustratio – a ritual purification, usually involving a sacrifice

manica – handcuffs; also refers to the long sleeves of a tunic

marita – wife

maritus – husband

matertera – a maternal aunt

maximus – meaning great or 'of greatness'

medicus – a doctor; army field doctor

miles - literally means 'soldiers'; a lower level grade in Mithraic religion

missum – used as a call for mercy by the crowd for a gladiator who had fought bravely

mithraeum - a place or shrine where the god Mithras was worshipped; usually a cave

murmillo – a heavily armed gladiator with a helmet, shield and sword

nomen – the *gens* of a family (as opposed to *cognomen* which was the specific branch of a wider *gens*)

nones – the fifth day of every month in the Roman calendar

novendialis – refers to the ninth day

nutrix – a wet-nurse or foster mother

nymphaeum – a pool, fountain or other monument dedicated to the nymphs

officium – an official employment; also a sense of duty or respect

onager – a powerful catapult used by the Romans; named after a wild ass because of its kick

optio – the officer beneath a centurion; second-in-command within a century

palaestra – the open space of a gymnasium where wrestling, boxing and other such events were practiced

palliatus – indicating someone clad in a pallium

pancration – a no-holds-barred sport that combined wrestling and boxing

parentalis – of parents or ancestors; (e.g. *Parentalia* was a festival in honour of the dead)

parma – a small, round shield often used by light-armed troops; also referred to as *parmula*

pater – a father; also a top grade in Mithraic religion

pax – peace; a state of peace as opposed to war

peregrinus – a strange or foreign person or thing

peristylum – a peristyle; a colonnade around a building; can be inside or outside of a building or home

phalax - a long, curned, bladed weapon used by the Dacians

phalerae – decorative medals or discs worn by centurions or other officers on the chest

pilum – a heavy javelin used by Roman legionaries

plebeius – of the plebeian class or the people

pontifex – a Roman high priest

popa – a junior priest or temple servant

primus pilus – the senior centurion of a legion who commanded the first cohort

pronaos – the porch or entrance to a building such as a temple protome – an adornment on a work of art, usually a frontal view of an animal

pteruges – protective leather straps used on armour; often a leather skirt for officers

pugio – a dagger

quadriga – a four-horse chariot

quinqueremis – a ship with five banks of oars

retiarius – a gladiator who fights with a net and trident

rosemarinus – the herb rosemary

rudus – a heavy wooden *gladius* or sword used for practice and to build strength

rusticus – of the country; e.g. a *villa rustica* was a country villa

sacrum – sacred or holy; e.g. the *Via Sacra* or 'sacred way'

salii – the dancing priests of Mars who performed ritual dances in Rome's streets during the Festival of Mars

schola – a place of learning and learned discussion

scutum – the large, rectangular, curved shield of a legionary

secutor – a gladiator armed with a sword and shield; often pitted against a *retiarius*

sestertius – a Roman silver coin worth a quarter *denarius*

sica – a type of dagger

signum – a military standard or banner

signifer – a military standard bearer

sistrum – an ancient instrument or rattle made up of tiny cymbals

spatha – an auxiliary trooper's long sword; normally used by cavalry because of its longer reach speleum - literally a cave or grotto

spina – the ornamented, central median in stadiums such as the *Circus Maximus* in Rome

stadium – a measure of length approximately 607 feet; also refers to a race course

stibium – *antimony*, which was used for dyeing eyebrows by women in the ancient world

stoa – a columned, public walkway or portico for public use; often used by merchants to sell their wares

stola – a long outer garment worn by Roman women

strigilis – a curved scraper used at the baths to remove oil and grime from the skin

stylus – a bronze or wood 'pen' used to write with ink on papyrus, or on wax tablets

taberna – an inn or tavern

tablinum – an office or work space where documents are stored and business is conducted

tabula – a Roman board game similar to backgammon; also a writing-tablet for keeping records

tauroctony - name giving to Mithraic act of killing a bull; the god Mithras is often portrayed in scenes of the Tauroctony

tepidarium – the 'warm room' of a bath house

tessera – a piece of mosaic paving; a die for playing; also a small wooden plaque

testudo – a tortoise formation created by troops' interlocking shields

thraex – a gladiator in Thracian armour

titulus – a title of honour or honourable designation

torques – also 'torc'; a neck band worn by Celtic peoples and adopted by Rome as a military decoration

trepidatio – trepidation, anxiety or alarm

tribunus – a senior officer in an imperial legion; there were six per legion, each commanding a cohort

triclinium – a dining room

trierarchus – the captain of a ship or fleet

tunica – a sleeved garment worn by both men and women

usij - false priests of the Daevas in Zoroastrian religion; arrogant and lacking in goodness

ustrinum – the site of a funeral pyre

vallum – an earthen wall or rampart with a palisade

veterinarius – a veterinary surgeon in the Roman army

vexillarius – a Roman standard bearer who carried the *vexillum* for each unit

vexillum – a standard carried in each unit of the Roman army

vicus – a settlement of civilians living outside a Roman fort

vigiles – Roman firemen; literally 'watchmen'

vinerod – a stick, or short staff, carried by a centurion that gave him the right to strike citizens

vitis – the twisted 'vinerod' of a Roman centurion; a centurion's emblem of office

vittae – a ribbon or band

yazad - good divinities (ie. immortal gods) in Zoroastrian religion; head of the Yazad is Ahura Mazda, he who created Mithras

Become a Patron of Eagles and Dragons Publishing!

If you enjoy the books that Eagles and Dragons Publishing puts out, our blogs about history, mythology, and archaeology, our video tours of historic sites and more, then you should consider becoming an official patron.

We love our regular visitors to the website, and of course our wonderful newsletter subscribers, but we want to offer more to our 'super fans', those readers and history-lovers who enjoy everything we do and create.

You can become a patron for as little as $1 per month. For your support, you can also get fantastic rewards as tokens of our appreciation.

If you are interested, visit the website below to go to the Eagles and Dragons Publishing Patreon page to watch the introductory video and check out the patronage levels and exciting rewards.

https://www.patreon.com/EaglesandDragonsPublishing

Join us for an exciting future as we bring the past to life!

ABOUT THE AUTHOR

Adam Alexander Haviaras is a writer and historian who has studied ancient and medieval history and archaeology in Canada and the United Kingdom. He currently resides in Stratford, Ontario with his wife and children where he is continuing his research and writing other works of historical fantasy.

Historical Fiction/Fantasy Titles
The Eagles and Dragons Series

The Dragon: Genesis (Prequel)
A Dragon among the Eagles (Prequel)
Children of Apollo (Book I)
Killing the Hydra (Book II)
Warriors of Epona (Book III)
Isle of the Blessed (Book IV)
The Stolen Throne (Book V)
The Blood Road (Book VI)
The Eagles and Dragons Legionary Box Set (Books 0-I-II)
The Eagles and Dragons Tribune Box Set (Books III-IV-V)

The Carpathian Interlude Series

The Carpathian Interlude - Complete Trilogy Box Set
Immortui (Part I)
Lykoi (Part II)
Thanatos (Part III)

The Mythologia Series

Chariot of the Son
Wheels of Fate
A Song for the Underworld

Heart of Fire: A Novel of the Ancient Olympics

Saturnalia: A Tale of Wickedness and Redemption in Ancient Rome

Short Stories

The Sea Released
Theoi
Nex (or, The Warrior Named for Death)

Titles in the Historia Non-fiction Series

Historia I: Celtic Literary Archetypes in *The Mabinogion*: A Study of the Ancient Tale of *Pwyll, Lord of Dyved*

Historia II: Arthurian Romance and the Knightly Ideal: A study of Medieval Romantic Literature and its Effect upon Warrior Culture in Europe

Historia III: *Y Gododdin*: The Last Stand of Three Hundred Britons - Understanding People and Events during Britain's Heroic Age

Historia IV: Camelot: The Historical, Archaeological and

Toponymic Considerations for South Cadbury Castle as King Arthur's Capital

Eagles and Dragons Publishing Guides

Writing the Past: The Eagles and Dragons Publishing Guide to Researching, Writing, Publishing and Marketing Historical Fiction and Historical Fantasy

To connect with Adam and learn more about the ancient world visit www.eaglesanddragonspublishing.com

Sign up for the Eagles and Dragons Publishing Newsletter at www.eaglesanddragonspublishing.com/newsletter-join-the-legions/ to receive a FREE BOOK, first access to new releases and posts on ancient history, special offers, and much more!

Readers can also connect with Adam on Twitter @Adam-Haviaras and Instagram @ adam_haviaras.

On Facebook you can 'Like' the Eagles and Dragons page to get regular updates on new historical fiction and non-fiction from Eagles and Dragons Publishing.